Final revelations . . .

'Mary,' he said, as she got her key from her purse.
She looked up at him, silhouetted against the moon.
'You're lovely tonight. I was almost afraid to look
when I came in for fear you might not be there.
And yet, as I stepped on that porch, I felt
your presence . . .'

Mary's pulse seemed to be beating so rapidly
that she felt giddy. It was true, then. Everything
that had happened – every word, every gesture –
had seemed only to draw them closer.

'I . . . I was terribly glad to see you, too,' she said,
so softly that he had to lean forward to hear her.

He reached out and put one hand lightly on
her arm.

'Will you have that picnic with me Friday that we
talked about? If I bring a basket at noon, can you
go with me?' *To the ends of the earth,* her eyes
replied . . .

Revelations

PHYLLIS NAYLOR

SPHERE BOOKS LIMITED
30/32 Gray's Inn Road, London WC1X 8JL

First published in Great Britain by
Sphere Books Ltd, 1981
Copyright © Phyllis Naylor 1979

TRADE
MARK

Printed in Canada

To the clover,
the sawdust,
and all six verses of
the final hymn

Revelations

ONE

Certainly there was sadness. But woven, too, in the fabric of her emotions were surprise, regret, anticipation, terror, and a feeling, somewhere in the loins, that poetic justice had been done. Why the loins and not the heart, she didn't know. Who was vice and who was virtue was decidedly unclear.

She was thinking about dropping the "aunt" altogether. There would be none of that "Aunt Mary Martha," as Verna's boy used to call her. What had she ever done to deserve a name like that? Why not Magdalene instead of Martha? Jezebel, even? "Mary Magdalene." "Aunt Jezebel." She hadn't done much to merit those either, but at least they got attention.

She swiftly coiled her long brown hair into the usual twist at the nape of her neck and pinned it securely. On the outside, the perfect Mary; inside, a wayward maid servant. Hagar, that was her. Hagar, bringing up Ishmael all by herself.

God help me, she thought, and the panic spread through her again.

The phone rang as she put on her jacket. She hoped it was Liz and not Verna. She prayed it was Liz.

God, let it be Liz, she said as she lifted the receiver. It was Verna. So much for selfish supplications.

"I thought you'd have left by now."

The statement made the call seem obsolete.

"Just going out the door," Mary said.

"You've got to allow for traffic, Mary! I could go along in case you have trouble parking. Somebody's got to be waiting for him."

Mary had known this would happen. All week she had silently rehearsed her answer and was furious at the tremor in her voice when she finally said it aloud: "I really think it's better if he meets us one at a time, Verna. I've no idea what kind of state he's in."

"Well, go on then," her sister instructed. "He'll be in a real state if he gets to the airport and nobody's there. And I hope you had the good sense to put on a girdle. You've been looking so vulgar. . . ."

Good. Mary stood with one hand on the phone after she'd hung up, perspiration on her palm. *Good, good, good!* A little vulgarity never hurt anybody. That's what Liz would say. The spandex girdle with overlapping self-fabric panels had been donated to Goodwill over a month ago and she wouldn't buy another. Liz had even suggested offering it up as a burnt sacrifice on the outdoor grill, but who knows— it might have exploded or something. All that constraint going up in smoke. . . . You just don't go around setting fire to spandex.

She stepped out on the porch, locking the door behind her, and the pounding of her heart began again. Jake was coming to her, to *her!* She and Verna were still reeling from the shock. Mary was not even sure, in fact, that she *wanted* him, and yet, to have been chosen. . . .

The old two-seater swing at one end of the porch hung lopsided because of a kink in the chain. She'd have to fix that. Just as she and Warren used to sit there on lazy afternoons pushing their feet against the floor in tandem, so would she and Jake. . . .

She backed the car out of the drive and sped down the narrow road. A large plastic M on her key chain, dangling from the ignition, jiggled against one knee. She wondered what Jake would think about her, her car, her name. . . . Mary Martha Myles. How could her parents have known, thirty-four years ago, that her initials would read like the Minnesota Mining and Manufacturing Company, and that whenever people saw them, they would think of Scotch tape?

Perhaps she should have brought a gift for Jake. But a thirteen-year-old she hadn't seen since he was six? No, better to meet him empty-handed and be honest about it. All she had to offer was her home and herself, and she a spinster aunt. . . .

Mary tried to remember what she had been like at thirteen: serious about silly things and ignorant of the profound; intimidated by the wrong people, shocked by the rest. At thirteen she had felt noble about things which rather nauseated her now, and guilty about more offenses than were listed in the whole of Deuteronomy.

But had she really changed so much? How was it she could have reached the middle thirties still feeling like the same scared eighth-grader she once had been? How was it that her body had grown taller, her breasts full, her thighs round and fleshy, and yet the image she kept of herself, as though preserved in a locket, was that of a young girl in braces—with hardware on her spirit as well as her teeth? A chastity belt for beginners.

She nervously clicked on the car radio and just as suddenly turned it off again. Liz Grossman should be meeting Jake's plane, that's what. Liz would know what to say. She'd lean her curly head against his, link arms like she'd known him forever, and go strolling through the airport talking to him like a Dutch uncle.

"Jake," Liz would probably say, "if you want to cry, go right ahead, because tears and cussing are the only sane response to being shit on. And life really dumped on you this time."

Mary smiled to herself. Liz could talk like that, but she couldn't—not in a million years. It would take a complete metamorphosis to turn her into Liz Grossman, beginning with the soul. She longed for a transformation, but was trapped inside her own skin. Her very bones held her prisoner.

It had all begun at seven o'clock Wednesday morning. Mary had just put her poached egg on her plate and unfolded the *Washington Post* when the phone rang. Twelve hours later, the egg was still there, and Mary could not remember whether she had eaten anything at all.

The call had been from a friend of her brother's in Santa Monica. Warren and his wife, the friend said, had been killed early that morning in an auto accident on the freeway. He was sorry to be the one to break the awful news. . . .

In shock, Mary had begun packing to fly to California with Verna when another call came from Warren's lawyer. A will had been filed, he said, stating emphatically that there should be no funeral, no service, no wake, and no mourning. Instead, it was the wish of Warren and Sue that their bodies be cremated without ceremony and the ashes scattered over the San Fernando valley by helicopter. And it was the sincere hope of the deceased that this would be followed by a seven-day binge in their beach house near Malibu.

It was Warren's will, all right.

"What about Jake?" Mary had asked numbly. "Where will he go?"

"It doesn't say," the lawyer told her. "But I just talked with the boy, and he says his parents told him he would live with his Aunt Mary should anything happen to them."

Mary had slowly lowered herself down on the telephone stool and stared at the wall calendar without seeing it. Could they do this? Could people just will their child on you, to be inherited like a clock? A clock you could auction off, but Jake. . . .

"They never mentioned that to me at all!" she had gasped.

"I see. . . . I suppose it was more of an understanding between them and the boy—so he wouldn't feel stranded. Children worry about that, you know." The lawyer had waited.

"Where is he now?"

"With friends of the family, and I'm sure they'd keep him a while longer till you think things through. Fortunately, they'll take care of the . . . uh . . . helicopter arrangements, so you need not concern yourself with that."

Still, Mary's thoughts had spun wildly, a kaleidoscope of feelings that kept her mute, until suddenly she thought of Verna and the possibility that Jake might go to her.

"When should I come and pick him up?" she asked.

The lawyer had sounded both relieved and embarrassed. "Jake said he would rather fly out east himself. Thinking that you might be agreeable to this, I . . . uh . . . took the liberty of checking airline schedules. If it's convenient for you, we could arrange to have him arrive there at two-fifty Friday afternoon. He'll bring a few bags with him and we'll ship the rest express. I'll be in touch with you shortly about the estate."

Now, as Mary recalled the conversation, the contradictions were all too apparent. She had not really wanted him to come, and yet he seemed to belong to her somehow. It made no sense at all.

She caught a glimpse of her face in the rearview mirror and was astonished at how pale it was. Her eyes stared back at her, large, gray and uncertain. It was a long way from Santa Monica and the beach house at Malibu to a bungalow in Charles County, Maryland.

She was within thirty feet of National Airport when the scent stopped her. It could have belonged to any one of the men she'd passed on the crosswalk, but his identity did not matter; it was the feeling that was so consistent. Whether of musk or camphor or pine or leather, a man's scent had an extraordinary effect upon Mary. She was almost embarrassed by the pleasure it gave her.

She paused, startled by the rush of it, giddy. Each

time it happened, in the last year especially, she had felt one step closer to something that lay just below the surface. Again, despite her struggle to catch it, it slipped over the edge of her mind and mingled once more with the grayness. But she knew it was there and welcomed it with surprised delight, like letters from an anonymous lover.

When she reached the glass doors to the lobby, however, both the scent and the pleasure had evaporated, and Mary went in, feeling uncomfortably out of place.

It was not like being in church on Tabernacle Sunday or shopping in La Plata. These people were different—self-assured, confident, determined. She felt as though she were the only one there without a flight plan and retreated at once to the women's lounge. "Excitable kidneys," Verna always said to her. Verna never referred to anything lower than the kidneys if she could help it.

Mary stopped to survey herself in the mirror, wondering if she should have worn a dress instead of a suit. She looked so severe. Why on earth hadn't she put on something soft and maternal that Jake could bury his face in? *It's all right, Jake*, she would say. *I know, I know.* . . . Would he be as likely to bury his face against a stiff polyester jacket? Probably not.

She went back to the waiting area. A crisp, staccato voice over the loudspeaker announced the arrival of the plane. An airport employee sat laconically on a stool in the corridor, looking down toward the escalator where the first passengers would appear. Mary moved over toward the rope. And finally she saw him.

He was a head shorter than the others, fair-haired and slight, his shoulders hunched as he struggled to keep a flight bag on an enormously long strap from bumping the ground. Down the passageway he came, stopping once to stuff his sweater into the bulging bag, then lumbering on toward the lobby.

He's certainly a young thirteen, Mary thought. Half his body seemed to be legs—long, spindly things with clumps of feet that occasionally kicked each other as they walked, almost tripping him. His arms were short in proportion, his chest small, his face narrow and lean. His hair was disheveled from the flight, and he looked groggy.

"Jake!"

The boy's eyes moved swiftly through the crowd and fastened themselves to her. He smiled just a bit.

He was still on the other side of the rope which was lined now with relatives of an elderly couple just ahead of him. The grandmother was leaning over, hugging each grandchild in turn, blocking the crowd of passengers behind her. Jake, his arms dangling at his sides, looked over at Mary and shrugged. At last the older woman moved on and the bottleneck eased. By the time Jake was clear of the rope, however, the spontaneity had waned, and Mary knew that he would not bury his head against her and that sofness wouldn't have helped.

"Jake!" she said again and came up to him, arms outstretched.

He stopped and put his flight bag on the floor, fumbling with the strap, trying to shorten it. When he finally stood up, Mary decided that even a hug would be awkward.

"It was a long flight, wasn't it?" she said simply.

"Yeah. About five hours."

She could tell that there were to be no words of sympathy uttered here, no tears, no mention of the catastrophe. Yet it seemed unnatural not to say something.

"I'm so glad you're here," she said, faltering. "And I'm so sorry. . . ." It was definitely ambiguous.

He stood looking straight ahead, his eyes following the other passengers. The corners of his mouth sagged just a bit. "Yeah," he said again. There was an awkward pause, and he swallowed. "Well. . . ." He pulled the claim checks from his jacket pocket. "I guess we'd better get the suitcases."

He walked with her through the lobby. As though worn down by his task of caretaker of the cantankerous flight bag. Jake gave up trying. He let it sag, swinging back and forth an inch from the floor. Now and then he managed to kick it with his right foot, sending it flying sideways against Mary's legs.

They planted themselves at the baggage counter.

"How was the weather?" Mary inquired politely.

"Okay except for Kansas. We went through a storm there. A man across the aisle threw up, but I didn't."

"Gracious!"

Again the silence. The luggage kept coming.

"Do you remember me at all, Jake? Do you remember when Verna and I came out there to visit when you were six?"

"Yeah."

Jake's two bags arrived together. She picked one up and Jake the other and was surprised at how light hers seemed. Jake must have packed them himself, throwing things in every which way without trying to conserve space.

"I don't think we'll need a sky cap," she told her nephew. "I managed to find a parking space in a lot fairly close."

Bumping and jostling, they made their way to the

main door and followed the sidewalk down to the parking lot. Mary got out her key to the trunk.

"Should I put this in there too, Aunt Mary?" Jake asked, pointing to his flight bag.

It was to be "aunt," then, after all. Well, if Jake felt comfortable with it, she wouldn't object. At least it defined her. Mary Martha—a supplier of needs. It had always been so.

"Well, the first thing you've got to do, see, is have him circumcized."

"*What?*"

Liz had thrown back her head, howling, her feet lifting off the floor and her hands coming down hard on her knees. "Oh, Mary!" she had shrieked. "My God, you're the innocent."

It was not a term Mary found endearing. "You're joking, of course," she'd said.

Liz had shaken her head hopelessly. "Of course!" The joking had seemed inappropriate, however, and Liz had sensed it too.

"Okay," she'd said. "How can I help? Talk it out? Analyze it?"

Mary had leaned back against the sofa, arms limp, palms turned upwards. She had fled to her friend's apartment the night before Jake arrived, entering breathlessly, perspiring and shaky.

Liz had viewed her sardonically over the Budweiser in her hand. "Look. You come flying in here—hyper-ventilating, practically—and tell me you're the guardian of a thirteen-year-old boy. Then you ask me what

to do and go catatonic. I don't know whether to con-
gratulate you or bury you."

They had met sixteen years ago at the junior college with no other bond between them than Philosophy 101. Liz—shorter, a month older—wore her curly
hair close-cropped, ears exposed, huge tinted glasses
enlarging her eyes. No one ever referred to Liz Grossman as pretty. "Vivacious," perhaps, but not "pretty."
She was a strange combination of intellect and earth-
iness, which was enormously appealing.

What an absolute child I am, Mary had thought,
feeling the contrast between them.

"What are you thinking?" Liz had urged. "Talk, for
God's sake."

"I act like a kid," Mary had said. "Always asking
advice, never trusting myself. . . ."

Liz had nodded without answering—the neutral
stance of the social worker.

"Oh, Liz, I don't even know if I *want* the boy!"

"How could you know? You've hardly had time to
think. One minute you're free as a bird and a phone
call later you're a mother! Sure you don't want a beer?"

"Half a can, maybe." Mary had watched Liz unfold
her legs, pad out to the refrigerator, and return with
the beer. Slowly Liz had poured the liquid into a
glass. "Venial sin," she'd said when the beer covered
the bottom, and then as the level rose, ". . . mortal
sin . . . purgatory. . . ." She'd stopped at half
a glass. "Did I get it right? Or does purgatory come
before mortal?"

Mary had smiled and took the glass. "Mortal sin
from the very first drop. Oh, Lord, if the congregation ever knew. . . ."

"This is one place you're safe. Thank God for sanc-
tuaries."

They had sat together awhile without talking. Then, from Mary, "I guess it's the timing, Liz. After Dad went to Verna's last year, I realized I had a place of my own for the first time in my life. I was beginning to like the idea. And now. . . ."

"Now a thirteen-year-old kid's moving in with you."

"A thirteen-year-old boy. . . ."

"Any possibility of his going to Verna's instead? She's home all day . . . has a house."

"No. I'd never agree to that."

"Why not? After taking care of your mother all these years, Mary, you're entitled to a life of your own."

"But maybe this is it. Maybe it's what I've been waiting for."

Liz had made no answer, and Mary had sat turning the glass around and around in her hands. Finally: "I read once that every woman, to be fulfilled, must both possess and be possessed. I've never done either. Do you realize that, Liz? Never in my entire life."

"Jake's not coming as a possession, Mary."

This time it was Mary who laughed, perhaps a bit too sardonically. "Wrong. I inherited him. He was willed to me—like a clock." The half glass of beer went back on the coffee table.

"All of two sips," Liz had commented.

"I know. I've never been able to let myself enjoy the stuff." There was quiet for a while. Then, "Was it difficult for you Liz, when you broke away?"

"From the synagogue? Actually, my grandmother made it very easy."

"Your grandmother?"

"Yeah." Liz's eyes had crinkled a little at the corners. "I'd been getting home later and later on Fridays. There was this man—we used to walk around—talk—and sometimes I'd get home after sundown. Finally my grandmother said that she was locking the door at dusk on the Sabbath. The next time I came home late, she wouldn't let me in. So this guy took me to a Unitarian discussion group that night, and I sort of went from church to church after that. Dad never forgave his mother, which is my only regret. Old Grandma Bertie probably did me a favor, but all Dad could say at her funeral was how she'd driven away his Elizabeth." Liz had stretched out her legs and her face became pensive. "It's sad, you know, when you feel you're walking away healthy and whole from something, and yet you leave everybody else in pieces."

"Does it have to be that way?"

Liz had shrugged. "I don't know. Grandmother Bertie used to repeat that old saying, 'When children are young, they step on yours toes, but when they grow up, they step on your heart.' Makes you feel guilty every time you have a damn birthday!"

They'd laughed.

"So you're going to take Jake in," Liz had said finally. "For richer or poorer, in sickness and health . . . acne, cold sores, the works. . . ."

"He was Warren's," Mary had told her, "and now he's mine."

They left the city behind and were heading south again: past the drive-in theater, the fruit market, the condominiums, until the highway narrowed to two lanes, and the greenery on either side became thick. Jake sat with his head turned to the right, saying nothing.

"The last few days must have been awful for you," Mary ventured, glancing over at him. "I won't ask you a lot of questions if you'd rather not talk about it, but . . . any time you want to share your feelings, I hope you will."

There was no answer, just a noticeable swallow.

"I suppose it will take us a while to get to know each other, so we'll both have to be tolerant," she went on. "Living in Maryland is going to be a lot different from living in Santa Monica, I'm afraid."

Jake turned his face toward the front of the car, but still did not look at her.

"Do you live near Aunt Verna and Uncle Sam?"

"Not too far away. They live in La Plata, and Dad—Grampa Myles—lives with them."

"You live in an apartment?"

"No, the same little house where we all grew up. Didn't your father tell you that?"

"I don't remember."

"Mother had arthritis and other problems, so I stayed on to take care of her. After she died last year, I got a secretarial job at our church. Then Dad had a stroke, and we decided he'd be better off at Verna's since I was working. Trouble comes in batches, they say."

Again the silence. Then Jake's voice: "Who says?"

Mary looked at him. "What?"

"Who says that trouble comes in batches?"

Mary blinked. "It's just a saying, Jake. Why?"

"It sounded like a fortune cookie or something."

Mary laughed. "Let's hope this is the end of our

bad luck. I think the Myles are due for some good times, don't you?"

The road rose and fell. On either side, the shoulder sloped down into a grassy ditch, and beyond the ditch the bank of clay soil showed streaks of purplish-red.

"It's sort of primitive out here, isn't it?" Jake commented.

"Compared to Santa Monica, maybe. But we don't feel that way about it. Not with Washington so close."

"You go into Washington a lot?"

"Well, not as often as I should. Maybe now that you're here we could take some trips—see some things."

They passed a tavern advertising country music every night; more dense trees; open stretches of tobacco fields; a sign saying, "Turkey Shoot—Sunday Noon to Sunset," and another sign, "Charles County Welcomes You," followed by the Gospel Union Church of Christ. Mary drove on past advertisements for steamed crabs, bloodworms and minnows, Arabian horses, and Veterans of Foreign Wars, finally turning left off the highway. She steered the car along winding back roads lush with trees, miles of woods which opened up occasionally for a house and some plowed fields, then closed again, blocking all sunlight from the road. She passed a one-room post office and turned on still another road where small unpretentious houses sat on one- and two-acre lots. At the fourth house from the corner she turned in.

"This it?" Jake asked.

"This is it. This is where your father and Verna and I grew up."

"What is it? Some kind of farm?"

"Good Heavens, no!"

"What are those things out back, then?"

"Used to be chicken coops, but we haven't raised chickens for years. Just old out-buildings that don't amount to much. Come on in."

It was a white frame bungalow with green shutters and the silhouette of an Irish setter on the screen. The front porch ran the width of the house, and the yard was dotted with pine trees, a wide maple in the center.

"That tree," said Mary proudly, nodding toward the maple, "will be absolutely gorgeous in another two weeks." She turned the key in the lock.

There was no entrance hall. The living room had a fireplace and furniture that was old but comfortable: overstuffed arm chairs, scratched end tables, lamps with yellowed shades a bookcase full of worn volumes and ancient *National Geographic*s. . . .

The kitchen was small and connected to an even smaller dining room with furniture entirely too massive for its size. On the left of the house, a hallway led to two bedrooms separated by a bath, and stairs mounted to one large attic room above.

"Verna and I slept upstairs, and Warren got the back bedroom," Mary explained. "I thought you'd like to have it now. You can fix it up as you wish."

The boy looked at the narrow bed and the walnut dresser, the desk and the straight-backed chair, and said nothing. Mary waited. "Would you like me to help you unpack?" she asked finally, "or would you just like to rest awhile?"

Jake sat down on the edge of the bed. "I don't know. Rest, maybe."

"Okay, you just take your time getting used to the place. I'm going to put a meat loaf in the oven. We'll be going to Verna's tomorrow, but today we'll just take it easy. I know how exhausted you must be."

She went out, closing the door only halfway so he wouldn't feel too shut off.

Zombies! she thought, covering her face with her hands. *Both of us! We can't seem to talk to each other. Warren's dead, and we can't even cry!*

It was only when dinner was baking that she realized how tired she was herself—a dull, gray sort of exhaustion that came over her occasionally like a veil. She'd told Dr. Dobbs about it the last time she'd had her physical. He had listened quietly, concerned as always, and then, as though changing the subject, "Still belong to the same church, Mary?"

"Faith Holiness? Of course. Why?"

At first he hadn't answered. He appeared to be listening through the stethoscope. Then, as he turned away, "Oh, I just wonder sometimes if it suits you."

"I've been going there all my life!"

"Sometimes people's needs change without their knowing it. Maybe your body's trying to tell you something."

"What on earth does my fatigue have to do with going to church?"

He had laughed then. "Maybe not a darn thing. It was just an idea."

"How about my thyroid medication?"

"You're taking all you need."

Mary sat now at the kitchen table, her head resting on one hand. Perhaps it was prayer she needed, not pills. Maybe now that she had a nephew to raise, the

Lord would speak a little louder. Communication had become somewhat difficult lately. She leaned forward, concentrating.

"Dear Father," she began and paused. The kindly old man who had always looked sorrowfully but benevolently down on her in the past seemed to have become less distinct over the years, and now remained blurred and mute no matter what she confided in him.

All her life she had felt that only Verna and her mother had the inside track because they could name the year, month, day, and hour when salvation occurred. With Mary there were no such statistics. She had grown up feeling close to God because she was never allowed to forget that he was present.

This was not entirely acceptable at Faith Holiness. The only authentic conversions, those that could be documented, had a date attached. But since being saved was, after all, a personal matter, no one could really prove that Mary Martha *wasn't*. So each summer at the revival meeting, when the call went out for witnesses to stand at the front for Christ, Mary dutifully went up beside Verna, and nobody turned her away. Somehow, they all must have decided, she had come in the side door of salvation when no one was looking.

Mary, however, had never felt like one of the flock, secure in the fold. It was as though she were straddling the fence, not enclosed by it. On one side were all the contented born-again sheep, peacefully munching, and on the other was darkness, a void, a scary unknown. Yet the sheep on the fence, draped over the top like a sandbag, was looking out, not in.

It was her philosophy class, actually, which had stirred up the trouble. She had been warned about

college even before she'd enrolled. Verna said that
unless you entered as a born-again Christian, your
mind would be permanently warped. So when Mary
had taken her seat warily on that first day, it was only
the fact that a girl behind her seemed to be praying
in Hebrew that kept her from bolting from the room.
She had later discovered that a few "Oy veys" said
out of exhaustion did not constitute a proper prayer,
even in Yiddish. But then, however, she and Liz had
become friends, and clung to each other as they entered the unit on moral responsibility and deter-
minism.

There had been selected readings from Socrates,
Hume, and Bertrand Russell. But it was a paragraph
from Mark Twain's *The Mysterious Stranger* that
captivated the girls, drawing them to it again and
again. They carried their philosophy books around
with them in the cafeteria, reading sections aloud to
each other. They had become obsessed with Twain's
conclusion that it could be only a "hysterically insane" dream that there is

> . . . a God who could make good children as
> easily as bad, yet preferred to make bad ones;
> who could have made every one of them happy
> yet never made a single happy one; who made
> them prize their bitter life, yet stingily cut it
> short; who gave his angels eternal happiness un-
> earned, yet required his other children to earn it;
> who gave his angels painless lives, yet cursed his
> other children with biting miseries and maladies
> of mind and body; who mouths justice and in-
> vented hell; who mouths morals to other people
> and has none himself; who frowns upon crimes,
> yet commits them all; who created man without

invitation, then tries to shuffle the responsibility
for man's acts upon man, instead of honorably
placing it where it belongs, upon himself; and finally, with altogether divine obtuseness, invites
his poor, abused slave to worship him! ...

Mary had longed to share this passage with her
family, but she didn't dare. Verna, she knew, would
attribute all her questions to (1) the devil; (2) the
professor; or (3) that Jewish girl. Her mother would
say simply, "A little knowledge is a dangerous thing."
Nobody would actually take on Twain.

A few weeks later in class discussion when one of
the students recounted how H.L. Mencken, an
avowed atheist, rose up on his deathbed and quipped,
"Bring on the angels!" Liz led the class in laughter
and Mary followed. It was the second chink in their
separate beliefs, and Mary did penance that night by
going without dinner. Yet, even as she lay in the
darkness with hunger gnawing through her, she
thought again of old man Mencken and laughed,
burying her face in the pillow. And then, as though
that weren't sacrilege enough, she had masturbated.
Sin upon sin upon sin.

She tried now to forget all this and focus on the
prayer at hand.

"Dear Lord, our Father," she whispered, "please be
with me. I know I have wandered away from you in
the past. I know I have doubted you. I know that I'm
unfit to bring up this young boy, but I ask you, God,
to please show me the way and help me say the right
thing—especially tonight."

There was no sign, one way or another. God
chastised by way of the silent treatment. She stood up
and slowly started the salad.

An hour later she decided that perhaps Jake had been left alone long enough and went to look in on him. He was lying on the bed, staring at the ceiling. His luggage had been opened and the contents placed here and there. A pile of *Mad* magazines lay beside him, a stamp album, and a book by Tolkien.

Mary sat down on his chair.

"Hungry, Jake?"

She wanted to enfold him in her arms. She longed to say, *Let it out, Jake! Just let the feelings out, honey!* Instead she leaned forward and put one hand on his knee.

"Jake, the whole world must look upside down to you right now. It must seem that God's deserted you and tossed you clear out here to Maryland where you hardly know anybody. Is that about how you feel?"

There was still no answer, but a tear glistened at the corner of Jake's eye and trickled down onto the spread. He sniffled once.

Mary patted his knee and waited. "I can't take the place of your parents, Jake, and I won't even try. But I'm glad you're here with me now, really glad. You're welcome in this house, and somehow we're going to pick up the pieces and work things out. Kids have gone through really awful things before, you know, but they usually manage to pull through, and you can too."

Again Jake sniffled. Mary sat back.

"Life's not very fair, you know. Some people get all the breaks and some people get all the knocks. My goodness, I certainly haven't had a great life, but I'm healthy, and I've got a job. . . ."

"What did you ever want that you never got?" Jake asked softly.

It was the first time anyone had asked her—the first time Mary had confronted it directly. Love? Excitement? A sense of worth, perhaps? Or was it as simple as possessing and being possessed? She could hardly say that to Jake.

"It sounds strange, but I don't really know," she told him. "Whatever it was I always wanted, though, sure hasn't happened to me yet."

TWO

It was strange, because there *had* been a time when Mary thought she knew what she wanted. She'd been only twelve, of course, and Warren eleven, but they used to sit out on the swing together barefoot and talk about where they would go when they got to be twenty.

It was assumed they would go somewhere—inconceivable to both that they might remain in Marbury. Marbury was the kind of place you grew up in to get out of, and if you ever came back, you could stand down by the road, looking as far as the eye could see, and count on the fingers of one hand the number of changes that had happened while you were gone. A tree had been felled by lightning, perhaps, or Mr. Conway had added a bedroom at the back of his house, but that would be all. It was the kind of place that, if you were buried there, people would remember your funeral forever after, and how old Mrs. Gatston, an invalid herself, had sent over a chiffon pie.

At the time, Mary had been most interested in horses and imagined she might work for a veterinarian somewhere. Run a stable, maybe. For a while a neighbor had let her ride his mare in the field behind the house, and this had been her heaven.

The horse, she discovered, could see her regardless of the direction from which she approached. It would follow her with its enormous eye, and the muscles along the sleek flank would ripple with anticipation. The animal would shift slightly as Mary mounted and then clop, high-hoofed, over the threshold of the barn and out to the warmth of the pasture.

At first Mary could manage only a trot, thudding down hard as the horse's back came up to meet her, her feet rising and falling in stirrups which needed adjustment. But as she grew more confident, and the animal sensed her mastery of it, she proceeded to gallop, the powerful horse at her command. Around the field she would ride, the wind on her face, her teeth bared. She galloped as though she could escape herself, fly out of her own skin, and finally, when she felt the mare's sides heaving in and out like a magnificent set of bellows and heard the animal snort through its black nostrils, she would slow it to a walk, a stately promenade.

Mary would keep the pace steady then, leaning forward against the horn of the saddle, the horse's rhythm becoming her own. She could feel sweat between the calves of her legs and the horse's body, feel the animal quiver as it cooled, sense its pleasure as it tossed its mane, droplets flying.

There was something about it, however, that displeased Mrs. Myles. She never told Mary exactly what. But she'd had a talk with the mare's owner, and shortly afterwards Mary had been told that the horse could not go out again, that it was time she found better things to do.

Warren wanted to take up sky diving or soaring. Anything to do with flying. They talked about it endlessly, sitting on the porch swing after dinner, thigh to thigh, the big family Bible—opened to Psalms—resting on both of them equally. He would take off from the hills around Chapel Point, Warren would tell her, sweeping out over the river, heading west toward Welcome, Hill Top, and Ironsides. He would skim the tops of the trees in the Doncaster State Forest, cross the Potomac where it curved back up again, and sail on into the state of Virginia, as simple as that. All it took was a pair of wings.

"You children working on those Bible verses?" Mrs. Myles would call from her big chair inside where she sat half-crippled with arthritis. "It's Verna who's doing the dishes herself, you know. . . ."

"Who shall ascend into the hill of the Lord?" Mary would ask loudly, "or who shall stand in his holy place?"

"He that hath clean hands and a pure heart. . . ." Warren would bellow.

Sometimes Warren took the Bible away from Mary and read from the Song of Solomon instead of the assigned verses, his voice young and lusty, breaking now and then with merriment.

"How beautiful are thy feet with shoes, O prince's daughter! The joints of thy thighs are like jewels, the work of the hands of a cunning workman. Thy naval is like a round goblet, which wanteth not liquor: thy belly is like a heap of wheat set about with lilies. Thy two breasts are like two young roes that are twins, thy neck is as a tower of ivory. . . ."

Mary would lean back in the swing, her hair hanging over the edge, face flushed, eyes closed, her knees, pressed tightly together, remembering the mare in the pasture and the feel of the saddle and the sweat on the calves of her legs. . . .

"They're talking dirty again, Mother," Verna

would complain loudly from inside, having sidled up to the screen with the dish towel.

"Solomon 8, verse 8," Warren would croak, his voice ringing in devilment: "We have a little sister and she hath no breasts: What shall we do for our sister in the day when she shall be spoken for?"

Then he and Mary would shriek with laughter as Verna would bolt out the door and grab the Bible away from them, leaving them to the soft, lilac-smelling dusk and the rhythmic creak of the swing.

Something happened to the dreams, however, as puberty gave way to adolescence and twenty came closer with each passing year. Somehow Mary sensed that old dreams would die out, but she always thought they would be replaced by something else. She and Warren had grown more introspective, absorbed in their own changes. New bodies brought new guilts, and at fifteen, they no longer sat thigh to thigh on the porch swing reading from the Book of Solomon. Still, all those years, Mary remembered. And when Warren suddenly left Marbury without her, on a night that wrenched her very soul, it was something she could never quite forgive. She wondered if she'd ever had a dream of her own in the first place, or if it had been Warren's all along.

On Saturday Mary woke at nine, surprised that she had slept so late. There was a boy to feed. She got up and hastily threw on her robe. There could be no more lounging about looking unkempt before breakfast—no reading the newspaper nude on hot July mornings. She wondered if she resented it already.

In the hall she stopped. Jake's door was wide open, his bed unmade and empty. She walked quickly to the living room. He was gone.

"Oh, God!" she breathed, leaning against the wall.

And then she heard sounds coming from the back yard, noises she could not readily describe. She went over to the dining room window.

Jake was squatting on top of the old chicken coop. He had the clothesline prop in one hand and was poking it down an abandoned chipmunk hole.

"There! That'll teach you!" he was saying to no one in particular. Then he stood up and, using the long stick as a vaulting pole, sailed out from the chicken shed and landed on the grass.

"Aaaaaagggggggggh!" he yelled, and lay still, spread-eagled on his back. Mary stared.

Instantly he was on his hands and knees again, this time crawling slowly toward the shed with his back low, buttocks in the air, looking first over his left shoulder, then his right.

"They're coming up from behind!" he gasped suddenly, whirling around and flattening himself against the shed. Then, with a whoop, he sprang to the top of the chicken coop again, hopped over to the roof of the old rabbit hutch, and this time, using the pole as a lance, thrust it right and left, eyes intent, fierce, whirling this way and that, jabbing at the air around him.

Mary stood there wondering. Had the child forgotten already? Was a boy's grief so short-lived? What would the neighbors think?

Then, just as suddenly, Mary realized she did not care what they thought. The boy needed a respite from turmoil—a chance to work things through in his own way. Strangely confident of this decision, she washed, dressed, then put on a fresh apron. The phone jangled by the door.

"Hello?"

"Mary! Is everything all right?"

Did she just imagine it, or did Verna sound chronically peeved these last few days?

"Of course."

"Well, the least you could have done was call me. I finally drove by your house last night to see if your car was there, but of course you didn't invite me, so I didn't come in."

"Verna, we've had a lot to do, and Jake was so tired. Everything's fine now, and he's out playing in the back yard."

"*Playing?* Who's he playing with?"

"No one. Just exploring around."

There was a pause. "He's not upset, then?"

"Of course he's upset! But you can't expect a thirteen-year-old to mourn all the time. What can I bring over for dinner this evening?"

"Have I ever asked you to bring food when you come to my house?"

"No, but I just thought . . . well, there are two of us now. . . ."

"Just be here at six," Verna commanded.

There were waffles, sausage, and apple sauce waiting on a yellow cloth when Mary called Jake to come in. He had put on yesterday's clothes again, and there

were dirty blotches on both knees of his gabardine
slacks.

"Might want to change clothes after breakfast,
Jake," Mary said, smiling warmly. "Hungry?"

"I guess so. Boy, you sure must have had a lot of
chickens!"

"Well, a few dozen, anyway."

He took off his jacket, threw it onto a chair, and
sat down. He was looking at her intently.

"What's that?" he asked finally.

"What's what?"

"That thing you've got on."

"This? An apron, for heaven's sake! Haven't you
seen an *apron* before?"

"Yeah. I thought just old women wore them. Is it
something religious?"

Mary burst out laughing. "Jake! I declare! Of
course not! Where did you ever get an idea like that?
It's white, that's all."

Jake shrugged. "Dad told me once you and Aunt
Verna were religious."

Mary frowned. "Well, an apron's got nothing to do
with it."

She sat across from him and, as always, bowed her
head for silent prayer. When she raised up, Jake had
already helped himself to one of the waffles and was
watching her. She ignored it and began dishing up
the apple sauce.

"What would happen if you didn't?" he asked.

"Didn't what?"

"Didn't pray. If you forgot or something?"

"Nothing at all."

"Then how come you do it?"

"It's a matter of courtesy, Jake. God gives us our
food and I'm thanking him for it, that's all." She

wondered if he could see the hypocrite in her. Habit. That was more like it.

Jake took another sausage and went on eating.

"I remember," he said, absently wiping his fingers on the cloth, "when we used to do that in nursery school."

Mary reached over and moved his napkin a little closer to his left hand. "Pray before meals?"

"Yeah. 'God is great, God is good, and we thank him for our food.' We used to do real dumb things like substitute other words for 'food.' One guy in particular, Herbie Kline, that was his name, he would always look around while we were praying and say things like, 'and we thank him for our scissors,' or 'and we thank him for the paper.' Corny stuff like that, and it would just break us up. Gee, we'd laugh at anything. But one day he was feeling really smart, and he thought the teacher was over by the sink, and when we all bowed our heads he said, 'God is dumb, God is stupid, and we thank him for our poopie!' We absolutely shrieked. We went into convulsions practically. The teacher took away the cookies and juice, but we still couldn't stop laughing. She said that God had decided we wouldn't have any juice and cookies for a whole week because of it. I always wondered how he got that message to her so fast."

Mary laughed. "Doesn't seem quite like the Christian spirit, does it? How about more waffles? Could you eat another?"

"I think so."

"That's good." Mary hastily got the eggs and milk from the refrigerator and made a new batter. "You look as though you're feeling better than you did yesterday. Not as tired. Did you sleep well?"

"Yeah."

Suddenly Jake was silent and serious. He sat tracing lines through the leftover syrup on his plate. Mary stood by the waffle iron, watching the gauge.

"Today's Saturday, isn't it?" he said finally.

"Yes."

"This is the day they're going to scatter the ashes. Jerry—he was one of Dad's friends—he told me they were going to rent a helicopter and do it. He asked me if I wanted to stay over the weekend and go along, but I didn't. I mean, I'd like to have gone up in the chopper, but I wouldn't want to scatter the ashes."

"Of course. That's understandable, Jake."

"It's . . . it's sort of strange when you think about it, you know? I mean, having them spread all over like that, like there's no place I can go where they really are—a grave or something—because they're everywhere. I don't know how to explain it. I wish there had been graves, that's all."

Mary felt her eyes brimming suddenly. "I know, Jake." She wiped her cheeks with one corner of the apron. "But that's the kind of funeral they wanted, so I guess that's the way it had to be. It's hard to imagine Warren gone, though. He was always so energetic, so full of life. . . ."

"It was somebody else's fault, too," Jake said, anger rising in his voice. "A car veered over into their lane. The police said there were skid marks. Dad swerved off the road to get out of the way and hit a concrete post. The other driver didn't even stop! I'd like to chop him up in pieces and scatter *him* around!"

"Was it late at night, Jake? I forgot what they told me."

"It was more like morning. Mom had been out late and Dad went to get her. . . ."

Mary turned suddenly and fiddled with the waffle iron. "Well! It's golden brown—just perfect!" She lifted the waffle out with a fork and slid it quickly onto Jake's plate.

He sat staring at his left hand and then suddenly stood up. "I guess I'm not hungry after all, Aunt Mary."

She watched him lean against the doorframe, looking stoop-shouldered and small. "That's okay," she said. "Maybe we'll snack on it later."

Verna Stouffer looked like a woman who hoped for the best but was armed to the teeth should she be mistaken. She was an inch shorter than Mary, some forty pounds heavier, and eleven years older. She also had a husband, more or less, and a son of sorts. These gave her a certain security, though not quite equal to that which she found in having been born again. An indelible wrinkle over the bridge of her nose made her appear to be frowning, which she was, much of the time, salvation or no. Warren used to comment both on the wrinkle and the eleven-year lull between Verna's birth and Mary's. He said that their parents, having put up with Verna for so long, must have thrown caution to the winds and opted for a little joy in their lives.

Verna's husband, Sam, was built like a box, and he smiled constantly when there was company about, almost never if there was not. He was even shorter than Verna, wore a size 17 shirt collar, and was strong enough to have carried Grandpa Myles—a big man himself—up two flights of stairs when he fell once in the basement. His face was red-brown and weatherbeaten, and it was a family secret that he had not lived intimately with Verna for eight years. But the marriage enabled her to put a "Mrs." in front of her name. And in Charles County, that was important.

Mary was never quite sure what emotional glue it was that held the two together, because Verna never talked about their separate lives. As Mary pulled in the drive by Verna's house, she wondered how she could explain it to Jake.

"Do they have any kids?" Jake asked.

"A son, but he's in the Navy. Didn't your father ever mention your cousin Bill?"

"I don't remember. Is this their farm?"

"No. That's up near White Plains. Sam stays up there most of the time." Mary hesitated. "The truth is, Verna and Sam don't live together much at all. The only time Sam comes down here is when there's company or something."

Jake nodded, seemingly unperturbed, and got out by the beech tree.

They were instantly greeted by a big half-breed collie who was going crazy, barking and circling, his tail wagging all the while.

"Tibs! Hush! Be quiet!" Mary said, extending one hand. The dog came over apologetically, licked her palm, sniffed at Jake, and then, satisfied that all was well, did a mongrel round-dance of welcome, leaping up every so often to lick Jake's face.

Jake laughed delightedly.

"See how Tibs loves that boy!" Verna came bustling down the side steps, wiping her hands on a towel. The wrinkle above her nose was sharper than ever, but she was clearly happy to see Jake.

"My goodness, what a fine looking boy!" she said, coming up to him and yanking his head against her bosom, holding him fast.

Sam, smiling broadly, followed her down the walk. "Don't break the kid's neck, Verna. You're fifty pounds heavier than when you saw him last, remember."

Verna ignored him.

"Bless your heart, Jake, but you're just a little tyke, too young for all that's happened to you," she clucked. "Isn't he small for thirteen, Sam? Mary, you've got a responsibility now, you know, to feed this boy good."

"Glad to see you, Jake," said Sam, extending his hand, and Jake shook it. "How you doin', Mary?"

"I've been fine. And busy. But it's nice to have someone else in the old house with me."

"Been tellin' you for years to get yourself a husband, but you'd never listen. All spring chickens grow up to be old hens eventually, you know."

Verna turned her back on Sam, put an arm around Jake's shoulder, and marched him toward the house.

"You know what we're having for dinner? Ham. I've got a big platter full, and if there's one thing I like, it's a boy who eats! I won't even tell you what I've made for dessert. You'll just have to wait and find out, but you save room for it, hear?"

Mary and Sam followed behind.

The dining table was already set with rose-patterned plates and there was no time for socializing first. Sam Stouffer liked his meals at six sharp, and Verna, knowing he wouldn't come to dinner at all unless he could count on it, didn't fail him.

"How 'bout if you sit over here close to me?" Sam said to Jake, motioning to a chair on the left side of the table. Mary took a chair across from Jake, leaving Sam and Verna to sit at the ends. There was still an extra plate beside Mary, however.

"Who's that for?" Jake inquired.

As if in answer, the dining room door banged open, and a large gaunt man in a wheel chair came rolling in. A few feet from the table he stopped, his eyes staring wide and curious at the boy across the table.

"Now, Dad," said Verna, carefully maneuvering his chair up to the table. "That's Jake, Warren's boy. Remember, I told you yesterday that he was coming?" Her voice had the ring of an overworked school teacher.

The old man's mouth dropped open and his tongue seemed undecided about where to go first. He tried to lift his right hand, but it fell heavily back his lap. His lips moved at last.

"Dong do it no how," he said, and drooled slightly. Jake gawked.

"He's had a stroke, you know, Jake," Verna explained.

"We're having ham, Grandpa," said Sam loudly, as though his father-in-law were deaf.

The old man stopped staring at Jake and focused hard on Sam.

"That's Sam, Dad," said Mary.

When at last they were all settled, Verna looked expectantly down the table her husband. All heads bowed except the old man's and Jake's, who stared unabashedly at each other. Mary lifted her eyes and watched them, amused.

It was the only religious rite that Sam still observed, as far as Mary knew. It confirmed him as head of the house—an absentee landlord, so to speak.

"Our heavenly Father, thank you for this day and this food, bless-it-to-nourish-our-good-Amen," he said, and reached for his napkin.

"Merry dingle," said the old man with much expression, and began studying the small bits of food that Verna was putting on his plate.

"Well, Jake, what do you think of Maryland?" asked Sam.

Jake accepted the platter that was offered him, selected a piece of meat, and passed it on. "I like Aunt Mary's backyard," he said.

"Aunt Mary's backyard!" Sam threw his head back and guffawed. "You should see our farm up at White Plains. Seventy acres. Why, you just don't see open space like that around Santa Monica, I'll bet."

"We'll put Tibs in the station wagon and drive you up there tomorrow after church," Verna said. "Would you like that?"

Jake looked at Mary.

"I know he'd like to see it sometime," Mary said, and again she noticed the slight tremor in her voice, "but I'm not sure about tomorrow, Verna. Let's see how things work out."

"Catsup!" bellowed Grandpa Myles suddenly. His voice, along with his spittle, seemed to explode over the table.

"What's the hell's he want to put catsup on?" Sam asked.

"He means butter," said Verna, and put a blob of it on Grandpa's mashed potato.

"Catsup!" roared the old man again, indignantly.

Mary went out to Verna's kitchen and returned with the catsup bottle. She poured some in the center of his plate. With his left hand, Mary's father picked up a small piece of ham and swirled it around in the sauce.

"Thank you," he said precisely.

"How come sometimes he talks right and sometimes he doesn't?" Jake asked softly.

Grandpa Myles stopped chewing and looked intently at Jake. The boy blushed.

"When he tries to talk," Mary explained, "all sorts of things come out. It's very frustrating for him."

"Can he understand us?"

"We're not sure. We think he understands most of it. But he doesn't usually find the right words to answer back."

Jake looked at the old man. "I like your shirt."

Grandpa Myles stared even harder at Jake, and finally down at his red flannel shirt.

"Chollie," he said, and smiled.

"Now what's this about eating only one ear of corn and giving up?' demanded Verna, passing the plate to Jake.

"You said to save room for dessert," he told her.

"Listen, you come out on the farm with me next summer, Jake, and I'll put muscle over those bones," Sam said, squeezing Jake's upper arm playfully. "Verna's not the only one who can cook around here. You ought to see the spread I can put on a table. Isn't that right, Mary?"

"Your uncle's a pretty good cook, Jake," Mary obliged.

Grandpa Myles tried to lift a spoonful of peas to

his mouth and sent them flying all over the table. Verna scraped them up with the edge of her knife.

"You haven't seen your cousin Bill yet, either," she said to Jake. "He's in the Navy. Did Mary tell you?"

"It's done wonders for the boy," Sam added. "Made a man of him. Good place, the Navy. You'll be a sailor yourself some day, Jake, I'll bet."

Jake shook his head. "I'm going to be a pacifist."

In unison, Sam and Verna lifted their heads and stared at Jake. Mary, across the table, watched in surprise.

"A *pacifist!*" said Sam. "Who put that in your head?"

"I told Mother once I didn't want to kill anybody and she said I didn't have to. I could be a pacifist."

"Well, for heaven's sake, Bill hasn't killed anybody either," said Verna, frowning. "Just because you're in the Navy doesn't mean you go around shooting."

"You travel," said Sam. "See the world. Learn yourself a trade."

"But if there was a war I'd have to," said Jake. "And I don't think I could ever kill anything. Not even a horse or something."

"Hell, kid, the next war there's not going to be much shooting," Sam told him, pushing away from the table. "Fire a few missiles and blast the hell out of them. That's the way it's going to be."

"No," said Jake. "I'm going to be a pacifist. I already wrote it in my journal."

"Chollie," said Grandpa Myles.

The night breeze swept noiselessly into the room, leaving a scent of leaves and earth. Then it faded out again, and the curtains fluttered to a standstill, hanging pale and limp in the moonlight. Always before, autumn had seemed to Mary more like a shroud, trailing a dry, dead smell in its wake. But tonight there was a freshness to the wind that gave the small bedroom a feeling of newness and life.

She lay on her back, knees bent, one hand resting lightly on her abdomen. Idly she stroked her stomach through the thin cotton grown and wondered if this was how it felt to be pregnant—this strange feeling of expectancy. Autumn, this year, had brought with it a beginning, not an end, and it was the first time she could remember contemplating November without being depressed.

She heard Jake get up and go into the bathroom. She heard the trickle of water as he urinated, the sudden loud flush of the john, the squeak of the faucet, and finally a rolling, clunking sound as the plastic cup slipped from his hands and tumbled into the sink. Then there were footsteps in the hall again, and the soft click of Jake's door at the other end.

He belonged here now; it was official. In the space of four days, her life had taken on a new dimension, an unexpected pleasure. How was it that last Tuesday she had gone to sleep in the same bed, feeling either too hot or too cold, bored, depressed, and constipated, and now was eager to sleep so that she could hurry and wake up again, curious to face whatever tomorrow would bring?

What tomorrow usually brought was nine-to-four in the office of the Faith Holiness Church. What tomorrow usually brought was another day the same as the one before. Life was a circular freeway with familiar markings at regular intervals—work, shopping, dinner, Verna's, work, shopping, dinner, church—and no exits in sight.

She had longed to wake up some morning and *not* see old Mr. Buddinger walking to the mailbox at the end of his drive. She wished she could shop in a store where beef did *not* go on sale every Thursday, and there were other cheeses besides Swiss and cheddar. She wanted to amble down a street where people did not know the names and birth dates of her parents and what her brother and sister had done to bring either disgrace or glory to the family name.

For thirty-four years she had lived in Charles County—in that very house—and still there was a part of her that could not call it home. Why, then, had she stayed?

Until a year ago, the answer had been obvious. Her mother, finally bedridden during Mary's second year in the junior college, needed constant care. After Mary got her diploma, it seemed only natural that she would assume the responsibility. If she'd had big plans, things might have been different. If Mary had had a career waiting, perhaps other arrangements would have been made. She was partly responsible for her own predicament, that she knew.

But Mary had been adrift at sea. Warren, by some unspoken, unwritten agreement, had been supposed to take her with him when he left Marbury once and for all. Hadn't they talked about it when they were eleven and twelve? Hadn't they winked at each other across the table at fifteen and sixteen when Verna or their mother talked about the wisdom of settling down in a stable community? Hadn't they choked once, in a laughing fit, when their father talked about how Warren might like to buy old Mr. Buddinger's house some day?

Suddenly, however, on a night Mary would never forget, Warren had left for good, and he'd left alone. Weeks afterwards, Mary had still felt paralyzed by it, half expecting him to send for her, but knowing that the master plan had been a pipe dream all along. There had been no plan except to get out—some time, in some way—and it was everybody for himself.

As for a career, what could she have done with two years of college and no major whatsoever? How was she supposed to have responded when neighbors said to her crippled mother, "Thank the good Lord you've got Mary Martha"? Her life had been predestined, that's what. God in all his wisdom knew that Warren would get away and Mary would not.

And so, for fourteen years she had taken care of her mother, who grew more complaining and difficult with each passing week. For fourteen years she had attended to her daily baths and enemas and various medications while each Christmas her father had said, "This one will be her last," and Mary believed him.

Had she known then that the first year would stretch to fourteen, would she have stayed? Had she known that she would go to bed night after night, for five thousand one hundred and ten nights, alone and untouched, would she have stood at the back door and screamed?

She wasn't sure. The fact was that she *had* stayed, and she had not screamed. And even after her mother's death and her father's stroke had set her free, she stayed because she felt she had become a stranger to the rest of the world. She was, quite simply, afraid. Changes, which one might make lightly at twenty, were discussed and dissected and revised again and again at the age of thirty-four.

Verna had never once, she claimed, even thought of leaving Marbury. Living there was a comfort. The church people would help her any time she asked—they were that sort of Christians. If someone fell ill, the neighbors simply took over temporarily—cooking, cleaning, running errands. Where else could you find a community where the doctor still made house calls, Verna always asked—where people still visited each other on Sunday afternoons?

It *was* a comfort, in a way—the familiar rhythm of life going on as it always had, a life you could count on. Mary herself, for example, liked to sit on Verna's screened porch on hot afternoons, waiting for the first faint stirrings of the breeze that always blew in about four. But she hated the way Verna always said, when she felt it, "Here it comes!" She hated its monotony, the total lack of originality. She hated the very expectancy, the predictability, of being bored. If she could just have the breeze without the comment, change without risk, growth without disillusionment. . . .

But now Jake was here, and whatever change she made in her life, if any, would involve him. The bubble of panic surfaced again in her throat. Had she, once more, waited too long? Should she have made her move quickly during the last year and got out while she still had the chance? Would Jake, and the new responsibility he brought, keep her here in Marbury the rest of her days, or was he a messenger, of sorts, from Warren—a guide to get her out?

She took a deep breath and closed her eyes against the moonlight on the opposite wall. Her fingers slowly swept her belly in wider and wider arcs till at last they settled on the spongy mass of pubic hair below. One finger searched out the cleft, burrowing down in the soft furrow, making her gown wet beneath the finger.

Suddenly she withdrew her hand and placed it firmly on the sheet beside her. For heaven's sake, she thought, there was a young boy not two rooms away. If she was going to bring up Jake in Marbury, she was going to have to act like a proper aunt. And yet. . . .

Her schizoid self. Her hand returned, and she welcomed it. Somehow she would have to decide where her soul belonged, whether here in Charles County or the beach house in Malibu.

THREE

It would help, Mary decided, if she knew for sure she were saved. At least it would be a place to start. If she *wasn't* saved, if there *were* no grace, and God was going to go on not speaking to her like this, well. . . .

"You'd think I'd have something to show for it if I was," Mary said.

Liz Grossman lowered her glasses and peered at her over the frames. "Should I be able to tell just by looking? You want to turn around slowly, or what?"

The same old Liz.

"I need answers," Mary said, "not jokes about something that's been a part of me all these years."

Liz had come over Sunday evening only to find that Jake was in bed.

"He's asleep already?" she'd asked. "I thought I'd at least say hello."

"He's been so tired. It's emotional, I'm sure," Mary had told her. "Come on in. We made a fire."

It had rained that morning, so there had been no drive to the farm in the station wagon. Nor had Mary and Jake gone to church.

"He needs time to pull himself together before we go introducing him around," Mary had explained timidly when Verna called.

"You're being overprotective, Mary. Didn't you see how he enjoyed himself at my place last night?"

"But there are so many people at church," Mary had protested. "They'd pounce on him."

"You're only making excuses. As the twig is bent, so grows the tree," Verna had said, and hung up.

Mary had resolved it by waiting to see what time Jake woke up, and he obliged by waking up too late to make the service. So they'd stayed home. They had puttered about the house, sorted through several boxes of Warren's things in the attic, and finished putting away Jake's clothes. In the evening Mary had built the first fire of the season, and Jake had lain a long time before it, chin on his hands, silently staring. Mary had let him be.

Now, with Jake asleep again at the end of the hall, Mary and Liz sat on the rug next to the hearth over tea that had gone untouched.

There was no hint of humor in Liz Grossman's eyes now. "Listen," she said, "don't talk to me about taking religion seriously. Haven't I sat through countless Bar Mitzvahs and gone back home for Passover every year of my life? I understand religion, Mary. I understand the symbolism and the sacrifice and all that. But what I don't understand is why a thirty-four-year-old woman has to go her whole life doing penance by denying herself cosmetics and movies and dances and jewelry and cigarettes and beer and card games and . . . have I left something out? Bathing suits, maybe? Good grief, Mary, you fundamentalists have more rules than Moses could have imagined! How do you ever manage to procreate, for God's sake? And I don't mean your personally. . . ."

Mary picked up her tea cup and set it down again.

There were times she felt peeved at Liz, and this was one of them. "So I don't wear make-up and you don't eat pork. I don't go to movies and you don't eat oysters. What's the difference?"

"The difference, sweetie, is that the only time I don't eat pork and oysters is when I'm home for the holidays, and you know it. Then I observe tradition for my father's sake, for all the generations who have gone on before me, for the reassurance of relatives who worry about my leaving the faith. You know what I had for lunch today, Mary? Bacon, lettuce, and tomato, with butter, yet! And you know what? I won't lose a second's sleep over it. Listen: regardless of what you've done with your life up until now, you've got another thirty-four years ahead of you. Are you going to go on forever being so damn prim?"

"Stop it!" Mary's voice had an edge that neither she nor Liz had heard before. It startled them both, but Liz seemed pleased, as though she'd dredged up something long overdue. Mary, however, flushed. "I'm not as prim and proper as you think," she said quietly, her eyes on the fire. "I'm not nearly as innocent as you imagine." Suddenly she drew her knees up close to her chest and rested her head on them, face down. "Oh, Jesus, Liz, I'm not even sure I'm a virgin."

The silence in the room seemed unnatural. A small, sudden crackling of the fire was an explosion in contrast. Liz dropped her hands at her sides and stared at Mary.

"You know," she said, "if you told me you were, I wouldn't be surprised. If you told me you weren't, I'd be surprised but not shocked. But when you don't even know . . . ! My God, Mary, I'm fascinated!"

Mary leaned back, her head on the couch, and watched the shadows darting about on the ceiling. Wasn't this the way it had always been—Mary, betwixt and between—between adult and child, sexual and chaste, liberal and conservative, sinner and saint? How it would help her to know the condition of her virginity as well as the state of her salvation, she wasn't sure, except that it would define her. If she'd been living one way, for example, when she was destined for another. . . .

If you asked any of the two hundred and twenty-nine members of the Faith Holiness congregation what they thought about the morals of their church secretary, they would all give her, she was sure, a vote of confidence. She could tell by the way they said good morning to her on Sundays or patted her arm at weddings. After all, where had the girl ever gone that she could have gotten herself deflowered? The dates in high school had been shy, hand-holding affairs with local boys, and if any of them had ever got under the waistband of her panties, half of Charles County would have known within forty-eight hours. Even when she'd enrolled in the junior college, she was always home by evening to look after her mother.

What the two hundred and twenty-nine members did not know, however, was that Mary Martha had been eating her lunch each day in the parked car of Lester Sims. He was a big fellow, a little on the pudgy side, who went to school mornings in Charles County and worked in a hardware store afternoons somewhere else.

They had begun eating lunch together on the campus and later, when the weather grew chilly, in the front seat of Lester's Buick. They shared their hard-

boiled eggs and salami sandwiches, and sometimes
Mary made a cake and brought in two pieces. By the
time the weather got really cold, they were parking out
behind the maintenance building and had moved to
the back seat with a lap robe thrown over them. By the
second week of December, Lester's hand had indeed
found its way under the waistband of Mary's pants.

"There was a boy at school during my second year,
after you left for the University," Mary told Liz hesitantly, and lapsed again into silence. The details were
too embarrassing. But they haunted her, nonetheless.

The last day before Christmas vacation, Lester had
told Mary he might not be coming back to school in
January—the boss wanted him to work full-time or
not at all. Mary had wept, not because she would
miss Lester particularly, but because she would miss
having a place to go over the lunch hour, someone
waiting for her. And then she was flat on her back
with her knees spread, and Lester—all one-hundred-
ninety pounds of him—was hulking over her, telling
her how he couldn't help himself, begging her to be
good to him, and she had felt like Mother Earth at
planting time and had enveloped him protectively in
her arms. His huge plow of a penis was sliding back
and forth over her, and suddenly she had been
bathed in warmth and wetness, and Lester had collapsed on top of her, crooning out his gratitude.

She had not gone to class that afternoon but to the
women's room instead to sponge off the stiff white
patches from her clothes, and there she discovered
that her face and neck had broken out in red welts,
making her itch all over. She had tried to examine
herself, to discover if Lester had actually penetrated
her, but she wasn't sure. A little, maybe. Did it have

to be all the way? Was there a semi-virginal state, perhaps, that did not interfere with salvation?

Still, she had not felt particularly guilty because
Lester had been so grateful. It was more like the
Good Samaritan. Two days before Christmas, however, she realized that her menstrual period was late.
Then, in a burst of fear and remorse, she had gone to
see the old pastor and, weeping, wanted to know how
she could tell if Jesus still loved her. The old man
didn't ask what she'd done, but simply got down on
his knees with her and prayed and told her afterwards that she could consider herself a new woman in
God's sight. That afternoon she began menstruating
and knew that God had heard her prayer. Two
months later, when the minister died with Mary's
half-guessed secret in his heart, Mary knew that she
was finally free and that only Lester, wherever he
was, knew whether she was or was not still a maiden.

"We . . . were in his car once," Mary said finally, knowing she'd have to tell Liz something, "and
he . . . he came all over me. I wasn't sure if he
really went in. . . ."

Liz folded her arms across her chest, eyes laughing,
but otherwise serious. And gentle. "Did bells ring and
violins play and the earth move, Mary?"

"No. The car shook a little, that's all."

Liz sighed. "Doesn't prove a thing. I was just curious, that's all."

"Is that the way it usually is?" Mary asked. How
could this be so, when the movie advertisements in
the *Post* showed women leaning back with eyes
closed, mouths open, abandoning themselves to ecstasy? True, they were not crammed in the back of
Lester's Buick, but they were certainly enjoying something great and wonderful.

"The earth moves only once in a while, Mary. For me, anyway. Has something to do with the mood, the man . . . maybe it's connected to the lunar cycle, who knows?" Liz reached for the tea, and then she too sat quietly, her face over the steam of the cup.

There were times when her friend's eyes appeared far older than they really were, Mary decided, and suddenly she wanted the familiar wise-cracking Liz back again. She tried to think of something clever to say herself—about how they had started out with the question of Mary's soul and ended up at the other end. But at this moment feelings seemed best shared through silence, and so she watched the glow of the embers at her feet and said nothing.

It seemed almost too cruel to wake Jake the next morning. Mary stood in the doorway watching the slight figure in the T-shirt and pajama bottoms breathing deeply through half-opened mouth. A bare leg was wound around on top of the covers, and an arm dangled off the side of the bed.

"Jake," she said softly. "The first bell is at 8:40. I'll be driving you this morning."

One eye opened, the pupil rolled back, and Jake was asleep again. Mary turned on the desk lamp and set some clothes out for him. "Jake," she said again, "we have to leave in twenty-five minutes."

"O-*kay!*" the boy snapped irritably, waving her away. Then his eyes opened and he stared at her in confusion. "Okay," he said again, more politely. "I'll be there in a minute."

As they drove up to the school, yellow buses were already parked at the circular drive, emptying themselves of teenagers. The young people called to each other in maddeningly loud voices, knocked books from each other's arms, bumped and jostled and moved slowly toward the low sprawling building that held them captive till 3:15.

Mary sensed Jake's reluctance to get out. "It's a big place," she said.

"It's ugly. Boy, is it ever ugly! In Santa Monica our school was really nice."

"Well, I guess it's what's inside that's important. Maybe you'll find people warm and friendly. I certainly hope so."

He opened the door and stepped out.

"Do you want me to come in with you, Jake?"

"No. I'll go by myself."

"The principal's office is just inside the door. He said he'd show you to your homeroom."

She watched him stride up the walk behind the other students, shoulders haunched as though trying to bury his head in his collar. Tears welled up in her eyes and then quickly disappeared. She *was* being overprotective. She turned the key in the ignition and drove away without looking back.

The church office was two miles in the other direction. Mary drove leisurely. In the past she had always liked Mondays because they meant an end to weekends. Mondays meant a new start. It was easier to fantasy about the seven days that had not yet happened than to reflect on the seven that had just passed. Today, however, Mary felt no special pleasure in sitting down at her desk.

Reverend Ralph Gordon was tall and gaunt and

spoke with a trace of the southern drawl he had acquired as a minister in Georgia. He had married his childhood sweetheart, who was now heavier than he by some fifteen pounds, and they had come to Maryland as confident of the move as they had been of each other twenty-five years before.

"His hand is on the tiller," Pastor Gordon always said after he had made a decision, and no one could argue with that without taking on the Almighty.

He was, in every sense, a fundamentalist preacher. He believed that there were no myths in the Bible because every word of it was true. Every commandment, law, rule, and practice was divinely inspired. Every event described therein had happened: Daniel in the lion's den, the plagues, the Red Sea, the Ark. That there were contradictions, that times had changed, that women then were exhorted not to braid their hair or that innocent animals were sacrificed as gifts to the Almighty seemed to him customs which could be judiciously ignored. That some of the Old Testament fathers impregnated their wives' maid-servants or gave issue unto their brothers' widows was a matter which the preacher did not even acknowledge. He ate ham and sausage at church suppers because Jews did not, and that seemed reason enough.

Ralph Gordon also believed that universal order began with the shoes in one's own closet, and this extended to the church office as well. Books were arranged by subject, and there were separate journals for baptism, weddings, and funerals. There was even a log for recording conversions, but this had proved something of a trial. Backsliders invariably caused people to wonder about the authenticity of the big event, yet there it was, all down in black and white.

In general, Mary and the pastor got on rather well. She was prompt about getting out the weekly newsletter, careful about his calendar, sympathetic in listening to grievances of various members, and meticulous in making arrangements for church functions. They shared the same small office in the basement of the church next to the kitchen, and if someone needed to talk to the pastor privately, he led them to one of the Sunday school rooms and closed the door.

The only area of contention between them was the reference folders. Every week the pastor placed a stack of newspaper and magazine clippings on her desk to be filed in the huge "Resource" cabinet kept for ready reference. There, in four long drawers, sat hundreds of folders in alphabetical order, bulging with a lifetime of collected clippings, beginning with "abasement," "abstinence," and "abundance," through "worship," "youth," and "Zion." What the pastor was looking for under "fornication," for example, Mary might have filed under "love," and what he had searched a half hour for in the folder marked "sin," Mary had filed under "pleasure."

"Approach your work more prayerfully," he told her once, "and God will show you how."

She was aware, of course, that the entire Faith Holiness Church was an anachronism. She knew that any group that could survive the swinging sixties and the indulgent seventies without taking on a little eyeshadow or dancing or canasta, even, was something else. *My God,* she'd thought when she had visited the junior high school and noticed the number of girls with pierced ears, *even my ear lobes are virgins!*

There was a specialness, however, in being apart. Hadn't she been taught that as long as she could remember? The fundamentalists were something different, their taboos a badge of distinction, their beliefs their source of strength. Stares and taunts, her mother had always told her, were only disguised manifestations of respect and envy. *Who shall ascend into the hill of the Lord? or who shall stand in his holy place?* The two hundred and twenty-nine members of the Faith Holiness Church, that's who.

During the last fourteen years, however, Mary had felt less and less special. When people stared at her chalk-white face in the department stores, she was not certain it was out of respect. When the girls who went braless in hot pants had been married off before anyone else, and Mary stayed home with her rheumatoid mother, she did not feel that she was the envy of anybody. And when, on her few chaste dates with Marbury's eligible bachelors, she compared the subjects they discussed with the ones on the cover of *Redbook* and *Cosmopolitan,* she wondered if "The Myth of the Mutual Orgasm" was something she would ever be able to talk about, or whether it was still light years away.

How she ended up in the church office as secretary just when she was on the verge of her freedom, she wasn't quite sure, except that after her mother died, everybody agreed that she would need something to "occupy" her. The next thing she'd known, Verna had called with the "wonderful news" that Pastor Gordon was looking for a secretary—one of the faith. And because she'd need experience and references to go anywhere else, she took it. Catch-22: to get out of Marbury, she'd have to stay in it.

On this particular Monday, Mary was surprised to find the minister waiting for her when she came in.

"Hanging around here on your day off?" she said. "I thought you'd be out enjoying the sun after all the rain we had yesterday."

"I wanted to see you," the pastor smiled. "How did it go? How's the boy?"

"Holding up better than I'd expected. He doesn't talk easily—not about that, anyway. But I think he will in time. It's a new experience for us both."

"He's lucky to have an aunt who cares about him," Reverend Gordon said. "Young people are more resilient than we imagine. He'll be okay. The important thing is to lead him to Christ, and I know I can count on you."

The Madonna Mary. Mary Madonna Myles.

She got off early that afternoon and waited for Jake. She wandered into his bedroom and opened his closet door, marveling again at the newness of seeing a young boy's clothes in her house. It was as though the walls and woodwork had taken on a different color since he'd come, as though it were autumn outside but spring inside. She half-expected the hat rack to bloom.

At three-twenty-five, the school bus rumbled down the road and squealed to a stop in front of the house. Jake came plodding across the grass, notebook under his arm. Other faces stared curiously from the windows of the bus as it moved on.

"Thought you didn't get off till four," Jake said when he saw her.

"Reverend Gordon let me leave early." She held the screen open. "How did it go?"

"Okay."

"Were you able to find all your classes?"

"Yeah. One of the guys showed me around."

"Good! You made friends, then!"

He shrugged.

"Hungry?"

"Yeah, I guess so."

He threw his jacket on a chair, went out to the kitchen, and ate some cookies standing up. Mary wondered at his silence.

"Anything bad happen at school, Jake?"

"Huh uh. Why?"

"Just wondering. How about good things? What was the nicest part of your day?"

"Coming home," Jake said, and reached for the milk.

The feeling was mutual. Mary smiled to herself, got out the vegetables for stew, and sat down at the table to pare them. Jake leaned against the kitchen wall watching her, his back sliding lower and lower, inch by inch, till he checked himself, stood up straight again, and once more began the slow slide. Mary tried not to notice.

"Who was here last night?" he asked finally.

She looked up. "Liz Grossman, a friend of mine. Did we wake you?"

"I don't know. I heard somebody yapping about pork and oysters and bacon and tomato sandwiches, and then I went back to sleep. Gad, what a mouth."

Mary laughed. "You'll like her, Jake. Really."

He shook his head. "Huh uh."

"Why do you say that?"

"Whenever somebody tells me I'm going to like someone, I don't. It's really weird."

"Okay, then, *don't* like her," Mary said, playing the game, "but she's my best friend."

"What's she got against oysters?"

"Nothing. She's Jewish and observes tradition—sometimes."

"Weird," said Jake, and took another cookie. "How'd you meet her?"

"In college. We took a philosophy class together. The next year she went to American University in the District, and I stayed at the junior college. I didn't suppose we'd ever meet each other after that. But life's funny. . . ."

"Yeah? What happened?"

"She got her master's degree in social work and married a man with multiple sclerosis. I got my diploma and stayed home to take care of mother. So we both ended up with invalids on our hands."

Jake sat down across from Mary. "Boy, you sure take a long time to tell a story."

She was half-pleased, half-startled by his insouciance. If he was this flip after three days, what would he be like in three years? Warren's genes, all the way.

"Liz's husband died," she said simply. "She got a job as social worker at the hospital in La Plata, and when we took mother there, I met her again."

"How'd he die—her husband?"

"He fell down the stairs."

"Jeez! How old was he?"

"Thirty-seven."

"Christ! Couldn't he have hung onto something? Grabbed the banister or something?"

"I suppose he tried, Jake. People with MS lose control, you know. . . ."

Jake sat turning the bag of cookies around and around on the table. "When it looks like I'm going to die," he said finally, "I'm going to do everything I can to keep it from happening."

"You can't go around expecting it all the time, Jake. Sometimes it takes you by surprise. . . ." Mary stopped, knowing what they were both thinking.

"Just the same, I'm going to try."

Coming home to Jake was different from stopping by Verna's. Verna was predictable. Her life had settled down in its well-worn ruts and her main topics of conversation were (1) Sam—what a trial he' was; (2) Bill—what a worry he was; and (3) Grandpa Myles—completely impossible. Men, in other words, were really messing things up. Someday, she always said, God would call Grandpa home, but until then he was the cross she had to bear, and if Christ could make it to Calvary with his, she could hold up for another few years.

But Jake's conversations were not so predictable, or his life either. Mary expected to find almost anything at all when she arrived home each afternoon at four, and on Friday of the first week she found Brick.

He was sitting at the kitchen table playing cards with Jake. Taller and heavier, he had curly brown hair which half-circled his acne-covered face. When Mary came in he looked up, then glanced at Jake and waited.

"Spades," said Jake, studying his hand. "Aunt Mary, this is Brick Adams."

"Hi, Brick. Nice to meet you."

"Hi." The voice was low in pitch, contrasting sharply with Jake's. Mary waited a moment, found herself totally ignored as the game went on, and finally retreated to the bedroom to change clothes.

Who do they think they are, taking over my kitchen like that? she thought. *Cards, yet!* The spinster-aunt rose up inside her and clucked her tongue.

Jake was more animated that evening, however, than Mary had seen him yet, and he smiled occasionally when he talked.

That's what's been missing, Mary thought as she listened. *The smile.*

"Brick's the one who shows me around at school," Jake explained. "When I asked the way to the gym, someone sent me to the girls' locker room, and Brick stopped me just in time."

"Well, thank goodness for that!" Mary laughed.

"Yeah. He's okay. Collects stamps, too. He invited me to come over Sunday and look at his first-day covers."

"We'll be going to church Sunday morning, Jake. Save time for that. Otherwise, it's fine with me."

Jake toyed with his fork. "What church is it?"

"The same church your father and Verna and I were brought up in—Faith Holiness."

"Dad never went to church in Santa Monica."

"I'm not surprised." Mary wondered if she sounded cold. She felt cold. "Your mother never went either?"

"No. She was an agnostic."

"Oh." Mary cut her broiled chicken into smaller and smaller pieces. The irritation she had felt earlier surfaced again. Warren must have known the bind she was in back here in Marbury. Why push their kid off onto her? What was this, a sick joke?

"I think I'm an agnostic too," Jake said. "That's not like an atheist, is it? It just means you're not sure."

Mary salted her meat, eyes on the table. "I don't know how anyone who looks at the sky and grass and trees can doubt God's existence, Jake. Life itself is a miracle."

"My folks aren't alive."

"But that's not God's fault, Jake. You mustn't blame him for that. He just made our beautiful world, that's all. It's people who mess it up."

"Then how come he made people like that?"

Mark Twain's thoughts exactly. She struggled. How were you supposed to raise a child, anyway? Inflict your same doubts on him?

"I suppose he could have made us puppets, with him pulling the strings, but what kind of a world would that be?"

"It'd be okay."

"I don't know. Most of us appreciate having freedom of choice. Whatever happens, we bring it on ourselves."

Jake sat back and pushed his plate away. "Why do you pray, then?"

"I told you. To thank God for all the good things, and there *are* good things. To thank him for our food."

"But he didn't grow it. The farmers did. Why don't you pray to the farmers?"

"God sent the sun, the rain. . . ."

"You said he doesn't help."

"I certainly didn't say that. Sometimes he *does* intervene when we pray earnestly enough."

"Then he *can* do something about us if he really wants to."

Mary felt the walls closing in on her and did not answer. She should not have accepted this child. She should have referred the lawyer, when he called, to Verna. She should have explained that Verna had a bigger house, a husband, a son, a dog, and a mind like a steel trap.

"I guess he didn't want to help my folks," Jake went on. "He could have stopped that car from driving on the wrong side of the road, but he didn't."

"Oh, Jake, don't be bitter. I don't understand it either. But some day we will."

"When?"

"When we meet God."

"After we're dead, you mean?"

"Yes. . . ."

"That's too late." He sounded flip. Obnoxious, even.

"You're being arrogant—exactly like Warren."

"Well, he was my father!" Jake said, suddenly belligerent, and stood up. "Who would you expect me to be like?" He left the table and strode down the hall to his room, shutting hard, but not quite slamming, his door.

Mary sat motionless, her heart pounding rapidly. What on earth had she done? The boy had been here less than a week, and already she had provoked him into arguing with her, not only over a God she didn't understand, but Jake's dead father at that! He was right. Whom did she expect him to be like if not the man who had raised him? Did she think she could undo thirteen years of training in less than a week?

Did she even want to? And yet, she had this responsibility . . .

Her first impulse was to call the pastor, tell him what a theological mess she had made of things, and persuade him to come over and talk to Jake. Her second impulse was to scrap the first, resign her job, and move to Greenwich Village.

She felt a wide sweep of anxiety flood through her, subside, then flow again. She was trapped. She had accepted him here and it was official, but they weren't going to get along. That was obvious. Their backgrounds were poles apart. It was like marrying someone you had only met once before in your life. She resented the intrusion of this young stranger with all the doubts which she had tried so hard to hide. And he probably resented her. But where else would he go? To send him to Verna with all his questions would be throwing him to the wolves.

Numbly she stood up and began clearing dishes off the table, her thoughts racing on ahead. Suddenly she put down the dish towel and started toward Jake's room, just as he came out. They stopped, looking at each other.

"Jake," Mary said, carefully choosing her words, "if we're going to get along, we have to respect each other's differences. I guess we didn't do such a good job of that just now. For my part, I'm sorry."

"Yeah," Jake said. "So am I. You just turned me off—talking like that about my dad."

"Yes, I know. I shouldn't have."

There was an awkward standoff.

"You still going to make me go to church?"

"I can't make you do anything. I'd like you to go with me, but if you decide not to, well—that's that."

"How long does it last—the church service?"

"About an hour."

"Well, maybe I'll go, just to see how I like it."

"I'm glad."

Jake seemed satisfied with the way the argument ended. He opened his math book on the dining room table and sat down to work on his assignment, his shoulders hunched over his papers, one knee drumming up and down to some secret inner rhythm.

With Mary, however, the problem was unresolved. There would be more questions, and she knew that even Pastor Gordon, if asked, would be unable to answer them to Jake's satisfaction. As far as Verna was concerned, it was blasphemy even to question. A bit of Malibu stirred inside her as she slowly hung up the towel, wishing the whole conversation had never taken place.

She was barely out of the kitchen when the phone rang. In contrast to the silence in the house, Liz Grossman's vibrant voice seemed out of place.

"Listen, I'm going to Charlottesville again tomorrow, and I thought I'd stop by and visit Jake tonight. Is this a good time?"

"Well . . . I'm not sure. He's doing homework. Let me check." Mary put her hand over the mouthpiece. "Jake, it's Liz Grossman. She's going out of town over the weekend and would like to meet you before she goes. Is it okay if she comes over for a little while this evening?"

Jake exhaled loudly. "Okay," he said. "Let's get it over with. Bring on the battalions."

Mary supressed a smile. She uncovered the phone. "Bring on the battalions."

Jake whirled around and stared at her.

"The batallions, eh?" said Liz. "What's he after—blood?"

"That's the mood around here tonight."

"Oh. Got'cha. Really, though, you think I should come?"

"Can't hurt."

Mary hung up and sat down on the couch with the paper.

"Jeez!" Jake said, still staring. "You didn't have to tell her that!"

"Might as well be honest," Mary said calmly. "You don't like my church, don't like my friends . . ."

"I haven't even *been* to your church. I haven't even *met* your friends!"

"Exactly."

He stared at her some more, then slowly returned to his homework, shaking his head. "Jeez!" he said again, and the knee started bobbing up and down once more.

Liz Grossman lived in a condominium on Indian Head Highway, a half hour's drive from Marbury. She arrived in jeans and a suede jacket.

"Let me put on my glasses so I can see what the kid looks like," she said, sliding them over her ears. She peered at Jake through the huge blue-tinted lenses and slowly approached the dining room table. "Well! Hmmmm. . . ."

Mary laughed and Jake managed a smile.

"Liz, this is Jake," Mary said. "The one and only."

Liz promptly sat down across from him and tucked

her legs under her. "So how's it going?" she asked, and surveyed the homework spread out before him. "Algebra?"

"Yeah. Five pages. I'm still trying to make up for the work I missed."

"Oh, right. School much different from the one in Santa Monica?"

"Well, it's hard to tell yet. I think the schools out there are better. More advanced. Once I catch up in all my classes, it'll go pretty slow. That's what Brick says."

"Friend?"

"Yeah."

How easily she does it, Mary thought, watching from the side. *Liz simply walks in a room and relates, as simple as that.* She felt suddenly envious, but hated herself for her insecurity.

"Hungry, Liz?" And then, as a joke, "A bacon-to-mato sandwich, maybe?"

Liz looked at her. "A sandwich at this hour of the night?"

Mary laughed feebly. "Just wanted to prove to Jake you weren't afraid of pork." The joke fell flat. Nobody laughed. Jake looked at her aghast.

"Yeah?" Liz said, turning back to Jake. "So what else do you want to know about me?"

Jake blushed fiercely. "Jeez!" he said.

Oh, God, thought Mary. Then, to Liz, "He heard us talking the other night about dietary restrictions. He was curious, that's all."

"She blabs everything," said Jake.

"Oh, why not?" said Liz. "We're good friends. Besides, I don't mind talking about my traditions, relatives—the works. They may be old-fashioned, and some are a little crazy, but they're mine, you know? I mean, when you belong to somebody, you're special even if you can't stand each other."

Jake scratched his head with one end of his pencil and looked at her, then at Mary.

"Listen," said Liz, "if you want to know about relatives, let me tell you about the Passover Pig."

Jake put down his pencil.

"I've got this brother, see, who lived in Georgetown," Liz began, "and if you know Georgetown . . . you don't know Georgetown? Well, it's like—places in San Francisco, I suppose. You've got all these students and artists and musicians milling around and, well, that's where he lived. But he's a good Jew. Really. He observes the rules and traditions, and still my relatives worried about him because they didn't see how anybody could observe the Sabbath in Georgetown. Listen, am I boring you? I mean, keeping you from homework or anything?"

"It's Friday night," said Jake. "I've got the weekend."

"Okay, where was I? Oh, yeah. Well, this one year my brother decided to have the Seder in his apartment and invite the whole clan to reassure them—namely, my grandmother. He was going with a *shikse* then, and. . . ." Liz stopped at Jake's quizzical expression. "That's a gentile—your kind of people. I mean, it's not derogatory or anything, just a term. And this girl helped him prepare the table. Oh, my grandmother would have choked if she'd known, but she didn't. Everything was there—the roasted lamb bone and the roasted egg and the karpas and charoses—everything. Come Passover, we all go to Harold's apartment. He's got on his skullcap and the table's all prepared and my grandmother's smiling, and everybody's relieved that Harold's a proper Jew. Even his girl friend was out for the day so as not to upset anybody, and we're all thinking, 'At last, the perfect Passover, with no quarreling, no forgetting, no upsetting of tradition.'"

Jake was leaning back in his chair now, smiling with anticipation, and Mary knew that Liz had won him over.

"Well," Liz continued, her eyes on Jake, "right next to Harold's apartment was this guy who owned a pig. Now you see all kinds of things in Georgetown. I mean, you see men with safety pins through their noses and girls without any . . . never mind, but anyway, anything goes in Georgetown. And this guy that lived next to Harold had this pig, and every day he'd put a red leash on it and walk it up and down Wisconsin Avenue in front of the Safeway."

"What happened?" asked Jake.

"During Seder, as you know—no, you don't know— during Seder it's traditional to keep the front door open a little in hopes that the prophet Elijah will walk in and announce the coming of the Messiah. So here we all are around the table, prepared by this *shikse* that Grandmother doesn't know about, and we'd just got through the third filling of the wine glass when suddenly we hear the front door opening wider. Everybody turns and stares. And then, instead of Elijah, here comes this pig, right up to the Passover table and grunts. . . ."

Jake was beside himself. It was the first full-fledged laughter Mary had heard since he'd arrived, and she could tell by the tone of it, that all reserves were down, all barriers had crumbled. For Liz, at least; not necessarily for her.

On Sunday morning Jake arrived at the breakfast table in a long-sleeved nylon shirt with the faces of the Rolling Stones on his chest.

"I'm afraid I'll have to veto what you're wearing," Mary said reluctantly. "It's a great-looking shirt, but I doubt the congregation would understand."

Jake looked himself over. "What's wrong with it?"

"Our young people aren't supposed to listen to rock music. Some of them do, of course, but the older folk don't approve."

Jake stared.

Mary put the newspaper aside. "Look, I'd better be honest with you about our church. It's a small denomination—strict—and there are a lot of things we aren't supposed to do."

"Like what?"

"We can't drink liquor or smoke. The women are supposed to dress modestly, and we don't go to movies or play cards or dance."

"Broth-er!" said Jake. "I don't believe it!"

Mary smiled a little. Must sound pretty restrictive for a kid raised in California."

"It's sick!" said Jake. "I mean *sick!*"

"Oh, I don't know. We're a lot healthier than the so-called normal society with its drunkenness and dope." She paused, expecting an argument, but Jake said nothing. "Besides, we *are* changing some. When I was growing up, we didn't believe in mixed swimming or theater. Boys and girls had to go to the beach in separate groups, and it was considered a sin to put on a costume and be in a play. But last year at Easter, Pastor Gordon said we could attend the local passion play, and it was really a thrill."

"What the heck kind of play is that? Boy, he sure picks 'em!"

Mary blushed, then laughed. "It's not what it sounds. It's a dramatization of Christ's crucifixion. It was very inspirational."

"Well, you won't find *me* living like that, not going to shows or anything," Jake declared, settling down in his chair—an immovable mass. He glared down at the table. "Jeez!"

"That's entirely up to you. I just thought I'd better tell you this in advance. When I came home Friday and found you playing cards with Brick, I kept thinking how Verna would react if she knew."

"Who's going to tell her?" Jake asked incredulously.

"Well, I'm not, of course. But you've got to watch yourself when you're around our church people. No sense in purposely upsetting anyone."

Jake tipped his chair back until it was balancing on two legs. He was watching Mary carefully.

"You want to know what Dad used to say?"

Mary managed a smile. "I'm not sure that I do. . . ."

"He used to say that Aunt Verna was completely bananas, but there was still hope for Mary."

She should have smiled, but instead her pulse quickened and an electric warmth spread through her. Warren hadn't given up on her then, after all these years. He hadn't forgotten. He hadn't simply catalogued her as one of the Marbury women and never thought of her again. . . .

It was as though he were speaking to her now, as

though he had sent Jake to get her out, to take her away from all this, to plan the escape. . . . Jake's face seemed blurred beyond the steam of her coffee cup—ethereal, almost transparent.

"What else did Warren tell you about me?" she asked, and her voice sounded strangely high and little-girlish. Even she was aware of it.

Jake was watching her. "I don't know. Sometimes he'd say, 'Mary would like this,' when he read something funny in the paper. Stuff like that. . . ."

But Warren never sent her the clippings he said she would like—rarely wrote to her at all. The hard facts came barreling in, rolling over the excitement. Still, she knew now that Warren had thought of her, and had sent his child, the fruit of his loins, to her, to *her*. . . .

She lifted her cup and let the steam form a veil between her and the boy. She didn't want Jake here now, at this moment, wanted to remember in private. Had Warren, by some chance, realized she had followed him that night? That she had not stayed behind with the others, but had run after him down the road, hair flying, her face wet, her fingers on the buttons of her blouse?

But Jake would not be ignored. "Is that why my Dad went to California?" he was asking. "Because of the church? Because he couldn't go to the beach with girls or see movies or things like that?"

How much should I tell him? Mary wondered. All of it, perhaps, some day.

"That was a big part of it, Jake," she said. "Warren didn't belong here. I think we both sensed that. And then, one night . . ." She stopped. "Well, I guess he just decided he'd had enough. And after he got to California, he became involved in real estate along the coast and decided to stay. He met your mother, you were born. . . ." She stood up suddenly and began clearing dishes from the table. "So, now that I've told you what to expect, in the worst possible terms, I suppose you've changed your mind about going to church with me this morning."

"No way!" said Jake. "I'm curious as hell. Wouldn't miss it for anything."

FOUR

She timed it so that they arrived only moments before
the first hymn. After the service, she knew, people
would crowd about him—the old women in their
black hats, pinching his cheek and asking if he knew
John 3:16 or something. One ordeal was enough.

They sat halfway down on an outer aisle. Heads
turned and friendly faces smiled in their direction.
Mary smiled back. Jake examined the offertory envelopes, flipped through the hymnal, turned around to
count the numbers of pews behind them, and finally
settled down as the choir rose for the anthem.

Mary felt a strong empathy for the boy beside
her—the hard edge of the seat digging into the backs
of his skinny legs. She tried to put herself in Jake's
place, squinting to block out the familiar sights
around her so as to see them with a new perspective.
A plain church—plain and severe. An all-purpose
floor in a one-purpose room.

And the people. Did they look like people in Santa
Monica? What was there that told her right away
they were different? If she saw any of them at National Airport, for instance, wouldn't she know they
belonged here at Faith Holiness? The men looked
uncomfortable, for one thing. *All of them?* Mary
glanced around. Yes. To a man. All except Ralph

Gordon, their shepherd. Shepherds always had an assurance about them. And the women? Corpses. No eye shadow, no blush, no lipstick. Chalk-white faces turned up toward the choir. How long had they all been dead, and why was Mary just noticing it now?

She remembered another morning she had sat in this church on the very same side of the aisle, in fact, when she was Jake's age. Thirteen. The magic year of puberty. She had come with her family that morning to hear a visiting faith healer, Sister Ernestine, talk about "Jesus' Cleansing Power." She had watched the small woman in the nurse's uniform stand up there on the podium, with golden curls all over her head and thick glasses covering her eyes, telling about the afflictions she had cured—gall bladder, ulcers, arthritis, prostate, and gout-things Mary had scarcely heard of.

She had watched a long procession of parishoners come up during the service to be healed and had shifted uncomfortably in her seat as the small lady placed her hands on or near the offending organ, praying all the while. Mary had seen a huge woman with a twisted foot stand up and shout that she had been cured, and then start to cry when she discovered she couldn't walk after all. And she had seen people whisper secret afflictions into the blond curls of the faith healer, who nodded gravely and prayed silently under the curious stares and imaginings of the hushed crowd.

And then, just before the service had ended, Mary had felt a warm, wet flow from her own body, trickling down between her legs and onto the pew beneath. It had been only her second menstrual period, a week off schedule, and she had sat with her thighs pressed tightly together, thinking only of her white dotted swiss dress.

The service had ended then, and she had not dared move. Her parents were already migrating toward the center aisle where the faith healer stood, and then they were turning to introduce the family and found only Verna and Warren behind them, while Mary remained back on the pew, head down. Her mother had called to her to come meet Sister Ernestine, but Mary had not moved, her face crimson.

"Is she ill?" Mary's father had asked, and then the faith healer herself was coming toward her, a small crowd in tow. Verna, already a woman of twenty-four, kept whispering, "Who are you trying to kid, pretending to be crippled? What kind of attention-getting device is this, not being able to stand up?" Warren had watched with amusement.

"*Why* can't you walk, Mary?" her mother insisted, but a half dozen other people were also leaning over to hear.

"I . . . I just can't," Mary had whispered. *Oh God make them go away just turn around and leave me alone don't come near me anybody. . . .*

And then the faith healer was sitting down beside her in the pew, taking Mary's hands in her own, and said that she knew what was troubling her. She said that she suspected God had told Mary not to leave until Sister Ernestine had come over and prayed with her. She whispered to Mary that she knew she was in the clutches of a terrible habit, and that the habit was preying at Mary's heart, leaving her no peace. But Mary's hands, she had said, holding them tightly, could be pure as snow again if her heart was pure. And then, in front of everybody, she had told Mary that from that moment onward all she had to do when she felt tempted was to command her hands to stop in Jesus' name, and God would keep her holy. Warren had doubled over in silent laughter.

Sister Ernestine had kissed her then and told Mary's parents that the girl ought to be left alone for a while—that she was sure Mary would get up and come out when she felt she had been forgiven. And so everyone had gone outside, Verna casting suspicious glances over her shoulder, and finally, when everyone had driven off but the Myles, Mary got up and came out. When her mother saw the dark red spot on the back of her dress, she had said disgustedly, "For heaven's sake, Mary, why didn't you just *tell* me?"

And that was how Mary got herself prayed over by Sister Ernestine.

The anthem had ended and it was time for everyone to join in the first hymn of the morning. Mary rose and Jake stood dutifully beside her, frowning quizzically down at the words.

> *Yield not to temptation,*
> *For yielding is sin,*
> *Each vict'ry will help you*
> *Some other to win;*
> *Fight manfully onward,*
> *Dark passions subdue,*
> *Look ever to Jesus,*
> *He will carry you through.*
> *Ask the Savior to help you,*
> *Comfort, strengthen and keep you,*

He is willing to aid you,
He will carry you through.

The congregation sat down again with a great creaking of pews and coughing and rustling.

Pastor Gordon stood for the morning announcements. His big hands gripped the sides of the lectern, and he turned smiling toward Mary and Jake.

"I want you to know that we have a very special visitor with us this morning." The minister's voice reverberated across the sanctuary. "Most of you have heard, I'm sure, of the tragic death of Warren Myles, but now his son, Jake, has come to make his home with our very own Mary. We want to give him a big welcome to our church. We greet him as a friend and pray that in time he will be moved by Jesus Christ to join the fellowship as a member. Jake, would you stand up for a minute, please?"

Taken by surprise, Jake disentangled his feet like a baby stork, pulled his sport coat into place, and finally stood up. At first Mary thought he was nervously scratching his forehead and chest, and then she realized that he was making the sign of the cross.

Oh, my God, she breathed, staring.

Necks strained to see the young boy, faces smiled, and there were murmurs of "God bless you," and "Praise Jesus." When Jake sat down again, a woman behind them reached forward and patted him lovingly on the shoulder.

As the offertory plate went around, Jake whispered, "See that girl in the blue dress?"

Mary followed his gaze and nodded.

"I think she's wearing lipstick."

"Could be," Mary whispered back, and concentrated once more on the piano solo.

Jake leaned over again. "What will they do with her?"

"Nothing, Jake. They disapprove, that's all."

"They won't kick her out?"

"Shhhh. We'll talk about it later."

The sermon was not one of the pastor's best. He rambled on for twenty-five minutes about David's grief for Absalom and spent another fifteen tying it in with God's love. Jake sat still because a large horsefly had lighted on the back of his hand, and he was experimenting with how much movement the fly would tolerate.

The closing hymn and benediction came at last, and then the postlude. There was no pipe organ. A small stiff-backed woman sat at the upright and played a march of some kind, and soon Mary found herself standing on the sidewalk out front with Verna and Jake and a small crowd of well-wishers.

"You've come to the right place, lad," said an elderly man, shaking Jake's hand.

Verna hugged him hard against her bosom, her customary greeting. "I want Mary to bring you up to the farm this afternoon," she said. "I've got to pick the last of my tomatoes before the frost sets in, and you can explore the place with Tibs. How does that sound?"

"Okay," said Jake, smiling a little.

As Mary was turning toward the car with her nephew, someone stopped her, taking both her hands in his.

"Mary."

Marbury's most eligible bachelor—a balding, round-faced man of thirty-five—blocked her way.

"So this is the boy." Each word the man spoke was accompanied by a slight shake of Mary's hands. He dropped them then and reached for Jake's, repeating the ritual. "So this is the young man who's come to stay. Well, how do you do, young fellow? We're glad to have you, let me tell you."

He was a mild-looking man with an exceedingly clean shave. His thinning sideburns were trimmed precisely. At that very moment, the breeze shifted, and the scent of his shaving lotion flooded Mary's nostrils. She felt no attraction toward this man, no wild impulse to throw herself in his arms, and yet the scent stirred something within her, so close to the surface now that it was like a word on the tip of her tongue, a name almost remembered, a tune so near to consciousness that it could almost be hummed. What *was* it that haunted her, possessed her, filled her with a liquid sweetness she could almost taste? She stood motionless, waiting, hoping that another second of silence would finally lift the curtain. Then she felt Jake's eyes upon her, and she knew that the moment, once more, had passed her by.

"Jake, this is Milt Jennings," she said.

"How do you do?" said Jake.

"I've known your Aunt Mary for a long time, a very long time," the man went on. "When I heard that you were coming, I said to myself, 'that's the best thing that could happen to Mary Martha.' And now you're here."

"Now I'm here," Jake said in mock seriousness. Mary turned her face away.

"I'm not going to impose myself on you now," Milt said, meaning it for Mary but saying it for Jake, "but I want the three of us to have dinner together some time."

"Of course, Milt," said Mary. "After things get settled down a bit."

Milt dropped Jake's hands and again took Mary's. "Good," he said, beaming at her. "Good," he said again, and shook both her hands simultaneously.

"Who the heck was *that?*" Jake asked after they got in the car.

"An old friend of mine. Milt's been around for a long time." She tried not to laugh.

"He likes you, doesn't he?"

"Milt's friendly with everyone."

"Oh, you know what I mean."

There was no evading Jake's questions. "Yes, he thinks we ought to get married."

"Do you like him?"

"I don't dislike him, Jake. I just can't picture myself married to him, that's all."

Their car moved out of church traffic and headed onto open road.

"You said we'd talk about it later," Jake reminded.

"About what?"

"About the girl wearing lipstick and what they'd do if they found out."

"Honestly, Jake! What do you think they'd do? Burn her at the stake?"

"Well, all those things you said church members couldn't do. What would happen if somebody *did?*"

"It depends on the offense. Sometimes we don't do anything. Sometimes we have a special prayer service for someone we're worried about. If a member does something really awful, he has to repent publicly in front of the congregation before he can be admitted to membership again."

"Wow! Do they have to confess out loud?"

"No, but in a small community like this, everybody

knows about it anyway. The guilty person has to take communion at a special service where he's publicly forgiven. Pastor Gordon doesn't say what the sin was, just refers to it in a general way."

They passed the main intersection of town and headed up the hill to the other side.

"Jake, did you ever attend a Catholic church?" Mary asked suddenly.

"Huh uh."

"I was wondering why you crossed yourself this morning when Pastor Gordon introduced you."

"I saw it on television. Some commandos came into a church where a guy was hiding and said if he didn't stand up they'd kill everyone there, so he crossed himself and stood up."

"Did you think you were supposed to do that too?"

"I didn't know. Anyway, they shot him, so I guess crossing didn't help."

Mary laughed, and Jake joined in. "You felt you were facing a firing squad, maybe?"

"No. I just thought maybe I was supposed to do it."

He slumped down then and leaned his head against the back of the seat, long legs crossed at the ankles, hands over his stomach, staring out the side window. His sudden moodiness seemed a punishment somehow for the laughter of the moment before.

"Do you suppose they're dust now, Aunt Mary?"

This time she understood his train of thought. "Yes."

"Just part of the dirt, huh?"

"Part of the soil, Jake, and the rivers—part of everything that gives life. Best of all, they gave life to you, and I'm grateful to them for that."

Jake turned his face away then, and they continued home in silence.

The afternoon was typical October. The trees had not quite peaked, but still made ruffles of yellow, peach, and bronze against a striking blue sky. Jake was impressed.

"It's so *pretty* out here!" he said, resting his arm in the open window as they approached the old farm house near White Plains.

"It's pretty everywhere in Maryland in the fall, Jake. I didn't used to like autumn much, but this year it's different."

Verna was standing in her garden next to the drive when Mary pulled in. Tibs came dashing out of nowhere, barking and yipping, and went almost insane with pleasure when Jake got out. Verna reached out her arms for Jake, but he was already racing back and forth along the drive with Tibs, making abrupt U-turns and shrieking with laughter as the large dog skidded to a stop and tried to reverse himself.

"Land, Jake, you're going to have that dog even crazier than he is," Verna laughed, and turned to Mary. "Why, Tibs is going to get so attached to that boy he won't let him get out of his sight."

The low grind of a tractor sounded from beyond the barn, growing louder as Sam came into view on the old machine. Jake stopped racing Tibs and looked at it.

"Come on, Jake, you've got to learn to drive this thing!" Sam called above the roar of the motor.

Jake rushed over and climbed aboard, sitting on one of the Sam's big knees. Sam wheeled the tractor around, heading for open field again, and Tibs scampered alongside, barking.

"Well, that's the last of the tomatoes I'm going to pick," Verna said as Mary followed her into the house. "Can't trust Sam to look after them the way I do, and I'll not be coming back up here again till spring. The frost'll take the rest."

Mary hung her sweater inside the door and started peeling apples by the sink.

Verna sat heavily down with a pan of lima beans. "Mary, did you see what Jake did in church this morning?"

"The sign of the cross, you mean?"

"Yes. What got into the boy?"

"He was just flustered, Verna—didn't know what was expected of him. I wish Pastor Gordon hadn't embarrassed him like that, though."

"*Embarrassed* him? Is it an embarrassment to welcome a homeless boy to a loving congregation?"

"You mean an orphaned boy, Verna."

Mary's sister ignored her. "The boy has got to feel he *belongs* somewhere, that he's a part of a family. . . ."

"Of course. That's what I want for him, too."

The grandfather clock in one corner ticked on, the only sound to break the silence except for the dropping of lima beans in the pan.

"Did you ever hear from the lawyer?" Verna asked after a bit.

"Yes. The will has to go through probate, and it will be a while before any of the money comes through. It won't be much, but I didn't suppose it would, knowing Warren. He left a lot of debts. The lawyer said the most Jake could hope for was $3,000 a year till he's eighteen. We'll manage, though."

Verna dropped her hands in her lap. "Mary, you know this is just plain crazy. We're living in three different houses, you and Sam and I, and there's room for the lot of us in any one of them. Why don't you sell, and you and Jake come live with Dad and me? You could go on working, and I'd do the cooking—easier on you and better for Jake. You know how Dad took to the boy last week. . . ."

Mary pressed her lips together. "We're doing fine, Verna. Don't worry about us." She looked around suddenly. "Where *is* Dad? Didn't I see him out on the glider when we came in?"

Verna followed her to the door. "You *ought* to come and live with us. Unless, of course, you and Milt are planning to mary. . . ."

"I'm not thinking of marrying anyone." Mary stepped outside and walked over to the lilac bush where her father sat, hands resting loosely in his lap. He turned his head when he heard her coming and leaned forward excitedly.

"Bo!" he said hoarsely. "An his going near the fen ding dang it."

"What is it you want, Dad?" Mary asked, sitting down beside him.

Grandpa Myles looked out toward the field. "Bo!" he said again. "Chollie bo!"

"Boy?" asked Verna, trying to interpret. "That's what he's saying, Mary. He wants Jake to come back. Why, that boy could change his life if he were around more often. Give him something to look forward to—Jake coming home from school each day. . . ."

"We'll come to visit often," Mary said, and silently rocked the glider back and forth with her foot.

By the time the tractor returned, the apple cobbler was bubbling in the oven and roasting ears were steaming on the stove. Jake sat down beside his grandfather at the table, and the old man kept turning sideways to stare at the boy. Once he put out his hand and touched Jake's hair.

As the meal progressed, Jake—his cheeks ruddy, his eyes mischievous—played games with his grandfather by reaching over every so often and stealing a lima bean off his plate. At first Grandpa Myles looked at the small thin hand reaching over and stared at it curiously. Then he began to laugh each time he caught it—a loud, sudden laugh that seemed to come from someone else.

"Look at him!" said Verna. "Why, I haven't seen him laugh like that in years!"

Sam helped himself to the chicken and passed it around again. "Why, this lad has a natural talent for driving a tractor. You know that, Mary? You should have seen him make those turns at the end of the field."

"I can drive it myself without a license as long as I don't take it out on the road," Jake added. "I'm going to plow one of the fields next summer."

"You'll do a fine job of it, I'm sure," Mary said, a fixed smile on her face. Did they know what they were doing? Did they realize they were trying to take away the only person who had ever really belonged to her? To possess or be possessed. . . . She was rapidly getting to the age when no one but Milt Jennings would ever want her. Warren had sent this child to rescue her from Verna, from monotony, from Marbury, and lead her to the land of milk and honey. Just where it was, or how Jake was to go about it, she wasn't sure, but she wasn't going to give him up.

After lunch, Mary and Verna put their father in his wheel chair, and Jake pushed him back and forth along the blacktop drive, Tibs walking slowly beside them. Once, coming back, Jake speeded up a little. The old man gripped one of the arm rests tightly but said nothing. When Jake slowed down again, however, he beat the palm of his left hand against the wheel and made high-pitched noises that stopped only when the chair went faster.

"My stars!" Verna laughed. "Dad's enjoying it, all right, but you'll have him in such a state he won't be able to sleep at all. We'd better calm him down now, Jake, and see if we can't get him to rest for an hour or two."

So Jake and Tibs were off again, exploring a grove of sycamore trees behind the house, while Verna took Grandpa Myles inside. Mary strolled out to the barn, hands in the pockets of her denim skirt. Sam followed, sucking on a toothpick.

"Well, how's it going, Mary?" he asked, coming up behind her and putting one arm about her shoulder. "You've had the boy two weeks. How does mothering strike you?"

She smiled and turned so that the arm slid off. "Great!" she said, "I love it."

"Kid needs a father, though. If you're going to keep him, you should get yourself a man."

"Of course I'm going to keep him! Why on earth not?"

Sam laughed. "You're not a bad-looking girl, sweetheart. Not too late to marry, you know. Remember what Ben Franklin said. . . ."

Mary leaned against the barn. "Yes, I know, you've told me."

". . . Older women make good mistresses because they're so grateful." He laughed delightedly, then stopped. "He never meant my Verna, that's for dang sure. The longer I keep away from her, the more grateful she gets."

"Oh, Sam, you're exaggerating," Mary said. "She told me once she wished you'd move back in with her. She gets lonesome in that house all alone with Dad."

"You know what she gets lonesome for, Mary? For somebody to harp at across the table, that's what—somebody who can say something besides 'Chollie.' She gets lonesome for somebody to take out the garbage or repair the toilet or put Ben Gay on her back, maybe, but she sure don't miss havin' a man between her legs, no sir! She don't miss that at all."

"Sam, don't."

"It's true, Mary, and you know it. If Verna'd had her way, the doctor would have sewed up her hole right after Bill was born. I only laid with her a couple times after that, and it wasn't worth it. It wasn't worth it at all."

"Sam, for heaven's sake, that's between you and Verna."

He shook his head. "I haven't had such a good life, Mary—Verna actin' the way she does, and Bill. . . . Heck, the doctor should have sewed her up *before* Bill was born. I could have done without him, too. Look, Mary, it's the wrong women that's married and the wrong woman that's single. . . ." He came closer again.

Mary pushed herself away from the barn and walked briskly back toward the house.

"I'm going to help with the dishes, and then Jake and I have to be going," she said.

Sam grinned after her. "You're a nice-looking girl, Mary, but Jake can't appreciate it the way some people can."

Some people were never the right people, Mary mused. The ones who appreciated her were usually married, like Sam, or else they appreciated her for the wrong reasons.

"We appreciated your help at the missionary luncheon," Louella Kramer had written on a sheet of note paper with meadowlarks in the upper left corner.

They appreciated her loyalty, her compassion, her dedication, her humility. . . .

Who besides Sam appreciate the shape of her calves? Did Milt Jennings ever notice? Who appreciated the softness of her bosom or the nape of her neck or her chestnut-colored hair? She was imperfect, she knew—terribly imperfect—but still there were things one could admire. . . .

There was once in her life—just once—when she decided that Sam was better than no lover at all. It was a memory she did not care to relive. Whenever she thought of it now, she reminded herself that she had been young and terribly immature. But somehow that never helped.

She had been twenty-two at the time and had already played nursemaid to her mother for several years. Friends she had known in high school were getting married. Already they had been fondled, penetrated, impregnated, even, while she—explored only by Lester Sims—remained at home in silent submission to her duty. Verna, long since married, already referred to her sister as the "little maiden lady." People assumed that she would remain so unless she became Mrs. Jennings.

It was one of those nights, hot and steamy, when Sam had driven down from La Plata with some cupboard doors he had finished for Mary's mother.

He had freshly showered, and his body smelled of soap and a newly ironed shirt. A man's scent. Even then it had had a hold upon her. It was a pleasant smell, his mood was gentle, and his presence seemed strangely welcome to a sullen young woman who longed for an intermission in the monotony of her life. Not that she would actually do anything, of course. . . .

Of course. She stood on the porch, her back against the house, arms behind her, with Sam beside her, talking. From inside she heard her father hammering away at the cupboard hinges and heard her mother's suggestions, but out on the porch it was hot and still, with only a wisp of a breeze on their faces. The moon, big and honey-yellow, smiled benevolently down on them, on what Mary suspected was about to happen.

Sam was standing too close to her, yet she did not move away. He was talking about the heat, about going someplace where it was air-conditioned, about how Mary needed a break, a chance to get away, and suddenly his hands were on her breasts, one on each, and his big farmer's thumbs were circling and pressing down on her nipples.

"Sam!" she said, and pushed his hands away, but still she did not move.

She had asked for it, she knew. She had wanted it

as much as he. She had stood there, back to the wall, virtually offering herself, and at the touch of his hands, awkward as they were, she had felt aroused. Verna's husband. The naughtiness of it, the nerve, the sin. . . .

He sensed the ambivalence, smelled the chase, and closed in once more on his quarry.

"I'm sorry, Mary," he said, "but it's all dead between me and Verna. It's her way, you know. I've got to have a warm, givin' woman. A man can't live without it."

"Sam," she said again, disapprovingly, but even she knew that her tone was unconvincing. And suddenly Sam had his arms around her and his groin against hers. His mouth found hers, and she let him kiss her, let him pull up the back of her dress with one big hand and caress her bottom.

"Oh, Jesus, Mary," he panted. "Let's go somewhere."

She was insane, she knew, even to think it. She didn't like Sam, but she wanted to be noticed, to be fondled, to be bedded and loved. Her resentment of her situation had the upper hand. She longed to make a statement, a protest—to do evil if necessary—anything to release the feelings that were inside.

"I've got to get a bag," she said, pushing him away again.

"You don't need no bag," Sam told her.

"No, I'm going to get it." She left him there and went into the house.

"Sam's driving me to the shopping center for a while, Mother," she called out. "Back in a couple of hours."

It meant nothing to her parents, and they barely responded.

Upstairs, in the room she had once shared with Verna, Mary took a suitcase and began throwing things in it: lingerie, raincoat, shoes, her savings book. . . . What had Warren taken the night he'd left? How long had it taken him to pack?

She slipped back downstairs and out onto the porch again.

"Christ!" Sam said when he saw her. "You got you a damn suitcase!"

They got in the pickup truck, and Sam started the motor. He looked over at her and grinned.

"I want to go to Washington," Mary told him.

Sam's smile faded. "Mary, girl, we don't have to go to Washington! I know a place. . . . I *been* there."

She didn't want to hear. "Washington, or I'm not going."

"Shit! It'll take me forty-five minutes to get there, and twice as much for a room. We won't have hardly any time!"

"I told them we'd be gone several hours," Mary said adamantly, and Sam barreled on out to the highway.

They would probably die in a crash, Mary thought as the pickup truck careened around other cars going north. It would serve her right. Serve Sam right, as well. They would be found there together, with the contents of her suitcase, for all the world to see, and Verna would never say a kind word about her sister for the rest of her life. She would probably never refer to her again as the "little maiden lady" either, and perhaps for that it would be worth it.

They reached an open stretch of road, and Sam put one hand on her crotch, his eyes straight ahead.

The passion that had erupted earlier in Mary—the

simple animal hunger—was replaced then with disgust. She tried to recapture it, tried to imagine him hovering over her in a bed, panting and pushing and leering down at her. She shuddered, and Sam mistook it for pleasure and went on digging with his fingers. She slowly pushed his hand away, and he put his arm around her shoulder. She let it be.

"We're gonna have ourselves a time tonight!" he told her. "I'm gonna love you ever' which way, Mary." He laughed aloud with anticipation.

They reached New York Avenue, and Sam started looking for a hotel.

"Keep an eye out for one of them signs that says 'rooms,' Mary. Might be we can find one of them that'll do just as well. Son-of-a-bitch town to park in, though."

The Greyhound bus depot came into view.

"Here," Mary said suddenly. "Stop here."

"Where, for Christ's sake? That's a fire hydrant."

"Just pull in for a minute."

Sam swerved into the open space near the curb, and Mary slid out, pulling the suitcase behind her.

"I got to park this thing, Mary," he told her, confused.

She slammed the door of the truck without answering and headed for the bus depot. She felt like an absolute bitch. What a terrible thing to do.

"Mary!" Sam bleated after her and honked the horn. She did not turn around, and he continued honking.

Even as she walked inside the depot, however, she knew she was playing a game. She knew she did not have the courage to carry it through. Where would she go? Where would she sleep? And her parents . . . dear Lord, what on earth would they say?

She knew, as she sat down on a bench waiting for Sam to come after her, that it had all been done for the devil of it, for the change, for the break in an otherwise staid life, for the feel of a man's fingers, even Sam's fingers, on her breasts. It had been done to show someone—if only Sam—she was not what people believed her to be. At the same time, she hated herself for leading him on. There was a name for women like her.

Sam came into the depot fifteen minutes later, vacillating between relief at finding her and exasperation. He sat down beside her and put one hand over hers there on the bench.

"Mary, baby, what's come over you? What'd you mean, walkin' off like that? You ain't scared of me, are you? I'm gentle. . . ."

There was no use pretending anymore.

"Oh, Sam, it's all wrong and you know it!" Mary listened to the spinster tone of her own voice and wondered why he just didn't slap her.

"Hey, now, you was all ready back there on the porch," Sam said, trying to understand.

"Well, I thought about it on the way here, and it's wrong. I'd never be able to face Verna again."

He slapped his knee, not her, in disgust, turned away, and then looked back at her. "Hell, Mary, we come all this way to Washington. . . ."

"I'm going to California to find Warren." She didn't look at him when she said it.

Sam's eyes widened. "No, you ain't, Mary. You get yourself right back in that truck. Your folks ever know I took you here to the bus station and there'd be hell to pay. Come on."

"I can't ride with you, Sam. I'd feel too guilty."

Sam looked around quickly and lowered his voice.

"I didn't do nothing you didn't let me do, did I? How come you're Miss Righteous all of a sudden, huh? How come you get a man all heated up and then you turn on him?"

She could sink no lower, Mary knew, and yet she continued the charade. "Just because I let you kiss me didn't mean I was about to go to bed with you."

"Well, I'd like the hell to know what it did mean, then. If it's only kissin' I want, I can go kiss my old granny."

She turned away from him, silent, loathing both him and herself.

"Come on," Sam said, looking at his watch. "I won't touch you on the way back, Mary. You want to go to California, you got to do it without any help from me. Verna's cold enough as it is, without layin' this thing on my head."

He picked up her suitcase, and she got up slowly and followed him to the door. Two women, watching from another bench, nodded knowingly to each other. Mary enjoyed that. That and Sam's hand on her bottom back there on the porch. They were the only parts of the evening worth repeating.

They did not say a word to each other all the way home. Sam drove more slowly, hunched silently over the wheel.

If I had any charity in me at all, I'd say I was sorry, Mary told herself. *I'm as guilty as he.* But there was no charity to be had. She was angry at the world, at the breaks life had given her, at the fact that of all the men in Marbury, only Sam had tried to seduce her. And so she'd taken it out on him. As they neared home, and still Sam had not spoken, she almost wished she had let him.

The pickup truck stopped, and Mary got out. She

lifted the suitcase down and then waited a moment, hoping Sam would say something, anything, but he said nothing, his eyes straight ahead. She walked up to the house as he drove away, hid her suitcase in the bushes where she could retrieve it later, and went inside. Her parents, reading in their respective chairs, did not even look up. No one suspected, so no one even cared.

The matter was never mentioned again between Sam and Mary. He had taken all the guilt on himself, she knew, yet somehow she feared that an apology on her part might be interpreted as a change of heart—a pass, even. And so it was years before Sam was jovial towards her again, before he was remotely flirtatious. But it was a cautious fondness, a narrow line that he trod, and he was always quick to back off if Mary gave the slightest sign. She gave it often. Since the night on the porch, Verna's husband never aroused the slighest longing in her. Guilt had once more taken the upper hand.

The color and warmth of October gave way to the nothingness of November. Trees which had stood resplendent in dresses of wild orange only a few weeks earlier now stretched themselves naked and stark against a gray sky.

Mary didn't even notice. A chill in the air outside meant an excuse for a fire. It meant drawing the shades and making a haven of the house that had been humorless for so long.

Jake liked to bathe early, put on his pajamas, and

lounge about the living room till bedtime. Mary was surprised at how rapidly he seemed to feel comfortable with her. Each new sign that he was losing his reserve pleased her, but sometimes she wondered. Had he buried his grief only to have it emerge misshapen and confused later on?

One night she was sitting on the sofa, leafing through the *National Geographic* when Jake came in wearing his pajama bottoms, his back still glistening from the shower. He smelled of soap and Breck shampoo mingled with the unique odor of rumpled pajamas. He stood swinging the tops around and around to dry his face, then came over and belly-flopped on the couch beside her.

"What're you reading?"

"About a one-man expedition to Antarctica," she told him

"Look at that wall of ice. I can't even imagine temperatures like that."

"I always wanted to go there," Jake said. "I always wanted to go where hardly anybody else ever goes."

"What would you do in Antarctica?"

"You learn all kinds of survival things." Jake rested his chin on his arms. His thin body reached from Mary's thighs at one end to where his toes curled over on the other. "I read a book about it once. When men go outside, see, they always go in pairs. And if one of them accidentally touches something metal with his bare hands, the other pees on them to thaw him out.

"What?"

"That's true. I read it."

"My, you're full of fascinating information." Mary put her feet up on the hassock, leaned back, and rested one hand on Jake's bare shoulders.

"You'll probably go there some day, Jake," she said, and rubbed his back idly with the palm of her hand. "No reason you can't do about anything you want. You're young, you're smart, you don't scare easily. . . ."

"Where would you like to go, Aunt Mary? If you could go anywhere in the whole world, what's the first place you think about?"

"New York."

"New York!" Jake raised up to stare at her, then flopped down again. "That's dumb! Why wouldn't you want to see India or Russia or Brazil or some place like that?"

She wondered about it herself. "Those other places just seem too impossible. I don't like to think about things I can't have. Just gets me eager for nothing."

"Boy, if everybody felt that way, nobody would ever have gone to Antarctica at all. Nobody would ever have tried to build an airplane or cross the ocean or anything. You have to have dreams. . . ."

"I guess so."

"I don't want to be afraid to try things," Jake continued. "I told that to Mother once and she said I was right." And then he lay very still and did not speak for a long time.

Mary sat waiting, kneading the skin on his back with her left hand, then switching to her fingers and lightly tracing large circles. She could tell by the way he burrowed his body down in the cushions that he was enjoying it.

"This sort of reminds you of your mother, doesn't it?" she said finally, determined to help him say whatever he was thinking.

"No."

"No?"

"Huh uh. She never rubbed my back. She hardly ever touched me."

"That's nonsense. Of course she touched you."

"Not like this. She didn't believe in it."

"Why not?"

"She said it would excite me. She read it somewhere."

Mary's hand came to a dead stop.

"She said that attractive women shouldn't be too affectionate with their sons," Jake told her.

Mary grunted indignantly and began rubbing Jake's back again vigorously. "Well, you've nothing to worry about ugly, old me, then. I think that's all a bunch of nonsense. And if I feel like a hug now and then, I'm going to help myself."

Jake smiled. "Okay."

They were quiet for a while.

"Do you miss them, Jake?" Mary asked finally.

Again the thin face rose from the couch cushion and rested on his folded arms.

"I feel sad whenever I think about them," Jake said, "but I don't think about them all the time."

"I understand."

"When it first happened . . . when this friend of Dad's called and told me about it . . . it was like a big cut down in my stomach. Like somebody had hit me there and taken my breath away. I couldn't believe it. And when I realized it was true, I didn't think the ache would ever go away—that it would stay there the rest of my life. But after a while I got to where there were stretches in between the aches and then the spaces got longer. Now the bad times hit me only once in a while, not a lot. . . ."

"I'm glad." Mary patted him reassuringly. "You're

going to come through this okay, Jake. You really are."

He got up finally and went to the dining room table to do his homework. Mary watched as his elbows sprawled over the table top and his bare feet stuck out at a wide angle. Every so often he tipped back on the legs of the chair, stared up at the light fixture, and then, problem solved, bent over the paper again and wrote it down.

It seemed to Mary as though he had lived here always, as though he had climbed up on that same chair as a three-year-old, feet tucked under him, until his body had elongated, year after year, into the gawky teen that he was now. It seemed to her that she had always known him, that he had always been hers. Perhaps she was remembering Warren.

She picked up the *Geographic* again to finish the article.

"That's not true, you know. What you said." Jake's voice again.

"What's not true?"

"What you said about yourself—about being ugly." Jake did not take his eyes off the paper in front of him, writing all the while he spoke. "I think you're pretty, sort of. . . ."

Mary smiled at the qualification. "It's not going to stop me from hugging you," she warned. "Not a bit."

It was only a few days later she noticed that Jake was not eating well. At breakfast he ate the egg but not the toast.

"I'm not hungry," he said. "I'll eat it later."

At dinner that evening, he ate his potatoes and beans but left the pork chops. "Maybe later," he said.

"It'll be cold, Jake."

"That's okay."

It was as though some drastic change had taken place in his appetite. Later, as he'd said, the toast and pork chop disappeared, but it wasn't normal that he should eat only a few bites to feel satiated. Weren't those symptoms of some awful disease? The liver, maybe?"

"You feeling okay?" Mary asked him. "Got any worries?"

"Huh uh. I feel fine."

It was not only the reduced appetite, however. There was an evasiveness about him now that had not been there before. Phone conversations ended abruptly when Mary entered the room, and Jake began coming and going at odd hours.

Just growing up, needing his privacy, Mary told herself, but even she didn't believe it. The change was far too sudden. Jake seemed to have lost his best friend as well, for Brick Adams was never there any more when Mary got home from work.

Yet Jake spoke with someone on the phone each evening before he left the house, and he would return a half hour later with no explanation at all.

"Going for a walk, Jake?" Mary asked casually one evening when she saw him putting on his jacket after dinner. "It's a beautiful night. May I come along?"

Jake did not look at her as he pulled up the zipper. "Uh . . . maybe some other time, Aunt Mary. I've got to . . . meet somebody. Be back in a little while."

A girl, Mary thought after he had gone. Of course.

That was it. The phone conversations . . . the secret meetings . . . the reticence . . . the poor appetite. . . . What was she worried about? Perfectly normal behavior. . . .

But doubts remained. In passing by the phone during Jakes' whispered conversations, she had heard a male voice at the other end. It was no girl Jake called every evening. And suddenly she had an overwhelming feeling that Jake was in trouble.

She lowered herself into a chair near the door. Homosexuality? Furtive meetings in someone's garage? She felt ill. How would she ever explain this to Verna? Then she remembered the way he seemed to hold his jacket so close to him as he went out the door each night, as though hiding something next to his skin.

The second supposition hit. Drugs. Wasn't one of the symptoms a decrease in appetite? Had his eyes been watering lately? Were they glazed? She hadn't noticed. As soon as he came home she would look at his eyes. Night sweats. That was another. Or was that diabetes?

She got up and ambled from room to room, her mind whirling, a tightness in her chest. Mary Martha louses up again. How could it have happened in two months' time right under her very nose? He had seemed so normal, had been adjusting so well, and then, almost overnight. . . .

That's what they always said. That's what parents always told the judge when they hauled a son into court and said he was beyond their control. But how was she to have known?

The question was irrelevant. Verna would have known. *Didn't you ever search his room?* she would ask. No. *Didn't you ever check his closet, his pockets, his shoes, his mattress, his wallet?* No. Absolute trust. Total naiveté. The court would take him away and appoint Verna his guardian. At least Verna would see that he went to church school each week. Mary had not required perfect attendance. Mary, Verna would say, had not required enough of anything.

By the time Jake came back at nine-thirty, she was limp and too tired to have it out with him then.

"Better wipe your feet, Jake," she said, her voice flat. "You've been getting mud on the carpet lately."

"Oops. Sorry." He hung his jacket in the closet and started down the hall toward his bedroom.

"Jake?"

"Yeah . . . ?"

"Let me look at you for a moment. You haven't seemed too well."

He waited reluctantly, frowning slightly, while Mary looked him over. "I feel okay," he said.

"Let me see your eyes."

His eyes were on his shoes, but he slowly raised them to look her in the face. They did not look glazed, they looked guilty. He went on down the hall, and Mary curled up on the couch, shivering with a sudden chill.

Thursday night, as soon as dinner was over, she saw him get his jacket from the front closet.

"Going out again, Jake?"

"Yeah. I'll be back in a little bit."

She came to the kitchen doorway and looked at him. Obviously he was holding something under the left side of his jacket while trying to get his right arm in the sleeve. She walked toward him.

"Jake, what do you have under that jacket?" Her voice shook.

He looked at her and swallowed. "You mean this?" He pulled out his history text. "That's all."

"What are you doing with it?"

"I'm just . . . going over to Brick's. He forgot to bring his book home from school and we're having a test tomorrow."

"How about you? How will you study without it?"

"Oh, I already have. I won't need it."

"Jake, could I see the book, please?"

He looked at her, the color rising slowly up his neck and covering his ears, as he handed over the book.

Get ready, Mary told herself. *Show no shock. Be prepared for anything—heroin, marijuana, condoms, pornographic pictures. . . .*

She flipped through the pages. Out fell two slices of salami and one of American cheese.

Mary stared at the cold cuts there on the floor and then at Jake. He had his head turned to one side, chin touching his shoulder, shoulders hunched, hands in his pockets, profoundly embarrassed.

"Jake?" She stood transfixed. He had a secret pet, maybe—a dog he was feeding somewhere. That was it! A dog she could understand.

Jake shifted to the other foot and stared at the floor.

"I'm sorry," he said into his shoulder. "I guess I should have told you."

Mary sat down on the arm of a chair. "What's this for, Jake? Have you got a dog somewhere?"

Jake stared at her. "A dog? Heck no, it's for Brick. I thought you guessed."

"Brick! You're feeding Brick?"

Jake took a deep breath. "Well, his parents won't give him anything decent to eat, see." He knelt down and picked up the cheese and salami. "I guess I thought you knew about him."

"How can I know about him? I haven't even seen him! Where is he, chained in a cellar somewhere?"

"No, it's . . . well, it's about his acne, see. I thought maybe his Mom would have called you. His folks have this idea that if they put Brick on health foods for two weeks, maybe his face will improve. They fix him a special lunch to bring to school, and they make him come right home at 3:30 and won't let him go anywhere to make sure he doesn't eat any junk food, and he's starving to death, Aunt Mary! He's absolutely starving!"

Mary slid down into the chair, her hands over her mouth, relief flooding through her. Then her shoulders began to shake and she doubled over, head in her lap.

Jake stared. "What's the matter?"

"Oh, Jake . . . if you just knew!"

"It's not funny," Jake declared. "You should see what his Mom puts in his lunch! Cottage cheese sandwiches on brown bread! Cucumbers and celery! Prune yogurt! It's awful! Every day we take the stuff his Mom sends and mix it all up together on somebody's tray to see what color it turns out, and it's always green. Can you imagine what that does to Brick's insides?"

Mary leaned back and shook her head. "So you've been feeding poor old Brick."

"Well, all of us have, sort of. I mean, all us guys chip in and give him bites of our cheeseburgers and pickles and candy bars and stuff. It's at night that he goes nuts. So I've been . . . well, I've been taking him things and leaving them on his window sill. He said if it wasn't for me, he'd be dead by morning."

Mary thought of the cold pork chop and the un-eaten toast. "He's almost a mile down the road. You've been walking there every night?"

"I cut across the field by the gas station."

"How much longer does he have to go before his two weeks are up?"

"Couple days."

"His face any better?"

"Not much."

"How about if we put together a lunch this time—a piece of pie, a sandwich. . . ."

Jake looked at her delightedly. "*Can* we? You don't care? You won't tell his Mom?"

"I don't know a thing," said Mary. Warren would have loved her.

FIVE

There was a large framed photograph in the dining room of Opal Myles. It showed Mary's mother—fur coat, black stockings—in front of a cinder block church. She was standing beside their first pastor, a man in wire-rimmed glasses, and together they held a placard bearing the words, "Faith Holiness Church of Marbury, Maryland, February 3, 1931." Jake said it was the ugliest picture he ever saw, but what did he know?

It was Opal Myles who, in large part, was responsible for the founding of the Marbury Church. Having come from Atlanta and the First Faith Holiness Congregation, she had worked tirelessly as a young woman to start another church in Maryland. She had asked for donations, proselytized, witnessed, and eventually converted a young farmer, who turned over the entire profits from his wheat crop to the foundling church before he married Opal.

By the time Verna was born, the church had been not only built but framed in wood siding as well. When Mary came along, an addition had sprung up on the back for the choir, and by the time Warren joined the family, the drive had been paved. It became known in the Myles household as "Mother's church," and as far as Mary's father was concerned, it stayed that way forever. He continued to attend every Sunday, but he never again donated an entire crop of wheat.

Females outnumbered the males in all the Faith Holiness congregations. It was a fact that the pastors viewed with alarm, but even the addition of men's supper clubs or male quartets in some of the churches did not significantly alter the condition. It was inherent in the faith that women were the most avid supporters; their men stayed home on Sundays, sat silently in the pews without active participation, or were among the few zealots who volunteered for everything and often became pastors themselves. All that was required was a two-year course at a training school in South Carolina and an overabundance of faith.

· There were several things that Opal Myles had believed in with all her heart: that the Bible was divinely inspired; that men were animals with Satan's lusts; and that Marbury, Maryland, was destined some day to be the home of the Second Coming.

By the time the three Myles children were grown, Verna, the first-born, had long since ceased to believe in Marbury as the location of the Last Judgment. She had been out of Charles County only a few times in her entire life—once to visit Warren in California— but that trip had convinced her that there were other places in the United States far more breathtaking than the road in front of the Marbury Post Office.

Mary had stopped believing in both Marbury and Satan's lusts. She had never felt the antagonism toward men that both Verna and her mother seemed to feel, not even after what happened in the back seat of Lester's Buick. *You've never had to live with a man,* Verna once told her. *You don't know how it is.*

Perhaps this was true, but fraternization still seemed the most logical course.

It had been left to Warren to discard all of his mother's beliefs, and he used to do so with relish. He told Verna that if God ever came to Marbury, it would only be to take a crap. He told Mary that when he married, it would only be to a girl whose lusts matched his own. And he told Opal Myles herself that if every word of the Bible was divinely inspired, then God was a dirty old man. Warren was not his mother's favorite.

Mary was not sure what she believed now, and Jake didn't help.

There were times she felt she should marry Milt Jennings and get it over with. It would help solidify her faith, and would certainly satisfy Pastor Gordon, who liked nothing better than to unite members of his flock.

"Another nest for the kingdom," he always said.

It would satisfy Verna, who had a need for Mary to settle down.

"I don't know how I could be more settled than I am," Mary told her once. "I've lived in the same house in the same town my whole life."

"I'd just feel better if you had an anchor," Verna had replied petulantly. "Being single the way you are, you could just walk off some day into who knows what."

It was, Mary had to admit, an absorbing fantasy. "Who knows what" could be anything at all, from going to work in the appliance department at Sears Roebuck to hijacking a Wonder Bread truck and holding the driver hostage.

She could, some day, simply dye her hair, cut it short, put on a pair of dark glasses, and take off. She could start a whole new life in Denver or Aspen or Acapulco, even—take up belly dancing, study Russian, or get into Zen.

With the exotic out of the way, more practical possibilities came to mind. She could move to the District and enroll in the Washington School for Secretaries. Take a course in computer learning, maybe. She would drop the "Martha" from her name completely, buy a whole new wardrobe including a halter top, and learn to drink wine.

By the time her imaginings had carried her this far, however, she became swamped in details. To afford an apartment in Washington, she would have to sell the house. To sell her house, she would have to let it be known she was leaving. And to tell the people of Marbury that she was going away would be like inviting the inquisition, a wake, and a shunning all at the same time. She had thought of just leaving in the middle of the night and letting an agent sell the house. She wouldn't miss Verna or Sam or their booze-happy son, but when she thought of her father, stranded there at Verna's, it gave her pause. And now there was Jake.

If she married Milt Jennings, Jake would have a father substitute, though Milt was to fatherhood what Blue Bonnet margarine was to butter. He *would* marry her, though. Marbury's most eligible bachelor had proposed regularly every New Year's Day for the last five years, and had vowed to go on proposing until Mary said yes. It was a rather gloomy prospect, Mary felt, and put somewhat of a pall on Christmas.

She had known Milt all her life, she believed. At least there was a moon-faced boy in the junior department who used to grin uncontrollably when he won the Bible race for that Sunday.

"Matthew 6:21," the teacher would call out.

And as the gold-leafed pages of each child's Bible flipped madly, the moon-faced boy usually got there first:

"Forwhereyourtreasureistherewillyourheartbealso," he would shriek.

"Luke 11:10."

Another frantic race, rustlings, moans, and then the moon-faced boy again:

"Foreveryonethataskethreceivethandhethatseeketh-findethandtohimthatknockethitshallbeopened."

Mary did not particularly care for Milt Jennings when she was ten.

When she was in high school, Mary and Milt used to date occasionally, meaning that they sat together in church and sometimes held hands under the hymnal. When Mary enrolled in the local junior college, Milt went to a business school and three years later joined his father's accounting firm, specializing in income tax. He was the tax expert of Charles County. Now that his parents were dead, he had inherited the family home and was looking about, more or less, for a wife, though he did not seem particularly driven by any animal urge that Mary could detect.

Mary was not sure just why it was she could not love him. He was steadfast and straight as an arrow. He would be kind to her, and neither gambled nor drank. He remembered birthdays and anniversaries, commemorating almost anything at all. He still phoned each year on the anniversary of the day he had kissed her when he graduated from business college. ("My impetuousness," he referred to it wickedly.) But she felt no more emotion toward Milt than she felt toward a boiled potato.

There was something more to her feelings than this, however. There was another image of Milt that came to mind occasionally in which his face did not look so beatific or his eyes so placid or his smile so benign. She had seen him this way only once, sitting at the back of the church during a special penitential communion offered for the soul of Warren Myles.

Warren had been seventeen at the time, newly graduated from high school. He was a slight, yet strong young man, with wavy hair the color of sand, a chin with a cleft in the middle, and eyes that laughed continually. He was the most attractive boy, Mary had felt, in the whole of Charles County, and she marveled that two people as ordinary-looking as her parents could have produced him. He teased both Verna and Mary constantly, but because Mary laughed and Verna didn't, his joking with Mary was gentle. Warm, even. It was like a secret language, and though they no longer sat on the swing together as they did at eleven and twelve, they communicated other things through jests and innuendos. It was nothing specific—just a general impatience with the people in their lives, a subtle mocking of the customs, a boredom with rural Maryland, and the unspoken assumption that some day they'd be free.

Not that Warren never annoyed her. There were times when Mary felt ages apart from her brother, infinitely older and more mature. There were things he did that even she could not condone, and then she found herself retreating into a mold—a set—that had seemed to be pre-formed and waiting for her. There were times when she felt exactly like Verna, and this confused and dismayed her. Was it predestination, maybe? Could your very soul turn against you and, like an engine set on a certain track, take you where you didn't want to go at all? Was there a point in your life where, regardless of your dreams or wishes or idealized expectations, custom and training and indoctrination took hold and only a miracle could set you free?

She used to wonder. If this were true, predestination hadn't caught up with her brother yet. He had been like a puppy on a leash, straining to break loose. He'd had a knack for raising a ruckus, arousing controversy, "going against the grain," as his mother put it. He was continually shocking and mocking, and making a general nuisance of himself. Yet he was a boy, as his father used to say, who could charm a hag out of hell. He knew his Bible verses and his Beatitudes by heart.

Ask him, ". . . if the salt have lost his savor, wherewith shall it be salted?" and Warren would answer, clear as a bell, ". . . it is thenceforth good for nothing, but to be cast out, and to be trodden under the foot of men." Old ladies loved him. To them he was gallant and courteous and complimentary. The women of the church used to gather around him after each service, vying for his personal attention. And yet those eyes. . . . Everyone in Charles County had suspected him of revelry of the wildest sort because of his eyes, but no one knew anything for a fact.

And then one night this boy with the devilish eyes had stood in front of the Faith Holiness congregation, head down, a devil no longer. This boy who opened doors for old ladies and flirted with his Sunday school teacher stood with arms hanging limply at his sides as the parson, now deceased, had read the composite scripture saved for this occasion only.

"For all have sinned and come short of the glory of God. For out of the heart proceed evil thoughts, murders, adulteries, fornications, thefts, false witness, blasphemies. For all that do such things, and all that do unrighteousness, are an abomination unto the Lord thy God. . . ."

There was no need to wonder which of the above-mentioned sins pertained to Warren Myles. Though the offense was never mentioned in the service and was, theoretically, a matter between Warren, the minister, and God, it was known to every adult member of the congregation and half of Charles County as well.

One of the church deacons, the rumor went, had been suspicious that his barn was being occupied on late summer evenings and had hired someone to hide out and observe.

The details, for something supposedly secret, had been rather specific. Warren Myles and a girl had entered the barn about nine-thirty, it was said. First they had shared a bottle of Taylor's sauterne. Next they had smoked cigarettes, lighting up their faces and furnishing identification. And finally they had undressed shamelessly there in the light of the hay-mow window and done unspeakable things. All the tale bearer could bring himself to report was that fornication itself had taken place not in the usual manner, but with the girl standing against the wall, and this after considerable dalliance.

It was the "unspeakables" that were dwelt upon in every shop, back room and sunporch of Marbury. Some had speculated that the girl was stretched on a

ladder. Others had the couple lying head to toe. As
the stories made the rounds, an animal of some sort
was added as an extra attraction—a dog, a sheep, even
a goat. It had seemed to Mary that the fantasies of
the congregation far surpassed anything that Warren
could have thought of himself.

She had watched the repentance ceremony in agony and humiliation, both for her family and for
Warren. Like Verna, she had been furious at him for
bringing this disgrace on them all, and yet—as she
had raised her eyes and seen him standing there, rejected—she had felt a sudden rush of compassion and
tenderness that was greater than anything she had felt
before. She had longed to run up and shield him with
her body from their stares, to share this moment with
him somehow, to let him know he was not alone, that
there was still one person in Marbury incapable of
throwing the first stone.

He had consented to come, she believed, because he
had felt he could count on the ladies to forgive him.
He had thought he could depend on their admiring
looks, their secret adulation. He had thought he
could stand up there the envy of every red-blooded
man in the congregation, make his repentance in a
loud, clear voice, and stride out smiling, making a
mockery of the whole thing.

It had not worked out that way. The eyes of the
women were cold as ice. He had betrayed them. Once
he had been caught, fornicating in the flesh with a
girl that none of them could ever be, a girl outside
the faith, even, there was neither forgiveness nor compassion any longer. Instead of standing straight with
merry eyes, he had found himself staring down at the
floor like a whipped dog. Mary had felt that, at that
moment, something was dying in Warren that would

be lost forever, but there had been enough of Verna in her to hold her to her seat, to prevent her from making a spectacle of herself. She detested her own cowardice, and blushed at her own shame.

When the communion had ended, the congregation had risen for the final hymn of atonement, faces lifted smugly in song:

> *I was sinking deep in sin,*
> *Far from the peaceful shore,*
> *Very deeply stained within,*
> *Sinking to rise no more;*
> *But the Master of the sea*
> *Heard my despairing cry,*
> *From the waters lifted me,*
> *Now safe am I.*
> > *Love lifted me! Love lifted me!*
> > *When nothing else could help,*
> > *Love lifted me....*

Suddenly, in the middle of the chorus, Warren had sprung down the aisle, through the front door, and out into the night. Mary had stood, face turned toward the door, numb with shock. Voices had petered out until only the pianist was left on the final verse of the hymn.

"Amen," the preacher had said, and had come over to where Mary and Verna stood with their parents. "God will touch his heart," he had told them. "It was just more than he could face. Tell him his sins are forgiven, to go and sin no more. He is welcome back into the fold."

All over the sanctuary little groups were huddled together, shaking their heads and clucking their tongues. The minister had knelt then with Mr. and

Mrs. Myles and Verna, but Mary had walked mechanically back up the aisle, away from the others, unspeaking, unseeing. Once she was outside, the cool night air, rich with the fragrance of clover, bathed her face, and the paralysis lifted. Mary had felt sensation again in her cheeks, her fingers, her loins, her feet. . . . And suddenly she had found herself running down the road, crying, her hair streaming, tossed and tangled behind her. Faster and faster, like a thing gone mad, she had run, her fingers on the buttons of her blouse.

"Mary?" her father had called from far, far behind her, but she was out of sight. She had left the road, crashing through underbrush, leaping over a stream, then running across a meadow barefoot, her shoes in her hand, her blouse open and her breasts exposed to the moonlight. She had been sure he would be there, sure she would find him. . . .

It had been after eleven when she'd arrived home. She had been greeted with a chorus of frenzied questions and accusations. Why had she walked off like that? Where had she gone? Wasn't it enough to be embarrassed by one member of the family in a single night?

"There's *hay* on her back!" Verna had exclaimed, her eyes narrowed and searching.

But Mary had told them nothing. Not a word. Not a syllable. Slowly she had gone upstairs and sat down in a crumpled heap at the window, her head buried in her arms. Warren, they'd told her, was gone. His clothes and a few possessions were missing. He had left no address, written no note.

A month later a postcared had come from Warren, addressed to no one in particular. He said he had hitchhiked to Washington and taken a bus from there to California. He would never, he'd said, come back to Marbury as long as he lived. And he never did. Over the years he sometimes called home around Christmas. He announced his marriage to a girl named Sue and later sent pictures of Jake. But he never came back. And Mary relived that night over and over a thousand times in fantasy, but she could never make it happen again. Warren had left without knowing, and the magic of the moment was gone for good.

Thanksgiving Day was cold and bleak—gray clouds, gray trees, gray fields and road and hedge. Mary had promised that they would have dinner with Milt Jennings, and neither she nor Jake was looking forward to it.

"The sky looks awful," she observed dully, "like it's about to throw up."

This brought an instant peal of laughter from Jake.

"Sometimes you sound like Dad," he said, and laughed some more.

Actually, Mary was sorry she had said it. It expressed the grayness she felt inside, and she hadn't meant to prejudice Jake.

At two o'clock they were ready and waiting, Mary in a green wool dress that was buttoned up to her neck. Jake sat stiffly on the couch, pulling at a string on his shirt cuff.

"Well, well, well!" Milt had grabbed one hand from each of them and pumped them up and down.

"What a privilege I'm going to have today!" he said, beaming. "What a privilege!"

They rode out to the Old Mill Restaurant where he had made the reservation. Jake sat in the back seat, snapping and unsnapping the seat belt, making loud clicks that Milt seemed to pretend not to hear.

"It was good of you to invite us out," Mary said.

"My pleasure, my pleasure."

Had he always repeated phrases like that? Mary wondered, looking out over the frozen farmland. Had he always behaved like an English nanny—protective, hovering?

The Old Mill was actually a prefabricated unit complete with polyurethane mill stone and styrene beams. A large wheel at the side revolved continuously from noon till eleven P.M. when the water was shut off. It was a chief attraction in Charles County, competing only with the drive-in theaters for non-believers and a mobile snake farm which had come to the area the year before.

There was a thick red carpet on the floor, brown-and red-checked tablecloths, and a large buffet laden with nuts, mints, relishes, and fruit.

"This is a real treat," said Mary.

Jake said nothing.

They were ushered to their table by a waitress in colonial dress. Jake accidentally stumbled on the hem, jerking her backwards, and then bumped into her. He was overcome with embarrassment.

"I'm so sorry," said the waitress diplomatically.

"That's okay," murmured Jake.

They sat down and looked at each other across the table.

"Well!" said Milt, opening his menu. "I want you to order anything you like—turkey, prime ribs, lobster. . . ." His eyes traveled up and down the list. "Jake, what appeals to you? A turkey leg with dressing! I'll bet that's what the boy wants!"

Jake studied the menu. He was definitely ill at ease; Mary could sense it. There was something about Milt's manner that made him even more self-conscious than usual.

"I'll have a cheeseburger," he said.

Milt's menu lowered and he looked incredulously at Jake. "Not on Thanksgiving!"

"I'm not too hungry," said Jake.

Milt turned helplessly to Mary.

She shrugged. "No point ordering something he won't eat. I'll have the duck with orange sauce, Milt."

They made small talk, Mary and Milt, till the appetizers were delivered. Mary shared her shrimp cocktail with Jake. He collected the toothpicks with the cellophane fringes and toyed with them idly, drawing even deeper into himself.

"Jake seems to be enjoying school," Mary said after a bit. "He's made some friends and likes his teachers."

"That's a good sign, liking the teachers," said Milt. "A person who doesn't get along with teachers when he's young doesn't get along with his boss when he's grown, you know that, Jake?"

"Yeah. I guess so."

The duck came surrounded by orange slices. Milt's prime ribs arrived with crab apples and parsley. The cheeseburger was delivered on a pewter platter with cherry tomatoes and olives stuck on toothpicks which fanned out all over the bun. The sight of it brought a wheeze of laughter from Jake. He drank some water and covered his mouth guiltily.

As Mary nibbled at the duck, Milt talked on at

length about Charles County being God's country, the ideal place in small-town America to bring up a Christian boy. He talked about his big house and how, if he had a young helper, he might even buy a horse that this young helper could ride. He said how happy his dead parents would be to know that there was life again in the old Jennings place, and how it was his fondest wish that he could someday share that lovely home with someone.

It occurred to Mary that there was suddenly an abundance of houses in and around Marbury needing Jake. Where had all the youth gone that a kid had to be imported all the way from California? If it were God's chosen place for raising children, what happened to those children when they were grown? She wondered idly if perhaps God's plan was to keep Milt Jennings a bachelor all his life so there would be no more moon-faced children shouting out Bible verses at the top of their lungs.

"Such a gray day outside, and so cheerful in here!" Mary said, hoping to change the subject.

Jake started to smile. And then a loud nervous giggle escaped through his lips. "You know what she said this morning?" he asked Milt.

Milt gave Jake his full attention and smiled benevolently. "What did our Mary say?"

The "our Mary" produced another sputter from Jake. "She said the sky . . . looked awful . . . like it was going to . . ." and suddenly he went into a spasm of laughter.

"What? I didn't hear the rest," said Milt, wondering.

"Oh, it's not important," Mary said quickly.

"She said . . . she said . . . ," Jake gulped, fighting for control, "it looked like it was . . ." He doubled over. ". . . going to . . . *throw up!*"

He bleated the last words so loudly, and was so wracked by laughter, that his chest heaved in and out. Some diners at nearby tables turned momentarily, and then pretended indifference and went on eating.

Jake grabbed for his glass and tried to gulp the water, but a second burst of howling erupted from his lips, and the water went spewing all over the table, splattering Milt's tie. This, and the expression on Milt's face, made Jake almost hysterical.

Mary watched her nephew in both embarrassment and concern. The laughter had become self-perpetuating. The sound of one outburst seemed to spark another. She handed him her napkin and he covered his mouth, but by now half the diners had turned to stare. Milt feigned total unconcern and went on eating, his face beet red, and at the sight of this tremendous display of fake calm, Jake suddenly howled again, his stomach pulled violently in, his shoulders shaking. His face was contorted. He was in agony.

Mary reached over and put one hand on his arm, and for a moment it seemed to have a calming effect. The laughter stopped, and Jake wiped his eyes. At that very moment, however, the head waiter appeared with a coughdrop on a large white plate and asked Jake if he thought that would help.

Instantly a wild shriek filled the dining room, and Jake doubled over again. He was beyond control.

"Let's go outside, Jake," Mary said sympathetically, and stood up. "We'll take a walk somewhere."

The young boy staggered awkwardly to his feet, convulsed, tears streaming down both cheeks, and they made their way through the tables of gawking patrons till at last they were outside.

Almost as soon as the door closed behind them, Jake's laughing stopped. He leaned weakly against the building, hands on his sides, miserable.

"I don't know what got into me, Aunt Mary," he apologized, humiliated. "That's never happened before in my whole life! Oh, Christ! I'm so embarrassed. I'll bet Milt's furious!"

Mary put one arm around him reassuringly. "He'll get over it," she said, as they walked back and forth along the drive. "So will you, Jake. It happens to all of us. It's just part of growing up."

"Did it ever happen to you?"

Mary nodded.

"When?"

"In church once. When somebody was being baptized. My mother was mortified."

"What happened?"

Mary thought for a moment, then laughed. "I wet my pants."

They both laughed out loud together, and it seemed to defuse the smoldering convulsions in Jake.

"I don't know how you stand me," he said at last.

"I stand you very well."

"*He* doesn't."

"Oh, I don't know. He's not used to young people, that's all."

Again the silence. They reached the end of the drive and turned around again.

"You're going to marry him, aren't you?"

Mary stopped, her arms folded across her chest, and studied him. Then she bent over and whispered conspiratorially, "Not if I can help it."

Jake leaped off the curb and spun around. "Whoopee!" he said, and they laughed again. "I thought maybe having dinner with him obligated us or something."

"Only to be considerate and polite," Mary told him. "Think you can go back in there now?"

He shook his head. "Let me stay out here till you finish. I didn't want any more anyway."

She went back in. People looked at her momentarily as she sat down and picked up her fork. Faces turned away again.

"What was the matter with him?" Milt asked.

"Just growing pains, that's all. Self-consciousness. It happens to the best of us."

"I don't ever remember doing anything like that," Milt said. He wasn't smiling.

"Don't try too hard," Mary said politely. "You might remember doing something far worse."

It was Liz's idea to take Jake Christmas shopping in Georgetown. On a freakishly warm Saturday, early in December, she called during breakfast.

"He'll love it, Mary. And the weather will bring everybody out. Why don't you drive over and we'll leave from here?"

"I thought you were going to Charlottesville on weekends."

"I'm re-evaluating that relationship," said Liz. There were times when the social worker in her took center stage. How easily she managed to put the intricate motions of a man and woman into clinical phrases.

Jake sat happily in the back seat as they left Liz's

condominium in her car. "Will we get to see your brother?" he asked. "The one who had Passover in his apartment?"

Liz laughed. "He's not there anymore, Jake. He never got over the feeling that he was a disappointment to the family somehow. My grandmother always wanted him to be a rabbi, my father wanted him to go to Harvard and become a doctor, and one of my cousins had a jewelry store in Miami and wanted Harold to go into business with him there.

"But Harold just wanted to be left alone with his Jewish customs and his girl friend, and finally he figured he couldn't please anybody, not even the girl friend who said he made love like a piece of lox on a bagel—he just laid there—oops! sorry, Mary—and so you know what Harold did? He packed up and moved to Louisville. The last I heard he was selling kosher hot dogs at the Kentucky Derby, and he's willed his body to Harvard Medical School to make Dad happy. I mean, really, he's such a nice guy if people would just leave him alone. . . ."

Both Mary and Jake were laughing.

"Boy, you've got a great family, Liz," Jake said, leaning forward and resting his arms on the back of the front seat.

Mary felt a flicker of jealousy again.

"Oy vey," murmured Liz. "They're not so amusing when you live with them twenty-four hours a day, kiddo. Grandmother always said I was her first big disappointment because I didn't keep the Sabbath, and Harold was her next. Her last big disappointment was the day she died. She'd always wanted to die during Passover to make sure all the relatives would be there. Instead, she popped off on Christmas Day when half the clan was off to the Bahamas. Every so often I dream she's going to come back to life just so she can die all over again during Passover."

Georgetown was so crowded that the sidewalks themselves seemed alive and moving. Improvised stands displaying leatherwork and handmade jewelry had sprouted up on the sidewalks, attended by tall sinewy girls in wrinkled cotton dresses and bearded young men in heavy thong sandals. Couples necked and fondled openly in doorways, and a girl atop a trash container sat with her dress hoisted up to her thighs, her bare legs wrapped around a standing youth who was licking her collarbone. Dogs of assorted sizes trotted along beside their owners on leashes, cats were held in arms or draped over shoulders, and one ponytailed man walked down the street with a live parrot perched on his forearm. Jake showed no special interest in the necking couples, but gawked in admiration at the parrot.

It was not, Mary realized, a place she could ever have come to by herself. She would have felt like an alien from another galaxy. But somehow, with Liz on one side of her and Jake on the other—guardians of her body if not her soul—she felt less conspicuous and awkward, and reveled in the anonymity she never achieved in Marbury.

The freedom she saw about her seemed contagious—the touching, the looks, the laughter—and she felt a tingling sensation on her skin, as though she were beginning to molt, to throw off her old inhibitions and take on a new personality, one that neither Verna nor her mother would ever recognize, much less approve.

Jake felt it, too. Sometimes he charged on ahead, a spring in his step, eager to poke his head into the next shop and discover its contents before the women caught up with him.

"Pots and pans!" he would call back over his shoulder, and bypass the store with the brightly-colored fondue kettles in the window for an incense-smelling place of black-light posters and rock music.

By one o'clock, Jake had ideas about presents for everyone on his list and begged to go off for an hour by himself. They lunched first at Swensen's and then let him go, Mary and Liz lounging in a booth by themselves over coffee.

"This was a great idea," Mary said. "Why are you the one who always thinks of these things?"

"I didn't invent Georgetown, you know," Liz told her. "It's been here all along. Just seemed like a good weekend to do it."

"You're not going to see Greg anymore?"

"I don't know." Liz put down her cup and pulled her sweater around her shoulders. "There are problems."

"Like what?"

"You'll never believe it."

"I'll believe anything."

"Sex. I think Greg majored in it."

"That's bad?"

"I'm swimming in it, Mary! I go to Charlottesville, and I've got my clothes off as soon as I'm inside the door. Two whole days of romping around in bed, week after week. I feel I'm in some damn experimental breeding program or something."

It was difficult, Mary decided, to feel sympathy.

Liz leaned her arms on the table. "Listen, did you ever go anywhere by Greyhound, through all those sleazy little towns, and see those diners with big signs saying, 'Eat'? Nothing else—not 'Steak and Seafood' or

'Welcome to Joe's' or even 'Homecooking'—just 'Eat,' like one of the commandments or something. And the more often they told you to 'Eat,' the less hungry you got? Well, that's the way it is with Greg and me. As soon as I get in his apartment his hands are under my blouse. It's as though there's a big sign over his sofa saying 'Fuck,' and suddenly I don't feel in the mood anymore."

Mary listened, fascinated. For a brief moment she felt that perhaps she *had* shed her skin, that she had metamorphosed into somebody else, and that for a short time she could actually feel what Liz was describing, difficult as that was.

"I want to be seduced," Liz said dejectedly. "I want music and tenderness and talk and 'Will he or won't he?' There's just no question when it comes to Greg. He will—on the sofa, behind the sofa, under the sink, in the lawn chairs. . . . His imagination knows no bounds. I don't know if I could stand being married to him, even though I think I love him."

"Oh, come on, Liz, there's more to Greg than that. The man's a Ph.D.—a biologist. It's just that you only see each other on weekends."

Liz sighed. "That's what I keep telling myself. He's going to Romania for a month this summer to study the mating habits of hamsters with a noted mammalogist. Jesus! Can you imagine a man majoring in mammalogy? I mean, the more I think about this, Mary, the sicker it gets!"

It was impossible to take this seriously. Mary was almost drunk with a surplus of good feelings: of Jake looking so happy, of cold ice cream and hot coffee, of sunshine flooding through an open doorway in December. She smiled lazily.

"Maybe that's what's the matter with him, he's

been watching hamsters too long. Maybe that's why you get laid behind the sofa and under the sink," Mary told her.

Liz took off her glasses and looked at Mary. "Did I hear you say 'laid'? I didn't know it was in your vocabulary."

"Neither did I," said Mary, and laughed. The day was all too delicious. Everybody should be eating ice cream. Everybody should be sitting in Georgetown on a Saturday afternoon. Everybody should have 'laid' in his vocabulary.

"Anyway," Liz continued, "he wants me to go with him this summer—spend my vacation in Romania."

"Sounds like a good idea. You'd get to see what he's like for a whole month, not just weekends."

They sat for a time without speaking, watching the other customers, comfortable with the silence.

"It's an escape, that's all," Liz said finally. "Do you ever feel that you're only experiencing a small percentage of what life has to offer, and panic because it goes by so quickly?"

All the time, Mary thought. But Liz was speaking of herself.

"There are days I get really frightened, Mary. I feel I should be doing something big and great—writing a symphony or painting a picture or climbing a mountain. Something for which I'd be remembered. I mean, when I die, what will I have done? I go to work, go to bed—with or without Greg—shop, eat. . . . Romania's not going to cure me. It's got to be more than that. Sometimes I think I'd like to buy a sailboat and just keep it handy. Then, if I ever decide I was in a rut and there was no way out, I'd just put a few things in the boat and take off. I'd simply drift along and see what happened. My whole life, from then on, would be uncharted. It would go against everything I am now—organized, efficient, disciplined. . . . The moment I untied the rope and trimmed the sails, it would be a whole new me. Do you ever feel like that? Do you ever worry that sometime something deep down inside you is going to get the upper hand, and you'll never be the same again?"

"If it only would," Mary said aloud, half in jest.

"Be serious for once."

Mary turned to Liz wide-eyed. "Do you know what you're *saying? Me?*"

The irony wasn't lost on Liz. "Okay, then, *don't* be serious. It becomes you. But at least listen to me."

"I'm listening! I'm listening!"

"No matter what I do, I'm in a rut. I'm a stereotype. You know what I'm talking about?"

"No."

"Look. When I was in high school, I decided I wouldn't be one of those typical Jewish girls who's looking for a rich doctor to marry. That was *my* stereotype, see. I was going to think about myself—a lifetime career. So after college, I went to the university. When I was too busy to come home for Yom Kippur, my family said I was the typical Jewish girl—as soon as she goes away she forgets all about her people. But when I broke my neck to get out of classes and come home, they said, 'Well, look who's come to honor us with her presence, Miss Uppity herself.'

"I wasn't taking too good care of myself then. I was trying so hard not to look like I was just going to school to get a husband that I went out of my way to look frumpy. I was overweight, my skirts were too long, and I was wearing some kind of crepe-soled shoes that were only a step up from Keds. Well, I went to visit my aunt in Philadelphia once between semesters. When I got off the bus, she kissed me, looked me up and down, and tisked, 'The typical Jewish social worker.'

"So I cleaned up my act. I lost weight, I had my hair cut, I went on a shopping spree, and instead of going around looking serious like I was out to save the world, I did my best to be pert and saucy and attractive. And when I visited my grandmother a few months before she died, she clucked her tongue and said, 'Flippant, that's what you are—like usual.' No matter what I did or said, or how I looked, it was never right. I always offended somebody. I didn't have the good sense to live for myself—please myself.

"Well, I know it in my head, but not my heart. Somewhere in all this is the real me. You'd think I would have found it by now. I don't know if the real Liz was Clyde's devoted wife, or Greg's current mistress, or Mrs. Grossman, the social worker, or whether I'm still the same mixed-up Jewish girl who sat behind you in Philosophy 101 back in Junior College. Or maybe I'm all of those at once. . . ."

It was amazing, Mary thought, that anyone else could feel this way, especially Liz—Liz the sophisticate. Was it inherent in their gender, perhaps? Or was it a part of every human being, male and female—something inside that never grows up, never knows for sure?

"I think you're all of them at once, Liz," she offered. "Personalities develop tentacles, you know, that creep out in a dozen different directions, grabbing first at one thing and then another. No one can possibly know you unless he sees you as a composite—wise and foolish, adult and child, organized and impetuous. . . ."

How good it sounded, coming from her! She could

hardly believe she had said it. It was as though she *were* experiencing a metamorphosis—as though she and Liz were changing places. And Liz nodded as though she understood, as though she had seen the truth of it. How good to be the sage for once instead of the student, to be asked rather than told.

Jake returned with a look of absolute rapture on his face. "All of them!" he said, "I got something for *everyone,* Aunt Mary. Even you, Liz. Oh, wait'll you see what I found for Gramps."

By the time they got back to Dumbarton Street where Liz had parked, the sun had gone behind a cloud, and December was fast rolling in upon them again. But Mary was riding too high to notice. It was only after they turned onto Indian Head Highway that she realized she was cold. She had slipped back into her own skin again and felt as though she had left something important behind.

SIX

~~~~~~

She did not know if she only imagined it or whether a rift was developing between her and Ralph Gordon.

Mary went into the church office on Monday determined to pay particular attention, to grasp the coolness if it were there and look it in the face. As it was the pastor's day off, however, he did not stop in until eleven o'clock, and then only to check his calendar for the following day. He said very little.

Guilt rose up in Mary, an empty feeling in the chest that she had experienced so often in the past. She had disappointed him somehow.

She mimeographed the church newsletter a day before it was due. She dusted his entire bookcase, sharpened all his pencils, emptied his out-box, tallied and averaged last month's offerings, checked on substitute teachers for the following Sunday, cut out a review of a new book on John the Baptist, ordered some new attendance pins for the junior department, called a plumber about the sink in the men's room, phoned all the ailing parishioners to see how they were doing and left the report on the pastor's desk, and spent an hour designing a Christmas masthead to appear on the newsletter during December.

But the guilt remained like a sodden mass of wet

socks at the bottom of her soul. She recognized the
feeling well. It was an old friend, inherent in her
faith, her family, the very soil of Marbury, Maryland.
But this time she was afraid it had something to do
with Jake.

Her suspicions were confirmed the following afternoon. Jake and Brick were horsing around the living
room when she got home. They had made slingshots
of rubber bands and were catapulting macaroni
shells at each other. The carpet was littered.

"Just don't step on those things or you'll grind
them into the rug," Mary cautioned, going out in the
kitchen to start dinner.

"We'll pick them all up," said Jake.

"Ha! Got'cha!" Brick chortled in his foghorn voice.
Whap. A shell hit him in return and he yelped.
They were chasing each other then, running around
and around the dining room table, pulling out chairs
to block the path of the other.

"Hey, knock it off!" Mary said. "Go out in the back
yard with those things if you want to run."

They went into the living room again and sat down
across from each other, perched on the edge of their
chairs, sling-shots poised, laughing.

The doorbell rang.

"See who it is," said Brick. "Probably that moony
girl following you home. I'll bet she would, too!"

"You see who it is!" said Jake. "You just want to
zap me when my butt is turned, that's all."

"Whoever it is will be gone by the time you guys
decide to open the door," said Mary, coming in from
the kitchen. "I'll get it."

A large woman stood on the other side of the storm
door. She was dressed in a bulky car coat with red
knitted gloves. Her face was pink and radiant.

"Mary!" she said warmly, heartily. "I've come to see Jake."

"Come in, Bernice. What a nice surprise."

The minister's wife was in her fifties. She had been born with the cord wrapped around her neck, and she always said that the doctor saved her life, but that God had saved her soul. On her fiftieth birthday, in fact, she had worn a homemade banner that proclaimed, "Half a century for Christ."

> *Jesus wants me for a sun beam,*
> *To shine for Him each day. . . .*

Mary had sung that song as a small girl in the primary department. And once she met Bernice Gordon, she was convinced that she had seen the original, unexpurgated edition—a sunbeam, indeed.

At the sound of the woman's voice, Jake sprang up off the couch and stood rigidly in the center of the room. Brick sat across from him, snapping the rubber band between his fingers.

Bernice Gordon took in the room and the macaroni at one glance and didn't seem bothered in the least.

"Jake, how good to see you!" she said, and sat down in a chair near the door.

"Hello," said Jake. "Uh . . . Brick, this is my Bible class teacher, Mrs. Gordon. Brick Adams."

"Hello, Brick, how are you?" Mrs. Gordon smiled warmly. "I'm not going to stay too long. I can see I've interrupted a game of some sort. No, don't apologize, Mary. I've raised two boys myself." Brick sat with his eyes on the rug, fiddling with the rubber band.

"Could I get you a soft drink, Bernice, or some

tea?" Mary asked. "I've already got the water on for me."

"Well, now, tea would warm me up, Mary. I take lots of sugar, you know." She turned her attention again to Jake, who now sat on the edge of the sofa. "We've missed you the last two Sundays, Jake." She pulled off her red gloves. "Everybody's been asking about you. I wanted to find out if it was that Jacob and Esau thing that made you stop coming. I said to myself, 'I'll bet that's why he quit. He didn't want to be Esau.'"

Brick stared.

"You see," Mrs. Gordon went on, turning to Brick, "Jacob and Esau were Isaac's sons, and it was Esau who had the birthright. We've been doing some role playing. . . ."

"I've just been sort of busy," Jake said, looking down at the macaroni.

"Well, Jake, the Lord gives us seven days a week, you know, and only requires one back in return." She was not scolding. Her voice miraculously carried no reprimand at all. She stated it as simple fact. "Maybe you'd like a friend to come with you." She turned again to Brick. "I'll bet you like M&M's."

Brick looked at her curiously. "What?"

"M&M's." She took the tea Mary handed her. "We're starting a Bible bee next Sunday, Brick, and we'd just love to have you come. Every time you memorize a Bible verse, you get an M&M for each word in it. Even 'Jesus wept.' See? You know a whole verse already, and you've got yourself two pieces of candy."

Brick glanced over at Jake, then back at the big woman again.

"First Corinthians 13:1 gets you 25; Genesis 1:26

gets you 50! You get credit for the verses you memorize at home as well as the ones you learn there."

Brick rolled the rubber band up and down one wrist. "I don't think I could ever come to your class," he said, looking serious. "My folks would never let me."

Mrs. Gordon's face became a study in compassion. "Are they nonbelievers?" she asked softly.

"Vegetarians," said Brick.

The large woman blinked. "What?"

Instantly Jake took it up. "It's his face, see," he told her, and Mary knew what was coming. "Brick can't eat anything sweet because of his problem."

"Acne, Jake, call it acne, for God's sake," said Brick.

"Because of his acne," Jake corrected. "If you give Brick all that candy, they'd really be upset. I mean, Brick's a fast learner."

Mrs. Gordon looked from one to the other, then quickly recovered. "Well, it doesn't have to be candy, Brick! How about gold stars? Why, you'd earn a whole box of stars to put in your Bible booklet."

Brick shook his head. "Huh uh. There's all kinds of sugar in glue. Man, you don't know what a box of gold stars can do to a guy's face. . . ."

"Yeah, he's . . . like . . . allergic to Bible classes, see," Jake put in. "His folks would be really mad if he went."

Bernice Gordon seemed dumbfounded, then realized she was being taken. She finished her tea quickly, sucked at the sugar in the bottom of the cup, and put on her gloves again.

"Well, I just wanted to stop and see how you were, Jake," she said. "I certainly *hope* you'll be coming back." She got up and touched Mary's arm as she passed. "It's such a *responsibility*, isn't it, raising a boy by yourself! Well, God bless you—you, too, Brick." And finally she was gone.

Mary sat down and faced the boys. "That was simply uncalled for!"

"What?" Jake asked wide-eyed, but he struggled to keep from laughing.

"You know very well."

"Well, she didn't have any right to go after Brick like that." Jake leaned back and folded his arms across his chest. His eyes met Brick's, and they exchanged a quick smile that turned sober again when they saw Mary's face.

"She had every right to extend an invitation. She was just being polite and friendly. The least you could have done was be courteous."

"We were, Aunt Mary!" Jake protested. "Telling her that Brick's allergic to Bible class is a lot more polite than saying no, isn't it?"

"She's not that stupid."

"She *is* stupid. You know what she said the second Sunday I was there? A lot of the kids were missing, and she figured she had to do something to get them back, so she told us that the next Sunday she was going to show us something we had never seen before and would never see again. She said to go tell all our friends, and the next Sunday there were thirteen people there, all waiting. You know what she did? She cracked open a peanut, held up the kernel, and said, 'Nobody's ever seen this little kernel before . . . ,' and then she popped it in her mouth, '. . . and nobody will ever see it again.' And she swallowed it."

"Gross!" said Brick.

"Then she talked about how maybe this was our

last chance to hear God's word and that if we didn't answer his call, he might never knock again. She's out of her tree, Aunt Mary!"

"She's doing the best she can with the education she has," Mary said, struggling to stay loyal.

"Well, I'm getting tired of these weirdos," Jake said defiantly. He seemed to enjoy having an audience. "I don't know how you got hooked up with them in the first place."

Brick snorted out a laugh which he tried to disguise as a cough. Jake grinned with pleasure, watching him all the while.

"Because they're my people, Jake," Mary said, and her voice was shaking. How dare he humiliate her in front of Brick! How was it he thought of Liz's relatives as wonderfully funny, but hers as merely odd? "This is the place I was born and brought up, and your father, too."

"And the first chance he got, he took off," said Jake, getting up. "C'mon, Brick, let's go outside."

Brick stood up uncertainly. "Uh . . . so long," he said, and followed Jake out the door.

Mary sat without moving. He was like Warren, all right—the same smart-aleck sophistication under that elfin face, that same look of innocence. She was surprised and fearful of the feelings he had evoked. She had wanted to walk across the room and slap him hard. She had wanted to shake that grin off his face and throw them both out, he and Brick. There was an anger against Warren she had refused to admit, and more of Verna in her than she realized.

What insolence—to speak like that to an aunt who had taken him in! If he said things like this to her face, what kind of stories was he telling about her at school?

She understood now the pastor's coolness, his wife's visit, Verna's comments, too. She had been far too lax with Jake, far too permissive. She and her nephew would have it out, once and for all.

She did not have it out with Jake, however. By dinner that evening, both seemed to have lost the urge to argue, apologies were alluded to, and somehow it seemed more important being friends. It was no more possible to stay angry with Jake than it had been with Warren. Also, when Sunday came, and the Sunday after that, Jake slowly dressed without comment and rode to church beside Mary. It was not a wholly satisfactory solution, but it bypassed a quarrel.

Mary was not even sure there *was* a satisfactory solution. Both Sundays she watched him get out of the car, thin lanky legs bent like a spider's, and then walk, shoulders hunched, to the side door for Bible school. Both Sundays, when youth and adult classes were over, she waited in the customary pew till Jake came in and sat beside her, a low sigh coming from his lips. Both Sundays, it seemed to her, Jake was a little less of what he used to be, exhibiting more and more of the Marbury syndrome.

"Guess who's coming for Christmas?" Mary said one morning after a call from Verna. "Bill. We just heard."

"What's he like?" asked Jake.

"It's hard to say. A little like your father, I guess—a little like Sam. He looks a lot like Sam, in fact, Not much at all like Verna."

Days passed in the gradual crescendo of holiday fever. Mary got out the old recipes her mother used to make and spent her evenings baking. The warmth and fragrance attracted Jake to the kitchen.

"Let me put the dots on," he said impulsively, and went about the table decorating each cookie carefully."

"Bet you used to help your mother do this, didn't you?" Mary said, flouring the board again.

"Huh uh."

"No? Tell me about her. I only met her once. What was she like?"

"Pretty."

"Yes, I remember that."

"And she liked to make pottery. Sometimes she made jewelry-things on strings to wear around your neck. Stuff like that."

"She sent me a bowl once for Christmas that she had made. It was beautiful. Mother dropped it accidentally."

"Yeah." Jake was quiet a moment. "Well, anyway, that's what she liked to do."

"What did you do together?"

Jake stopped decorating and stared hard at the cupboards, trying to remember. "I don't know."

"Ever go for walks? Read? Just talk?"

"I guess so. Yeah, she used to read to me sometimes—bedtime stories, I think that's what the book was called. Except that they weren't very good. Once I took a little truck to bed with me, and I was running it around under the covers while she was reading, and she got mad and said she wouldn't read to me anymore. And she didn't, not for a long time."

"All because of a little truck?" Mary shook her

head. "Well, you did have *some* good times, didn't you?"

"I guess so. It's just that . . . well, she had ideas about the way things should go, and they just never went that way. Like Christmas. . . ."

Mary waited.

Jake shook his head uncertainly, as though afraid of being disloyal. "She was strange sometimes. She liked to do things whenever she felt like it, you know? I mean, one Christmas Eve it snowed in California around midnight, just a little bit, and it hardly ever snows. She woke me up when she saw it and tried to put my boots on over my pajamas. She wanted me to go outside with her and walk in the snow, and I just wanted to go back to sleep. I was crying. Dad said to let me be, and then Mom got mad at him too. She said I'd probably never see snow again in Santa Monica and that I'd ruined Christmas for everybody."

"Oh, Jake, she *wanted* to have good times with you," Mary said earnestly. "She just didn't know quite how."

"Yeah, I supose so."

The day before Christmas there was an inch of snow. Jake was out in it before breakfast, yelping and whooping. He made tracks all around the chicken coop, spread-eagled his long adolescent body on the ground and made patterns by rolling this way and that. Brick came over around ten, and they leaped and laughed and rolled down on each other from the roof of the rabbit hutch.

Mary watched delightedly from the window. If Warren and Sue could somehow see him now—know that he was happy here. Parenthood had its moments. She was beginning to get the hang of it, beginning to feel more secure.

Brick was invited to stay for lunch. Then there was joking and kidding and glorying in the fact that there were nine days before school began again. Finally, at four, as Brick opened the door to leave, a small package tumbled on his foot.

"Hey!" he said, picking it up. "Santa Claus already!" He looked at the tag. " 'To Jake'! I'll bet it's that dumb girl."

"What girl?" asked Mary.

"Oh, some dizzy redhead who's been hanging around Jake at school," Brick explained.

Mary saw the color rise in Jake's face. "Well! Sounds interesting! Want to open it in private, Jake?"

"Naw," he said nonchalantly, ripping into the foil and tearing it down one side. "I don't care what she gives me."

It was from "the girl," all right. There was a small card inside, bordered in gold, that said simply, "Merry Christmas. Shirley." And underneath the tissue paper was a wallet with her picture in it.

"Jeez!" said Jake, staring at it, "I don't even need a wallet."

"What a lamebrain," Brick scoffed. "Putting her picture in it!"

"She doesn't look like a lamebrain to me," said Mary, picking it up and looking more closely.

The girl was big-breasted and had a smile that seemed to split her face in half. Not exactly pretty, not exactly plain, she looked simply like a girl caught up in puberty before she knew what to do with it.

Mary handed it to Jake, and he tossed it disgustedly down on the rug.

"Jeez!" he said again, but his face was still flushed.

Brick playfully punched him on the shoulder. "You

gotta thank her now, Jake. You got to call her up and say you always wanted a wallet with her mug in it."

Jake looked imploringly at Mary. "I don't, do I?"

"Well, you ought to thank her some way. Either a note or a phone call. But you have to say something. She'll be wondering. . . ."

"Can I use the wallet without her picture in it?"

"It was a gift. You can do whatever you want."

"Okay." Jake picked the wallet up off the rug. "Here, it's yours," he said, holding it out to Brick. "It's a present from me to you."

Brick backed off. "Hey! No way! Get it off me, man!"

"Just put it under the tree, Jake," Mary laughed. "Don't let it ruin your vacation."

The snow was gone by the next morning, but it was Christmas nonetheless.

"Bill's plane was due in at eleven last night," Mary said, as she and Jake put their presents in the car. "I suppose he'll be sleeping late, but I told Verna we'd come early to help with the dinner."

Sam met them at the door wearing a new yellow vest. Mary gave him a quick kiss. "Merry Christmas, Sam! Merry Christmas, Dad."

Jake followed her and put the presents under Verna's tree.

"Chollie!" As soon as Mary's father saw Jake, he began to smile and gabble, leaning forward on the sofa. "He bay be five go yadder, go year gone!"

Jake looked up at Mary. "What did he say?"

"Go yadder ank glank, sit nown yadder," the old man continued excitedly.

"I'm not sure," said Mary. "Perhaps he wants you to sit down beside him."

Jake took one of the presents from under the tree, wrapped in bright green paper, and put it in his grandfather's lap.

Verna came in from the kitchen.

"Well, well, Merry Christmas, everybody!" she said. "Where's my boy? Got to give him a big Christmas hug!"

Jake went to her obligingly, then sat back down.

"Opening presents already?" Verna exclaimed.

Jake picked out our present to Dad this year," Mary told her. "He's eager to see his reaction. Where's Bill?"

"Asleep," Sam said. "Didn't get in till almost midnight, then we sat up and talked till four in the morning. Dead to the world, he is. He'll be glad to get out of uniform and into his old things. What's the matter, Grandpa? Can't get the paper off?"

The old man was picking futilely at the box with one finger, his other hand lying uselessly in his lap.

"I'll help," said Jake, and tore off the wrapping. "Should I take off the lid, too?" he asked his grandfather.

"Put down yaddee ank, yaddee yadder ank."

"I guess he wants me to take off the lid," Jake concluded, and lifted the top. Then he reached his hands under the tissue and pulled out a music box.

It was a chunky wooden affair with three carved musicians glued to the top.

"Watch," said Jake, his eyes merry. When he turned the handle, the strains of "Joy to the World" issued from the box, and the arms of the three wooden figures moved back and forth on their instruments.

The old man was delighted. He laughed quickly, loudly, looking around the room and then at the box again, explosive little gurgles escaping from his chest. His pleasure delighted Jake in turn.

"Merry Christmas," Jake told him.

"Merry . . . merry . . . chollie merry nang," said the old man. And then, as an afterthought, "Christmas."

"What's all the ruckus?"

The voice came from the stairs, and heads turned to see Bill grinning at them, buttoning the cuffs of an old flannel shirt. "Can't a tired sailor get a little sleep around here?"

"Merry Christmas, Bill!" Mary said. "How nice you could be home for the holidays!" She caught the smell of bourbon as he came over and kissed her, and suspected he had been awake for some time.

"Long time no see," Bill said, and then his eyes met Jake's. "Well-l-l-l-l, who the ding dong is this?" he asked, faking surprise.

"Jake, this is your cousin Bill," Mary said. "It's hard to believe you two have never met."

"Put'er there, old buddy," Bill said, extending one hand, and Jake grinned, shaking it hard.

Sam and Verna's boy was nineteen, and he looked like Sam already. He had a large stomach, large arms, short stocky legs, and a tattoo on the back of one hand which looked like a montage of the American flag, a naked woman, a dollar sign, and the prairie rose.

"So how's Aunt Mary treatin' you, kid? Beat ye every night, does she?"

Jake giggled self-consciously.

"He's a joy to have around, Bill," Mary said. "We get along fine."

Christmas dinner began gaily. Verna turned out a splendid leg of lamb and there were canned vegetables from her garden, relishes, and hot rolls with apple butter.

"Ma, we got us a cook on board our ship that beats any food I ever had in the Navy, but it sure don't beat this," said Bill, reaching for another roll. "How 'bout you, Gramps? You want another?"

"Think I maybe don nang," replied Grandpa Myles.

"What the hell's that supposed to mean?" asked Bill. "How you know what he wants, Ma? Talks plain foolishness."

"Be patient with him, Bill, like I do," Verna replied. "You only see him a few days a year, so you can put up with it."

Sam sat down his fork and rubbed his stomach, pausing between bites. "Well, Jake, what you think? Still think sailors are so bad?" he asked playfully, and then turned to Bill. "Kid says he wants to be a pacifist."

"A pacifist?" said Bill, stuffing a piece of meat in his mouth. "What you want to go and be that for, Jake? The Commies come sweeping over here, you aren't going to try and stop 'em? Just let 'em come?"

"Seems like nobody ever comes here, we're always

going somewhere else and fighting," Jake said, embarrassed at the unwanted attention.

"Well, I say let the boy be whatever he wants," Verna declared. "It's Christmas, and I don't want any arguing at my table. Long as he turns out to be a Christian, it's all that counts."

It was uttered like a benediction, and so the conversation ceased and Bill began eating again. But Verna, having had the floor, seized the opportunity to say something else while they were all quiet, polite, and listening.

"This is a special Christmas," she continued, "having Bill home on leave, and Jake here too. You know what would make me the happiest woman on earth? I don't need presents—not a one. If Sam and Bill would go with us to church this Sunday, if all of us could walk in there as a *family*—Jake and Mary, too—it would be the most wonderful gift of all."

Verna either did not know or had ignored the fact that Bill had brought a glass of whiskey with him to the table and had been drinking it along with the meal. Now she realized that she should have stopped while she was ahead, for at the mention of church, Bill gave a loud laugh, startling his grandfather.

"I'll go to church when hell freezes over and I'm through ice skatin' with the devil!" he roared, finding it uncommonly funny, and winked at Jake. "Christ! That's the last place *I* want to go when I'm home on leave, Ma! Now don't you start that up."

"All right, Bill, you don't have to talk that way," Verna said, her expression pained. "You've said your piece and I've said mine, so let's drop it." But it was too late.

Bill lifted his glass and gulped some more, then

belched and laughed again. Jake put down his fork
and watched, fascinated, and his attention egged Bill
on.

"What the hell would I want to go look at all them
sour-faced women for? I seen me enough sour-faced
women to last me a lifetime."

Mary started the roast lamb around again, hoping
to distract him, but the platter stopped at Bill's place
and he ignored it.

"Blamed icicle women!" he grunted.

"Okay, Bill, let's drop it!" said Verna firmly. "Let's
just *drop* it."

Bill leaned his big arms on the table and concentrated on Jake, grinning.

"You know why I joined the Navy, Jake? To get
away from sour-faced women, that's what. Decided I
wanted to see what the other end of a woman looked
like for a change, and I want to state. . . ." He
picked up his glass, gulped down what was left, and
banged it down again. ". . . I want to state une-
qui-quivo-cal-ly . . . that the women in Japan are
put together just like the women here in the U.S.A."

"Bill!" Verna's face was ashen.

Sam smiled a little, his eyes on his plate, and went
on eating rapidly.

"Yes sir, they're put together straight just like
American girls are. Not a sideways piece among 'em."

Verna stood up and carried some dishes out to the
kitchen.

"Aw, Bill, cut it out, now," said Sam.

Bill leaned back and folded his arms across his
chest. "Okay. I'll change the subject. I'll talk about
any goddamned thing you want. I'll talk about Jesus
Christ or John the Baptist or the Book of Rev-

elations. You name it. What do you say, Jake? You know the Lord Jesus Christ as your personal savior?"

Jake thought about it as Verna came back in. He swallowed the piece of bread in his mouth.

"I think I'm an agnostic," he said, almost inaudibly.

Sam looked up and Verna stopped dead in her tracks half-way between the kitchen and the dining table.

"A . . . an egg what?" Bill said, squinting across the table.

"A person who's not sure," said Jake.

"Mary, what in the world's going on over at your place?" said Verna, quickly transferring her anger. "First he's a pacifist and now he's an agnostic? Tell me that!"

Mary flushed. She had meant to have a talk with Jake. All along she had kept it in the back of her mind, but had never got around to it. And now, suddenly, he was being attacked, and she felt like defending him.

"He's got a mind of his own, Verna," she said, her heart thumping. "I can't make his decisions for him."

"Well, you can guide him, can't you? What's a guardian supposed to do, anyway?" She turned to her nephew. "Jake, some of these ideas can lead you right straight to hell. You know that, don't you?"

"Just because I'm not sure?" Jake's voice was still soft, his lips dry.

"That's the unforgivable sin—turning down God. Not believing. Matthew 12:31."

"I'm not sure I believe in hell either."

Bill gave a loud whoop. "Hey! You tell it, Jake!"

"Well, whether you believe in it or not, young man, it's there and waiting for those who disobey the Lord."

Jake sat absolutely still, looking at Verna, and she took the opportunity to finish her speech.

"It doesn't pay to make enemies of the Lord, Jake."

"I thought Jesus said to love our enemies," said Jake. "Mrs. Gordon taught us that in Bible class."

Verna didn't see the trap. "That's right."

"Then how come God wouldn't forgive me?"

Another bellow from Bill. "Heeeeyyy, Jake! Go, Jake, go! Whooooopeeeee!"

"I mean, I just can't worship somebody like that," Jake continued earnestly, buoyed up by the cheering. "Anybody who would throw a guy in hell just because he wasn't sure. . . ."

"I won't have this kind of talk at my table!" Verna cried, her face coloring. "And Christmas, too! I won't have it!"

"Shut up."

All eyes turned to Grandpa Myles. The old man was looking straight at his elder daughter. The family stared.

"Yad do up, Verna," he continued, his stare unwavering. "Yad do up gang shut." He said it with such expression that there was no question what he meant, and that he had been following the conversation.

"Well, listen to that!" said Sam, amused. "He *does* make sense sometimes. First intelligent thing he's said since his stroke." He hid a smile under his napkin.

Verna got up again and began stacking plates, her face still crimson and her mouth set. "We'll have dessert later," she said. "I don't feel like serving it now."

And they all moved slowly, cautiously, into the living room to open their gifts.

"I think you should know," he said, "that I won't go on asking forever."

They sat side by side on the couch. Mary and Milt. A feeble flame tried a solitary dance in the fireplace before settling down to a more sedate glow.

"Of course not," she said. "I wouldn't expect you to go on asking. You've been very kind to me—to us—and I appreciate all of that."

New Year's Day had been cleverly orchestrated. Bill had called around noon to say that he was going to take Jake "out on the town" and would bring him back by five. Verna had obviously suggested it. Mary had not approved of the idea, but Jake wanted to go and Bill had been sober, so she'd given in.

Everybody knew that Milt, as usual, would be going to Mary's to make his annual proposal. Everyone would be waiting. Everyone expected that *this* time, with Jake needing a father and all, Mary would say yes.

Milt turned suddenly on the sofa and grabbed her arms, squeezing them hard.

"I'm a man with needs, Mary. Maybe I've never let you know that. Maybe the fault is mine. But I want you. . . ." With that, his hands left her arms, flattened themselves against her back, and pulled her to him. His lips pressed hard against her mouth.

It was a new sensation, coming from Milt. It felt

good to be grabbed, to be held, to be kissed and squeezed and pressed against. And then he ruined it.

"Therefore shall a man leave his father and his mother and shall cleave unto his wife; and they shall be one flesh," he said. "I'm a man of The Word and I believe in doing the Lord's will, Mary." He took her hands again and pumped them up and down. "I want you for my wife." With that he slid halfway off the couch so that one knee was resting on the floor, the other digging into Mary's thigh. It was too ludicrous for words.

Milt was, Mary decided, congenitally incapable of saying something without ruffles and flourishes. It was impossible for him to do anything simply, without drama, merely because he felt like it. There had to be a commandment lurking somewhere behind it.

"Oh God, get up, Milt," she said, feeling mildly nauseated.

He tried to pull her toward him again, but she pushed away.

"I can't, Milt! I can*not* marry you now or ever, and you'd hate me within a month if I did. We just weren't meant for each other, and that's that."

"Mary Martha, how can you say that? We've always been meant for each other. Everyone knows that."

"Everyone but me." Mary stood up and left Milt still perched awkwardly on one knee. He got up too, hurt and embarrassed.

"Look," Mary continued. "Do you think I've enjoyed saying 'no' for five years? I've tried to be gentle, Milt. I've tried to let you know how it is without hurting your feelings. I don't *want* to marry you. I'll *never* want to marry you. We're just not right for each other. You don't know me half as well as you think you do. I'm not even sure I know myself. There's a whole side of me that nobody's ever seen."

"We've all sinned and come short of the glory of God," said Milt.

"I'm not talking about sin, damn it!" Mary exploded suddenly, and it was as though her outer dried-up layer of dead skin was being peeled from her in one large piece. She shivered with the ecstasy of it. "I'm talking about aliveness, joy, feeling, passion!"

He stared at her.

"I'm changing, Milt! People do change, you know. They grow. They get outside themselves and develop in new directions. But you haven't changed at all."

He was offended. "I've been to college, Mary. I've got my firm. I'm a successful businessman in Charles County. I've got a house. . . . You flatter yourself if you think you're the only one capable of changing."

"But there's been no change between us, Milt. You still sound like a . . . boy back in Bible class."

"Just because I want God in my home, a Christian wife?" Milt asked righteously.

"I want God in my home too, Milt, but I'm not about to marry a Moses. Every time you open your mouth you've got a pronouncement to make, like you've just come down from Mount Sinai or some place."

"Mary! You amaze me!"

She amazed herself. "Listen, Milt, I'm not the girl you once knew. I'm going through a metamorphosis."

"Menopause?"

"Metamorphosis. I'm becoming somebody else. I can feel it."

"I don't understand you at all. Are you into spiritualism?"

She sat down wearily on the hearth and looked up at him. How could she marry Milt? She couldn't even communicate with him.

"No. I'm into life. Into learning about myself and where I'm going and discovering that I don't want to end up like Verna, that's all. I've no idea where it will end. But you're not in the picture, Milt. You just aren't. You've wasted five years waiting around for me, and I hate to see you waste any more. I'm not the only single woman in the congregation, and I wish you the best of luck. Honestly."

"I want *you*, Mary."

"Milt! Jesus! What does it take? A Mack truck? I don't love you. I'm not even sure I like you."

He stood stunned, looking at her. "That's an awful thing to say, Mary, after all these years."

She was crying now, from tension. "I know it, Milt. But I had to. There's no other way I can get through to you. Please never ask me again."

He walked to the door, took his hat from the telephone stool, and said, without turning around, "Okay, Mary, I won't ever ask you again." And he left.

She continued to cry for the relief of it, not from sorrow. She had not meant to hurt him, not *wanted* to hurt him, but she had. The crying stopped as suddenly as it had begun, and she felt her body relax. It was over. Thank God in heaven, it was done with. Still, meek and baby-faced as he was, Milt had left like a wounded buffalo, a spear in its side, and such animals were dangerous. She smiled wanly. Any animality at all, coming from Milt, would be an improvement.

She put another log on the fire, crumpled some paper under it, and sank down on the rug. She *did* want love, that much she knew. But she was no starry-eyed seventeen-year-old who thought that love would solve all her problems. She read the women's magazines. She read Ann Landers and the medical columnists and the feature articles in the *Post*. She knew about jealousy and distrust and impotence and frigidity and the endless varieties of problems appearing in "Can This Marriage Be Saved?" She knew that there were troubles no matter what you did, and that giving up her single status for being married would only be trading one set of problems for another. But still, she'd like the chance to try. . . ."

She ran one hand up and down the calf of her leg, caressingly. Her body would get no firmer, no more supple or smooth. The veins on her thighs were already beginning to show. A trace of panic swept over her. If no man ravished her in the next few years, perhaps none would ever want to. Could time have passed so quickly? How could she have just let it go? And yet, what, really, could she have done? What options had she now? Would it have been better to marry Milt and let his pudgy hands caress her than to go all her life without being explored at all?

For some reason she thought of Warren. He had wasted no time with his life. He had thrown himself into the lap of lust and reveled in it. Whether he had won or lost, she hadn't decided. There was more to life than what Warren had lived for, and she didn't want Jake to end up the same way. But she would never make a Milt Jennings of her nephew. Of that she was sure.

What had she, Mary Martha Myles, to remember after all these years? What moment of passion would warm her when she was eighty, make her thin lips smile with the mere thought of it? What else besides that one ridiculous grope in Lester Sim's Buick?

There's hay on her back! Verna's words seemed to ring out so suddenly that Mary sat up and looked around. Sitting there alone in an empty house made her remember things that were better off forgotten, she decided. She turned on the radio and went to the kitchen to make coffee.

SEVEN

It was almost six o'clock before Jake came home. Bill let him out and drove off without bothering to come in. That meant he was going somewhere for a drink.

"I was beginning to worry. Have a good time?" Mary said.

"Yeah. It was neat." Jake took off his jacket.

"What did you do?"

"Went bowling. Played some pinball and got ice cream—stuff like that." Jake ambled on out to the kitchen, got the sandwich Mary had made for him, and returned. He glanced around, commented on the anemic-looking fire, and sat down. "So what did you do all afternoon?" he asked curiously.

"Nothing special. Milt Jennings came over and we talked awhile."

Jake waited. Mary picked up a magazine and leafed through it.

"Is he your lover?"

Mary started. "What did you say?"

"Is he your lover?"

"Jake!"

He shrugged. "Well, I just wondered. You told me you wouldn't marry him, but you keep seeing him."

"I resent the implication."

"Jeez! You'd think I'd touched the Ark of the Covenant or something!"

"Don't throw your limited Bible knowledge at me. And just because I'm your aunt, don't think you can pry into my life like that." Her voice was crazily sharp. What on earth was the matter with her? She *had* no lover, that was it.

"Holy Toledo! I'm sorry, I'm sorry! I should have kept my mouth shut. Boy, are you ever square."

"That's *enough*, Jake."

She continued flipping pages and felt him glaring at her across the room. "Okay." She put the magazine down. "I overreacted. Good grief, if Milt heard what you'd asked he'd have a spasm."

"On old M.J. anything would look good."

Another minute of silence passed.

"Mother and Dad had them, you know," Jake said finally.

"Spasms?"

"Lovers."

"Jake, I'm not sure they'd want you to tell me about that."

He shrugged. "Then they shouldn't have died and left me with you." He said it without malice. It was as though he were beginning his transfer of allegiance—something he had to do. He stared into the fire. "That's where Mom went the night she died. Only she had an argument with her boy friend, I guess, and called Dad to come and get her. That's when they were killed—on the way back."

Mary covered her eyes, waited for the sting of tears to subside, then dropped her hands in her lap. "Was Warren upset—about where she'd gone?"

"Not too much. He knew about it. But I could tell he was glad she was coming home. He woke me up and said he was going to get Mom. I didn't go back to sleep after that. I lay there listening for their car—for the door to open. And then the phone rang. . . .

"Oh, God. . . ."

"For a while Mom was going to some musician's apartment every morning after Dad had gone to work. I knew because the kids at school told me her car was always there. Once I forgot my lunch money and I couldn't go back home to get it because I didn't have a key, so I went over to this guy's apartment and waited out on the steps. I figured she wouldn't be there very long, but it seemed like hours, and then I got scared she was never coming out again and started crying. . . ."

"How old were you, Jake?"

"Nine." He stopped and took a deep breath. "Finally a neighbor came by and asked what I was doing there, and I told her, and she knocked on their door. Mom was real mad. She said I had no right to follow her like that."

Mary waited. What could she say? What kind of consolation, when Jake himself knew infinitely more about such matters than she?

"Dad had them too, though. He had girl friends, and he and Mom used to argue about them. I met one of them once."

He needed to talk. It was coming out now—a verbal rush—as though pent up for months, even years. . . . Mary listened sadly.

"Mom was gone all week, and I was supposed to spend Saturday night at a friend's house. But about midnight I got sick and came home. Dad gave me some medicine, but after a while I threw up all over the place, and when I went in his room to tell him, I saw this woman in the bed. Dad just introduced me to her and called her a friend. Boy, they must have really thought I was dumb. Or maybe they just didn't care." His voice had lost its flatness. He seemed taut, on the verge of emotion.

"I don't know what to say, Jake. I didn't have much contact with Warren after he went to California. I'm just . . . sorry for you. . . ."

"He wasn't a bad father," Jake said quickly, defensively. "I mean, he didn't hit me or anything. . . ."

"But . . . ?" Mary's voice was gentle.

"But he . . . he. . . ." Jake's eyes closed momentarily as though to block back tears, and the corners of his mouth sagged, his chin quivering. "He just didn't care very much about . . . me. Neither did Mom. I was the Grand Accident, you know. The Big Surprise."

"Jake, how do you know that? How does any kid know that for sure?"

"They told me. Dad did, anyway. He said that they hadn't really planned on having children because it would affect their life-style, but that after I came, he was glad. That's what he said. I never believed him, though."

"Why not?"

"Because he kept talking about how we'd be real pals when I was older. And I was getting older all the time, but it seemed like we just got further apart. I never knew what he was waiting for."

Mary was crying openly, silently. "J . . . Jake, I can't change what went on in your home. All I can say is that Warren missed a lot. He was the real loser. But you're here now because I really want you, not because I had to take you in. Can you believe that?"

He was looking into the fire again, and Mary could

see tears glistening on his eyelashes. He nodded without speaking.

"You've been needing a home you could count on," she told him. "Have *I* been a disappointment to you, Jake?"

He shook his head.

"Not ever?" she asked.

"Not yet."

Why was she surprised? Mary wondered. If she had been asked about Warren's life-style, isn't that what she would have guessed? Was the hurt she felt for Jake alone?

It was for Jake that, seven years ago, she and Verna had flown to the west coast. It didn't seem right to either of them that a nephew should be growing up in Santa Monica whom they might never see. Photographs were not enough. And Warren, they knew, would never come home.

They were met at the airport by Warren, Jake, and a young woman in a poncho and long, embroidered skirt.

"This is Sue," Warren told them as though the boy at his side didn't exist. And then, as an afterthought, "and this is Jake."

They rode along the freeway in Warren's Porsche, Verna with Jake firmly ensconced on her lap. Sue sat with her face turned toward the window, smiling occasionally, and saying very little. Warren did all the talking—climate, business, prices—and Verna coun-

tered with comparisons to the way things were back
in Marbury.

The three days were pleasant enough. Sue—though
she kept her distance emotionally, smiling as if some
inner joke amused her—cooked decently and had
made some semblance of cleaning the house before
they got there. She was slim, tanned, her lips as bare
as Mary's, but with heavy indigo on her eyelids. Because she taught art in a private school during the afternoons, Warren took his son and his sisters
sightseeing—the park, the beach, the stores—and en-
tertained them till Sue came home again and started
dinner.

There was affection for Jake, Mary had felt, but
not on a parent-child basis. Warren and Sue talked to
him as though he were a miniature adult.

"You're angry because you can't have any more ice
cream, but you've been told what cholesterol does to
your blood, so I don't see why we should discuss it
further," Sue told him one evening.

After dinner Warren would take the boy on his
lap, but more like Edgar Bergen with Charlie McCar-
thy. There was none of that downy head on a father's
chest, but rather an after-dinner ritual in which Jake
sat dutifully, yet willingly, on his father's knee, and
Warren would put one hand on his back to keep him
from tipping. After ten minutes or so, during which
Warren talked to his sisters, he would give his foot a
little tap and Jake would slide off.

Mary followed Jake once to his room.

"This is an interesting place," she said, looking
around at his posters and drawings, and sat down on
the edge of his bed.

Jake stood in the middle of the floor, hands in his
pockets, watching her curiously. He should have been

dressed, she decided, in a gray flannel suit, vest, and watch chain rather than Keds and Snoopy T-shirt. It would have suited him better.

"Those things over there," she asked, "what are they?"

"Lego," he answered without emotion. He sidled over to the table, surveyed the toy buildings impassively, and turned once more to her.

"You can make all kinds of things, can't you?"

"Yes . . . ."

He never offered himself willingly, she discovered, but had to be drawn out slowly. An hour later she and Jake were hard at work trying to construct a drawbridge, but it took that long to convince him that she was truly interested.

It was not till the third day, the day before they were to leave, that Mary had a chance to talk with Warren alone. Verna had found some mending that needed doing and vowed to finish the job before they left. Jake had been invited to a birthday party so Warren and Mary went for a walk along the boulevard. They walked slowly, Mary enjoying the strange mixture of hot sun and cool breeze, Warren taking slightly longer strides, chain-smoking, but amiable.

"So how goes it, Mary?" he asked after they had walked a few blocks. "Anything changed since I left?"

She laughed as though they were using their secret language again—the double talk, innuendos. "Nothing worth mentioning. You know that."

"How's Mom?"

"No better."

"You have to care for her full time?"

"Dad relieves me occasionally. That's how we managed to make this trip. But someone has to help her around, dress her—and we sure can't afford a nurse."

"It's a rotten deal for you, Mary. How did you get stuck with it? What would happen if they didn't have you?"

"But they do. There was no one else. I'd just graduated—didn't have definite plans, and Verna had her hands full with Bill. He's been a troublemaker since his first day in school, and Verna says she's spent more time in conference with the principal than Bill's spent in the classroom. We could hardly have dumped Mother on her too."

"And so, the faithful Mary Martha. . . ."

"Right."

They walked for a while in silence.

"What would happen if you didn't go back, Mary?"

She glanced at him to see if he were joking. "You can't be serious."

"Completely."

"What would Mother do?"

"Move in with Verna, I suppose. Bill's a teenager now. . . ."

"And worse than ever."

"Look, Mary, Verna chose to stay. Mom and Dad chose to stay. You didn't. Why should you be the one held prisoner against your will?"

"What could I do here, Warren? What can I do with a junior college degree in liberal arts?"

"Go back to school and get the rest . . . teach in a private day school like Sue's doing. Pay's terrible, but the requirements aren't much. You've got guts. You'd find something and could live with us until you did."

It was not as though the idea had not already occurred to her. On the plane going west Mary had felt like a convict making a cross-country trip with her custodian. Once, when Verna had dozed, she gleefully fantasied her getaway. She had wondered if Warren might suggest it.

"I'd hate doing it to Dad," she said finally, wrestling with the idea.

"Yeah. Know what you mean." They came to a low wall beside a bank and sat down. "He's always been pretty decent, level-headed. . . . Just never learned to open his mouth and talk back," Warren said. "It was the one thing I regretted when I left that night—that I didn't say something to Dad."

Mary felt a coldness on her arms. The one thing he regretted? The only thing? "You went so suddenly," she said. "It took us all by surprise."

"Yeah. Well, it was the last straw. Gave me an excuse to do what I'd wanted all along. No sweat." He slapped his knee as though to end the conversation.

"You know," Mary said, afraid the opportunity would be lost forever, "right after you left the church, I ran after you, but I was too late. . . ."

He looked at her and laughed. "You must not have run very fast. Took me twenty minutes to pack up my stuff and get the hell out."

"I didn't go home," she confessed. "I went to the barn—where you and that girl had been. I figured you'd be there, just to show them. . . ."

"What for? Once the gossip got around, they shipped that girl out of Marbury so fast I never did find out where she went."

"I know. But I just . . . thought you'd be there. . . ."

He put his arm around her and gave her a quick squeeze. "Just as well. You couldn't have talked me into staying if you'd tried. But maybe I could have persuaded you to go with me."

He stood up and fumbled in his shirt pocket.

"Damn. I'm out of cigarettes. Let's walk on down to the shopping center, Mary."

She followed him reluctantly. She wanted to grab his hand and pull him back down on the wall beside her. She felt the need—no, the desire to confess, but he'd already begun to walk away.

It was a jovial family dinner that evening. Even Jake seemed more animated. Verna and Mary had brought him a clown marionette, and he gave an impromptu show at the end of the table, enjoying the attention. They all clapped when he was through. Even Sue seemed more open.

Mary lay awake for a long time, thinking about Warren's offer, weighing its sincerity as well as the practicality. Had he really meant she could live with them, or was it an offer he felt obliged to make? Could she adjust to their life-style, to Sue's aloofness, and would she soon be able to support herself, or would she cling to them like a terrified parasite? And what about her parents? She would not even allow herself to imagine Verna's reaction. It would be awful. She would make a terrible scene, ruining whatever good had come from their visit, and the rift in the Myles family would be wider still. And yet. . . .

It was almost two in the morning when she heard stirrings in the next bedroom. Low voices, murmurings, and then, after a while, the slow, steady, rhythmical creak of the bedsprings.

She listened with her mouth open, captive, embarrassed. . . . Is this what it would be like if she stayed, she'd wondered—Warren with his slim, supple wife in one bedroom, maiden aunt in the next, listening? Would the difference in their lives, living side by side, be so obvious, so vast, that it would be painful for her to stay and awkward for Warren to keep her?

The rhythm of the squeaking bed quickened, there was a dull thud of a headboard vibrating against the wall, and suddenly Mary heard a deep animal moan that she knew to be Warren's, followed shortly by a guttural cry and then a gasp from Sue. And then the house became as quiet as it had been before, as though the act had never taken place. Verna slept on in the next bed, breathing deeply, oblivious to the passion which had been expended beyond the wall. Mary rolled over and buried her face in the pillow.

The next morning Mary packed her bags along with Verna, kissed Jake, said her goodbyes, and only briefly let her eyes meet Warren's. A question passed between them that neither could answer, and then they were all in the Porsche again and heading for the airport.

Dr. Dobbs' office was a large examining room divided in the middle by a screen. On one side was his desk and a couple of chairs, on the other his examining table. When he came to the door of the waiting room, he invited both Mary and Jake to come in.

He was a rather small man, but gave the impression of enormous strength. Perhaps it was his jaw, or the large forehead, or the thick unruly gray hair that curled down the back of his neck. He was smiling—a full, generous smile.

"Glad to meet you, Jake. Any friend of Mary's is a

friend of mine." He shook his hand. Jake returned the smile. "How's it going?"

"Okay."

"Looks like your aunt's feeding you all right. Any particular problems?"

"No."

"I just thought it would be a good idea if Jake had a checkup," Mary said. "He says he hasn't seen a doctor for several years, so he may need inoculations or something."

Dr. Dobbs nodded. "I like to get to know my patients when they're well. Then if they get sick I'll know what they were like before. You look pretty healthy to me, Jake. Why don't you step back there and strip down to your shorts and socks."

Jake seemed refreshingly unselfconscious with the doctor, Mary thought. He did as he was told, padded back out in his jockey shorts, his clothes neatly folded in his hands, and asked where he should put them. Mary admired his firm thighs, his straight flank, the leanness of his long body.

Dr. Dobbs went back with his stethoscope and Mary listened to his familiar directions: "Cough, breathe in . . . that's right . . . breathe . . . good." "Follow this light with your eyes. No, don't turn your head . . . that's right. . . ." "What kind of sports do you like, Jake?"

She was showing him off, she knew, like a proud mother lion and her cub. She beamed when Dr. Dobbs came out and pronounced him fit.

Jake followed, pulling on his jeans.

"When will I get . . . you know . . . hair and everything," he asked.

Dr. Dobbs' eyebrows raised just a fraction. He turned around in his chair. "Oh, that! Well, now,

Jake, I wish I could give you a timetable, but puberty comes when it damn well pleases. Had any pimples on your face yet?"

Jake shook his head. "A lot of other guys have hair all over," he said. "Boy, you should see them in gym! Chris Meyers even has it in his ears."

"Well, Chris Meyers'll have a lot of competition one of these days, so don't worry about it. I can't guarantee hair in your ears, but you've got everything you need to be a man, so don't get uptight. Okay?"

"Yeah."

When Jake had dressed, Dr. Dobbs sent him to the small lab next door for blood and urine tests. Mary smiled and shook her head when the door closed behind him.

"Isn't he something?" she said.

"He's terrific." Dr. Dobbs smiled and finished writing his notes. "You're looking good yourself, Mary—enthused, relaxed. It's working out all right, then?"

"Pretty well. We have our moments, but . . . well, we've been able to talk them out."

"That's the most anyone can ask." He leaned forward again and idly tapped his pen against the desk blotter. "You bringing him up in your church, Mary?"

"More or less. He's not very enthusiastic."

"Sure it's wise?"

"No, I'm not sure of anything. Ask me anything at all about raising a boy and you'll find me wishy-washy."

They laughed together.

"It's all I know, Dr. Dobbs," Mary said, growing serious again. "All I can give him is what I am."

He didn't respond for a moment. Then finally, "There's a big world out there, Mary. Don't be sur-

prised some day if you find out that it's a part of you,
too."

Evidently Shirley Delvaney thought that Jake
looked good also. There began to be phone calls,
questions at first: what was the date of the science test
again? Did Jake happen to get the fourth problem on
page ninety? Would he possibly know where she
could get a confederate flag to use in a skit for history?

Jake was formal, and spoke tersely in a monotone:
"Hello . . . oh, hi . . . yeah . . . I don't think
so . . . huh uh . . . you're welcome."

Why does the girl keep calling? Mary wondered.
He obviously doesn't care for her.

"*Her* again," he would often say when the telephone rang in the evening, and usually he was right.

Toward the end of January, however, there was a
definite, though subtle, change in his tone. Instead of
standing with one foot forward as though ready to
bolt when he took her calls, he began sitting down on
the stool by the phone, his back to Mary, and the
terse answers gave way to studied quips, derogatorily
affectionate:

"Yeah, well you always were a little slow. . . .
Big deal. So what else is new? . . . Say something
intelligent for a change. . . ."

Instead of waiting for Mary to answer and call him
to the phone, he now lifted the receiver himself, usually on the second ring.

"Brick has a girl, too," he confided to Mary once,

by way of explanation. "Her name's Gloria, and boy, is she ugly. Braces and everything. Brick says she's nice."

"Looks aren't everything."

"Yeah, I know. If they were, I sure wouldn't go around with Shirley."

"Why *do* you like her, then?"

"She's easy."

"Easy?"

"You know—easy to be around. I feel comfortable with her."

"Oh." Mary was relieved.

The evening before Valentine's Day, Jake decided he ought to buy Shirley something to repay her for the wallet he never used.

"I suppose candy or something like that," he said, as they got out of the car at the shopping center.

"How much did you want to spend?"

"A dollar, maybe."

Mary led him past Fannie Mae's and took him in the drug store, Jake looked over the Whitman chocolates, exclaimed over the price, and finally settled for a cellophane package of three chocolate-covered marshmallow hearts for a dollar twenty-nine by the Casonova Candy Company.

Mary helped him wrap the box. "Want me to drive you over to her house?"

Jake was shocked. "No! For Christ's sake, I don't even know where she lives! Boy, if I ever went to her house it would be all over school. I'm just going to hand them to her before class sometime."

And so he set out the next day with the package discreetly tucked inside his notebook.

Mary drove to work smiling about Jake, and did not notice the minister's thoughtful glance.

"We're going to have an old-fashioned revival the third week of July," he told her when she was seated at her desk. "I've heard great things about this preacher. He's increased attendance fifty percent with an eighty percent sign-up for the Lord."

"You're bringing in someone else, then?"

"I've hired a professional. I've been working too hard. Bernice says so. I'll be a part of the service each night, but it will be good to sit back and let someone else run it, plan it, advertise it. . . ."

"No professional jealousy?" Mary joked.

He looked offended that she should even ask. "Not where the Lord is concerned, Mary. We're all brothers in His sight."

They worked silently at their separate tasks. Mary was deep in attendance records for the high-school department when she was conscious that the minister had swiveled his chair around and was looking at her, fingers folded under his chin.

"You're changing, Mary," he told her. His voice was kind, and he bore a sad smile on his face. "Did you know that?"

"Changing?"

"Yes, I can't quite put my finger on it. . . ."

"For the better, I hope."

He didn't answer. Mary put down her pen and looked at him. "*Not* for the better!"

"I'm not exactly sure. You seem more casual. Maybe it's the effect of having that boy around."

Mary tried to sound pleasant. "He's not just 'that boy' and he's not just 'around.' He's my nephew, and we're a family. I guess he's bound to influence me some."

"Of course." The minister's eyebrows were drawn

together in a frown. "I'd just like to see more influence in the other direction, too."

"He's been coming to Bible class every Sunday, now," Mary protested.

"Yes, but Bernice says he sits there looking bored and asks inflammatory questions. Sometimes attitudes like that are contagious."

"Well, if you want me to keep him home. . . ."

"That's not what I meant."

"He's only been here five months. Personally, I think he's doing marvelously for a boy who's been through what he has."

"You're quite right. I didn't mean any criticism, Mary. And we started out talking about you anyway, not Jake. I just wanted to make sure that you realize this is a serious profession, your job no less than mine. We do have a lot of older people in our congregation, so you have to be especially careful."

"Whom did I offend?"

"Well, now, I don't want to go naming names."

"Good grief, how many are there?"

"It's not the number, Mary. It's your attitude. You have to be more careful what you say."

What on earth made the man so verbally constipated? Mary wondered. Would he never be able to get it out?

"*What* did I say?"

"Someone overheard you using the Lord's name in vain when you were using the mimeograph machine last week. Others have reported a light-heartedness that they feel is out of place in a church office. Remember that many of our callers are in pain—physical and spiritual—and they want to hear a comforting voice on the other end of the line, not a flip retort."

"When was I ever flip to anyone in pain, Ralph?" Mary insisted. "I need to know."

"Well, Myra Olstead called here last week. . . ."

"Yes. You were out. She was hysterical because her daughter's moved in with a man, and she thinks God's punishing her because she let Joanne go around in shorts last summer. She says the girl is deliriously happy and never coming back home again."

"And do you remember what you said then?"

"I told her that if Joanne was deliriously happy, it didn't look as though God were punishing anybody."

"That's the type of thing I mean, Mary."

"I should have told her she was right—that God's got this grudge against her?"

"She needed prayer, Mary: guidance; support. She wanted someone to talk to Joanne."

"Good grief, Ralph, have *you* ever lived with Myra Olstead? I mean, can you imagine what it would be like? All the angels in heaven must be rejoicing because Joanne finally got away. If I brought the girl back again, God would have it in for *me*."

"It's not for us to judge Myra Olstead."

"Or her daughter either, then."

"All I'm saying, Mary, is that you are too quick sometimes. You don't think before you answer. In the future I want you to refer all such calls to me."

Mary nodded. "I'll try to remember," she said, and felt her facial muscles settling back into the old familiar mold that reminded her of her mother's photograph. The Marbury Syndrome. And to think she'd almost lost it! How had the new smile crept in so unaware? How had the twinkle in her eyes and the laugh in her voice taken over without her knowing it? Jake was infiltrating every fiber of her body. . . .

She stopped by a bakery on the way home and got

some chocolate cupcakes with white icing and red hearts. When she reached the house, Jake was sitting on the couch reading a science fiction book. He merely grunted when she came in and did not even raise his head. She set the package down and looked at him, wondering. There was a decided scowl on his face.

"Well," she said, after a bit. "Did she like it?"

"Who?"

"Shirley. The candy."

"She *sat* on it."

Mary put one hand over her mouth, suppressing a howl that she knew was out of place. "What?"

"I put it on her seat in history class, and she didn't even see it."

"Oh, no!"

"That dumb jerk. She just sat on it."

"But wasn't she even . . . appreciative a little?"

"How can you appreciate three flat blobs of marshmallow gluck? It was oozing out of the cellophane. She said 'Yech!' and held it up for everybody to see, and somebody got hold of the card and told her it was from me, and I just wanted to die."

"Oh, Jake."

"You know what they looked like—the hearts?"

"What?"

"Those cow pies in Uncle Sam's pasture."

The howl came in spite of herself. Mary doubled over, Jake smiled a little, and finally they were laughing together. Chalk one up for mirth. The Marbury Syndrome had lost out once again.

EIGHT

~~~

"It'll be good for you."

Like a health tonic? Maybe so.

"Greg's coming here this weekend. He has an old classmate living in Washington, and suggested we all go out together." As simple as that. Liz always made the mountains seem low, and the crooked straight, and the rough places plain.

"What would we do?"

"Nothing terribly sensational. No orgies or anything."

It occurred to Mary that she had never dated anyone outside of Charles County. She didn't even *know* any men outside of Charles County. It was ironic that she should feel frightened. For thirty-four years she'd lived to get out, and now that she had the chance, even for an evening, she was digging her heels in the carpet and holding on for dear life. You didn't have to worry when you went out with Faith Holiness boys—Warren excepted. You knew that hands would stay where hands belonged and that kissing, even, wouldn't become an issue till the sixth or seventh date. The older the men got, the more sedate they became—an inverse correlation between age and libido.

On Saturday she tried several dresses before settling on the same green wool she had worn on Thanksgiving. This time, however, she tied her long hair back with a scarf and unbuttoned the neckline down to her bra. From the back of her dresser, she took out some rouge, mascara, and lip gloss which she'd purchased the day before in La Plata. Carefully, slowly, she began the maiden voyage on her face.

She stared at the woman before her, and the large gray eyes—accented now with mascara—stared back uncertainly. What a difference a few simple cosmetics could make—to think that the person before her had been hiding there all this time, just waiting for a chance to come out. She blushed happily and went into the living room to show Jake.

"How do I look?" she asked and stood still for inspection.

He was playing solitaire on the coffee table; he gave her a quick appraisal and returned to the game. "Like you've got a date with Albert Schweitzer," he said.

Her shoulders sagged. "Still prudish, huh?" She went back to the bedroom, pausing a moment in the doorway. "What do you know about Schweitzer, anyway?"

"Some guy gave a report on him at school."

Inside the bedroom, Mary took off her dress, removed her slip, and put the dress back on again. This time she started with the buttons at the bottom and undid them up to her knee. She looked in the mirror. Albert Schweitzer once removed. Impulsively, she undid the buttons halfway up her thigh, revealing only panty hose beneath. A horn tapped lightly outside; they were already late.

"*God help me,*" she said aloud. Sacrilege.

Jake looked up when she came out of the bedroom

again and stared at the way her skirt flapped open. "Jesus! Some cat's gonna howl tonight!"

She gasped, grabbed her coat, and fled out the door. "If Verna calls. . . ." she said over her shoulder.

"If Verna calls, I'll tell her you're out with a Mormon missionary," said Jake.

She didn't really see what the men looked like until they were seated in a rustic bar and grill in Virginia. They looked as though they'd both been raised on the same rations. They were lean and slightly graying, and they each had a shaggy look about them, like prize-winning Irish wolfhounds. One wore a tweed sport coat, the other a corduroy with leather patches on the elbows, and Mary wondered if—as old married couples begin to resemble each other after a while— two college roommates could have influenced each other through a sort of collegiate osmosis. Phillip, her date, was the better looking of the two, if only because his face was a bit more square and his eyes not as deep set as Greg's. Mary looked at Greg and tried to imagine him undressing Liz the moment she entered his apartment. She could imagine it very well.

"This is cozy!" Liz said, looking toward the fireplace where logs were blazing. A blackboard over the bar listed specials for the day, and the bartenders all wore derbies. "Mary, you look particularly attractive."

"She does indeed," said Phillip.

Mary would have preferred no comments at all.

Compliments merely pointed up the fact that she
didn't usually look so pretty. She tried to pull the
edges of her dress together in front, but they kept
slipping open, and she could hardly button them
now, having walked the full length of the bar with
noticeable glances from both Greg and Phillip. She
shivered, and Phillip caught it. He helped pull her
coat up around her and then sat with one hand resting casually on her shoulders—so easy, so spontaneous.
So obvious.

He was certainly nice enough, however. He had
gallantly paid her his complete attention in the car
coming up. How long, she wondered—and how many
women—did it take before a man could behave so ef-
fortlessly? If Milt Jennings, for example, were given a
crash course—say, for three nights a week—was there
still hope, or were Marbury men doomed from their
twentieth year on? What had her father been like as a
young blade? He must have felt *something*—some stirrings in the heart, some lust in the loins—to go and
contribute an entire wheat crop to the church of his
fiancée. How long had the flame continued, and
when had it flickered its last? Or had it? She realized
she knew nothing whatsoever about the sex lives of
her parents. The questions seemed suddenly important, as though through these she could find her own
place in the scheme of things.

A large-bosomed waitress in a tight black uniform
came over with a small tray of cheese and crackers.
Greg's eyes fondled the woman's breasts.

"What would you like?" she asked.

Greg smiled up at her. "Nothing that's on the
menu," he said teasingly.

Liz rolled her eyes. It was obviously a much-re-
peated line.

"What are you having?" Phillip said, turning to Mary.

She stared up at the blackboard and read it hastily.

"I guess I'll try the barbeque," she said.

Instantly Liz and Greg looked up. Phillip, too, sat strangely quiet. What had she done? What social error had she committed that she hadn't learned about in Marbury? Had she ordered the most expensive thing on the list?

"We were just going to have a drink here, Mary," Liz said. "But if you're really hungry. . . ."

Oh, my God, why hadn't somebody told her? "No, no," she said quickly. "A drink's fine. Order one for me, will you, Phil?"

Phillip glanced at her silently. The second big goof of the evening. She was doing just splendidly. She thought of Jake in the restaurant at Thanksgiving. Maybe she should have a laughing fit, and *really* set their teeth on edge.

"Two old-fashioneds," said Phillip. How appropriate, Mary thought. She was feeling used and hurt and embarrassed.

"What's your field, Phillip?" Liz asked as soon as the waitress had left.

"Education," he said. "I'm editor of one of those hundreds of journals put out by the National Education Association. Technical stuff. Not very interesting, really."

Everything they did to cover for her seemed to make it worse, Mary thought. Great evening! A scintillating start!

It was, in fact, the craziest thing she had ever seen. For thirty-five minutes they sat there, nursing their drinks, then got up, paid the bill, and left. This time they went to a restaurant in the District, with torches inside the entrance, and were again given a booth in the bar.

"Two old-fashioneds," Phillip said again, before Mary could disgrace herself a second time.

Her stomach began to protest. She was, after all, a farm girl, and used to dinner early. Whoever heard of driving from one place to another just to eat a couple of crackers and order a drink? No one in Marbury, that's certain.

As soon as Mary had settled in against the wall, she realized the need to urinate.

"I'm sorry, will you excuse me?" she asked Phillip, and he got up quickly, taking her arm and helping her out of the seat. She went to the women's room wishing dully that the evening was over. Before she left she rubbed at the thin line of eye shadow that had settled in the crease of her lids, buttoned two of the buttons on her thigh, and returned to the booth. Phillip was already standing, waiting for her.

It took fifteen minutes for the drinks to arrive, and another half hour to consume them. Mary was dismayed to discover that she needed the restroom again.

"Excuse me, Phillip," she said again, and this time Liz followed her to the lounge.

"Mary, are you sick?"

"No, damn it, I'm starving," she said angrily. "I'm coming in here to nibble on the soap, what do you think?"

Liz looked at her more closely. "Sure you're not getting stewed?"

"Liz it's a quarter to nine! Sometimes I'm in *bed* by nine. I'm hungry."

She looked in the mirror to check her make-up again and found herself tilting rather strangely to the left. Maybe she *was* drunk. She was not sure of anything, except that she was going to have a Big Mac attack if they didn't eat soon.

"Okay, we'll order right away," Liz promised. "Listen, you really look great tonight, Mary. Honestly! Phil's impressed."

"Well, please quit telling me so," Mary said. "He'll be a lot more impressed if I can stop crawling over his knees to go to the bathroom."

They were ushered into the dining room, guided by a waiter in a tunic. There they were given a small recitation about the soup of the day, the chef's special, the origin of the steaks, the good wishes of the owner, and finally the name of the waiter himself.

"All but the date of his appendectomy," said Greg after the young man had gone, and they laughed together, Mary included. Maybe they weren't such bad people after all.

Dinner came, entrees were shared and commented upon, stories exchanged. Greg said that when he was traveling, he made it a point to eat at ham and turkey dinners sponsored by local churches because the food was so good. Phillip talked about being a member of the Washington Ethical Society, Liz mentioned going to a Unitarian church once, and then she paused. Obviously, there was a story coming on. Mary could tell. There was always a certain look in her eyes.

"You want to know why I never went back?" Liz asked. "I will tell you why I never went back. There was this guy, see, and when my grandmother locked me out of the house one Sabbath because I wasn't home by sundown, he took me with him to a Unitarian book discussion group where all these people were sitting around discussing Ibsen's *Doll's House*.

I'd never even heard of Ibsen, but it was sort of fascinating, and anyway they were kind and invited me to church that Sunday."

"Did anyone ask for this?" Greg teased, looking around the group.

Liz ignored him. "So I went to church with this guy—Eddie, that was his name. The first thing I discovered was that Unitarians are big on bumper stickers. The whole parking lot was filled with 'I brake for animals' and 'One world under law' and 'Nudists do it outdoors.' I mean, you can't help but be wary. Well, they had a soundtrack of *Godspell* going, and the program said that the service would be done by the worship workshop committee. All the chairs were arranged in concentric circles, see, and all at once here came these four middle-aged women—well, thirtyish, at least—dancing down the aisle in leotards and bare feet. They did the entire dance holding hands— you know, twisting over and under and through—and finally ended up in a heap at the center with their arms around each other."

The waiter came for the dishes, and Greg lit a cigarette, smiling. Phillip was smiling too, chin resting on his hands.

"Well, the director of religious education got up next and gave a short talk about how earth's survival depended on man's concern for his fellow man and how as evidence of that concern she was passing out a dish of sunflower seeds to show that what we sow we shall reap, and if we plant sunshine and love among our friends and neighbors, we get love in return."

"Sounds harmless enough," said Phillip. "Rather nice, in fact. What was so offensive?"

"Me," said Liz dolefully. "I just couldn't get the hang of it somehow. I mean, I'd been a good Jewish girl up to that point, I'd read the Haftorah and the blessings and the Prophetic selections, and somehow I just wasn't prepared for sunflower seeds. It wasn't till Eddie asked me where I was going to plant mine that I realized I'd goofed."

"Why?"

"I ate it."

All three burst into laughter, attracting stares from diners at the other tables. There was something warm and friendly about being included in such laughter, Mary discovered. She suddenly felt very good about the evening, the people she was with, and herself.

"Anyway," Liz continued, settling back in her chair, the ruffles on the sleeves of her purple blouse coming together as she touched the tips of her fingers, "we all got up to leave after the service, and when we got to the door, here was this man passing out paper reinforcements. I thought maybe it was like the wafer in a Catholic church, but I wasn't about to put it on my tongue unless Eddie told me to. And you know what we were supposed to do with them? You'll never guess. We were supposed to lick them and stick them on our foreheads to remind us that love is a never-ending circle."

Again the laughter, deep chesty laughs from the men, accented with Mary's more lilting soprano, like a perfectly tuned trio. It was delicious being a part of it all.

"Here we were," Liz went on, "all these sober-faced people going out to their cars with these little circles on their foreheads that looked like misplaced lifesavers or something. By the time we got to the corner, Eddie's had slipped down on one side of his nose, and I couldn't hold back any longer. I just sat there and howled. He never asked me to a service again. . . ."

"Hardly a representative sample," Phillip laughed.

Mary was warm and happy. Her stomach was full, and she was feeling just a bit drowsy. She smiled benevolently out over all of them, over everyone in the dining room—a blessing for the waiters and the cooks and the hat-check girl—for the town of Marbury, even—a blessing from the church secretary of the Faith Holiness Church who was probably on the verge of being fired. It seemed very funny to her, and she wondered if it would sound funny if she told it to the others. It was hard to compete with Liz Grossman's stories, however, so she kept it to herself and just went on smiling.

It was eleven when they left the restaurant, and Greg suggested stopping for one more drink at a mideast nightclub.

There were small tables pushed together in long rows and almost nonexistent aisles between them. Phillip helped Mary squeeze into a chair far down the middle of one row and took one beside her, while Liz and Greg sat across from them. The air vibrated with the amplified sounds of strange instruments pounding torrid beats and sensuous melodies.

"What are you having?" the waitress yelled above the music, from the end of the table.

Phillip called something back, then turned to Mary. "Gin and tonic," he said. "Hope that's okay."

"Sure, that's fine."

"What?" he said, leaning over toward her.

"That's fine!" Mary bleated. You could go deaf in such a place.

She was beginning to feel it now. Halfway through the drink she felt unusually sleepy, silly, and her mouth and tongue seemed slightly anesthetized. Her arms were absolutely limp. It was the most relaxed she had ever felt in her life. In a fog such as this, one might let a man do anything. Phillip had his arm around her, and she leaned her head on his shoulder. She caught the scent of his after-shave, and this time she wondered if, in such a comatose state, she might perhaps discover the meaning of its attraction for her. If she lay here listless, and let her mind wander, would the memory come back to her, that elusive slip of something that was always just out of reach? But Phillip was talking so she didn't pursue it.

"Better go slow with that drink," he said in her ear. "As soon as it's half gone, they'll be after you to order again."

Mary continued her idiotic smiling. She didn't know why she did it. Her mouth just seemed to tilt upwards without any help from her at all. Phillip tried to describe the various instruments up on stage—the ud, the bouzouki, the derbecke—but she heard little of it. She wanted to stay forever in this den of iniquity, this smoke-filled place of loin-tingling rhythms and dark-eyed musicians playing their hearts out to her alone.

Some middle-aged men, a bit tipsy, climbed up on stage and managed a rather graceful dance, holding their hands up in the air, each bearing a white hand-kerchief which he waved delicately, dancing together a simple little side-step. Mary wanted to join them. She wanted to let everyone know she liked being there—that she, too, was feeling joyful. But somehow her legs wouldn't move.

She was conscious of the music growing louder. Phillip shifted his arm slightly, and Mary sat up, groggy.

"It's Adrienne," Greg shouted from across the table, pleased. "We're in luck."

With a crescendo of drum beats, a red-haired woman, swathed in veils, came walking quickly from a side door and up on the stage, peering seductively down at the crowd with large, luminous eyes, the only portion of her face that was exposed. All the while she was clicking small cymbals attached to her fingers, her body weaving back and forth to the beat of the drums. Phillip took his arm from around Mary and rested his elbows on the table.

Mary's first thought, as the woman unveiled, was that they were kindred souls, pushing forty. The dancer's hair was obviously dyed, her waist thick, her thighs large, and small deposits of fat were just beginning to pocket her upper arms. But she was attractive nonetheless, and there was the wonder. She was beautiful—sensuous—and Mary realized it wasn't her body so much that the men came to see, but the animal vitality, the lusty joy of being alive.

Adrienne, the dancer, wiggled from one musician to another, thrusting her sequinned bosom in the man's face and shaking it rapidly, keeping the rest of her body still. Each man in turn responded by improvising wildly on his instrument, as though an electric current had passed between them. Show business, but effective, thought Mary.

Then Adrienne the Magnificent was on the floor, one leg tucked under her, her belly undulating, and doing something with her head which Mary did not

quite understand. It was as though she had an extra
joint—a hinge, somewhere—which enabled her head
to slide back and forth above her neck, her body motionless, and her eyes began a sort of Morse code as
she rolled them first to the right and then to the left.

Then she was crawling about the stage on her
stomach, a shimmering snake, one bare leg inching
forward in front of the other, till suddenly she was on
her feet again, the music was orgiastic, and she was
dancing faster and faster, her hair wild. Her back glistened and drops of sweat trickled down between the
cleavage of her breasts. Around and around she
whirled, her filmy skirt flying, her hair like a horse's
mane. Droplets of sweat flew about the stage, leaving
it wet with the exuberance of her body.

And suddenly the music was over and, her chest
heaving in and out, her mouth open in a breathless
smile, Adrienne took her bows demurely and, swath-
ing herself once more, ran back out the side door.

Mary could not seem to move. It was as though the
animality of the dancer's body had provoked a paralysis in her own. It didn't matter if Adrienne's real
name might be Sara Worfdorger, or if she had lived
in Arlington all her life. The fact was that she had
come up on stage and freed her body before all these
men—these strange men she did not even know. And
Mary remembered the night that Warren had left—
how she had run to the barn barefoot, her body, too,
glistening with sweat, her mouth open, her breasts exposed to the moonlight, and there, in the barn, had
undressed herself. . . .

She got up quickly, the paralysis gone, and
stumbled blindly toward the door, tripping over feet
and chairs as she went. Phillip, startled, got up and
went after her. Liz and Greg, seeing what was hap-

pening, picked up the bill and began making their way among the chairs. And the next thing Mary knew, she was outside, bending over the curb and throwing up behind a blue Mustang.

Liz seemed to feel responsible somehow. "Oh, my God, I shouldn't have let her drink so much," she said, and dashed back inside for some wet paper towels. "Mary, you going to be all right?" she asked as she swabbed her face. "You want to lie down?"

"I'm okay," Mary said. There was no way to tell Liz that the excitement had been in her soul, not her stomach.

Phillip sat with his arm around Mary in the back seat, stroking her forehead now and then as she leaned against his shoulder. He did not try to slip one hand up her dress or fondle her breasts with the other. He treated her tenderly, quietly, and Mary marveled that she could feel so at peace with him.

Liz chattered on about whether belly dancing was basically Turkish or Greek, and this evolved into exercise in general, jogging in particular. But it seemed very far away, and did not concern Mary at all. Phillip's fingers on her forehead felt unusually pleasant, caressing her temples, curling themselves around her ears. It was as though she were a young girl in the act of being comforted—familiar, somehow.

The musky scent of his cologne invaded her nostrils, and she languished in it. Casually, his hand moved up to the top of her head, the fingers threading themselves through her hair, his palm gently patting her head. . . . *There, there,* she half-expected him to say. *Go, my child, and sin no more.*

She started, her legs stiffening, her muscles taut. The memory of it! Of course, that was it! The summer evangelists, those gorgeous-smelling men in their snow-white suits, who knelt with her there in the tent. Those powerful men with the breast-pocket handkerchiefs who laid their hands on her head and flooded her being with their scent. Those huge men whose knees touched hers there by the altar, who accepted her totally and whatever sins she had brought them, who touched not only her senses but her soul as well, and sent her reeling back across the sawdust to her seat, cleansed and pure and free.

"You all right?" Phillip asked.

Her body went limp once more and Mary nuzzled her nose against his cheek, not caring, drinking in his fragrance, gulping it down, reveling in the memory.

"Wonderful," she said. "Simply wonderful."

Finally the car stopped, and there was her house like something out of a fairy tale. Mary felt she had been away for a long time—traveled around the world, perhaps—and it seemed impossible that nothing should have changed here in Marbury, that everything was just as she had left it.

Phillip took her to the door and made sure she had her key. He stepped inside with her, told her to take care of herself, that it had been a marvelous evening. Then he kissed her lightly on the lips, squeezed her hand, and left.

Jake had gone to bed. A note under the lamp said, "Aunt Verna said she'd call in the morning. Wouldn't believe the Mormon missionary bit."

The phone call the next morning was not from Verna but from Liz.

"How're you feeling?" The voice was cautious.

"Fine."

"Really? Listen, we thought it was a great evening. We all enjoyed it."

"I did too. I thought Phillip was exceptionally nice."

There was a pause. "Yes, he was. I guess Greg's known him for a long time."

Mary sensed the pause and instantly a cold awareness of something gone wrong swept over her. He *hadn't* liked her, then. He hadn't asked for her phone number, she realized. He hadn't said he'd like to see her again. It was clear now, after a full night's sleep.

"He didn't like me, did he?" she said flatly.

"That's not true. He thought you were extremely nice. He said so."

"But not very exciting."

"That wasn't it at all, Mary. He told us he'd been feeling a little depressed, that's all."

"Because of me?"

Liz sighed. "No. Because of his wife. He's married."

Mary sat down on the telephone stool. "Liz!"

"I didn't know, Mary, or I would never have agreed to the four of us going out. I didn't find out till after we took him home. Greg told me that Phil's wife had left him a week ago, that things hadn't been too good between them, and Phillip was depressed. Greg had wanted to cheer him up, and that's why he suggested we all go out. When we got him home, though, and Phil saw his wife's car in the driveway, he couldn't seem to get out of the car fast enough. So I guess that's that."

Mary leaned against the wall, tears running down the back of her throat. Angry tears.

Liz sensed it. "Mary, I didn't know! I was really angry at Greg for not telling me. He said he figured that Phil needed a lift, and that you . . . I mean being religious and everything . . . you couldn't do him any harm. . . ."

Mary blinked. Mary Poppins. That's who she was. She'd get it right, yet.

"Oh, God, Mary, the more I say the worse it gets," Liz apologized. "I'm really sorry. Greg's an ass, some- times, and I told him so. I told him how awful you'd feel if you knew."

No, they were wrong, Mary decided. She didn't feel awful. She didn't feel anything at all where men were concerned. And it was better this way. Expect noth- ing, feel nothing, and you'll never be disappointed. Expect the moon and stars and a full orchestra, and you get to throw up behind a blue Mustang on Four- teenth Street.

Winter was melting away early. It had snowed only twice, and by the middle of March the wind had a certain sweetness about it, as though blown across the crocuses that were pushing up beneath the maple tree. Whatever else you could say about Marbury, it was beautiful in the spring.

I belong here, Mary told herself. The statement lacked conviction, but it made her feel better to think it. The world outside was what she'd been told it was all along. Her visit to Santa Monica seven years ago, Warren's will, a date with a genteel man only to dis- cover he was married. . . . Life in the fold was not what it was cracked up to be, but life beyond the gate was worse. She set about her duties both at home and at work with new determination and loyalty.

Jake had outgrown all his trousers and at school, he reported, the kids teased him for wearing "floods." Sam had started the spring plowing early because of the unusually warm weather, so one Saturday Mary drove Jake to the farm and went shopping with Verna.

"He needs at least four new pairs of jeans and a couple long-sleeved shirts," Mary said.

"It's a shame I didn't save Bill's clothes," Verna commented. "The things I gave away! Oh, for heaven's sake, Mary, not those jeans! They wouldn't last a week! You've got to get extra duty denim with reinforced knees!"

Mary backed away from the counter displaying fancy jeans with embroidered stars on the pockets and followed her sister across the floor to where a sign said "Toughskins! Sears Finest!"

"Here." Verna grabbed a pair and held it up. "Feel the difference in weight. Why, those other jeans would have given at the knees in no time. You've got to be *aware* of things like that, Mary, if you're going to bring up a boy. Why don't you turn the clothes buying over to me? I've raised a son myself."

They sat across from each other in a small diner with green cafe curtains along the front windows and plastic ivy hanging in pots from the ceiling. Each picked at her chicken salad, her face unsmiling, staring occasionally out the window at passersby, lifting her water glass wordlessly. Jake was a subject that drove them apart.

"I asked Sam to come back," Verna said at last in uncustomarily soft tones. "I told him if he stayed this fall and winter with me in La Plata, I'd do for him in

White Plains in spring and summer—make his meals and fix him a good lunch when he's working the fields. Man can't run a farm good by himself. . . ."

"What did he say?"

"He won't come, Mary."

"He said that?"

"He said he's got used to being up there by himself and it don't bother him." Verna stopped chewing and pressed her lips together.

Mary was very quiet. Finally she said, "Sam needs more than just a cook and housekeeper, Verna."

Verna lifted her fork again without looking up. "We're getting on, Mary We're past all that."

"Sam's not."

The large woman pushed her plate away and sat staring across the room, hands in her lap. She seemed unusually docile, Mary thought. It was a side of her sister she had rarely experienced before.

"There are times," Verna began, and then stopped. ". . . there are times," she said again, in a small voice, "when I wish I'd been raised differently, Mary. I never did like it, you know—the physical side. You'd think that once a woman got to be forty-five and had given a man a son, he'd let her be."

"Forty-five's not old."

"I feel old. Maybe you don't think I've minded, Sam living out there away from me, but I do. Down underneath it hurts. And people—they know. They don't ask, but they know. It's not a good feeling for a woman, Mary, to have a husband who won't live with her. . . ."

"Maybe if you were more affectionate. . . ."

"It's hard, Mary. You don't know what it's like—a

man pushing up against you, pawing you, all that
fumbling around under the covers. . . ."

Mary took a drink of water.

"A lot of animal nonsense, that's what it is," Verna
finished.

"That's why Sam won't come back."

Verna took a deep breath that ended in a sigh and
then grew quiet. Mary's fork clinked out a solo as she
finished her meal.

"I think he'd come back if I had Jake with me,"
Verna said finally.

Mary felt the muscles in her throat tighten.

"If Sam had that boy to come home to, he'd not
stay up on that farm all winter, you can bet. It'd be
like when Bill was little again, and Sam'd take him
out and show him things. They had a good time,
them two . . . when Bill was little. . . ."

"Jake's a boy, Verna—a flesh and blood person.
He's not just something to use as bait to bring Sam
home again."

"Whoever said he was, Mary? Of course he's a boy,
and I'd love him to death. Think what he'd do for
Dad!"

"He was sent to *me*, Verna, and I don't want to go
on having arguments with you over Jake."

Verna's eyebrows came together in the familiar
knot that Mary had come to know so well.

"You're selfish, Mary!" she snapped. "You think of
no one but yourself! You've changed—changed for the
worse, I say, and don't think I'm the only one who's
noticed."

"You don't have to speak for anyone else," Mary
said, reaching for the check. "If someone's got something to say, he can tell me himself." Her heart
pounded rapidly. She was really asking for trouble.

Verna stared at her fiercely. "That's just what I mean. That's a fine example. You don't even talk like you used to—you go around sassing people back."

The drive to White Plains was made in silence. Once or twice Mary commented on a tree that was budding already, but Verna only looked in that direction and made no comment. Relieved, Mary gave up trying.

Jake was lying on the ground on his stomach. He had his head buried in his arms, and Tibs was frantically trying to get him to uncover his face. The dog poked his nose around Jake's head and whined. Jake was shaking with laughter.

He jumped up and came over to the car.

"Guess what?" he told Mary. "Uncle Sam wants me to stay up here this summer. He said I could come as soon as school was out and stay till September. I plowed half a field today, and I even turned the tractor around by myself."

Verna's face was instantly wreathed in a smile. "And what a *helper* you'll be to your uncle," she said. "Why, Jake, you'll grow a foot at least—all that work and fresh air, won't he, Mary? It's just the thing for him!"

"We'll see," said Mary, and felt that spring had suddenly reversed itself, and it was January once more.

NINE

Jake celebrated his fourteenth birthday on May 20, and received a Swiss army knife from Mary. He was delighted. Verna gave him a white imitation leather Bible; Sam, a pair of hiking boots; Mrs. Gordon presented him with a book mark with the Ten Commandments on it, and Liz sent him an envelope containing some cancelled stamps.

"Birthday chollie gun dang!" beamed Grandpa Myles, and laughed heartily, sending a shower of saliva over the tablecloth.

There had obviously been a private celebration at school of some sort, for Mary found crumpled wrapping paper in Jake's waste basket and a copy of *Penthouse,* with a semi-nude woman on the cover, under Jake's pillow when she changed the linen. She put it back guiltily, as though she had intruded on Jake's private thoughts. He was Warren's boy, all right. She tried not to think of Shirley Delvaney, who was too big-breasted for her own good, and what she might have offered Jake as a gift. They ought to bind up bodies like that.

It seemed, however, that Shirley had no intention of being bound, or Jake either, for that matter. He announced at the breakfast table one morning that he was taking her to the junior high semi-formal on June first. They would be doubling with Brick and Gloria, and could Mary please drive them one way?

Somehow Mary had imagined she wouldn't have to face this for years. But suddenly this boy of fourteen, with not even a pimple yet, was going to be surrounded by big-breasted girls in low-cut gowns—girls who, she was sure, wore their corsages on their wrists just so bodies could press together as they danced.

"Verna," she said, "will have a fit."

"She won't know," said Jake.

"She'll know. There's not one thing that's happened in Charles County in the last twenty years that she doesn't know about. Verna's got antennae out in fifty different directions."

"I'm going," said Jake. "I've been saving up my allowance for the tickets and corsage."

It was final. At least she could tell Verna she tried —more or less.

"The only problem," said Jake, "is what to do afterwards. The kids always go somewhere. Some of the parents are driving them to Ocean City for the night."

"Some parents are insane."

"Well, we're not going, anyway. Shirley has to be home at twelve-thirty, and Brick doesn't have any money to take the girls anywhere. We were . . . sort of wondering . . . well, could we come back here afterward and play records and stuff?"

"Of course!" said Mary, enormously relieved. "You know you can invite friends here any time, Jake."

The night of June 1 was warm and somewhat humid. Jake was struggling to get the ends of his tie in position when the phone rang. Mary answered.

"Jake's not going to that dance is he, Mary?" came Verna's strident voice.

How did she do it, that woman? Mary wondered. Jake caught the look on her face and mouthed, *Aunt Verna?* Mary nodded. He rolled his eyes.

"Yes, he is, Verna," said Mary.

"Mary!" Verna followed the exclamation with silence, as though she would win a recantation with it, but Mary waited her out.

"Have you gone mad," Verna said at last. "Have you no sense of responsibility whatsoever."

"He'll be all right. The kids are coming back here afterwards. Look, I really can't talk any more right now because Jake needs help with his tie."

She put the receiver down and found that her legs felt trembly. She had actually hung up on Verna.

"How did she know," Jake asked, curious.

"It was probably mentioned in the weekly newspaper. She keeps track of such things. If you want to know where men go to shoot pool or drink or anything else, ask Verna. She's an encyclopedia of sinful knowledge."

"Weird," said Jake.

Brick's father pulled up in front. Jake gingerly picked up the gardenia box and started for the door.

"Have a good time," Mary said brightly. "I'll pick you up at ten-thirty." Now that the decision was made, he might as well enjoy himself.

She closed the door behind him and stretched out on the couch. Fifteen minutes later the phone rang again. She let it ring until it gave one final chirp and stopped abruptly. She had more nerve than she'd thought.

At ten-twenty, Mary drove to school. The parking lot was crowded with girls in long gowns and their smartly dressed escorts. Parental cars were lined up for a block and a half.

Jake and his friends were waiting by the flag pole. They were laughing. Everyone was laughing. Everyone came out of the gym with a huge smile. It was as though, at the age of fourteen, there was a monstrous joke written in the sky, ever-present, and only the young could see it.

"Hello," Mary said cheerfully, trying to make out the girls' faces in the darkness, and then, as they climbed in the car, "how was the dance?"

"Great!" came a high-pitched female voice. "How do you do, Mrs. Myles! I'm Shirley Delvaney."

"I'm Jake's aunt," Mary explained, by way of correction. She waited for someone to open the front door and get in beside her, then realized that all four had squeezed in back.

There was excited chatter as they drove to the house. The girls were talking about someone who had made the mistake of arriving in a short dress and had gone back home in tears. The boys were talking about the live band. There were two conversations going on simultaneously, and yet somehow they were all responding to each other. It was amazing.

Inside the house, Mary began laying out a supply of ice and pretzels and potato chips, watching the girls out of the corner of her eye. Shirley looked as cheerful as the picture Jake did not carry in his wallet. In fact, she looked even more so. In real life, Shirley Delvaney smiled with her mouth wide open. Her eyes were deep set, so there was very little space between her brows and eyelids, but her figure was positively striking.

The other girl, blond, insisted on smiling without parting her lips at all, which gave her the appearance of an Albino cat. Once, when Gloria laughed in spite of herself, Mary noticed a glint of hardware and remembered the braces Jake had mentioned. She wore a dress with a slit up one side and, each time she sat, rested on the opposite hip to expose the other more fully. Brick never took his eyes off her once.

As Mary was putting the ice back in the refrigerator, she was conscious of the girls whispering in the doorway of the kitchen.

"Excuse me, Mrs. Myles," said Shirley. "Would you happen to have a rest room,"

"Certainly. Right at the end of the hall."

Mary smiled to herself as the girls hurried off, still whispering. A blare of rock music shook the walls as Brick put on the first record.

Mary got a book, a couple of magazines, fixed herself some tea, and took them into her bedroom. She was about to take off her shoes when the two girls appeared timidly again in the doorway. Shirley's face was flushed.

"Excuse me, Mrs. Myles," she said, and her voice fell to a whisper. "I'm afraid I've started my period, and I wasn't expecting it yet."

"Excitement," said Gloria.

"That happened to me once," Mary said, trying to put her at ease. She opened the drawer of her dresser, gave Shirley a pad and some pins. "Need any help?"

"No, we can do it," Gloria said.

"Hey, what's taking so long?" bellowed Brick from the living room.

Shirley quickly stuffed the pad into the neck of her dress as the girls went back to the bathroom.

"Just a *minute!*" Gloria said, and they giggled again.

Mary closed the door, took off her shoes, and settled down with her book. The loud, blaring rock was eventually replaced with soft vocals of love and passion. At twenty of twelve, she decided she had better put the pizza in the oven if they were to eat and have the girls home by twelve-thirty. She slipped on her shoes and opened the bedroom door.

It was pitch black in the hall. She groped her way down toward the kitchen, guided only by the small red light on the record player, and finally found the light switch. Instantly a muffled protest came from Brick. She glanced into the living room.

Jake was in the middle of the floor dancing sedately with Shirley, their arms extended stiffly, faces sober and drawn. But Brick and his girl friend were sprawled in one corner of the couch, and one of Brick's hands had found the slit in Gloria's dress and was caressing her fanny.

Mary leaned against the oven door. Yes, she *had* gone mad. No, she *didn't* have any sense of responsibility. None whatsoever. The girls could have been raped in the time she had left them alone in the living room. Brick's hands and who knows what else could have been inside of Gloria's dress for the last half hour! Should she stop the action? Would it embarrass Jake if she walked in there and turned on a lamp?

"Hey," came Brick's befuddled voice, his lips still pressed against Gloria's bosom, "out with the lights, Jake."

"No, man, let's leave 'em on," came Jake's shaky reply. "Aunt Mary's making the pizza."

"Fuck the pizza."

"Oh, come on, Brick," said Shirley. "We're hungry."

"So go eat and turn out the lights," said Brick. "I can get pizza any day."

There was a titter of laughter from Gloria.

"Hey, Brick," Jake pleaded. "It'll be time to go soon. Get up and be sociable."

"What do you think I'm doin'? I'm being social as hell," growled Brick. "Christ!" There was a rustling of sofa springs, and the next time Mary glanced in, Brick and his girl were dancing as though their groins were glued, but at least they had their feet on the floor.

"Thank you, Mrs. Myles," Shirley burbled when it was time to go. "It was just the best party, and it was nice of you to let us come."

"You're very welcome, Shirley. It was nice to meet you girls."

"Yeah, we enjoyed it," said Brick, straightening his tie and cramming his shirt down in his trousers. Gloria laughed again.

Jake went along for the drive home. Gloria was taken home first, then Brick, then Shirley.

He walked her up to the door where the porch light illuminated half the front yard. Shirley had started up the first step, then realized her mistake and tried to come back down, but Jake was standing too close so she was stranded there six inches higher than he. Suddenly he reached out, his hands on her waist, stood on tiptoe to kiss her mouth, then turned abruptly and bolted for the car.

"Let's *go!*" he breathed, sliding in the front seat

beside Mary, refusing to look up at the house where Shirley was, just as rapidly, disappearing.

The car rolled back down the drive, then out onto the road, and Jake leaned his head back, emitting a long sigh. Mary smiled in the darkness.

"I'm not ready for this," he said at last. "Jesus, I'm just not ready!"

The church, Mary decided, had given up on trying to convert Jake through her. She had expected Verna to call her on Saturday, but the phone did not ring all day. She had expected glares on Sunday from the Gordons, but they virtually ignored her and focused on Jake instead. Milt Jennings nodded stiffly to her and that was all. God had extended his Silent Treatment and made ambassadors of the whole congregation.

The dance had not been mentioned in Bible class, Jake reported later. Instead, Mrs. Gordon had passed out mimeographed slips of paper which read, "I——, do solemnly swear that I will never taste alcoholic beverages. (signed) —— (date) ——."

This had been followed by a lecture about the evils that the class would meet out there in the world somewhere, and how the best defense was the Lord Jesus Christ. Once they joined the church, they would find strength in numbers. This, he said, had been followed in turn by a temperance demonstration in which an egg had been dropped in a glass pitcher of pure alcohol. It promptly disintegrated before the very eyes of the class, and Mrs. Gordon said that this was what whiskey did to the lining of the stomach. Jake had not signed the pledge, and his teacher was not pleased.

On Monday, the pastor's day off, Ralph Gordon did not come into the office at all, even to say hello. Mary would not have been surprised if the grocer, the butcher, and the gas station attendant shunned her also, but it was only within the church that the prophets and the martyrs and the Four Horsemen of the Apocalypse shook their hallowed heads and watched her every move.

A new kind of loneliness swept over her. A cystic fibrosis of the heart seemed to be filling the cells of her soul. She was the sheep again that straddled the fence. She belonged neither in nor out—a woman without a country. All these years she had hoped that at least Warren had understood her, and now he was gone, leaving Jake as his shadow. But there was too much she could not confide in Jake.

"I'm lost, Liz," she said one Friday, having driven to her friend's condominium after work. "Being Jake's aunt just isn't enough, and yet he's all I've got."

"What did you expect?" Liz asked, and went on packing her suitcase for Charlottesville. "Whenever you think that one person's going to solve all your problems, that's when you get clipped in the chops."

Liz sat down on the edge of the bed and lit a cigarette. "I know how you feel, though. I felt that way when I married Clyde. I loved him—I really did love him—as a mother, a daughter, a wife, a mistress—a nurse, even. He was one of those all-purpose men, you know? Whatever you wanted to fantasy when you were in bed with him, you could find something about him that would do the trick."

She sighed, blew a deep lungful of smoke toward the ceiling, and took off her glasses, dangling them carelessly in one hand. "Everything I learned about feeling and caring, he taught me. It was as though— knowing he had MS—Clyde wanted to give as much of himself as he could while he was around. Every day was an event to be celebrated."

"Then he *was* everything to you."

"Not quite. He was also human. There were times, when a new paralysis set in, for example, when he just withdrew. He wouldn't even talk about it, wouldn't share his feelings. I never felt so much alone as I did then—even though he was there, and I knew I had his love. I realized then that no matter how much you love someone, no matter how close you are, you still have to be on good terms with yourself, be- cause you still go through life alone. Your pain, your illnesses, your body still belong to you alone, and when you die, you go out of this world alone. Clyde was alone when he fell, and no amount of love in the world would bring him back."

"But you've got memories, Liz. And there were so many good ones."

"Yes, but you can't curl up to a memory. It won't rub your back or kiss your breasts or take you some- where on weekends. I know women—widowed women like myself—who go their whole lives basking in what they once had—long ago. The only way I can get through the week is by realizing that Clyde was once a part of me—an important part—but still only a seg- ment, a phase. I'm different because of him, I'm hap- pier because of him, but having been married to him once doesn't make me whole. You can't live your whole life on memories, Mary." She waved her glasses toward the suitcase. "And so I'm off to Charlottes-ville."

"You told me once you thought you loved Greg, too."

"I do, but not in the same way. I guess you never love anybody the same."

We speak from different worlds, Mary thought to herself, silently watching Liz smoke. *She doesn't need memories because she can go wherever she likes and do what she likes and feel natural. I'm just as much a prisoner as I was when Mother was alive. I can leave Marbury, but for what?*

"I know that Jake can't solve everything for me," she said aloud, "but if we were closer, if we had a really strong relationship, I think maybe I'd feel ful-filled."

"Poor Jake," Liz said simply.

"Yes, poor Jake. I think that sometimes myself. All my love and concern is poured out onto him. It's like drowning a single scoop of ice scream in a quart of hot fudge."

Liz didn't smile. She rarely smiled at jokes Mary made. Mary Martha Myles was no comedienne.

"He won't stay fourteen forever, Mary, and if you keep him wrapped up in yourself, you'll stunt him as surely as if you kept him in a box."

"I'd never do that," said Mary, and knew, even as she said it, that there was no guarantee whatsoever.

The next day, she and Jake made plans to go to Washington together.

"We'll have a grand tour," she said, sitting at her dressing table and brushing her hair. "We'll see the monuments, the Capitol, the Smithsonian, the White House. . . ." She took her long red-brown hair and began forming the familiar bun at the back of her head.

"Hey, don't do that," said Jake, watching her from the doorway.

"Don't do what?"

"Pin up your hair that way. Let it hang loose this time. It's prettier."

Mary looked at herself in the mirror. "It's so wild, Jake. It would blow all over."

"So let it. You don't look so much like Aunt Verna this way."

"God forbid. For today, anyway."

They drove leisurely, the windows open, basking in the summer sun that flooded the front seat. The air was full of honeysuckle, and all the bees in Charles County were out scouting, racing each other for the sweetness.

The waiting line at the Monument extended twice around its base, and there was no parking near the memorials either, so Mary gave up and settled on the Air and Space Museum. Jake wanted to see everything in the shortest possible time, so they made flying tours through all the exhibits before driving to the Kennedy Center for a mid-afternoon lunch.

They sat in the Gallery Restaurant surrounded by photographs of celebrities—Mary with her shoes off, and Jake well-behaved in his slacks and sport shirt. Mary felt young herself, with her hair loose about her shoulders, free of the bun that had always balanced at the back of her head. He was like a spring, she decided, a well of spontaneity and surprises, a fountain of youth from which she could refresh her own life. He was faith in the future, hope for the present, and charity for all that had gone before and needed forgiving. It was Jake for whom First Corinthians 13 had been written. Her heart welled up with affection for him, and she wondered if he could feel it from across the table.

Afterwards they walked around the rooftop terrace. They could see all over Washington—the planes taking off from National Airport, the boats on the Potomac. They could see the White House and the long green mall. . . .

There was a puff of smoke from a hill beyond the river and then a dull boom. A second puff of smoke and another boom. Three times it happened, and then there was silence again.

"What was that?" Jake asked.

"A military funeral. Someone's being buried in Arlington Cemetery."

Jake stood very still. "That's *one* good thing about being a soldier, I guess. Boy, when you die, they see to it you get *buried*. I guess it's just pacifists and agnostics that get sprinkled around."

They drove back home ahead of the rush hour traffic and stopped at a playground Jake noticed along the way. It had a long slide with two humps in the middle, and he decided he couldn't live without trying it out. Besides, he had been the gentleman too long that day and nobody knew him here. He could get away with his childishness.

Mary laughed and pulled over. "I'm going to sit on a bench back here and get some sun," she told him. "When you're through exploring around, let me know."

He bounded across the field and into the fenced

play area, ran up the slide from the bottom, grasping it along the edges, slid down backwards, ran up the ladder, came down headfirst, a mass of legs and arms—an adolescent spider. Small children, playing in the sandbox, watched with awe. It did look a little incongruous.

Mary smiled to herself. Fourteen was indeed a strange age. Only a few weeks before he had escorted a girl to a dance in shirt and tie, subdued and proper. And look at him now. Fourteen was a time of transformations, forward and back again. He was oblivious of himself at that moment, oblivious to all except the fact that he was alive and the day was gorgeous and he was free as a cricket. Shirley Delvaney should see him now!

A larger boy entered the near-deserted playground on a ten-speed bike and sat for a few moments watching Jake from the gate. Then he slowly rode over, past the mothers who were chatting near the swings, and began circling the slide. He and Jake were talking. That was good. It would give Jake a companion for the next half hour or so and give Mary time to rest. Fourteen was also an age for wearing one out.

It felt sensuously delicious sitting out there in the sun, Mary decided, leaning back and letting the breeze toss her hair. How long had it been since she had worn her hair long and loose? Since the back seat of Lester's car? Was it that long ago? Was it shortly after that she had turned her hair into the prim twist at the nape of the neck, as though daring a man to run his hand through it? What a pity. . . . She tilted her head up to the sky and closed her eyes, feeling the warmth on her lids, listening to the drone

of bees. Maybe Charles County was the right place
for the Second Coming after all.

When she opened her eyes again and looked across
the field, she saw Jake climbing up the slide again
from the bottom, monkey-fashion, his back to the boy
on the bike. The boy was laughing and saying something—Jake was not paying attention. Mary watched
idly.

At the top Jake turned, sat down, and began his
descent. The boy reached out, a soda bottle in his
hand filled with sand, and sprinkled some in Jake's
path. Jake landed in a cloud of dust.

He turned, said something to the boy, and went
back up the slide again. The boy was now obviously
jeering at him. Jake was trying to ignore it. Down the
slide he came, and this time the boy tossed the bottle
itself onto the slide before Jake reached the bottom,
and the bottle rolled off the end with him. Jake responded by picking it up and flinging it over the
playground fence into the woods beyond.

Instantly the boy was off his bike, advancing men-
acingly toward him. Jake stared, taken by surprise—
then began to back up.

The big bully! Mary thought, leaning forward. *He
has just itching for a fight—just looking for an excuse.
Clobber him, Jake!*

The realization suddenly hit that the boy was much
bigger than Jake, taller than Brick, even. He was
heavier than her nephew by at least thirty pounds.
He had put up his fists and was taking little swings in
Jake's direction. Jake, bewildered, had put up his
own fists close to his chest for protection, and was
mumbling something, backing up as the boy advanced. Again the big boy's fists darted out, a jab, a

pause, another jab, just waiting for Jake to return a blow so that he could lunge at him full force.

Mary was on her feet in an instant and half-running toward the playground. A few of the mothers had turned to look. The boy went on jabbing, backing Jake into a corner. Mary's heart began to pound as she broke into a full run. Her temples were throbbing, and her throat felt thick with fury.

"Hey!" she yelled, and dashed through the gate. "What do you think you're doing?"

The boy stopped jabbing and turned around. Jake's face was ashen and, at the sight of Mary, his shoulders slumped with relief and embarrassment, and he turned his face away.

The boy made the connection, sidled back over to his bike and picked it up, sneering.

"Fuckin' baby," he taunted softly at Jake.

Mary walked straight over to him. "What do you think you're doing?" she demanded, the words erupting from her mouth. She felt a flow of rage and it was rapture to let it out. She wanted to grab the boy and shake him, throw him down and stomp on that leering face.

"What the hell do you care?" the boy retorted more softly, without looking at her. He stood, straddling his bike, arms folded over his chest, watching Jake in disgust.

"I care because you can't go around picking on other people like that," she said.

"I can do anything I want."

"No, you can't! And it's time you got that through your head. You're nothing but a bully."

She turned to Jake. He still stood with his face turned away, and she knew that there were tears in his eyes which only added to his humiliation.

"Come on, Jake," she said, "let's get out of this jungle. Let the madman go find someone his own size to pick on."

The boy hooted. Jake walked out the gate beside her. The mothers began chatting again. Mary glared at them too.

Halfway across the field, the boy yelled, "Mo-ther fucker!"

When they had almost reached the car, they heard the rush of tires behind them, and the boy came barreling toward them, swerving only at the last moment and missing them by inches before pedaling as fast as he could out onto the road.

They got in the car as the bicycle disappeared around the bend. Mary felt weak. Jake had one hand over his eyes and was crying.

"Let it out, Jake," Mary said. "I'm mad at him, too."

"That goddamned bastard!" Jake exploded, letting the tears run freely, as angry at himself and his helplessness as he was at the boy. His face contorted with his emotions. "Boy, if I had Brick here, we'd kill him! We'd wipe his face in the dirt."

"I'd help you," said Mary, and started the car.

"I didn't do anything to him! I just threw his damned bottle across the fence because he kept dumping sand on the slide."

"He was just waiting for a fight, Jake. He would have found any excuse at all."

". . . thinks he's so goddamned smart," Jake sniffled, and wiped his arm across his eyes.

A quarter mile down the road, they saw a bike parked on the shoulder. The boy was waiting for them, the leer ever-present on his face.

Mary pushed down hard on the gas. It would be so

easy to veer just a little off the road. An inch of the steering wheel would do it. It would smash in that sneering face and leave a tangle of flesh and twisted metal. For one brief moment she and Jake would have the satisfaction of seeing his sneer turn to terror, and then it would be all over. She gripped the wheel hard so the temptation would not overpower her, and they sped on by.

"Fuckin' fag!" the boy yelled at them derisively.

Jake stuck his head out the window and screamed, "Up yours, you goddamned piss-head."

He was crying again. He craved a noble revenge, Mary knew—thirsted for it, and had to settle instead for a fleeting shout from the safety of his aunt's automobile.

"A piece of shit," he said, fists clenched.

"A big, overgrown ape," said Mary.

"Stinkin' ass-hole," said Jake.

"Idiot. . . ."

"Dirty rat. . . ."

Mary began to laugh a little. "We're running out of names," she said. "Maybe if we keep on we'll get it all out."

Jake took a deep breath and began to breathe slower. "He was a lot bigger than me."

"Of course. That's why he picked on you. Cowards never choose someone their own size."

They rode in silence for a while.

"He could have hit you, Aunt Mary. You know it? The way you charged up to him like that, I was afraid you weren't ever going to shut up, and he'd grind us both into the ground."

They laughed together then, and the tension began to fade.

"He *could* have, too," said Mary, remembering the

boy's size. "I just didn't think about it at the time. I was so mad I . . . I wanted to kill him, Jake. For the first time in my life I really, truly felt like murdering someone. It's a scary feeling to think how little it took. . . ."

She had been like the mother rats in the scientific experiments who would risk anything at all when the lives of their babies were in danger. She had felt no fear whatsoever. Only fury—mad, blinding rage. And along with the rage she had experienced an overwhelming rush of love and protectiveness for Jake that she had never felt so strongly before, and somehow it seemed to have made him hers. She had delivered him at that moment, had saved his life. It had sealed the contract, mixed their blood, breathed her life into his veins and made them one. She would never let anyone harm him, ever. He was hers, and no one had better ever try to take him away.

TEN

~

Summer. If for once, it would arrive out of turn—in the middle of January, maybe. If she could look out some June morning and see fall foliage or a sunset, even. . . . But the seasons of the year, like the seasons of her life, were steadfast, unfailing. Somewhere it had been writ that her life should go on here in Marbury as it had gone on for thirty-four years, as predicted as old Mr. Buddinger walking down to the mailbox each morning, looking around as though both ends of the road had to be surveyed before he could tend to his business. Then, satisfied that all was well, he would open the door of his box, take out the mail, reach in with his left hand all the way to the elbow, then transfer the mail to his left hand and reach in with the right all the way to the elbow, and finally close the door again with a resounding *thap*. Without as much as a glance at the treasures he had recovered, he would then march directly back to the house where he could go over them privately, one by one.

God, help me not to be bitter, Mary prayed, dropping her legs over the side of the bed. *You gave me a child just when my life was most desolate. If I give Jake all the attention he needs, there won't be time for anything else.*

It was an imperfect rationale, and she knew it.
There was a hunger in her that Jake couldn't fill—
that he only made worse, in fact. He had encouraged
an exploration of her psyche, and it was on these
short, timid voyages into herself that she discovered
the hunger and recognized it as an old friend.

She had always known it—sitting thigh-to-thigh by
Warren on the swing, in the back seat of Lester's car,
on the date with Phillip. . . . It was more than
sexual cravings, more than a mere physiological swelling and throbbing of the genitals that she could easily
resolve herself. It was the yearning for a man-woman
relationship in the fullest sense—to possess and be
possessed by someone who understood not only her
but Marbury; someone who did not care about her
lack of sophistication, her self-doubts, but would see
her as raw material and set about to make her whole.
A miracle, that's what she wanted.

Mary had been dreading summer because of its
sameness—the heat, the sweltering humidity, the
listless pall that fell over the Maryland countryside in
the glare of a relentless sun. She dreaded the summer
revival because of the memories it would conjure up,
and now that she understood those memories, the
pleasure only made her feel guilty. She particularly
dreaded summer because Sam expected Jake to stay
with him in White Plains, and she would come home
once more to an empty house.

When school was over, however, Jake announced a
change of plans. He and Brick had seen an advertisement that temporary workers were needed for a carnival that was setting up in the huge vacant lot
beside the gas station. If he stayed at Mary's during
the week and went to help Sam on Sundays, Jake rea-
soned, he'd have the best of all possible worlds and a

perfect excuse for skipping Bible school in the bargain.

Mary let him go.

The carnival arrived on the first of July, and Jake and Brick were hired as odd-job boys. They sat on the roof of the rabbit hutch and talked about it as Mary weeded her small garden.

"The carnival's going to have everything," Jake told her. "Ned—he's the owner—says it'll fill the whole two acres when he gets the sideshow set up, and he's renting the pasture across the road for parking."

Mary tried to think of something neutral to say. "How long will it be here?"

"A month. Boy, we were really lucky to get work. Ned only hires five boys each place he stops."

"It's really going to be wild," Brick said. "He's got a fat lady so fat that there's a special car just for her."

"And there's a guy with three arms," said Jake. "Ned showed us a picture. He's got a small arm growing out of a regular arm."

"And the dog woman. Don't forget her."

"The dog woman?" Mary asked.

"Yeah," said Brick. "She's got hair all over her body. Ned said he found her down in Louisiana. Her parents had her locked in a woodshed, and if it wasn't for him, they'd never have let her out."

"The Good Samaritan himself," said Mary, and bent over her tomato plants again.

"You against life or something?" Jake asked her at dinner that evening. "You sure didn't sound very enthusiastic."

"No, I'm not against life. I just don't see carnivals as part of it, that's all. These traveling shows are a sin. They take people's money and cheat them with a bunch of fake thrills."

"They're not fakes!" Jake protested. "They're all real freaks! If it wasn't for Ned, they'd be locked up in an institution somewhere. This way they get a place to live, good food, a chance to travel. . . ."

". . . and get stared at like humanity's leftovers," said Mary. "If Ned was the marvelous person you think, he could find some other way to help them. Think about it, Jake, If you had hair all over your body, would you want somebody charging admission to customers to come in and stare at you?"

"I'd be so glad to have hair all over my body I wouldn't care," Jake quipped, and Mary tried not to smile.

"Besides," he went on, "the sideshow's only part of it. Ned's got rides and shooting galleries and bingo and fortune telling. It's all in fun, Aunt Mary! Jesus! People are supposed to have a *little* fun now and then! You can't go around praying all the time unless you want to end up looking like Aunt Verna."

"There are other kinds of fun."

"What? What do *you* ever do just for the heck of it?"

"What about that day we went to Washington?"

"Jeez, Aunt Mary, is that the only fun thing you ever did in your life? There should be dozens of times like that—hundreds! For once I'd like to see you really cut loose—just to see if you could do it!"

She sat in the darkened living room long after Jake had gone to bed that night, her hands limp in her lap, bare toes resting on the soft carpet, her hair hanging over the back of the sofa. She would never, she vowed, pin it up again. From that night on, just to prove she could do it, she would wear her hair long and loose about her shoulders. If she herself could not run free, she would at least unpin her hair.

What *did* she do for fun? The very words seemed out of place. All these years she and Verna had spoken of rest or relaxation—vacation, even. But never fun. Never pleasure. These meant secret, naughty doings in dark and dingy places, or silly acts without meaning or purpose. "Fun" was not a part of this congregation's vocabulary. The Savior was never portrayed as "having fun."

But she *had* cut loose—once. One night, when she was eighteen, she had run across a meadow barefoot, hair streaming out behind her, tossed and tangled, her blouse unbuttoned and her breasts exposed to the moonlight. On this night, the one unfettered night of her life, she had run to the place she had thought Warren would be—run blindly, half-mad with the ridicule he had suffered, driven by fury against the church which, having idolized him for so long, had humiliated him so completely She had run with the conviction that what had been done to Warren had been done to her as well—that the two of them were one, inseparable—and that the hurt Warren had experienced, she alone could ease.

Mary sat without moving, remembering. She could recall it as vividly as if it were happening again—the prickly grass on the soles of her feet, the smell of the clover, the crazy calls of a mockingbird, the rush of clouds across the moon, as though racing with her to

Warren's side. . . . She felt hot with fever, and her whole body seemed heavy, throbbing, . . .

She had run into the barn—the sin trap, the devil's lair—where Warren and the girl had lain.

"Warren," she had called, half-crying, and taken off her blouse completely. She would hold his head in her lap, croon to him, caress his face with her breasts, stroke his body with her hand. She would give herself to him completely, in whatever way he desired to be comforted. From that night on, they would be outcasts together and leave Charles County for good. It was the night they had been waiting for all these years and didn't know it—a night of running and horse and sweat and barns and flesh and flying with a sweet, sweet wetness. . . .

But there had been no answer to her call—no rumpled figure lying wild-eyed, in need of comfort, in the hay.

"Warren?" she had called again, moving slowly about the barn, peering through the darkness. Where else would he have gone? Where else could he so completely show his defiance? He most certainly would not have gone home.

She had stood there in the light of the haymow window, confusion welling up in her, mingled with anger and desire. It was as though every pore of her body were a mouth, sucking and screaming, hungry and raging, begging and blasphemous. . . .

"Oh, God!" she had shrieked, and torn off the rest of her clothes.

The girl who had never danced before danced then. The girl who had never stepped outside her own room immodestly dressed hurled herself wantonly over the hay. The girl who had sat so sedately in the same pew every Sunday of her life whirled in the moonlight as though willing the demons to possess her. She had been Tamar and Jezebel and Hagar and Potipher's wife, all at the same time.

And when at last she had collapsed, breathless, drenched in her own sweat, wet with her own secretions, she had opened her legs wide to the moon itself, waiting for Warren, listening, lusting with a thirst so deep that she had shuddered with the awfulness of it. But Warren had not come, and finally, thrashing and tossing, she had brought about her own climax and rolled in a heap across the hay.

For over an hour she had lain there waiting, at first for Warren, then for any member of the congregation who might come looking for her—anyone to whom she could expose her nakedness, her wickedness, and her contempt. But no one had come. The barn, empty even of animals, remained empty except for her, and Mary's pagan rite, the black mass of her soul, had been witnessed by God alone.

Her first thought, when she'd considered returning home, had been to walk naked and silent down the street and through the center of Marbury, clothes in hand, in rebellious protest. But as the passion subsided, the anger was replaced with a dull disappointment. The hypnotic lure of the moonlight turned to dust, and the barn, a refuge for rapture, became merely a barn once more. Uncertainty and a flicker of guilt began to eat away at her bravado. Slowly she had sat up and dressed.

Warren had not come. She had misjudged his intentions, misread his mind. Would he have come to her if he had known? Had he gone to somebody else?

As she'd walked home, the gravity of her offense loomed larger. She had quickened her pace, knowing that if Warren were home she could tell him what she had done. He would applaud her, revel in it with her, and the marvelous warmth she had felt before would seep into her veins once more.

Sam's car had been parked in front, so she'd known that Verna was there. Instantly she had been confronted with a screeching cacophony of exclamations and questions, and suddenly there had been a silence. She had felt Sam's eyes encircling her body, and then Verna's voice—Verna, only five years married—rising above the others; Verna, who had never willingly opened her legs to anybody.

"There's hay on her back!"

But she had heard no more questions, no more accusations, no more indignant cries of moral outrage, for above the tumult, one fact seeped through: Warren had run away. His clothes were gone. He had left without saying goodbye, even to her.

For two days, Mary had stayed in her room, talking to no one, eating little. It was a judgment against her, she had been sure. If she had stayed at the church with the others and prayed, if she had come soberly home, perhaps he would have been there. Only God knew what Mary had done that night, what demons she had invited, what lusts had pleasured her that would remain with her always. And so, for sixteen years, she had done penance. . . .

Now she leaned forward, dropping her head in her lap, feeling the softness of her hair fall around her knees. Sixteen years was a long time to feel guilty. How long would she go on wondering whether, if Warren had known, if Warren had found her there, if . . . if . . . if. . . . Her life was infected with "might-have-beens."

She had thought that once Jake moved in with her, the past would resolve itself. She knew that if everyone who had committed incest in fantasy were burned at the stake, Marbury would reek with the smell of scorching flesh. But knowledge in the head is not the same as certainty in the heart. And there was Jesus, after all, saying, " . . . whosoever looketh on a woman to lust after her hath committed adultery with her already in his heart." Did Christ never feel a prick of desire for some Nazarene matron? she wondered.

Anyway, Jake had not helped. And on this particular night, full of memories of Warren, he seemed less like a nephew than a love-child, the only link left between her and her brother.

"Mary, for God's sake, you don't need tranquilizers. You're already taking thyroid medication. What do you want to do—become a pill popper?" Dr. Dobbs leaned his head in one hand. "Something bothering you? Anything specific?"

"I'm just not myself. Verna says I'm changing for the worse, Jake says I'm not changing enough, the minister's disappointed in me. . . ."

"And what about Mary? She have any say in it at all?"

She smiled. "The older she gets, the more confused she becomes."

Dr. Dobbs swiveled his chair around. He was serious now as he studied her for a moment, started to say something, stopped, and began again.

"Mary, I've known you for a long time. You're attractive, you're intelligent, and contrary to how you seem to feel about yourself, you've still got a lot of living to do. Am I lecturing? You want me to stop?"

"No, I'm used to lectures."

He nodded. "Precisely. You get it coming and going, don't you? Verna, Sam, Ralph Gordon, Jake me—everybody's got a blueprint for the way you should live your life except yourself."

She remained silent. Guilty, as usual.

"What do *you* want from life, Mary? And where are you most likely to find it?"

She sank down lower in her chair. "So what do you want me to do, Dr. Dobbs? Move out of Charles County?"

"What difference does it make what I want you to do? What do you want? Charles County's a big place. There are all kinds of people here—fanatics like Verna, poker faces like Ralph Gordon, old renegades like me. . . ."

"I've got security to think about. All my friends are in the church. My job is in the church."

"And your heart and mind and soul and strength? I know my Bible too, Mary. Plunking your fanny down in a pew every Sunday doesn't count—not if your heart's not with it."

"You sound like Jake. You two must be in cahoots."

"And what does Jake say?"

"He says I never let myself have any fun—never cut loose—never do anything for pleasure's sake."

"Ah! Out of the mouths of babes. . . . I knew I liked that kid." He smiled. "Look, Mary, it's your life, and I really didn't mean to come down so hard. But . . . if you ever decide you need a change, I've got a brother who supervises a clinic in Fairfax. He's always looking for reliable people—secretaries, typists, receptionists. . . . I could recommend you. Would do you a lot more good than tranquilizers."

"I could never leave you," Mary joked, getting up. "Half the fun is listening to you nag me."

"That's my vice," said the doctor, walking her to the door. "Never learned to keep my mouth shut. But none of us was meant to be perfect, Mary, and I don't give a damn what Faith Holiness says about that."

The visit hadn't helped. *I feel so old,* Mary thought as she got in her car. *I want someone to rescue me, inject me with joy, and give me a few moments of spontaneity and bliss before it's too late. . . .*

Bill was home on leave for three weeks, and Verna called to say she was concerned about the effect the Navy was having on him. He'd arrived home drunk and been drinking steadily.

"He was drinking at Christmas, Verna—you knew that, didn't you?" Mary told her.

"Well, maybe he was, but not like this."

Bill became a phantom, then. Every day Mary heard reports on what "Verna's boy is doing." The rumors drifted into the church office, were whispered about in the grocery store, laughed at over at the gas station. Verna's boy had drunk himself senseless in the park one night and then, when roused by a policeman, had urinated on the officer; Bill Stouffer had been seen going around with a prostitute from Marlboro; Verna and Sam's boy had appeared at the snake farm one night, nude from the waist down, and paid twenty-five dollars for a rattlesnake which he forgot to take with him. He was arrested for speeding, reprimanded for loitering, and then he disappeared for a few days with one of the file clerks from the Naval Ordnance west of Marbury. He had only been home for six days and already had his name in the paper twice.

Jake, meanwhile, had started work at the carnival. His duties began at eleven every morning when he and Brick hosed down the rides, and ended at eleven at night when the rides stopped running. They had from four to six off each day, plus all day on Sunday, but the rest of the time they were kept busy picking up litter, feeding the ponies and donkeys, oiling the machinery, taking tickets, and running errands for the fat lady, the three-armed man, the dog woman, the girl without eyes, and the contortionist who could bend his arms and legs in a variety of poses. Jake spoke about them so compassionately that Mary half-expected to find them in her living room each afternoon when she got home. Instead, she walked in one day and found her father.

"He was sitting in the sideshow tent," Jake explained, coming out of the bathroom. "The fat lady said he'd been there since noon, that somebody brought him in and left him. I was just getting ready to call Aunt Verna."

He was interrupted by the ringing of the phone.

"Oh, Mary, thank goodness you're home!" Verna's words came tumbling hysterically over the wire. "Bill got it in his head to take Dad out for a drive, and they've been gone since eleven-thirty! I'm frantic!"

"Dad's here, Verna. Bill must have taken him to the carnival and left him. Jake just brought him home."

"Jesus help us!"

"Can chang chollie," said Grandpa Myles.

"Why not let us keep him here for dinner this evening, and you can pick him up later?" Mary suggested.

"Oh, Mary, Bill's going to be the death of me! To have taken that poor old man. . . ."

Grandpa Myles was clearly delighted to be at Mary's table that evening. He kept turning his head toward his daughter and smiling childishly, rolling his tongue around in his mouth, hesitating, trying to speak, and then coming out with something like, "Gang do it all the time nothing," or "put it down and nasser cholling." Finally tears came to his eyes, he stopped talking altogether, and ate silently.

Jake took over. He began telling his grandfather what he did when he got to the carnival each morning. He told him about the errands he ran, and the crowds, and the pick-pockets. Ned said they had to look out for, and the calliope, and the pony tent. He described the midgets and the eight-foot giant, and the fat lady who needed three chairs. When he got to the rides Grandpa Myles' eyes lit up, and he began to laugh again out loud.

"Let me take him back to the Ferris wheel and give him a ride, Aunt Mary!" Jake begged. "Tell Aunt Verna to pick him up there when she comes. He'd love it! Wouldn't you like to go back with me and ride the Ferris wheel, Grandpa?"

"Ch . . . cholling, . . ." said Grandpa, starting to get up. "Going, dong."

"He's an old man, Jake! He might fall out!"

"He won't. I'll ride with him. I'll stay right there with him till Aunt Verna comes. Please! Look how he wants to go!"

"Jake, that's crazy! Verna will be fit to be tied!"

"Then tie her up," Jake said defiantly. "Don't let her go and rob *us* of joy!"

Grandpa Myles laughed aloud and stomped one foot.

"All right," said Mary. "But I'm driving you there. I'll not have Dad walking along the road all that way. It's a wonder he didn't collapse before you got him home."

Verna arrived a half hour later, her eyes puffy from weeping. "Bill met some girl at the carnival and went off with her," she said, her lips trembling. "Just walked right off and left his grandfather. Louella Kramer heard about it and called me." She sat down and buried her head in one hand. "Pray with me, Mary," she said softly. "The gossip is more than I can stand. Every day another story, everybody talking about him behind my back. I'm suffering what Mother suffered with Warren, and nobody but the Good Lord knows why I have to do it.

"Dear God," she said, going right into her prayer, "you know where my Bill is this very minute, and you see what he's doing, and you know what he did yesterday and what he'll do tomorrow. It's out of my hands now, Jesus. I've done for him all the Bible said, and he's come to this." Verna raised up her face, eyes tightly shut, fervent with belief. "If it's the Navy, dear Lord, I ask you in Jesus' name to get him out of it. If it's bad company he's fallen in with, I ask you in Jesus' name to take him away from them. If it's me, God, if I haven't let my light shine enough on that boy, then show me what to do and what to say, and I'll follow you, Lord, wherever you might lead. . . ." Her voice faltered here and her head dropped again. "You take over, Mary," she wept.

Mary looked at her older sister and noticed for the

first time that her hands resembled their
mother's—wrinkled, thick-veined, and ugly. She saw
the gray in Verna's hair and the hump that was beginning at the back of her neck. Would a bit of pleasure
now and then have slowed the aging process, she
wondered. Was it possible for a body to be so void of
passion that it began to shrivel prematurely?

"Dear God," said Mary aloud, "teach us joy."

Verna's eyes opened. She sat for a moment staring
down at her lap, waiting for the prayer to continue.
When it did not, she said "Amen," and looked up,
wondering.

"Well," she said finally, and stood up. "Perhaps
Bill will be home by now. I'd better have some supper for him, just in case. Where's Dad?"

Mary braced herself. "Jake took him back to the
carnival to ride the Ferris wheel. They want you to
pick him up there."

Verna stared. "You let them?"

"Yes, I let them."

Verna wheeled about and headed rapidly for the
front door. The look of suffering on her face was re-
place by a look of astonished anger. She went out,
then turned, one hand on the screen.

"When Brother Dawes gets here for revival week,
Mary Martha, you'd better be the first one to offer
your soul, God help you."

He was a big man—a Samson, of sorts—with broad
shoulders and square hands. His stomach protruded a
bit, perhaps, but he kept it neatly concealed behind a

striking white suit which he wore with a deep blue
shirt and striped tie. His thick hair was dark, graying
at the temples where it curled back over the ears, and
his eyes, matching the color of the shirt, looked out
intently and mysteriously beneath full, shaggy brows.
He had a scar beneath his nose, the result of surgery
to correct a cleft lip, but most of it was hidden
beneath a neatly trimmed mustache which flared out
on both sides.

"Brother Murray Dawes," he said from the doorway of the church office, and strode confidently across
the floor, hand extended to grasp Mary's.

He seemed ridiculously out of place in Marbury, as
incongruous, Mary decided, as the Second Coming.
And yet he belonged as surely as old Mr. Buddinger
or Louella Kramer or the Reverend Ralph Gordon
himself. Hadn't Mary known them all her life, these
preachers in their white suits, these fragrant-smelling
men who descended on her community with the dazzling splendor of a Solomon? The memories they
evoked. . . .

"I thought the revival began next week," she said,
confused.

"It does. But I always come to town early. It gives
me a chance to know the people. . . ." He folded
his big hands in his lap when he sat down, and
looked at her intently. "You're a Marbury girl."

Could he tell that just by looking, Mary wondered.
What was it that gave it away—the dullness in the
eyes? The width of the hips? Was a hump already beginning at the back of her own neck, perhaps? Or was
it the corners of the mouth turned down at the edges,
the listless joylessness of piety?

"Yes," she said flatly. "Sorry it shows."

He smiled faintly and she flushed.

"Excuse that remark," she apologized quickly. "I didn't mean for my disenchantment to rub off onto you."

"You're remarkably candid," the big man said.

She stared at him for a moment, then busied herself with a stack of papers—shuffling, reshuffling. She was glad, for some reason, that she was wearing her hair long and loose.

"Well!" He glanced at his watch and stood up. "I'm here to take you to lunch. It's your pastor's day off, and he had a dental appointment, but he told me where I'd find you. He said you would drive around with me this afternoon—show me the lay of the land, so to speak."

"Really? I have the afternoon off?"

"That's what he said."

He drove a gray Dodge with black upholstery and gallantly brushed off the seat before helping Mary inside.

"I'm not dressed for anything fancy," she said, looking down at her wrap-around skirt.

"You are dressed," said Murry, "for green grass and warm breezes and billowy clouds. Before I leave Marbury, I promise you a picnic."

Why had he come here, Mary wondered—a man who talked like that? Every preacher had his own spiel, it was true, but this man was more like a poet. She was delighted—and wary.

They had to settle for Marbury's one diner, with the plastic seats and plastic ivy. Heads turned as the man in the spotless suit seated Mary at a table. Charlaton or saint, Mary decided, he was as welcome as the four o'clock breeze, and she was going to enjoy this day.

He seemed a complete extrovert, charming the

waitress, joking with the table boy, carrying on bits of conversation with people in the other booths, and yet it was as though those deep blue eyes never left hers—as though there was, beneath the laughter and talk and animated joking, a seriousness that only she could sense. The very air about him was electrically charged.

There were moments, however, when the extroversion seemed a facade for insecurity—when, for just a minute, the big man fumbled over his words, when a look crept into his eyes that made him more of an awkward adolescent, self-conscious about his cleft lip. And then, in a sudden burst of enthusiasm, his voice would become rich and full again, and the little boy in him would disappear.

"I grew up in Yazoo City," he told her as they set out for a tour of the countryside. "That's Mississippi, and you can't get more rural than that."

"You lost your accent, then."

"And picked up a couple more," Murray laughed. "Family moved to Indiana. My father was a salesman, and he had the six of us out selling shoe polish before I was ten. Would go and leave us off in some small town in the morning and pick us up again in the afternoon. Used to say he wouldn't come for us unless we'd sold the whole box, and at that age you believe anything. I thought up more ways to sell shoe polish you wouldn't believe. . . ."

They laughed together.

"So you became a preacher?"

He smiled broadly. "I became a preacher. Decided I'd rather save souls than shine shoes. Something glorious, you know. Tell me about you, Mary Martha."

"Where did you find that out?"

"Your middle name? Ah! You don't like it, then.

It's significant, you know, when a woman doesn't like her name."

Mary laughed delightedly. "Really? What does it signify?"

"That she has a deep yearning to be someone else, or do something else, or go somewhere she's never been before."

Did he have a special power, this preacher, that he could see inside her soul? Or was it simply the Marbury Syndrome? All small-town girls felt this way and he knew it.

"You're right," said Mary. It was useless to deny it. "I just don't want to end up like my sister."

He nodded. "She lives with you?"

"No, I've a fourteen-year-old nephew with me. His parents were killed in an auto accident last year."

"God bless him."

"If you like candor, you ought to meet Jake."

"He must be very special."

"He is."

As they drove back and forth across the county, circling Marbury and La Plata, Mary tried to figure out what it was that Murray Dawes wanted to see.

"I want to see where your congregation lives—the kinds of houses," he said when she asked. "I want to see where the women shop and the men go on Saturday nights. I want to see your amusements and your schools and your libraries—the baseball diamond, the parks. . . . I want to know Charles County as intimately as a man knows his wife. . . ."

Again Mary flushed. He seemed not to notice.

She directed him to the junior high school and the firehouse and the cemetery beyond. They drove past Sam's farm near White Plains, Sears Roebuck in Waldorf, the X-rated drive-in theater, the Valley View

Motel, past the gas station and carnival, and finally back to Mary's house.

"Mary," he said, and lightly put one hand over hers on the seat. "You have been gracious and honest and a ray of sunshine to a preacher who's beginning to feel a little gray. Thank you for a splendid afternoon."

The warmth of his hand lingered on hers even after she left the car. She was suffused with good feeling. She had wanted to stand at the window and watch him drive away, but the phone jangled maddeningly from the hallway.

"Mary! Where on earth have you been? I've been calling and calling the church office, and you weren't there."

"I had the afternoon off, Verna."

There was silence for a moment.

"Well, something funny's going on, because Sheilah called from the diner and said you were there for lunch with an absolute stranger, and she said that anybody could tell just by looking that he was no stranger to *you*. She said you were so dazzled you hardly finished your plate."

Mary wanted to tell her it was none of her business. She wanted to tell her that a white knight had ridden into town and carried her off. She wanted to tell her that she had felt more warm and comfortable and happy with Murray Dawes than with any man she'd ever met in her life. Instead, she sat down by the phone, described the preacher in businesslike tones, and said it had been an informative afternoon. She was regressing. Jake would not have been pleased.

There were flowers on her desk the next day. They were not roses or carnations, but a simple bouquet of lily of the valley and sweet peas. There was no note. She just knew.

She had dressed with particular care that morning, in a full-sleeved peasant blouse and skirt. She'd even added a faint trace of rouge to her cheeks.

But Murray did not come. Every time she heard footsteps in the sanctuary or a door closing at the back of the church or the sound of a car in the parking lot, her pulse quickened and her throat felt constricted. Each time, however, it was only a parishoner or the janitor or Ralph Gordon coming and going.

"You're looking especially nice today, Mary," the pastor commented when he came to his desk that morning. "Taking the afternoon off yesterday must have refreshed you."

"I enjoyed it. I think Brother Dawes had a good tour of our community. He seems terribly interested in it."

"That's what makes a good preacher. A man's got to speak to the concerns of the people. You can't just bring in a man from Chicago or Pittsburgh who doesn't know the community. If Brother Dawes does all they claim, we'll have a bigger congregation come fall, praise God."

But Murry Dawes did not appear. Mary ate lunch at her desk, afraid that if she left she might miss him, then felt disgusted with herself. She was a Marbury girl, all right. Let a handsome outsider come to town and she was instantly giddy. Didn't she realize that his livelihood depended on getting along with the office staff of every church which sponsored him? There were probably flowers on the desk of every secretary of every fundamentalist church from here to Richmond. That was his job. And yet, the look in his eyes the day before, the way he had put one of his big hands over hers in the car. . . ."

"Is Brother Dawes married?" she asked.

"I don't know," said the pastor without looking up from the theology book he was reading. "He didn't mention a wife. Probably not." And then, a moment later, he turned his head and looked at Mary, but she had busied herself with the filing.

At three-thirty, when she was checking the next day's calendar, he came. He was dressed again in his immaculate white suit, but his hair was tousled, and he looked tired.

Instantly their eyes met. She smiled—far too broadly, she decided later—and he returned it, full and warm. Her heart pounded.

"The flowers are beautiful," she said softly.

"In appreciation," he said, still looking at her. Then he turned to the pastor. "Mary gave me a grand tour of the community yesterday, Brother Gordon. And I've spent the whole day following up on it. I visited the hospital this morning, the home for the aged—I stopped and talked to farmers, went to an auction. . . . I wouldn't have known where to begin if it hadn't been for Mary."

"No one knows this place like Mary Martha," said the pastor. "Been here all her life. In the same house, as a matter of fact. Isn't that right, Mary?"

Please shut up, Mary thought, and turned away. But Murray was watching her again.

"I'll see you tomorrow," he said, his voice gentle.

Mary drove home without any sensations at all of

her foot on the pedal or her hands on the wheel. He *had* to be attracted to her. No man could look at a woman that way and speak to her in a voice like that and not mean it. How different he was from Milt, from Lester Sims, from Sam, from Warren, even—a man not only of God but of flesh and blood as well. He was the catalyst she had been needing to bring her many-faceted self together, to make her whole in body and spirit. Was it possible that God, in his infinite wisdom, had long since forgiven her the afternoon with Lester, the evening with Sam, the night in the barn, and had been saving her all these years for Murray Dawes? Mary Martha Dawes. Mary M. Dawes. Mrs. Murray Dawes. She was trembling.

Oh, stop it! she said to herself, frightened. He had never said that he loved her. All he had said, in fact, was "in appreciation" and "I'll see you tomorrow."

A dull panic filled her chest. She was overboard already, and they hadn't even launched the ship. She had already been ravished by him when he had only touched her hand. If she'd learned anything at all in her thirty-four years, it was that you can't count on something till it happens.

"What will be will be," she said aloud as she got out of the car.

"Where'd the flowers come from?" Jake asked that evening, noticing them on the table.

"Brother Dawes gave them to me. I found them on my desk."

"How come people call him 'brother'?"

"It's a form of address. Many churches call all the men 'brother' and all the women 'sister.' It's the recognition that Christians are brothers and sisters in God's sight."

Jake screwed up his face. "Weird," he said.

It was beginning to get to her, the glib way Jake responded to things he did not understand.

"You don't even know the man," she snapped.

Jake made a face again but had no comment. He leaned back in his chair, chewing on a stalk of celery.

"Brick's parents have a cottage at Rehoboth Beach," he told her. "They're going down the first two weeks of August, and they invited me to come along. They're going to let Brick have a party there, too, and we're going to invite Shirley and Gloria. I can go, can't I?"

Mary tried to imagine Gloria in a bathing suit and what it would do to Brick.

"I'm not sure it's safe," she said dryly.

"Why not? I can swim! You ought to see me!"

It would be a week after the revival was over. Perhaps Murray would stay on for a while. Perhaps, with Jake gone, it would give them a chance to know each other better. . . .

"What about your job?" she asked.

"The carnival's over the end of July."

"Then I suppose you can go. We'll see."

It seemed clear that Providence had a hand in her life and was planning the whole thing.

Liz dropped by the church on Wednesday at noon.

"If I don't see you now, I may not get another chance before I leave," she told Mary. "I brought some sandwiches. . . ."

Mary pulled a chair over for her and opened the leaves on her typewriter table to spread their lunch.

"Leave for where?" she asked. Everybody suddenly seemed to have a place to go except her.

"To Romania—for the Great Hamster Hump. We're leaving Friday. Can you imagine, Mary, four whole weeks with Greg just watching hamsters screw around? He'll be impossible!"

"Shhh . . .," Mary looked about to make sure that Pastor Gordon had already left the building. "You're down here in the Dark Ages, remember."

"Sorry."

"Why are you going if you feel that way?"

"Because I've got to make a decision about Greg. He wants to get married, and I have to know if I can spend the rest of my natural life with him, especially since I can barely make it through a weekend."

Mary smiled. "Everybody should have such problems."

"Yeah. Funny, isn't it? The grass always looks greener. . . . The only thing that helps me keep my perspective is listening to all the sad tales that come through my office every day—wives of men who are brain-damaged, amputees trying to find a job, parents trying to accept the fact that their four-year-old child is dying. . . . And I sit here griping about a trip to Romania, which most people don't get in their whole lifetimes. Wash my mouth out with soap, Mary."

She poured iced coffee from her thermos into a paper cup and drank it slowly, legs stretched out before her to cool off. "One thing I'll say for Faith Holiness, they sure keep a cool basement—a great place to work in July." She suddenly put down her cup and looked at Mary closely. "Do my eyes deceive me, or is Mary Martha actually wearing the slightest hint of rouge and a little mascara?"

"You've got great eyesight."

"And you're still sitting here—not nailed to a tree or anything?"

"I don't think Ralph even noticed. I try to be discreet."

"And since when did you start wearing your hair long, Mary? What's Jake doing—redecorating his aunt?"

Mary smiled again—grinned, actually. She had found herself grinning uncontrollably these days. Most women in love glowed, she reflected, rather than grinned.

"It's not only Jake," she began.

"Ah!" Liz leaned back, ready to listen, but just then there were footsteps on the floor above, then on the stairs coming down. Mary quickly dabbed her mouth with her napkin and brushed the crumbs off her skirt. "Ah!" Liz said again, and sat back to watch.

He towered there in the doorway, his magnificent body resplendent in white. His buckskin shoes were spotless, and the dark blue of his eyes seemed like two laser beams penetrating the space between him and Mary.

"Murray . . . ," she said, and felt her cheeks flooding with color. She didn't care any longer. Let him see. Let the whole world see.

"Liz," she said, standing up awkwardly, "this is Murray Dawes, our visiting evangelist. Murray, Liz Grossman. She's an old friend of mine from college."

Liz was still staring at the vision in the doorway, jaw slightly agape. Her eyes traveled up and down the height of him, pausing a moment on the buck-skins and then slowly climbing back to his face.

Murry came striding over, hand extended, just as Mary had seen him do the first day.

"My pleasure, indeed," he said. "I was about to of-fer my company for lunch—blue plate special in La Plata or something—but I see I'm too late."

Liz was suddenly herself once more.

"Have some," she said. "I wasn't sure Mary had brought a lunch today so I made enough for both of us. Chicken salad okay? Really, there's plenty. . . ."

"Love to." Murray took off his coat, loosened his tie, and rolled up his shirt sleeves. Mary could not keep her eyes from him. Every move he made, every gesture, every look of his eyes or inflection of his voice seemed perfect. If God ever came to earth again, he would undoubtedly come as Murray Dawes.

"So you've known each other for a long time," he said, taking a bite of the sandwich. "The friends I had in school are scattered to the far ends of the earth, I'm afraid."

"We only met again last year," Mary explained. "Liz had moved away and become a social worker. I didn't know she was back in the county till Mother was dying and I took her to the hospital in La Plata. Liz was assigned to the case. She was marvelous."

"Real friends are hard to come by," Murray said. "I've read that the average person makes only four close friends in his entire life. It's sad, isn't it, when you consider the number of people who cross our paths."

Will I be one of your four? Mary wondered, her eyes meeting his. She knew he was answering. She could feel the answer. She suddenly wished that Liz

had not come, and that she and Murray could share
this moment alone.

But Liz seemed to have no intention of leaving. "A
visiting evangelist," she said. "Is that like a consul-
tant?"

"Exactly." Murray took the apple slices she offered,
refused the cake, and ate them one at a time. "Most
ministers have their hands full with the weekly sermon, the sick calls, the budget, the board of
trustees. . . . I specialize in revivals. Takes a big
load off a pastor to know that he can put that part of
his ministry in the hands of someone else. And because tent revivals are my business, I can do things,
promotion-wise, that a minister wouldn't have time to
do."

"I've never been to a revival meeting," said Liz.
"I'd be fascinated."

"Come," said Murray, and he looked like the Good
Shepherd.

"She can't," Mary told him. "She's leaving for Romania on Friday."

"Vacation?" asked Murray.

"Sort of," Liz said. "I rode down today because it's
the last chance I'll get to see Mary before I go. She
looks absolutely blooming."

"She does indeed." Murray leaned forward and
grasped each woman by the hand, holding Mary's a
second or two longer and squeezing it tightly. "Now
. . . I've got to be going. Have a good trip, Liz, in
the best of health." He turned to Mary as he rolled
down his shirt sleeves and put on his coat. "I'll see
you tonight, perhaps? At the prayer meeting?"

"Yes."

He straightened his tie, picked up his hat, and with

a half bow, turned and strode back up the stairs and out the door.

Liz sat motionless, watching him go.

"My God!" she said finally. "He's unbelievable! A cross between Colonel Sanders and Mr. Clean!"

ELEVEN

He was believable to Mary, because she had sat beside him and felt his warmth. She had seen the scar on his lip, the mustache which camouflaged it, and the little-boy uncertainty that men sometimes reveal when they are around a woman who makes them comfortable. She knew that Murray was for real because she had smelled the animal fragrance of his sweat mingled with the starch of his shirts and his after-shave. And he was believable because he was the only kind of man Marbury *would* believe.

Would the people have come to a revival meeting led by some slow-speaking, leather-faced farmer from White Plains? Would they have bathed every night for a week and put on freshly pressed pants for a fast-talking man with slicked-back hair who sounded like a tobacco auctioneer from La Plata? Would they have put their crumpled one- and five-dollar bills in the collection plate if it were a neighbor from Newton or Waldorf or Bel Alton who led the singing?

In Charles County, summer revivals were the next best thing to Christmas, and in Marbury, you'd better not ruin Christmas. Once December was over, the only thing you had to look forward to was the revival, so you went all out and expected your church to do the same.

"I'll be going to prayer meeting tonight, Jake," Mary said as she headed for the shower after dinner. "If I'm not home before you are, don't worry."

"I won't. What could happen to you at a prayer meeting?"

What could happen was that Murray Dawes might kneel beside her and she would feel his knee against hers and their folded hands might touch and they could get up and leave together when the service was half over. That's what could happen. They could get in Murray's gray Dodge and drive out to the forest preserve and there, under the stars, Murray himself could pronounce them man and wife, and then, on top of the picnic table. . . . *My God*, she thought, panic rising up in her at her own presumptiousness. *What on earth is the matter with me?*

She put on a soft jersey dress and carefully applied her rouge, fading it out at the edges so that no one could tell for sure. Then she brushed her long hair into an upward flip, pleased with what she saw in the mirror, and allowed her fantasies to overtake her again.

As she drove to Louella Kramer's house, she wondered how Murray would react to her relatives. Jake was fine. Nor was she ashamed of her father. But the rest of them. . . . Verna had stopped coming to prayer meetings because she was getting arthritis of the knees, but she would be at the tent every night of the revival. Sam was a fifty-fifty chance. He might come once or twice, but he wouldn't go to the altar. The big problem was keeping Bill under wraps, and that was impossible.

Louella's house was in the center of Marbury, a block from the one-room post office. She was a spinster in her mid-sixties who continued to wear the dark print dresses with detachable collar and cuffs that had been popular fifty years back. Her hair lay close to her head in small precise waves, and her living room, cluttered with doilies, smelled of lemon oil and camphor.

"Now that Mary Martha's here, I want to make an announcement!" Louella said, clasping her hands and looking mysterious. "I found out just this morning that Brother Murray Dawes, the evangelist, is going to be present this evening."

A delighted exclamation traveled around the group.

"Girls," Louella continued, "tonight, with Brother Dawes to help us, our 'strength is as the strength of ten.' I want every one of you to pray as you've never prayed before."

There was a silver coffee pot on the table in the next room and a platter of brownies beside it. Bernice Gordon had already helped herself and was nibbling over a napkin spread on her huge lap. The doorbell rang, and Louella ushered Murray into the room.

Mary had expected that, as she got to know him, he would seem less awesome and begin to shrink in size. Instead, he seemed to have grown an inch or two, standing there beside the diminutive Louella. He must have had more than one white suit, possibly a closet of them, because this one, too, was immaculately pressed and, as usual, spotless. This time he wore a shirt a shade lighter than usual with a breast pocket handkerchief to match. His hair looked as though it had been conditioned and groomed by the most expert of barbers, and his smile, beneath the perfectly trimmed mustache, seemed to radiate to every woman in the room and touch her personally. Mary's heart raced.

He made a slight bow. "Ladies," he said softly, and the women began to coo back words of welcome. At first Mary thought he had not seen her. Then she was sure he was deliberately avoiding her, and her head reeled with all her foolishness. As Louella led him around the room, introducing him to each woman in turn, he grasped the woman's outstretched hand and looked into her eyes, and Mary wondered what had ever made her believe she was special. This was business—the way it was done in the big time. It was as phony as the starch in his shirt, but she had fallen for it—body, mind, and soul. And then he turned away from the woman next to her and his eyes fell on Mary—full of warmth and protectiveness. He clasped her hand in both of his and pressed it firmly in his palms.

"Mary," he said, and his eyes did not leave hers. It was as though he were asking her questions with his eyes, and all of Mary's doubts disappeared. To Louella, he said, "We've met, of course."

"Oh, of course! I keep forgetting! My goodness, Mary Martha, it's not fair! Church secretaries get to meet all the nice-looking men before the rest of us do."

A girlish laughter filled the room, and then Bernice Gordon said, "Oh, no, *I* got to meet Brother Dawes first. In fact, I was the one who saw his advertisement in the evangelical newsletter and said to my husband, 'Ralph, this is the man you've got to have for the revival this summer.' "

Murray Dawes slowly let Mary's hand go and took Bernice Gordon's. "God bless you," he said, and sat down a few chairs away.

The coffee was poured, the brownies were passed again and exclaimed over, and then Louella got out the list of prayer requests for that week from the Evangelical News.

"We have fourteen names tonight," she said, "and all but three have cancer. Brother Dawes, I hope you have a way with cancer and a way with the Lord, because we're going to need you."

He nodded without answering.

First, however, were the testimonials of answered prayers in a separate column on the first page. Louella, her cheeks pink because of Murray's presence, read them in a slightly breathy voice, with much expression.

> Four months ago I prayed for relief from terrible back pain and a day after I mailed my request for prayer, the pain lifted, praise God.

"Praise God," said the women in unison.

> Have had gall bladder trouble for years, but after requesting prayer, God has healed me and it doesn't hurt me much anymore.

"Praise Jesus."

The testimonials went on for ten minutes, and then it was time to take their places on the floor, each kneeling beside her own chair. In the quiet of the camphorous room, Louella read the first request:

I have a growth under my left arm that has not responded to prayer to date. Now I am getting another one on my neck. The doctor wants to operate, but I have put my trust in the Lord and request your earnest prayers. Brother T.L. Hart, Milwaukee.

"Jesus, help him," murmured a woman across the room. There was a brief moment of silence, and then Bernice Gordon began to pray, "Dear heavenly Father, only you can know how long this man has suffered and how long he must endure before you touch his body and make him whole. . . ."

"Lord Jesus," said someone.

". . . We ask you to take away his growths, our heavenly Father. Make him well again so that he can praise Jesus all his life. Amen."

"Amen," went around the room.

There were other prayers then. And finally the voice of Murray Dawes—confident, vibrant, and strong:

"Our Father God, who knowest all things before we know them, who holds us in the palm of his hand, tonight we are gathered here to pray for one of our brothers. Be of good cheer, you told us, and we are cheerful, God, because we believe. We are happy, Lord, because we have faith. We are confident because we know that you alone have the power to heal Brother Hart from the affliction that racks his body, and to give him everlasting peace."

Mary lifted her eyes and looked down the row. Murray had rocked back on his heels and, with back straight, tilted his face toward the ceiling, eyes closed. There was something about his look that was strong yet humble, luxurious yet simple, rich yet plain, and she wanted to crawl over to him, bury her face against his chest, place his big hands on her head, and beg him to hold her forever. She was a child again, and Murray Dawes her creator.

She flushed and felt electrified, as though God had given her a sign. She and Murray were meant for one another—the kind of couple that elderly pastors always said were needed in the church. They would travel from one city to the next, ministering, witnessing, and somewhere they would build a home, their hideaway. . . . And then she remembered Jake. The dream began to crack a little.

She became conscious of the silence after Murray's prayer, and finally Louella began reading the next request.

> Four months ago the doctors told me I have only a year to live. I have got a cancer of my small intestine that cannot be operated on. I have got my soul ready for the Lord, but believe he might spare me yet. Please remember me with prayers. Lillian Wheeler, South Bend, Indiana.

Again the prayers were offered, and this time Mary prayed one of her own. There was no set pattern for the praying. It was possible for one to remain in the circle all evening with nothing more than an occasional, "Yes, Jesus." (It was the power generated when one or more persons were gathered together in Jesus' name that did the healing, Mary had explained to Jake. "Sort of like witchcraft—a coven or something?" Jake had replied.)

Slowly Louella Kramer read her way down the list

of requests, and as the time on their knees grew longer, the prayers became shorter.

> I request prayer for my husband who has been backsliding after being a Christian for thirteen years. He has started drinking again and he hardly knows his children anymore. I am afraid for my older boy who will turn out just like him. Please pray. Sara Riley, Nashville, Tennessee.

This time several women began praying at once, and when one got the upper hand, her voice had an urgency and empathy that was unequaled in the previous prayers. Mary did not participate, watching Murray instead. His large frame was bent forward now over the chair, and he was resting his head in his hands.

"Dear Father," he began, "wonderful Jesus, maker of heaven and earth, controller of our destinies, we believe that you have your hand even now on our brother. We believe that even now that still, small voice is speaking to him from the depths of his spirit, from the dregs at the bottom of his glass, from the vomit and stench of his debauchery, and that if he has ears to hear, as the scripture says, he will heed your voice. Remember our poor sister, Sara Riley, in her travail, and remember her children and especially her oldest wayward boy. Heal that festering sore in the father's spirit, stop that demon call in the boy's soul, and reunite that family dear Father, so that they may praise your name forever more. Amen."

The moon was out full when the prayer group ended at last and the woman thanked Louella and headed home. Silently Murray Dawes walked along the road beside Mary, escorting her to her car.

"Mary," he said, as she got her key from her purse. She looked up at him, silhouetted against the moon. "You're lovely tonight. I was almost afraid to look when I came in for fear you might not be there. And yet, as I stepped on that porch, I felt your presence. . . ."

Mary's pulse seemed to be beating so rapidly that she felt giddy. It was true, then. Everything that had happened—every word, every gesture—had seemed only to draw them closer.

"I . . . I was terribly glad to see you, too," she said, so softly that he had to lean forward to hear her.

He reached out and put one hand lightly on her arm.

"Will you have that picnic with me Friday that we talked about? If I bring a basket at noon, can you go with me?"

To the ends of the earth, her eyes replied.

"What do you *do* at a prayer meeting? Just pray?"

Jake had brought Brick home to dinner with him Thursday evening. Mary fed them first so that they could be back at the carnival by six.

"If you'd come with me some time instead of just criticizing, you'd know, wouldn't you?" she said good-naturedly, setting a plate of tacos on the table. "We receive a weekly bulletin that lists special requests for prayer. Each week we pray for all the people on the list."

"How many is that?" asked Brick curiously.

"Usually a dozen or so."

"How come it takes all evening?" Jake asked, his mouth full.

"Well, we talk a little first and have coffee—read testimonials of people who have been cured by prayer. Then each request is read aloud, and we take turns praying for that person."

"Why don't you just pray for them all at once?"

Mary sat down in a chair beside the table. "Because that's a rather impersonal way to go about it. We feel that if we pray earnestly for each of the people on the list, mentioning them by name, it will have more effect."

Jake stopped eating altogether. "You mean that maybe God will pay more attention?"

"You might say that."

"I thought he knew everything. Mrs. Gordon's always saying that his eye is on the sparrow and he knows the smallest detail."

"That's true."

"Then how come he has to be reminded about all these sick people? How come he doesn't know already and do something about it?"

"He does know, Jake, of course. What we're really doing when we pray is showing God that we are sincere and that we trust him completely to make us whole."

Jake and Brick exchanged confused glances and ate silently for a moment or two.

"Then how come you have to try so hard to get his attention? Doesn't sound like you trust him completely to me," said Jake.

"Yeah," added Brick, warming to the discussion. "How come you have to ask him at all? If he already knows that these guys are sick, why doesn't he just come down here and do something about it? I had a grandfather who was a diabetic, and he got an infection in his toe, and Grandma prayed that the infection would go away. She lit candles over it and recited the rosary and sent in special contributions and everything, and you know what happened? He lost his foot! Grandma prayed for God to take away the infection in his toe, and he took the whole foot! Big deal!"

Mary leaned back in her chair and studied them. "What makes kids so cynical these days? You've got smart answers for everything."

Jake's head jerked up. "You're wrong, Aunt Mary! We don't have answers for anything! That's the problem. Nobody else does either. All we've got are questions and nobody knows the answers."

"What don't you understand?"

"Everything," said Jake. "Sometimes God answers prayers, and sometimes he doesn't. Sometimes you pray and it works, and sometimes it doesn't. I don't understand that."

"There are certain theologians who say that prayer always works, Jake. The outcome may not be what you hoped for, but in the long run it will be what is for the best. Maybe God won't solve things the way you like because you need to be taught a lesson, or because you wanted something that wasn't really good for you."

"He decided my grandfather's foot wasn't good for him?" Brick asked, disbelieving.

"Brick, I don't know anything about your grandfather, but there's always a purpose to what happens to us here on earth. Sometimes the reason isn't understood till the next generation or even the one after that, but we're all a part of God's plan."

Jake gulped down his milk and set the glass loudly

on the table. "I think it's a lousy plan. Look, Aunt Mary, you can prove *anything* like that. I could go around saying that I'm always right, and that it may not look like it now, but in fifty or one hundred years it will turn out to be true. In fifty or one hundred years nobody's around to prove it. It's just a bunch of excuses. No matter what happens, it's God's plan. If a guy gets well, it's because God answered your prayer. If a guy doesn't get well, then that's the way God wanted it for some reason you won't find out for one hundred years. God could kill off half the human race, and preachers would go right on saying that God, in his infinite wisdom (that's Mrs. Gordon's favorite line) . . . God, in his infinite wisdom, knows what's best. Bull shit."

"Jake!" She was not particularly surprised that he chose to argue with her when Brick was around, because he liked an audience. But she was startled by the sincerity of his argument, his earnestness, and the fact that tears had appeared in his eyes momentarily.

Jake got up quickly and went into the living room to get a hold on his temper. Brick remained uncomfortably at the table, staring down at a half-eaten taco.

"You're Catholic, then, Brick?" Mary asked, trying to get some civility back into the conversation.

"Well, I guess so. I still wear a medal and everything, but we hardly ever go to church. Christmas mass, maybe." He smiled slightly. "Dad said once that if God could take my grandfather's foot, no telling what he had his eye on next, and Dad didn't want to go through life as a triple amputee just 'cause God got a hankering for his elbows."

A howl of laughter came from the next room, and Jake collapsed in a chair, shrieking with delight, relieved of his tension. Brick laughed out loud then, and finally Mary couldn't keep from smiling either. Brick got up and went in the next room, playfully punching Jake to make him shut up, and Mary knew that dinner, as well as the theology lesson, was over for the day.

About ten-thirty, Mary was washing her face with Ponds when there was a light tap on the door. Only Liz tapped that way.

She came in looking different, somehow. Her eyes, her glasses, her short curly hair all seemed the same, but there was a cautiousness about her that seemed out of place.

"Good grief, Liz! Why didn't you call? Another ten minutes and I would have been in bed."

"Impulse," Liz said. "I won't stay long. I just felt that I had to talk to you in person before I leave tomorrow."

"If you want advice about Greg, Liz, I haven't the foggiest idea what you should decide."

"It's not about Greg." Liz sat down, looking unkempt in a wrinkled blouse.

"What's the matter, then?"

Liz sighed and her shoulders drooped. "Oh, damn it, Mary, I'm afraid you'll run off and do something stupid while I'm gone."

Mary's eyes widened. "Do I believe my ears? Liz Grossman has now joined in the clamor of concern! What shall we do about Mary Martha? We have a little sister, and she hath no breasts. What shall we do for our sister in the day when she shall be spoken for?"

Liz stared. "What the heck is that?"

"Would you believe the Bible?" Mary laughed.

"I'd believe anything. I'm not concerned about little sisters with no breasts. I'm concerned about a full-bodied woman who's about to be swept off her feet by a man in a white suit, with eyes of azure blue, that's what."

Mary's smile disappeared, and she studied Liz thoughtfully for a moment.

"Ah! Nobody ever warned me about anemic bachelors like Milt Jennings who might be congenitally impotent, for all I know. No one ever warned me about Phillip who needed a good-time girl while his wife was away. But let a man like no other ride into Charles County—a big, beautiful bear of a man—and suddenly the lectures are flying thick and fast."

"I didn't mean to lecture, Mary. I'm concerned, that's all."

"What's there to be concerned about? Am I concerned about what might happen with you and Greg? Do I come driving down to your apartment to make sure you know what you're doing?"

"Greg and I have been seeing each other for months, Mary. With you, it's all new. . . ."

The contrast, intentional or not, made a sharp cut.

"Little Mary Martha may get herself a man after all, is that it? And who will there be to pity if she does?"

"Mary, that's unfair. When have I ever said anything like that?"

"It's implied, Liz."

"There's nothing I want more for you. You deserve it! You've got it coming! But for God's sake, Murray could be one of those fly-by-night evangelists that absconds with all the money! He could have a wife and seven kids! How long have you know him? Two days? Three?"

"All my life," Mary said. "I feel I've known him all my life."

Liz put one hand over her eyes, then dropped it limply. "Listen, Mary. He may be the greatest guy who ever lived. He may be perfect for you. But give yourself time, huh?"

"You don't see me packing, do you? I've got Jake, remember?"

"Yes. Thank goodness for Jake. At least he'll help keep your feet on the ground."

The cut grew deeper. Liz had evoked his name like an ally. Liz the Sophisticate and Jake the Sensible united against the ridiculous whims of a maiden aunt.

"What is it really, Liz? Jealousy?"

"*Jealousy*? Mary, there's no hidden motive here, believe me. It's just that yesterday—the way you looked, the way you smiled, the way you talked—I've never seen you look like that before, so full of love and joy and expectancy. I just couldn't bear to have you hurt. I'd like to know that Murray feels the same way about you."

Mary heard, but the words were like barbs, sticking against the sides of her head, sharp and unwanted.

"Why is that so unbelievable?" she said, and felt her throat constricting. "He's too marvelous, is that it? Strong, sexy, intelligent, kind. . . . How could he fall for a scared, unsophisticated country girl like Mary?"

"I didn't mean that at all."

"Then what did you mean?" The words came tumbling out. "You couldn't stand that it was my hand he held so long there in the church yesterday, not yours? My face his eyes kept returning to again and again, not yours? Is that it? It's you who's been invited away for weekends in Charlottesville, you the doctors and interns always ask out, you who is so goddamned extroverted you can pick out any man you choose and have him licking your breasts, but it's me that Murray Dawes is interested in this time, and suddenly you can't stand it. Suddenly you're drenched with concern." She could not believe herself—could not believe she was sitting there talking that way to Liz.

"Mary!"

"All my life, Liz, when I got something that really meant a lot to me, somebody tried to take it away. There used to be a horse, Liz—yes, a horse!—that I loved more than anything else. And then one day Mother got it in her head that it wasn't good for me, and told the neighbor not to let me ride it any more. All the while I was growing up, Verna was jealous of Warren and me. Now she wants Jake. Even you—the way you buddy around with him when you're here— the 'good pal' bit, just to prove that Liz is really cool, really 'with it,' and Mary's the religious old biddy."

Liz shook her head slowly, her face pale.

"You know what?" Mary felt as though she were vomiting the words and couldn't stop them if she tried. "I don't think that half the stories you tell ever happened. I don't believe in the Passover Pig, I don't believe that your grandmother locked you out, I don't believe that the Unitarians stick paper reinforcements on their foreheads. . . . I think you make all that stuff up just to get attention—to get laughs. Well, I don't work that way, Liz. I am what I am, and this time I'm going to do what I damn well want with my life, and it's long overdue."

The screen door opened cautiously and Jake stepped in, looking quickly from Mary to Liz.

Liz stood up. "I don't think you're in any mood to talk tonight, Mary, and I'm sorry I came. It wasn't fair dropping in on you like this in the first place." She looked at Jake, but he stood rooted to the rug, watching them both. "I . . . had no idea that you felt that way—all this anger, all these months, direct-ed at me. I wanted you to know I'm worried, that's all. There was nothing more to it than that."

"Jeez, what's wrong?" Jake asked, but neither an-swered him.

"I've never worried about you, Liz," Mary said. "Don't concern yourself with me."

"Okay. Let's leave it at that." Liz walked over to the door. "Well, so long." She stopped a moment and looked at Jake. "Goodbye, Jake. Have a great sum-mer. I'm off to Romania for a month. I'll try to get some stamps for you—if Mary doesn't object."

She opened the screen and went out. Mary listened to her footsteps on the sidewalk, her heart beating so rapidly that her chest hurt. *It had to be said,* she told herself. She had to do it, for herself and Murray. She had to let everyone know, Jake included, that this time Mary Martha had a mind of her own.

The surge of adrenalin had been so great that she felt nothing more than the satisfaction of spewing it out, uprooting the words which had been stuck in her throat all these years, making sentences of the poison in her spleen. The feelings she had conjured up were so deep that it seemed they had come from somebody else.

And then suddenly Jake was saying something behind her chair, "Jeez, Aunt Mary, how come *she* got the shit in the face? How come you never did that with Verna or the Gordons or old M.J.? Why'd you have to do it to Liz?"

Outside Liz's car door opened, then closed again, and suddenly Mary sprang to her feet, flung open the screen, and rushed down the steps.

They sat together in the front seat, each crying noiselessly, head tipped back, tears running down cheeks and throats simultaneously. They neither talked nor touched. For five minutes Mary fought for control.

"I can't really apologize," she said finally, "because I must have meant it. But . . . like Jake said . . . he doesn't see why you had to get it in the face when there've been so many others."

"I just happened to walk in the line of fire, I guess," Liz said.

"Oh, God." Mary began to cry again, laughing at the same time. "They ought to lock up women in love, you know it? I'd sell you down the river, Liz, for Murray Dawes' little toenail. Are men like that, do you suppose? Or is it only us? Only me?"

Liz patted her hand. "I don't know, kiddo. All I know is that you can't go starving for thirty-four years and then be expected to act normal when a seven-course dinner sits down beside you."

"You've had so much, Liz," Mary said, and her voice was void of venom now. "You've been happily married, you've got Greg . . . you have a job where you meet new people all the time. . . . For once, I'd like to live my life the way I want it, without a lot of people telling me to watch out, like I'm a five-year-old about to pull down my pants for a funny-uncle or something. . . ."

"It's gone that far, then?" asked Liz.

Mary blushed. "An analogy, only."

They were quiet a while longer. Jake came to the screen, peered out at them through the darkness, then turned and went back to the kitchen.

"You're right, Mary," Liz said finally. "You should be free to do what you want, even if it's a mistake, and who ever really knows for sure? I don't. I could be making a huge mistake with Greg, yet you've never cautioned me to be careful. I had no right to come driving down here with unwanted advice." She paused. "You were right about something else, too. Some of my stories . . . The Passover thing. . . ."

Mary looked at her. "The pig? There wasn't a pig?"

"There wasn't even a Passover. I never had a brother in Georgetown. Hell, I never even had a brother at all!"

"Liz!"

"I'm an unmitigated story-teller, an inventor of tales. . . . All a cover of insecurity, I guess. I'm always so damn afraid I'm going to bore somebody. I mean, life is really mundane, you know? If I just talked about going to the Safeway, and writing up reports and getting my hair cut . . . well, who would want to listen? But I've never hurt anybody with my stories. They're all harmless, really. . . ."

"But your grandmother?"

"She *did* lock me out, Mary. That was the truth."

"And the Unitarians?"

"They *did!* They did stick reinforcements on their foreheads that Sunday. But they say that service was an exception, so I suppose, in a way, I misrepresent. I only tell the parts that are interesting. . . ."

"How can you live with yourself when it's so phony?"

"Aren't we all? Isn't there any phoniness in you? All these years you've spent in Marbury being sweet and kind and obedient. . . . Isn't there something a little phony in that? Don't you ever feel you want to take off and do something fun and wild and delicious?"

"Liz, that's what I'm *trying* to do, but everybody wants to hold me back!"

Suddenly they had their arms around each other, and there were tears again.

"Oh, Lord, Mary, if we were lesbians, we could comfort each other, but it just never appealed somehow. . . ."

They laughed together then, and the laughter healed. Liz sat back. "I've got to get home, Mary. We leave for New York at eight in the morning. But you have one hell of a good time while I'm gone. You've got thirty-four years of solitary to make up for, and there's probably nothing you can do with that Kentucky Colonel that can't be undone later if you have to."

They hugged once more. "You too, Liz. Whatever you and Greg decide, be happy."

Mary went into the house then, her eyes red, the Kleenex still knotted up in her hand. Jake was leaning against the kitchen doorway.

"What was that all about, anyway?" he said. "Or is it any of my business?"

Mary blew her nose again. "Love," she said, "and it's none of your business."

"You both in love with the same guy?" Jake asked, undeterred.

"No."

"You're in love with *Liz*?"

"Lord, no, Jake," she laughed. "Not like that."

"Well, is it anybody I know, then?" Jake insisted.

Mary walked on down the hall to her room. "No. Not yet."

She awoke Friday morning to the braying of donkeys from the carnival down the road. The braying and the jerky rhythm of the calliope had become familiar noises now, waxing and waning, carried across the fields and through the yards on a hot July breeze.

On the other side of Marbury stood a tent of a different sort. It had been erected the day before in the empty lot a block from the church, and its seating capacity was double that of the Faith Holiness sanctuary. A huge white banner with black letters had been stretched across the front announcing the dates of the revival. Murray Dawes had been going about distributing flyers. The green mimeographed sheets found their way to the bulletin boards of the grocery store and the barbershop and the post office. The revival, which would begin and end on a Sunday, became the general topic of conversation.

At noon, the big man stood tall and swarthy in the door of the church office with a basket in his hand, coatless, and without a tie. Ralph Gordon looked at him curiously as Mary quickly put the cover on her typewriter.

"I've come to steal your secretary for an hour," Murray said. "I promised her a picnic-in return for showing me about on Monday."

Mary wished, somehow, that it didn't sound quite so obligatory.

"Of course," said Ralph Gordon, his voice flat, and returned to the book in his lap.

"Ah!" said Murray, once they were outside. "If I didn't know better, I'd say the good pastor had an eye on you himself."

"But he's married!"

"So was King David, and then he saw Bathsheba."

Murray reached into the open window of the gray Dodge and retrieved a car blanket. They walked to the back of the church property where oaks and maples kept the ground below dark and cool. Mary helped spread the blanket and sat down at one end, wishing she were ten years younger and ten pounds lighter. Still, she felt girlish and attractive. It was Murray's doing.

He lifted the lid of the wicker basket.

"Voilà!" he said, and produced sandwiches wrapped in foil, little plastic containers of olives and potato salad along with waxed cartons of orange drink.

"It's not exactly gourmet," he apologized, "but it was the best the Safeway could do."

"It looks great." Mary divided the potato salad between them. "How are things going? Ralph said that the tent was up."

"Have you seen it? She's glorious! Billows out like the sails of a ship! I think I was born for this, Mary. Put me in a church with stone walls and fixed pews, and I'm like an animal, restless to get out. But give me a tent with God's breezes blowing in the open door and the sound of flaps fluttering and the smell of sawdust inside and the clover out, and I'm happy as a bug!"

Mary smiled. "It's wanderlust. You never got it out of your system."

"God's truth." He unwrapped the sandwiches. "What about you? Ever get the urge to leave Marbury? See new things? Travel a bit?"

"Yes, but somehow Verna always talked me out of it. Since Jake came, I've been thinking about it more. I went to California once to visit him when he was small. I liked that."

"You'd like other places, too. I don't go for the big cities, though." He chewed thoughtfully for a moment. "Nope. I'm a small town boy at heart. I like people, and you can't get at a man's heart in New York or Chicago or Pittsburgh. Can't hear the breeze, can't smell the clover—can't even wear a white suit more'n an hour without it getting all smudged. No, I like small-town people, small-town ways." He smiled at her. "So tell me about this nephew. What's he like?"

"Jake? He's. . . ." Mary put down her sandwich and shrugged helplessly. "He's shy and direct at the same time, gentle and arrogant, childish and mature, unreasonable and yet utterly logical . . . what can I say? He's fourteen, that's all."

"Ah, yes! I can still remember my fourteenth year. It was the first time I'd ever kissed a girl."

"Like Jake, exactly."

"She let me do it, and then she shoved me away. I never got over it." Murray laughed. "I thought I couldn't live if she didn't like me. I wasted a whole summer just pining away for her, even wrote a suicide note. It wasn't until the following September that she started to like me in return."

"Were you happy then?"

"By that time I had another girl."

They laughed together.

"Jake's interested in all kinds of things—girls, stamps, science, theology. . . . He keeps a journal too, of his thoughts. We have our arguments, though—mostly over religion. I'm afraid he gets the better of me. He accepts nothing on faith. It's hard for me to handle."

"It's adolescence, Mary. It takes time to learn that there aren't scientific answers for everything. It's only after a person has experienced love and grief and jealousy and hate that he discovers there are facets of life which can't be measured by any standards—can't be predicted or controlled or explained. And yet, as surely as he exists, he knows them to be present; he feels their hold on him. And he believes in something he has never seen or understood because he feels its power. Give him time, Mary. He'll come around."

It was five of one when Mary looked at her watch. "The time went so quickly," she said. "I can't believe it's over already."

"Picnics become you, Mary." His eyes crinkled at the corners. "You should do it more often. Stone walls and fixed pews aren't beneficial to your health, either."

She smiled. "I enjoyed it. Really."

But Murray didn't move. Mary could sense his eyes watching her as she put all the things back in his basket. Then his fingers were touching her cheek, lightly brushing back a wisp of hair. She felt them move on back to her ear, caressing the lobe tenderly. His face was sober now.

"Promise we'll see each other more next week," he said. "The singers arrive tomorrow, and I've got to spend some time with them, but I want to do this again."

Slowly she reached up and touched his fingers with her own. She wanted to run them across her lips, to bury her head on his shoulder, to feel his body next to hers, to grasp his beautiful head and kiss the eyelids. . . . Instead, her fingers lingered a minute over his and then dropped quickly down to her lap. Slowly he withdrew his hand, stood up, and wordlessly began folding the blanket. They walked back to the church office, their bodies swaying, touching occasionally. They had just reached the side door when Milt Jennings came out.

"Mary! I've been looking all over for you," he said, and then stopped, his eye taking in the picnic basket. At the same moment Pastor Gordon came striding across the parking lot from the parsonage.

"Milt, this is Brother Dawes, the evangelist," Mary said. "Murray, Milt Jennings."

"Glad to meet you, sir," Murray said, instantly extending his hand and enveloping Milt in his smile.

Milt shook it stiffly.

"Well, Milt," said Pastor Gordon, coming over. "Hot day, isn't it? Guess we all felt the need to get out in the shade. Bernice served lunch on the back porch, and Mary ate out under the trees. Murray, Milt and Mary have been friends for a long, long time—most of their lives, in fact."

This last remark was delivered so deliberately, so surely, that there could be no mistaking his meaning. But Murray handled it well.

"If you've known Mary all your life, then you are rich in friendship indeed," he said to Milt, and appeased the minister by adding, "She and Brother Gordon have done so much to make me feel at home in Marbury."

He left, then, with Ralph Gordon to check out the sound system in the tent. Mary went back inside, Milt following petulantly.

"I couldn't imagine where you were," he said. "I even called your house. I thought perhaps you were sick."

"My lunch hour is free time," Mary reminded him.

"Obviously."

She ignored the sarcasm and began scanning the work on her desk.

"I wanted to tell you," Milt said, "that I was driving by the carnival this morning and saw Jake there. I thought you ought to know."

"Yes, he has a job for a few weeks, he and a friend."

Milt stared, aghast. "A job!"

"He runs errands and hoses down the rides. I know you don't approve, but he has to decide things for himself."

"Mary, you need a strong hand with that lad! You really do. I'm not asking you to change your mind about me . . . though if you ever should, my feelings are the same. But—I'm surprised!"

"It's only adolescence. Every boy goes through it."

"Not like that. It's not the kind of adolescence I knew."

"No," said Mary, "it's not."

"When I was fourteen," Milt began, "I knew the books of the Bible backwards. There wasn't a king or a prophet or a disciple I didn't know. I spent my summers working for my father, learning about character. . . ."

"And you'd never kissed a girl, either. Never even tried."

"Of course not, Mary! You're the only one I've ever kissed. You know that."

"A pity," said Mary.

On Sunday morning, Mary drove Jake to Sam's for the day as usual, then went to church. Already most of the pews were filled. Those who were present would come again that evening to the big tent down the road, when the large man in the white suit, now sitting up front with Pastor Gordon, would be running his own show. They were sizing him up, comparing him with past evangelists and faith healers.

He already had them in the palm of his hand, Mary decided, overhearing the complimentary whispers that traveled back and forth among the pews. He had done his homework well, He had visited every sick parishioner, attended prayer meetings and luncheons. He had been a guest at the Kiwanis Club on Thursday and had his hair trimmed at the local barbershop. He had stopped at the post office to chat, shopped at the Safeway, patronized the local fruit-stands, eaten at every café and diner within a five-mile radius of Marbury, and he was able to call at least thirty parishioners by their first names. He had made sure, wherever he stopped, that they knew who he was and what he had come for. Once a sales-man, always a salesman. . . .

His eyes met Mary's, and for a long moment she drank in his gaze, returning his smile. And then his eyes moved on. Milt, sitting stiffly a few seats away, coughed.

When the piano music stopped, Ralph Gordon got up to introduce his guest: ". . . someone with us today you have all met. Brother Dawes is going to be with us through the greatest revival Charles County has ever seen. And I've invited him here this Sunday to lead us in the hymn singing. Brother Dawes. . . ."

Pastor Gordon was a tall man, but Murray towered even higher above the lectern. He placed his big hands on either side, and his deep blue eyes scanned the crowd as though communicating a silent message to every person present.

"My good friends in Christ," he said softly, and his face broke into a radiant glow, "you are here today not because of me, not because of Brother Gordon, but because you love your Savior Jesus and you want to love him more. I'm looking forward to seeing you again this evening for singing that will rock Charles County from one end to the other, for down-on-your-knees praying that will shake the devil himself, and for preaching and scripture and testimonials that will put Marbury on the map as a place where God's got the upper hand. Let's get in practice, every last one of us, with 'Heavenly Sunlight,' page twenty-seven. Let's sing all three verses, each one louder than the one before. Let's let people hear us all the way down to Pope's Creek."

They sang. With voices sliding up and down from one note to the next, they belted out their beloved hymn:

> *Walking in sunlight, all of my jour-ney;*
> *Over the mountains, thro' the deep vale;*

Jesus has said, 'I'll never forsake thee,
Promise divine that never can fail.
  Heavenly sun-light,
  Heavenly sun-light,
  Flooding my soul with glory di-vine;
  Hallelujah, I am rejoic-ing,
  Singing his praises, Jesus is mine.

Verna, guiding her father by the arm after the service, came up to Mary as she was getting in her car.

"Mary, I want to talk to you."

Mary turned around. "Hi, Verna. Hello, Dad. How are you feeling?"

"Fine," said her father. "Fine nang choorie."

"I'm just going to say one thing," Verna continued, getting right to the point. "Milt stopped by last night to talk to me. He's very upset about you and that evangelist. After all these years of him waiting. . . ."

"Waiting for what?" Mary said. "How many times do I have to say no, Verna?"

"Just the same, don't think folks aren't talking. At least five or six people saw you with him at Sheilah's diner the other day. And Milt told me about that picnic lunch. . . ."

"Did he?" said Mary coldly. "I can't imagine why it should interest either of you."

"M . . . Mary," said Grandpa Myles. "Milt . . . ," He was struggling with his tongue, working it around in his mouth, forcing it into odd shapes. "Milt is . . . nod dang done . . . good . . . non . . . not good bum." He stopped, helpless at his inability to speak.

"Milt's what?" Mary said, trying to understand. Her father fell silent.

"I'm taking Dad home to dinner," Verna said, ignoring the outburst. "As usual, you're invited to come, but I mean to have the last word on this thing between you and Murray Dawes."

Mary declined and drove home. So it was out now and people knew. They knew her sins before she committed them, almost. They had known what was in her heart the moment she'd looked at Murray Dawes. God help her.

In another week, the revival would be over, and Murray would be gone. If he left without her, everyone would pity her. If he took her with him—oh, God, what was she thinking about? She hardly even knew him. And what about Jake?

She changed into a seersucker robe and prepared a cold sandwich that she could eat in the shade on the back steps. Tonight she would see the charisma that everyone talked about when they spoke of Murray Dawes' revival meetings, and then on Monday—the pastor's day off—he would come by the office again.

Mary shivered with the thought of his voice, his touch. . . . Where would it all lead? How could she decide anything? Would he even ask, and what did she want him to ask? She felt frightened and confused, excited and reckless, the worst possible combination in a woman of thirty-four. . . .

She finished eating and had just stepped back inside when there was a light knock on the front door. *Verna,* she decided. Then, *Milt.* . . .

It was neither. Murray stood there in his white suit.

"I was passing," he said, "and had to see you ... if only for a moment...."

The door closed behind him. He looked down at her with such tenderness that Mary wanted to kneel before him. Like the Biblical Mary, she would gladly have washed his feet and dried them with her hair. Instead, when he held out his arms, she rushed toward him and found herself being hugged tightly against his huge chest till it seemed the breath had gone out of her. She could smell his shaving lotion, his deodorant, a faint trace of perspiration even, and her head felt giddy. Then his lips grazed her forehead, her ear and hungrily sought her mouth.

She reeled and his strong arms braced her. He kissed her lightly, again, and again, and again....

"Oh, Mary," he said, and held her to him.

For a full minute they stood there, holding each other, rocking, until at last a big sigh escaped from Murray's chest and he backed away just a bit to look at her face. Mary flushed. Her belt had come untied and the robe hung open slightly, revealing her bra and half-slip. Murray did not seem to notice.

"You don't know how long I've wanted to do that, Mary, how long I've been holding back...."

She closed her eyes and leaned her head on his shoulder. Would that the world would end now, so that nothing need be asked and nothing decided.

"I can't stay," he murmured. "Some people are expecting me. But I had to have you—this little bit of you—before the service tonight. I had to know that you felt this way about me."

"Oh, Murray, I do...."

He held her tightly. "I'm only a small-town preacher, Mary, dressed up in a white suit. You've got to know that. I'm nothing special at all."

"You're special to me."

He kissed her again, this time more passionately, afterwards burying his lips in her neck. And this time, pressing against him, Mary felt his hardness, and it seemed a wonderful thing—awesome. . . .

He moved back quickly, his face grave. Again he searched out her eyes. "I'll see you this evening?"

"Yes . . . yes. . . ."

He left without looking back, and Mary knelt down by the door in the place where he had stood, drunk with the joy of it. It was still too soon, too exquisitely real, to relive it just now. That night, she knew, alone in bed, she would go over every detail, every touch, every caress and kiss. . . . She would lie there wet with desire, knees bent, heart begging for Murray. . . . But just now she had to recover. How would she be able to sit through the revival without screaming out her happiness? She would see him standing up there, remember his hands and his lips and his hardness, and go mad. . . .

She was conscious of the phone ringing and wondered how long it had been clanging there beside her. Was she rational, even? Could she trust herself to talk sensibly? She stood up and lifted the receiver.

"Aunt Mary?"

It was Jake.

"Hello, dear." Yes, thank God, she sounded normal.

"Could you come and pick me up?"

"Already? I hadn't planned to come till after the revival this evening."

"I know, but I want to come home."

"You're not sick, are you?"

"No."

He offered no explanation. *Bill,* thought Mary, as she got in the car and headed toward White Plains. *I'll bet he was there, drunk as anything. That must be it.* She realized that she hadn't seen Bill once since he'd been home on leave. She hadn't missed him either. So much for Verna's boy.

Jake was waiting on a rock where the long driveway met the road. Tibs was beside him. He stood up as soon as he saw Mary and got in the car.

"Bye, Tibs," he said. "Go back, now. Go on, Tibs. Good dog."

The dog backed up and stood looking at him, head cocked.

"Where's Sam? Does he know you're leaving?"

"Yeah, he knows. Let's just go."

Mary backed out onto the road, turning the car around, and headed home. Jake was strangely silent.

"What is it, Jake? Was Bill there? Was that what happened—he was drunk?"

"No."

Mary waited a moment. "Did you have an argument with Sam?"

Again the silence. "Sort of," Jake answered finally.

"Well, Sam's temper gets the better of him sometimes, but he'll cool off. By next Sunday you'll both be glad to see each other again."

"No," said Jake. "I'm not going back there again."

Mary looked at him in surprise. "What is it, Jake? What's happened? I need to know."

He turned his face away from her.

"Something he said? Something about your dad?"

Jake shook his head. "He . . . he tried to . . . to touch me. *You* know. . . ."

Mary's arms went limp, and the car slowed down. "Oh, my God," she breathed, and relived a memory she would have preferred to forget.

Was it the Marbury Syndrome again? What was it that made refrigerators of the women and perverts of the men? What was it that polarized the sexes, that made them enemies? Was it the "brother and sister" complex of the church that de-sexed the adults in these small-town congregations, that made desire seem somehow incestuous? Was it the emphasis on duty and responsibility, and the negating of pleasure and fun that made love a joyless adventure and marriage a mere business proposition? Was Murray Dawes the only man alive who could combine lust and grace, passion and belief—who could enjoy a woman not only for her soul but her body as well?

"Jake, I'm sorry about that," she said. "Of course, you don't have to go back." She hesitated. "You know, there are times when I've thought about leaving Marbury, leaving these people. . . ."

"I don't want to go anywhere," said Jake. "I wouldn't want to leave Brick. I just don't want to go back to Sam's any more, that's all."

TWELVE

—〜—

Bill had spent only five nights at Verna's, and the devil knew where he was the rest of the time. He had arrived home on leave, Verna told Mary, with a pink satin pillow, a facsimile of Whistler's mother painted on one side in fluorescent green. It was garish, but a gift nonetheless, so Verna had put it in one corner of her sofa. It was not till the second day she discovered that in direct sunlight Whistler's mother appeared totally naked. Bill had brought nothing at all for Sam.

"Tell him I wanted to buy him a red-headed concubine," he had yelled as he drove off after his first day home, "but the only ones I could find are brunettes between the legs. I'd want 'im to have the real thing."

"Do you suppose," Verna had asked Mary, "that God arranged to have the revival here while Bill is home—that somehow the Lord will touch him yet?"

Mary doubted it.

Now, as the time of the first service drew near, she wondered what to do with Jake. With Bill running loose, it was almost too dangerous to leave the boy at home. Jake resolved it himself by deciding to go to Brick's for the evening. Mary was glad. She did not want him along on this night, with his questions and wisecracks. She wanted to think only of Murray and his arms and the delicious smell of his body.

Jake left reluctantly, however—standing in the doorway, one hand on the screen.

"Everything's just different lately," he said to no one in particular.

Mary put the last of the silverware in the buffet and glanced over at him. "What do you mean?"

"Just everything. Sam's acting weird, you're different. . . ."

"I am, Jake? How?"

He shrugged. "You're always at church now, or prayer meetings or something. And your mind—jeez! You're a million miles away, you know it?"

Mary moved back into the kitchen and vigorously wiped off the table. "It's always busy when the revival's here," she said. "I haven't changed, Jake. Not really."

She was glad when he was gone so that she could concentrate on the evening before her, glad to be alone with her hunger, her wanting, the delicious anticipation of all that was to come.

The field beside the tent was rapidly filling with cars, and already a second contingent was parking a block away beside the church. The road in between was thronged with people walking briskly along the shoulder, greeting each other in the twilight, glad for the coolness of evening. The tent itself was lit on four sides by flood lamps, and a steady swarm of moths bathed in the light of each lamp.

The air was like Murray had said it would be—rich with the fragrance of clover outside and sawdust in. Folding chairs were set up in rows with an aisle down the middle and one on either side. Up front, on a raised platform, was a lectern covered with purple cloth. An old man in overalls was tinkering with the microphone, scowling at no one in particular.

Murray, striking in his usual white suit, stood off to one side talking cheerfully with Pastor Gordon, stopping now and then to look out over the rapidly filling seats, smiling broadly and saying, "Welcome, brothers and sisters. Come on in. That's right, sister. You take a chair down here in the first row where you can see better."

On the left of the stage, beside the portable organ, stood the hired gospel trio, the Solomon Singers, that Murray had been advertising all week. There were two men and the wife of one, all wearing white satin shirts with red vests. Embroidered in silver spangles on one side of the vests was the word "Jesus," and on the other side, "Saves." The woman's hair was done up in a stiff bouffant style that contrasted sharply with the plainness of her face. All three were smiling, commenting to each other about the size of the crowd.

Verna and Grandpa Myles were already seated on the aisle halfway down. Mary slipped in past them and sat on the other side of her father. He reached over feebly and patted her knee.

It was a world that Mary knew well, and she felt as comfortable here, three seats from the aisle, as she felt in her own living room. Some part of her would be forever linked to small-town revivals on a summer evening. It was the fundamentalist's circus—a substitute for the movies they were not allowed to see and the television they watched guiltily, if at all. It was a change of pace for the farmers who lived year in and year out by the seasons, an opportunity for courtship for the young people who scanned the rows not for converts but for sweethearts. It had a fragrance not only of clover and sawdust, but of tired men and women, of mildewed hymnals, of dust from the road; whatever emotions it evoked in Mary, she knew it meant home.

There was a squeaking of chairs as people took seats—leathery, red-necked farmers stiff in white shirts and once-a-week neckties, their women in starched house dresses with a rose, perhaps, pinned to their bosoms in place of jewelry. The Solomon Singers had seated themselves behind the organist now, and he—a small man with a slight back deformity—began playing the first hymn, "I'm Redeemed." The old man in overalls turned a revolving disk that changed the blue spotlight to a warm red.

It was all permissible. Showmanship that would be out of place in the sanctuary of the Faith Holiness Church a block away was acceptable here—expected, in fact—because everyone knew that tent revivals were designed to attract the sinner in off the street, to lure him away from the gaming tables and pool halls, and whatever means were necessary were blessed by the Lord.

Suddenly the squeaking of chairs and the whispering subsided. The organ music grew louder, and Brother Dawes stood at the lectern, his white suit bathed in a warm glow. Mary's pulse quickened when she saw him looking at her, but his compassionate smile, this time, seemed to welcome the whole congregation to his bosom.

"Page one hundred thirty-two, brothers and sisters, 'I'm Redeemed,'" he announced, pulling the audience in at the very first. "Let's hear it now for Jesus Christ our Lord—those of you who are saved, and those who are still thinking about it, God bless you too. There's a place for every one of you here tonight. You are all welcome as rain, and you men out there know just what I mean by that."

The farmers nodded and smiled. He spoke their language. Murray Dawes, the big evangelist in the white suit, had been following the weather forecasts too, listening to the talk at the barbershop.

The organist played on, repeating the hymn over and over, shifting to a new key for variety, waiting for Murray to finish the introduction. They were obviously used to working together.

"I praise Jesus tonight that the seats are full," Murray said.

"Praise Jesus," said a few voices from the congregation.

"I praise Jesus that he should have sent me to Marbury, and that I've had the good fortune to be in your homes this past week and eat at your tables and pray about your concerns. I praise the Lord for the sun and the pure fresh air, and I know that before long he will give us the rain we so desperately need, so we can sing his praises all the louder. Right now, brothers and sisters, let's sing out page 132, all the verses. Let's sing it out so loud that they'll hear it all down the highway to the carnival. Let's sing it so loudly that all those sin-sick men and women staring at poor half-naked sideshow creatures will hear Jesus calling them and come home. Let's sing it now, one and all, for the Maker of heaven and earth, page one hundred thirty-two." With that, Murray Dawes' face took on a glorious sheen from the yellow glow of the spotlight. He knew the words by heart and needed no hymnal.

> *I'm redeemed, praise the Lord!*
> *I'm redeemed by the blood of the Lamb.*

I am saved from all sin, and I'm walking
 in the light,
I'm redeemed by the blood of the Lamb.

When all five verses of the hymn were over, Murray Dawes sat down and Pastor Gordon got up. He formally welcomed his own congregation to the tent as well as other county residents who were present. He told them of the wonderful things he had heard about Murry Dawes and the Solomon Singers, and he had the trio and the organist and even the old man in overalls stand up to be acknowledged.

It was time for the trio to perform. They arranged themselves in front of the microphone standing peculiarly sideways so that only the "Jesus" sides of their vests faced the audience.

It was a number designed to keep the young people in the audience—a popularized version of "What a Friend We Have in Jesus," and was accompanied by finger-snapping and a syncopated beat. This was followed by an even livelier number written by one of the singers himself, titled "When You Hear Your Savior Knocking, Let Him In." The big-booted farmers tapped their feet, the young people smiled appreciatively, and the mothers cast smug glances at their offspring, meaning, *See? I told you you'd enjoy it.*

After the second number, the spotlight turned blue again, and Murray Dawes got up to read the Scripture. He had chosen Sodom and Gomorrah, and it was clearly the favorite theme of everyone present:

"And there came two angels to Sodom at even; and

Lot sat in the gate of Sodom: and Lot seeing them rose up to meet them; he bowed himself with his face toward the ground; and he said, behold now, my lords, turn in, I pray you, into your servant's house, and tarry all night, and wash your feet, and ye shall rise up early and go on your ways."

Here Murray's voice became deeper and more mysterious as he answered for the angels:

"And they said, Nay, but we will abide in the street all night. And he pressed upon them greatly; and they turned in unto him, and entered into his house; and he made them a feast, and did bake unleavened bread, and they did eat."

The preacher's face now took on an entirely different look. The lips curled down at the edges, the eyes themselves seemed to snarl, and his voice rose to compete with traffic noise out on the road.

"But before they lay, the men of the city, even the men of Sodom, compassed the house round, both old and young, all the people from every quarter. And they called unto Lot, and said to him, where are the men which came in to thee this night? bring them out unto us, that we may know them. . . ."

The sound which Mary had heard halfway through the Scripture was unmistakable now. It was the familiar roar of an old car, far off down the road, coming closer, the noise growing irritatingly louder until suddenly, in a squeal of tires, it paused directly in front of the entrance to the tent. Verna sat frozen in her seat. And then a raucous drunken voice shattered the stillness:

"Heeeyyy, Preacher Boy! Hey! You in the white suit! You wanna know where there's some sin? C'mon, I'll take you!"

Murray paused, his eyes fixed on the car outside.

Verna covered her face with her hands. Two ushers went quickly to quiet Bill, but he was already yelling again. "Whooopeeee! I got me two takers! C'mon, brothers, hop in. I got me two, who'll make it four?"

A sob escaped from Verna's throat. Her face had grown beet red under the handkerchief. A woman sitting behind reached forward and touched her sympathetically on the shoulder. All over the tent, eyes turned kindly toward her and voices murmured, "You done your best with him, Verna."

Murray Dawes, his back straight, the Bible in his outstretched hand, moved off the platform and slowly down the center aisle, never once taking his eyes off the car outside. He stopped beside Verna, put one hand on her hot cheek, and gently pressed her head against his white suit coat, like a shepherd protecting the neediest of his flock. A second murmur of admiration traveled through the tent, and at that moment, with a final "Whoopeee!" the car roared off, the ushers returned, and Murray Dawes read the rest of the Scripture from the center aisle, his hand on Verna's cheek.

"And Lot went out of the door unto them, and shut the door after him, and said, I pray you, brethren, do not so wickedly. Behold now, I have two daughters which have not known man; let me, I pray you, bring them out unto you, and do ye to them as is good in your eyes, only unto these men do nothing; for therefore came they under the shadow of my roof."

Murray's lips curled again and he closed the Bible. "And they said, stand back. . . ."

There wasn't a sound anywhere in the tent—not a rustle, not a murmur, not a squeak of a chair. They had given themselves, every last one, to Murray Dawes.

The worshipers were left to ponder this depravity while the offering was taken. Murray sat soberly on the platform, his eyes staring out into the night. The people gave generously. Mary was surprised at the number of five- and ten-dollar bills in the plate. The Solomon Singers rose to sing, "What If It Were Today?" Then it was time for the sermon.

In the minutes which had elapsed between Bill Stouffer's appearance and the sermon, Murray Dawes had obviously worked out what was what. Not a murmur nor a look nor a gesture had escaped him. He rose, his big hands resting on either side of the lectern again, his shoulders hunched up, and he faced the waiting audience a full fifteen seconds before he spoke, as though overcome, himself, with feeling.

"Sisters and brothers," he said huskily, "your God is my God, your troubles are my troubles, your joys . . . and your humiliations . . . are mine as well. I do believe that Jesus himself sent us an example tonight. But it may be that that young man has a purpose none of us yet realize. It may be that, in the depths of his shame, we will see ourselves, and then— when God's purpose has been fulfilled—the boy will be brought to his knees, and accept the Lord Jesus Christ as his personal savior."

"Oh, Lord, let it be," wept Verna.

"I've seen it happen. I've seen the lowest of men reduced to mere lambs at the altar of God. So I do not look down on the drunkards or the adulterers or the gamblers amongst us, but try, instead, to see God's purpose. If our own eyes have been opened to our own grievous sins, if we ask forgiveness from our heavenly Father who loves us all equally, saint and sinner alike, then who are we to look for the mote in our brother's eye, ignoring the beam in our own?"

Mary had heard many preachers in her life and she was not, she had always thought, easily impressed. But she admired Murray enormously. Other preachers would have stonily ignored Bill's outburst. They would have pretended they were above the mere mention of such things. They would have ignored Verna's agony, fearing that to call attention to it would only make it worse. Murray Dawes was a master. He had taken Verna's embarrassment and shared it with her. He had suggested that perhaps Bill himself was a prophet of sorts, and that, of course, made Verna something special.

"Like Lot," continued Murray, "we are concerned about sin right here in our own city. We are shocked by the depravity we see around us. And yet we contribute to it ourselves. . . . Behold now, said Lot. Behold now, I have two daughters which have not known man; let me, I pray you, bring them out to you, and do ye to them as is good in your eyes. . . ." Murray's own eyes became like narrow slits of evil. He looked like a huge white snake behind the pulpit, bobbing his head about. "Do ye to them as is good in your eyes," he hissed.

It seemed to Mary as though no one around her was even breathing. The Solomon Singers, the organist, even the old man in the overalls, sat like statues.

Murray continued. "And did the men of Sodom accept his offer? Did they tell Lot to bring out his tender virgin daughters, then? No. They said, 'Stand back,' and the Bible tells us how they attempted to beat down the door in order to sodomize God's holy angels."

He poured himself a glass of water, and there was a soft, brief rustle of chairs as the listeners took a quick respite from their emotions. As Murray's glass went down, however, the tent became as quiet as a tomb again.

"There is depravity here in Charles County," Murray said. "There are gambling halls; you know where they are. There are taverns; you know where they are. There are houses of lust and corruption, and you know where these are too. But sometimes sin comes into our midst insidiously. Sometimes it creeps in at night like a tiny mouse, and it is only in the morning we discover that it has grown into a monstrous rat—a rat that offends our morals, warps our children, deluges our senses with grossness, quickens our pulses for yet another taste of evil, and numbs that still, small voice. . . ."

A man on the other side of Mary leaned forward slightly, waiting.

"You know what I'm talking about," Murray said softly. "You know what has invaded Marbury under the guise of fun and frolic. You know that if you drive down the very road where this tent now stands and on across the highway, you will come to tents of a far different sort. It is a carnival of sin, my friends, and we have let it in our gates."

Verna, who was fully recovered by now and feeling like a high priestess, cast a sidelong glance at Mary, then lifted her head triumphantly and gave her full attention to the preacher.

"Oh, my friends, don't be fooled. Don't think that

those are innocent pleasures for the young. Don't think that in simple games of chance and shooting galleries and strength-testing devices there is harmless amusement. Don't think that in rides which hurl the body at unnatural speeds and contort it into unnatural positions there is only momentary thrill. Don't think that in the tents at the back of the lot there are only poor unfortunate creatures waiting to be stared at. No, my friends, there is much more, and you don't have to take my word for it. Go and see for yourselves. God will protect you."

He stood up straighter now and looked around the tent, his eyes traveling up and down each row, resting on every face present.

"I have been all around your wonderful county," Murray continued. "I've seen the best and the worst. A Christian is not afraid to enter a place of abomination, for he brings righteousness with him and is protected by the angels, just as Lot himself was protected by the angels in his house. I have seen young girls, like Lot's daughters—young Marbury girls in sun dresses, their faces shining—get into that contraption at the carnival called the Zoom. I have seen the delight in their eyes turn to terror as their tender bodies are whipped around corners and down hills. And I have seen, brothers and sisters, I have seen their dresses blow so high that. . . ." He stopped, unable to go on, till finally, his voice low, embarrassed: "I have seen the young men standing there at the gate, watching like the man of Sodom—watching the girls unwittingly expose themselves before their lecherous eyes. And when the awful mechanical thing stops, the girls come out of the gate with their heads down, their cheeks burning, as though their very innocence has been taken from them.

"And the young men. . . . I have seen them, sturdy and strong, trying out their strength to ring a bell or testing their skill at the shooting galleries or trying their luck at the wheel of fortune. Did you know, my fellow Christians, did you know that many a gambler had his start at a wheel of fortune at a neighborhood carnival? Did you know that a taste for guns and violence has often been the result of shooting first at wooden ducks? Did you know that in Fort Worth, Texas, an accused ax murderer confessed that once he tasted the thrill of a sledge hammer hitting the scales at a carnival, he took next to axes and chopped his cousin into pieces?"

The people gasped, Mary among them.

"But that isn't the worst, sisters and brothers. Back in those tents, those sideshow tents where no one goes without a ticket, it's a one-way trip to hell, and only a genuine born-again Christian can get in there and back again without selling his soul to the devil.

"Did you know," he asked, and his voice was a whisper, "did you know that unspeakable things go on in those tents between the misfits? Did you know that sometimes the only pleasure they get out of life is to explore each other's deformities? Did you know . . . ?" He shook his head lowered his eyes to the floor, and waited a moment, hands clutching the lectern. "Well," he said finally "perhaps another night I will tell you things that I myself have witnessed. Right now words fail me. I am a traveling man. I have seen a lot but never in my life have I witnessed anything like that which goes on in those sideshow tents in the dead of night, when the thin man gets restless and the fat lady can't move, and the dog woman. . . ." He shook his head again.

He let off preaching about the carnival then and

went on to the pool halls and the bingo parlors, and thirty minutes later, when he had finished, there wasn't a community in Charles County that hadn't been called infamous for something. With each new name of a town, a head would nod somewhere in the room, or two people would exchange knowing smiles, and Mary, watching, decided that people would have been disappointed if Murray had let their particular community go unscathed.

The sermon ended with a call for believers. Suddenly both Pastor Gordon and Murray Dawes were standing together there behind the purple-clothed lectern.

"I'm not asking for sinners first," said Murray, "because I know what a decision it is to give your heart and soul to Jesus Christ. I know how wrenching it is to change your way of life and become a Christian. It's the greatest joy in the world, my friends, but I know it's not easy, so I just want you to think about it now and I want the believers to come forward.

"I want all you folks out there who have accepted Jesus Christ as your personal savior to get up out of your seats and come down to the platform here. I want you to kneel down before your Lord and Maker, and be a witness to those folks who are undecided. Will you come, my friends? Will you come and stand up to the men of Sodom, as Lot did?"

There was a great squeaking of chairs from all over the tent as people began to rise and make their way down the aisles. Some came soberly, some tearfully, some joyously, and some self-consciously. A third of the people stayed behind. Mary and Verna got up with Grandpa Myles between them and moved down the center aisle.

"God bless you, sisters," said someone.

"Just as I am, without one plea," sang the Solomon Singers softly, and after the first verse, hummed the tune over and over again.

Mary and Verna found a place on the sawdust among the other believers and knelt down, Verna wincing because of her knees. Murray had stepped off one end of the platform and Pastor Gordon the other, and they were making their way slowly along the people, patting heads, shaking hands, whispering encouragement.

Mary's eyes met Murray's, and for a long moment each drank in the face of the other. Murray reached out and touched her forehead, and Mary felt the wild electric charge pulsing through her again that she had felt that afternoon.

Murray slowly withdrew his hand and moved on to Grandpa Myles.

"God bless you, sir," he said.

"Chollie," said Grandpa.

When Mary pulled into her driveway at 10:30, Jake and Brick were just sauntering up the road together. They had a habit of walking each other home until finally, unable to decide which of them would make that final walk alone, they would compromise and part halfway between their houses.

She sat down on the porch steps and waited for them. They were eating long strands of licorice and, even in the darkness, their lips were black. They looked like demons.

"How was the revival," Jake asked, plopping down

on the step below her, with Brick a step below that. "Anybody get revived? Yuk, yuk."

"Nevermind the wisecracks," Mary snapped, and there was no humor in her eyes this time. "I want to know what goes on at that carnival. That's what *I* want to know. And I want you to tell me truthfully, Jake—you too, Brick. Everything."

Jake looked at her. "What do you mean, everything? Come on over and see some day. I keep inviting you. I'll bet Ned would let you have free rides and everything."

"Well, I've been hearing about that place, and I'm absolutely shocked, the things that go on. I can't understand why you haven't told me."

Jake and Brick stared at each other.

"What things?" asked Jake.

Mary wondered where to begin. "I want to know about a ride called the Zoom."

"You'd better not ride on that one," Brick cautioned. "That'll make you sick. And when someone barfs, I've got to clean it up."

"Does it go at unnatural speeds? Does it contort the body into unnatural positions?"

"You'd better believe it! That's what people pay for."

"And the young girls that get on in dresses. . . ."

"*What* girls in dresses?" Jake insisted. "Jesus, love of God, Aunt Mary, what have you been hearing, anyway? I'll bet old Milt's been filling your head with crap again. Milt or Aunt Verna, one or the other."

"I didn't hear it from either Milt or Verna. I heard it from someone who's been there, who's seen these things firsthand."

"So why would any girls get on in dresses?" asked

Brick. "All the girls wear jeans. I mean, I don't even *see* girls in dresses anymore. Except at dances and stuff."

"Well, this person said that girls sometimes get on wearing dresses, and when they do the wind blows them up over their heads and there's always a crowd of leering men watching from the gate."

Brick began to smile appreciatively. "Je-sus!" he said. "I must be working for the wrong carnival. Jake, you ever see any girls come in dresses, you let me know, huh?"

Either they were masters of evasion or she had it all wrong, Mary decided.

"Okay, forget about the rides. I want to know about those sideshow tents. I want to know exactly what goes on, and I want you to tell me everything, because if you don't, I'm going to forbid you to work there anymore, Jake, and I'm going to call your parents, Brick, and tell them just what's happening."

The boys stared at her dumbfounded.

"She's serious!" Jake breathed.

"You bet I'm serious."

"Okay," he said, wondering. "What do you want to know exacty?"

"For starters, I want to know what goes on between the fat lady and the thin man and the dog woman."

"Between the . . . fat lady . . . and the . . . Aunt Mary, you can't even *get* between the fat lady and anybody! I mean, she's sort of got a tent all to herself."

"And we don't even have a thin man," said Brick. "We've got a guy with one arm growing out of the other arm. But he dates the girl at the popcorn stand. Nobody dates the dog woman. At least, I haven't seen anybody date her, have you, Jake?"

Jake shook his head, still looking at his aunt.

"It's not when people are around that these things go on, I'm sure," said Mary, beginning to wonder about it herself. "It's in the dead of night."

"So what was somebody doing in the fat lady's tent in the dead of night?" Brick asked. "Trying to climb up her?"

Jake began to smile. "No, man, whoever told Aunt Mary this was in the dog woman's tent getting a good licking."

The boys exploded in laughter.

Mary got up. "I can see you're not in the mood for a serious discussion," she said tersely.

"Aunt Mary, I would if I could just get a handle on it," said Jake. "I don't know what you're talking about, that's all. Whoever told you that is just trying to make trouble. And I'll bet it was old Milt. Milt's got eyes where his balls should be, and he's always looking for dirt."

"Jake, for heaven's sake!"

"Well, whoever it was is a bastard," added Brick. "Wait'll we tell Ned what folks are saying about his carnival."

"That might be a fine idea. Maybe he'll fold the place and move on," Mary retorted.

Mary decided she was too weary to discuss it any more, so after Brick went home, she sat down in the kitchen for a soft drink. Jake joined her. He waited a few minutes, as though to be sure she wasn't angry with him, and then said, "You know those two weeks I'm spending at the ocean with Brick? Do you suppose we'll be sorry if we invite the girls down for a day? I mean, I'd sure hate to ruin a good time."

She tried to remain civil. "Brick's parents might be

sorry, but I don't think you would. Why? I thought it was all arranged."

Jake sighed. "Oh, I don't know. When Brick and I are together, we're really good friends. But when girls are around, we're always showing each other up—always trying to make each other look stupid. We even talked about it once—how we do this—and we agreed it's dumb and everything, but then the girls come along and we're at it again."

"That happens," said Mary. "Girls do it too, sometimes." *They ought to lock up women in love.* Weren't those her very words? She wondered what Liz was doing at the moment and felt a sudden craving for Murray.

"I wish I was . . . well . . . more comfortable with women," Jake said thoughtfully.

Mary looked up. Women, did he say?

"I see some guys—the way they walk with their arms around girls—you know, they lean over and kiss them and keep right on walking, stuff like that. Man, I wish that was me. I don't think I'll ever get to that point. I mean, I'd step on her feet if I tried that, or kiss her eye or something. How do men get to be that way, Aunt Mary—easy and everything?"

"Practice," said Mary. "Plenty of practice. Those guys you're talking about, Jake, are nineteen and twenty. When they were fourteen, they were stepping on feet and kissing eyelids, too." She thought of Murray again and then the carnival. "Don't worry," she added. "If you hang around that carnival, kid, you'll grow up faster than you think."

She did not feel as she had expected to feel when she went to work on Monday. She'd rather imagined she would float to the office on the heavenly sunlight which hymn writers glorified, find Murray waiting for her, and rush into his warm embrace. Instead, something seemed to have taken the edge off her joy. And that something was Jake.

Murray *was* waiting for her. He was sitting on the edge of her desk when she walked in, and his smile was so encompassing, his arms so welcoming, that Mary forgot all her reservations and rushed to meet him.

He stood up and whirled her around a little as he grabbed her, hugging her to his chest. His shaving lotion intoxicated her. She never wanted to leave, never wanted to do anything but stand there protected by his arms.

"I'm going to sit here this morning and keep you from working," Murray told her. "I'm going to watch the sunlight on your hair and the sparkle in your smile, and I'm going to distract you with kisses and caresses."

Mary giggled. She sounded unnaturally girlish—childish, even.

"Then I'm going to take you to lunch," Murray said. "I have an appointment this afternoon, but we'll see each other again this evening, won't we? You'll be there?"

"I'll be there," Mary promised. *Whither thou goest, I will go. Thy people shall be my people, and thy God, my God.*

He kissed her then, long and passionately, his hands encircling her shoulders, touching, gently touching. . . . She felt thirsty for him—delirious, as though her entire being could only survive by the touch of Murray Dawes. Her own fingers explored the back of his neck, his face, the crevices of his ears. How strange. She barely knew this man, really, and yet she loved him. Was she behaving like a woman who recognizes her one last chance, or was this the love she had been waiting for all her life? How could she tell? How did one ever know? What on earth had attracted Sam to Verna, for example? That was madness in the extreme, and yet it must not have seemed so to them.

"Let me look at you," Murray said, holding her at arm's length. "Oh, you're beautiful, Mary. You really are."

She wasn't. She knew it to be a fact that she was not. And yet she accepted Murray's version of her with pleasure. If he thought so, what else mattered?

"I hoped you'd be here," she said shyly.

"Where else would I be?"

"I'm sure every woman in Charles County, married or otherwise, would welcome a call from you," she said, settling down at her desk. "And after that humiliating incident outside the tent last night from one of my relatives, I wasn't sure you'd ever want to see me again."

"You don't know me, Mary."

"Oh, you handled it beautifully, Murray! The whole service—everyone was commenting."

He smiled graciously.

She started to sort the mail, then suddenly turned and faced him again. "There's more you should know. . . ."

Murray looked at her quizzically, then smiled. "I'm tough. I can take it."

"You know . . . what you said in your sermon last night—all the things about the carnival?"

"Ah! So you're guilty, then. You've been."

She laughed. That made it easier. "No, but Jake works there—in that pit of depravity, or whatever you called it. I thought you ought to know. Everyone's having a fit because I let him, but I can't see that it does him any harm."

Murray's smile never wavered. "He's young, Mary. He has plenty of time to repent. He's so young, in fact, that most of what goes on probably escapes him."

"I don't think so. He's pretty observant. After the meeting last night, I went home armed for battle, ready to have it out with him. He didn't seem to know what I was talking about."

"And . . . ?"

She shrugged. "It made me wonder, Murray, if you were exaggerating."

"What else did you feel about me then?"

"Lots of things. But good things, too."

"You're hedging. Besides the good things. What did you feel about me when you suspected I'd been exaggerating?"

He made it so easy. He looked so strong, so capable of understanding any criticism, any onslaught. . . .

"I was. . . ." She hesitated.

"Go ahead. Nothing you say will affect how I feel about you."

"I was afraid you were attacking the carnival because you know it's only temporary—run by an outsider. Everybody expects a preacher to rain down fire and brimstone—that's one of the reasons they come, but of course no one wants any of the flak to land on *his* head. Oh, I know you mentioned a few other places too in Charles County, but you didn't talk much about them. All your wrath went for that pathetic carnival that will be gone in another two weeks.

"It just seemed . . . well, sort of cowardly, Murray. Nobody really cares much if you attack it. After it packs up and leaves Marbury, it will be as though our sins went along with it, and we'll all feel righteous again, when actually the same taverns will be turning out drunkards on the roads at night and the same illegal bookie joints will be operating, and the same prostitutes. We'll feel victorious because we've driven out that pit of depravity, but actually nothing will have changed at all."

"You're a harsh judge of your neighbors, Mary," he said kindly, "but you're also intelligent. You see through me and other people more quickly than we see through ourselves, and you're partly right. I am reluctant to attack the local vices that have been a part of Charles County longer than you or I ever knew about them. I know I don't attack them with the same vigor I save for the carnival. And it's true that I exaggerate some. Some of the things I mention I've seen in other carnivals, some I've heard about here, and some I've seen for myself. I've been there, Mary. I know. I keep my eyes open. I listen. You can't expect a fourteen-year-old like Jake to catch the innuendos, the gestures, the way a salesman can, and I still am a salesman, however you want to look at it."

"But you made it sound so awful, Murray."

"I only said it was a ticket to hell for nonbelievers, Mary. Didn't I tell the congregation to go see for themselves? One trip won't send anybody to purgatory. And I don't think your nephew is about to lose his soul for working there. People have to find out things for themselves. I'm not afraid to tell folks to go look the carnival over and come to their own conclusions—the carnival or the pool hall or a tavern or whatever. If they don't agree, that's okay too. Christianity's nothing if it's handed to you on somebody else's platter. It has to be a personal thing. . . ."

A warmth slowly pulsed through Mary, dispelling the doubts—a trust and an empathy and a compassion, even, for this small-town preacher who was trying in the ways he knew best.

"You see, Mary, there's a reason for the way I preach. It's like selling. There are good ways and bad ways to make a point. And while it's true that some of the congregation may feel when the carnival leaves that we have driven out sin, there will be even more, I hope, who see it as only symbolic of all the vices left behind. They will see the similarities between the depravity and emptiness of the sideshow people and the depravity and emptiness of their own lives; they will see that the dishonesty, the phoniness, the tinsel, and the cheap thrills of the carnival simply mirror the tawdriness of their own souls. When the carnival finally leaves Marbury, and the pasture where it stood is cleansed again and pure, they will, I hope, feel that it is time to put their own lives in order once more. An outside preacher can't just ride into town and attack the vices they have lived with all their lives. Can't you see that? Small-town people are too threatened by that, Mary. Instead of drawing them to Jesus, it only drives them away.

"It's the best way, Mary. Whenever I find a symbol

in a small town, I use it. I'll be attacking the carnival all week, because I know that it works. I hope you can understand. . . ."

"I do, Murray." And then she was in his arms again, trusting that Ralph Gordon would stay away on his day off.

They had reached a point of wanting, Mary knew, where kisses and caresses would no longer suffice. They were not children who thrilled at driving themselves close to the sexual act, pretending innocence all the while, as she had done with Sam. Their hunger was open and honest. Murray's hand slipped down and gently pressed her close to him.

"Mary," he said, his voice impatient, breathless. Then he held her away, as though it were an effort to separate them. Their bodies were magnets.

The silent treatment was over and God was speaking to her through Murray, Mary was sure. It was as if the last shred of doubt and uncertainty had been wiped away, the last ounce of reserve. If her heart had hesitated before, his honesty had won her over. Her mind congealed around his interpretations and left no room for questions. It was an answer to prayer. God, as she had been taught to know him, must surely now exist, and in deciding to give herself to Murray, she offered herself to the Lord as well.

Later that afternoon, after Murray had gone, she laid her head on her desk, and poured out her soul.

"Oh Jesus, dear Jesus, sweet Jesus," she prayed, her forehead against the blotter, "please forgive me for ignoring you for so long. Please forgive my doubts and the half-hearted way I have believed. I believe everything now, Jesus—every word, yes, every word. I am yours forever, to serve you body and soul. . . ."

She stopped. Jesus and Murray kept changing places in her mind. "Please understand, dear Jesus," she murmured, but her thoughts were on Murray again.

THIRTEEN

His preaching that night seemed tortured, yet it added an intensity to the service that had Verna weeping openly and many others as well.

Again he condemned the carnival, and again the seats were filled. A dozen people waited at the back of the tent, unable to find room, and remained standing.

Bernice Gordon kept looking about the tent and smiling, and Murray did not disappoint her. He talked of the sensually starved freaks who inhabited sideshow tents all over America. He told of the leering carnival owners who traveled about the country with an eye out for deformities. When an unfortunate creature had been found, he said, shut away in a cellar or attic, the carnival man became a slave trader. He would pay a small price to take the unhappy misfit off the hands of relatives, and from then on the poor creature would be a slave of a different sort—no longer chained in a garage, to be sure, and most certainly free to come and go, but where would such a person go? Where might he wander outside at night, for example, without being stoned to death as some evil apparition?

In fact, Murray continued darkly, the souls of these creatures were often as warped and twisted as their bodies. There were instances, he said, where men—

like men of Sodom—had been so depraved that they could think of no sexual experience that would satisfy them any longer. They had tried other men's wives and other men's daughters, but each new experience made them desire something more. And finally, catering to these base appetites, one carnival owner rented his poor pitiful sideshow attractions out as prostitutes, and men who could no longer thrill at the rape of a small innocent girl could satisfy their lusts with creatures too unnatural to mention.

This time, instead of asking the righteous to come forward first as witnesses, Murray Dawes asked those with sin in their hearts to come forward so that God could forgive them and make them whole.

"You whose hearts are the heaviest are tonight the most favored in God's eyes. If you who have the most to repent will get up out of your seats now and come forward, if you will kneel down at the altar of the living God and say, 'Lord Jesus, take me, for I have sinned and I wish to be cleansed,' he will give you the courage of Daniel in the lion's den, the strength of Samson. He will walk down that aisle beside you, with you all the way."

At least a dozen people stood up and made their way to the altar while the Solomon Singers in their spangled vests sang, "Softly and tenderly, Jesus is calling; calling for you and for me. . . ." Those who remained in their seats watched discreetly. Up at the altar the sinners knelt together. One woman, weeping as she made her way down the aisle, threw herself at Murray's feet, wracked with sobs, and confessed that she had worked in a café once and done unspeakable things in the kitchen. Murray held her face in his hands and whispered something to her, trying to calm her down, but she kept wailing, "Oh, Jesus, come into me, please," over and over. Finally Bernice Gordon helped her back to her seat.

By this time so many people had come in off the street that a second collection was taken toward the end of the evening, and Murray said it would go toward the renting of more chairs for the next service.

Mary desired his body. She craved it, as though Murray were a living spring and she were dehydrated. She imagined their bodies together as she lay naked on her own bed that night, and opened her legs to fantasy. Jake came home much later than usual, but she did not get up to question him. She wanted only Murray and allowed no other thoughts to interfere.

There was no breeze. The maple, which usually protected the small house from the sun, had failed to cool them this time. The humid air filled every square inch of space. But it was not the humidity which made her gasp or her chest heave. Again she spread her sticky thighs and begged her phantom preacher to penetrate her. *Thy rod and thy staff, they comfort me. My cunt runneth over. . . .*

Jake was already up when Mary entered the kitchen the next morning.

"You came home pretty late last night," she remarked, and set about making the orange juice.

"Man, I was tired, too!" Jake said. "I don't think I've ever been that tired in my whole life."

"Why were you so late?"

"Customers! You should have seen them! We had

crowds of people coming all evening long. Ned says that when it's too hot to sleep, people look for something to do. We had the whole field full of cars by nine o'clock, and they were parked all down the highway as far as the cemetary."

"I'll be glad when the next two weeks are over, Jake, and the carnival moves on. You've been working too hard."

"Yeah. I'll be sort of glad when they're over, too, all those bug-eyed people coming through and staring like it's a nudist camp or something. You know what a carnival is, Aunt Mary? You should see it in the mornings."

He leaned his elbows on the table. "It's a lot of dirty rides that are gukked up with Coke and chewing gum wrappers, that's what—paint peeling off the booths and the smell of horse dung and donkey shit. Ned's grouchy because he says he always has a headache in the mornings, and somebody's got to go out and buy a half dozen jelly doughnuts for the fat lady. A carnival is fingerprints all over the front of the popcorn stand and the stench of watermelon rinds and taking the dog woman for a walk because she's feeble-minded and might get run over. It's everybody bitching at everybody else and arguing over small dumb things because the morning's the only chance they have to be themselves. When the calliope starts at two o'clock, it's tinsel-time again, and everybody's smiling, whether he feels like it or not. That's what a carnival is."

"Jake, that's really very good, you know? You express yourself so vividly. You should write it down in your journal. It's worth remembering."

He was pleased with the compliment. "Maybe I will."

"Would you mind if I invited Murray Dawes for dinner some evening this week? I'd like you to meet him. I think he'd be very interested in your description of the carnival. He's rather poetic himself."

Jake shrugged and fell silent. Then, after a bit, "I don't care. What's so great about him? You never have Pastor Gordon here for dinner."

"Why, of course I do. Not since you came, that's all."

"Yeah? Well, what's the matter with Murray Dawes? He can't afford his own meals or something?"

"Jake, what on earth's the matter with you? Do I begrudge you the opportunity to invite *your* friends over? When I think of all the meals I've cooked for Brick Adams. . . ."

"Yeah, you're right. I'm sorry." Jake took his toast and wandered about the kitchen with it. "Brick and I were talking about it yesterday—what we're going to do when the carnival's over. We're going down to Rehoboth Beach and just lay on the sand and let the ocean roll over our feet, and we're not even going to move unless we have to." He stopped talking for a minute. "When are *you* going to get a vacation?"

"I'm thinking about it. Maybe I'll go somewhere when you're away. I'll have to see what works out."

She did not know what she would do. She did not know what would happen to her or to Murray or Jake or the love affair. All she knew was that she would give herself to Murray Dawes before he left Marbury, and that God would forgive her. He could not have made her wait all these years for Murray and then expect her to wait any longer. Think of the Old Testament fathers and what they got away with—Abraham with Hagar, Judah with Tamar. . . .

Please forgive me, she prayed in advance, lest she forget to do it later.

He came to dinner Wednesday evening before the revival service. Jake had to be back to work at six, so they ate at five, and Murray was prompt.

"So this is Jake," he said, shaking the boy's hand.

"How do you do?" said Jake, and sat down on the sofa in front of the tray of crackers.

"Why don't you start with the cheese while I make the salad?" Mary suggested. "We're having a light supper—it's been so hot lately."

Murray helped himself to a generous slab, leaned back, and studied the boy beside him while Mary watched covertly from the dining room.

"I used to make a study of names," Murray began, smiling. "Jake is a form of Jacob. I suppose you knew that. A good Biblical name—why your parents chose it, I suppose."

"No way," said Jake. "If they'd know it was from the Bible, they'd have called me something else."

Mary suppressed a smile.

"Anyway, what's it mean—Jacob?" Jake asked, curious nonetheless.

"It means a 'supplanter.' Somebody who takes the place of somebody else—possibly by trickery. Do you know the story of Jacob and Esau?"

"Yaaggg!" said Jake, and dramatically clutched his throat.

"He knows," said Mary. "He's been Jacobed and Esaued to death lately."

Murray smiled and offered the boy the plate of crackers. Jake refused and Murray took another for himself.

"What does 'Mary' mean?" Jake asked.

"I could never find out," Murray confessed. "Everywhere I looked it up, it said, 'See Marie,' and when I looked up Marie, it said, 'See Mary.'"

This brought a chuckle from Jake.

"Ah, but I know what Martha means," Murray added, glancing at Mary in the dining room. "It means 'lady' or 'mistress.'"

She smiled.

"What's 'Murray' mean?"

"You would ask that." The big man's eyes twinkled. "It comes from 'Maurice,' and it means 'Moorish—mysterious.'"

"That's you, all right," Jake said, with complete aplomb.

They sat around the dining room table, and Mary pressured her guest to take his jacket off. Mercifully the heat of the last two days had given way to a bit of a breeze which blew gently through the open door.

"Mary tells me you keep a journal," Murray said as the rolls went around.

"Yeah. I want to be a reporter some day."

"Woodward and Bernstein kind of stuff?"

"It doesn't have to be that big. I just don't want to spend my life writing about fires and burglaries, you know? I want assignments that let me write what I feel."

"Mary told me you wrote a terrific piece on the carnival."

"Well, I haven't really written it yet, but I'm going to. I was just talking to her about it."

"Jake has Sundays off from work, Murray. I'm hoping he'll attend the final night of revival."

"Be mighty glad to have you there, Jake."

"Is that your work?" Jake asked. "I mean, is that what you do, travel around holding revivals?"

"Most of the time. Seems to suit me. I like to see new places—meet new people. In the winter months I sometimes take on an assistant pastorship—help out somewhere temporarily. But spring, summer, and fall, I'm on the road, a salesman for Christ."

"My dad was a salesman," said Jake. "He sold real estate in California."

"Good field, real estate. The west coast, too! Now there's a place I've never been. Always wanted to go. We're all salesmen, you know it, Jake? I'm a salesman for the Lord, your dad was a salesman of land, and if you turn out to be a reporter, you'll have to do a good selling job, too, if you're going to be convincing—stir up feelings and get action. Where's your dad buried?"

"He isn't."

Murray looked up, then glanced at Mary.

"He's dead, but he's not buried," Jake explained, and went on buttering his roll.

"He was cremated, Jake. You should tell people that," Mary said quickly.

"He was scattered," Jake insisted. "Scattered to the four winds." He pointed to a thin film of dust that was already collecting on the buffet behind them. "See that, Aunt Mary? That could be my dad right there."

Murray wheeled around.

"I mean, dust is blowing about all the time, and by now my parents could be in every state. Wherever I go they could be there too."

Murray was speechless, and looked at Mary for guidance.

"Maybe that's why they made their request," she said. "Maybe they decided that if anything happened to them, then having their ashes scattered would make you feel less alone."

Jake wiped his mouth and put his napkin down. "I don't think that's why they did it. Not really. I don't think they even thought very much about it. I think they just decided it would be a neat way to go, and wrote it down as a joke."

He pushed his chair away from the table. "Well, off to the loony farm. The night crowd starts arriving about six. Did you know that some folks come for dinner, Aunt Mary, and stay all evening? They just feed their kids hot dogs and then wander around the shooting galleries and stuff. Ned says if the crowds keep coming, he'll have to hire more people. Everybody comes to see the sideshow. Everybody wants to get in the tents. Ned says if he put an ordinary house-cat in a tent, people would pay to go in and look at it. As soon as you cover something up and put a wall around it, he says, everybody wants to see it. Take the tent away and nobody cares. I'm going to put that in my journal, too, when I get home. Well, nice to meet you, Murray. See you around."

"Okay, Jake. I enjoyed it."

As soon as Jake was out the door, Murray turned to Mary. "Now that . . . that is one bright kid! How do you cope?"

She laughed, pleased that the evening had gone so well. "I was going to ask if you had any suggestions."

They went into the living room to the sofa.

"However you do it, you do it well. I can see how you love him," Murray said.

"Yes, I really do. He's been fun to live with—to have around."

Slowly Murray pulled her toward him till her head was on his chest. "We're always in a hurry," he said. "There's never time to talk—really talk. How long before seven o'clock?"

"Forty-five minutes."

He sighed, and the sigh seemed to come from deep inside him. "We need a place, Mary. We need to talk, to love, to know each other. People are watching us all the time. It's not good for you."

"I know."

They sat quietly for a moment or two.

"Could you ever leave here, Mary? Could you be happy traveling around with me?"

"I feel I could be happy anywhere with you."

"Lovers always feel that way at first."

He pressed her to him. Mary felt him gently touch her cheeks, her throat, and then, very softly, her breasts. She lay willingly in his arms and let him touch her. It did not seem evil at all.

"Mary," he said huskily, "could you take next Monday off? Could we spend the whole day together? The evening . . . ?"

"Yes. . . ."

He kissed her.

There was an airmail letter in Mary's box on Thursday, postmarked Bucharest.

* * *

Monday morning

Dear Mary,

Greg takes forever on the john so it's a marvelous time to write letters. That's one thing you don't find out about a man until you've lived with him, not that it's important.

The drivers here are absolute maniacs, so we feel safer on foot and have been doing some sightseeing. But it rained yesterday and it's been raining ever since, so we're stuck in this hotel. We'll be going to the University this afternoon to meet the great mammalogist and then start our tour of the research stations to see the hamsters mate or whatever. I think they're the only form of life around here that does. The people we've met so far seem long-faced and humorless—infinitely worse than Marbury—but I've heard the Romanians are bright and fun-loving, so maybe it's only the weather.

Greg says I've got it wrong, anyway, about the study. He is, believe it or not, interested in the social communities of hamsters, their aggression, their patterns of dominance—the whole ethology bit—so perhaps there's more to him after all than those weekends in Charlottesville.

My feelings do seem to be growing for him, but they're not consistent, and that bothers me. There should be some point at which I feel I can joyously accept the risk, and this hasn't happened yet.

Still, when it comes—if it comes—it has more to do with psychology than logic anyway. I remember that from my first marriage. It happened one evening—the way Clyde looked at me or something he said—and suddenly I was overwhelmed

with love and compassion and maternal tenderness and joy. From then on it was as though
something had snapped in my brain and locked
it in the "go" position. I could explain or excuse
anything at all after that, and lost all my objec-
tivity. I've heard other people talk about this as
the "ping"—the moment you know you're in
love. In any case, I hope it comes soon with Greg
and me, because it would make all these rodent
inspections so much more bearable.

I'm glad you said what you did last Thursday—glad we both had it out. Maybe I *was* jealous, you know? I've gone out with lots of men in
white lab coats who wanted to talk about my
body, but never with a man in a white suit who
wanted to talk about my soul. It must be like going out with a rabbi and having him recite the
Torah with one hand on your knee, and there's a
certain appeal in that.

Whatever, disregard all my previous warnings,
Mary. He *is* a big, beautiful bear of a man, and I
hope you'll do whatever your heart and soul and
glands tell you to do.

                                        Fondly,
                                        Liz

P.S. Stamps enclosed for Jake.

That evening Sam came to the revival. Mary saw
him walking down the road from the church parking
lot, dressed in a rumpled seersucker suit. He walked

in a grim, determined manner, like a man whose mind is set on a difficult task, and who fears, if he lifts his eyes for even a second, one foot plodding in front of the other, that he might change his mind.

He looked so pathetic, so beaten down, so inwardly empty while she herself felt joyous, that Mary could not help but feel sorry for him. She waited until he reached the path leading up to the tent.

"Hello, Sam."

He looked up quickly, his color deepening. "Hello, Mary."

She waited.

"Uh . . . Verna's here, I suppose?"

"Yes. She left Dad with some friends tonight. He's been getting a little restless at the revival meetings."

Sam looked agonizingly toward the tent, shifted a little in his seersucker suit, but did not move toward the door.

"Jake didn't come, did he?"

"No. He's working at the carnival this month."

"Yeah. I forgot." He stood there, one side of his face twitching, and suddenly bleated, "Jake talk to you yet, Mary? About last Sunday?"

"Yes."

"Oh, hell, Mary! I'm sorry as can be! I don't know what come over me. Tell him I won't be botherin' him like that again, I swear it. Jesus, Mary! A guy gets so sex-starved he just—well, he just about takes up with anything."

Mary studied him. "I'll tell him, but if ever again you make any kind of advances toward Jake. . . ."

"I won't, Mary, for the love of God, quit actin' like I'm some old sop that goes after sheep. Isn't it disgrace enough that my own boy's stirrin' up trouble all over Charles County, and my wife lives off to herself? Jesus God, don't go tellin' Verna now about Jake and me. . . ."

"Verna doesn't know. She wants you back with her again."

"I know. Like livin' with a goddamned knothole, though, the way she just lays there. . . ."

"She wishes she weren't that way."

"She tell you that?"

"Yes. She said sometimes she's sorry she was raised the way she was. I don't know—maybe if you gave her a lot of affection, a lot of time, it might work out."

Suddenly Mary knew that she could no longer withold a confession of her own. Sam had been so open, so honest, that it had humbled her. If Murray had truly touched her spiritually, as she believed, if God were working through him, then she must give Sam an apology that was years overdue.

"I understand how you feel, Sam," she continued. "I didn't like what Jake told me, about what happened, but I do understand. And I need to tell you— all these years I've needed to apologize—for that night we went to Washington, that night on the porch."

He stared at her dumbfounded.

"It was my fault as much as it was yours," she told him. "I was leading you on, and I never had the courage to say so. I was behaving stupidly, Sam, but I put it all on you."

"Well," he said awkwardly, "it was a long time ago."

"Yes, a long time. . . ."

He shifted again, embarrassed. "I'm obliged, Mary," he said finally, and his voice was grateful. He turned then, and plodded on toward the door of the tent. The seersucker suit moved down the center aisle and paused hesitantly at the row where Verna sat.

When she stared up at him in disbelief, finally scooting over a seat to give him her chair, he sat heavily down beside her. For better or worse, he had done it.

Lest the men of Charles County feel that the preaching was directed solely at them, Murray's sermon took a new twist. Everyone knew, he said, how God had destroyed the cities of Sodom and Gomorrah. Everyone knew how God had urged Lot and his wife and daughters to flee the city as it was burning.

"Yes Lord, we know," murmured someone in the front row.

Everyone knew, Murray continued, how God had warned them not to look back.

"It's the truth," said someone.

"But some women," said Murray, his voice falling to that certain sad whisper again, "cannot forget the things that thrilled them, sinful as they might be. Some women want to hang on to that little piece of lust, that trinket of shame—to take one fond look at that foul thing which so depraved them. And so Lot's wife turned back—only for a second—and she was turned to a pillar of salt."

"Yes, Lord."

It was not enough, evidently, that she had apologized to Sam, Mary thought. What if Murray knew about her and Warren? About that night in the barn and the memories . . . what they did to her even now?

"And so Lot was left with his two daughters—Lot of Sodom and Gomorrah. And they went to live in a cave, Lot with his two virgin daughters, who had not known men. But Lot's daughters remembered how he had offered them to the men of Sodom. Lot's daughters remembered how he had bartered for the angels' safety by saying, 'Behold now, I have two daughters

which have not known man—do ye to them as is good
is your eyes.' What do you think this did to their
young impressionable minds? What do you imagine
those young girls fantasied? Who is responsible for
the corrupting of innocents, my friends—the seducer
or the suggester?"

Murray opened the Bible on the pulpit before him
and began to read: "And Lot went up out of Zoar,
and dwelt in the mountain, and his two daughters
with him; for he feared to dwell in Zoar; and he
dwelt in a cave, he and his two daughters. And the
firstborn said unto the younger, Our father is old,
and there is not a man in the earth to come in unto
us after the manner of all the earth. Come, let us
make our father drink wine, and we will lie with him,
that we may preserve seed of our father. And they
made their father drink wine that night; and the
firstborn went in and lay with her father, and he perceived not when she lay down nor when she arose.
And it came to pass the morrow, that the firstborn
said unto the younger, Behold, I lay yesternight with
my father; let us make him drink wine this night
also; and go thou in and lie with him, that we may
preserve seed of our father.

"And they made their father drink wine that night
also; and the younger arose and lay with him, and he
perceived not when she lay down, nor when she
arose. Thus were both the daughters of Lot with
child by their father. . . ."

Murray closed the Bible and looked into the faces
of the people before him. "Thus were both the
daughters of Lot with child by their father," he repeated. "You know what that is, my friends. That is
incest. And you all know that behind God's laws,
there is a reason. He doesn't just command us be-

cause He likes to give orders. Incest is wrong because it breeds misfits. That is the corruption of drink. That is the corruption of carnivals; they parade the products of accidents, of misfortunes and of incest before you. Take a good look, my friends. If you are Christian, you have nothing to fear. Go to the side-shows and look at these creatures, and you will see what Lot's daughters have wrought upon this earth. Each of them begat a son by her father, and even to-day—in carnival tents all over the country, in sanitariums, in hospital wards—you will see what happens when men look upon their daughters with lust, and sons look upon their mothers, and the bodies of sister and brother are joined in sin. Wives, return to your husbands; husbands, cleave only unto you wives. Sex in matrimony is holy and right in the sight of the Lord, and He shall bless your union. . . ."

It was as though the sermon were meant for her, Mary thought. It was as though the sermon were meant for Verna, too, and Sam. It was as though Murray were a wonderful magician sent to this town to sort out the troubles in people's souls, to set things right.

"Oh, Lamb of God, I come, I come," sang the Solomon Singers when the service was over.

"It's like a miracle!"

Verna called the next morning before Mary had even dressed. The jangling of the phone had wakened Jake also who now straggled into the bathroom in his pajama bottoms while Mary answered the ring.

"What is, Verna?" she asked groggily.

"Sam. He's come back to me, Mary—after all these years. He slept in my bed last night."

Mary rubbed her eyes and tried to wake up. "Then what are you doing up so early?" she yawned.

"What?"

"Never mind," said Mary. "Look, I'm glad for you."

"The way Sam went down to the altar when Murray put out the call—knelt right there beside me on his knees like we were being married again. When Murray asked him if he'd take Jesus back into his heart, he said yes, and there were *tears* in Sam's eyes, Mary! He's a changed man. I feel like driving up and down the street shouting out the window. I want to yell, 'Jesus lives! Jesus saves!' to everyone I meet."

"You'd better hold off on that, Verna."

"Oh, Mary, if only Bill would come to the revival. I've a feeling that Murray Dawes was sent to Marbury for a purpose. I think he came to get our little family back together again. Only three more nights and then he'll be gone. You've been fond of him, Mary, we all know that. But he's a traveler, and we'll never see him again. If he could just lead my Bill to Jesus before he goes. . . ."

"Verna, huh?" said Jake, when Mary came into the kitchen and sat down.

"Verna." She sat with her eyes closed a minute. Six o'clock. "You should get back to bed, Jake. You simply haven't been getting enough sleep. It was midnight again before you got home last night. I heard you come in."

"It's all the people, Aunt Mary! At eleven we had seventy-five waiting to get in the sideshow tent. Leah, the dog woman, she was so tired she just went to sleep while people were still coming through. And you know, some guy had the nerve to poke her with his foot and tell her to bark. Ned said if anybody ever kicked Leah again he'd throw him right out of the tent."

"Well, that was decent of Ned. I'm glad to hear there's a spark of charity somewhere in him." Mary yawned again. "It looks as though the carnival is going to walk off with half the money in Marbury before the month is over." She put some bread in the toaster. "Incidentally, what did you think of Murray when he was here the other night?"

"He was okay."

She waited. Why did young people have to be flogged, practically, before they'd tell you what you wanted to know?

"Did you like him?"

"Depends."

Drawn and quartered, she thought. *Boiled in oil.* "Depends on what?"

"On what you want me to like him as. If you mean as an ordinary guy, sure, I liked him fine. If you meant as a preacher, I haven't heard him yet. If you meant as a father or something, well, that's something else."

"I didn't exactly mean that. But I do like him a lot."

Jake slumped a little further down in his chair. His hair was still mussed, and there were pillow marks on one side of his cheek. Why did boys look so cherubic when they had just wakened? Mary wondered. Would he always look that way—even when those same cheeks sprouted whiskers?

When he spoke again, however, Jake's voice sounded deeper, as though it had matured overnight, as though sleep had aged him somehow.

"You sure you know what you're doing?" he said at last.

"What do you mean?"

"Well, he's a traveling man. . . ."

"Good grief, is that all anybody can find to say about him? Is it a crime for a man to like to travel, to see the country, to meet new people?"

"That what you want to do?" Jake asked.

"Well, I'm not sure." She was quiet for a long while. Finally, "What about you?"

"I like it here. Oh, some of the people are nutty, but I like you and Tibs and Grandpa Myles and Brick and the guys at school. It's like I belong. I've got a place."

"You'll always have a place, Jake. Always."

"Yeah? A room somewhere, you mean? Jeez, I was just beginning to feel I belonged here—like it was my town, you know?"

Did she detect the slightest tremor of his lip? Mary wondered. "I wouldn't expect you to travel around, Jake."

"What would we do, then? Stay here while he took off?"

Not even she could answer that. She unfolded the morning paper and passed the comics to him. "Look, you've already got us married, and we just met. Let's just see what happens, okay?"

"Okay."

She hesitated a moment. "By the way, I saw Sam at the service last night, and he apologized for what happened. He was embarrassed and really very sorry. You see, he and Verna . . . uh. . . ."

"Yeah, I know. He and Verna shacked up last

night. I heard you talking on the phone and guessed."

"That's right, as you so delicately put it. Maybe there will be a real reconciliation."

"Wait until Sam wakes up, though, and sees where he is. He'll clear out pretty fast."

The second picnic that Mary and Murray had talked about never took place. There were too many appointments that Murray had to keep, too many obligations. On Friday night, toward the end of the revival service, the microphone went dead, and Murray spent all of Saturday morning working with the old man in the overalls to find the trouble. By evening, however, all was in order.

For the benefit of those who might have missed the first six sermons, he gave a quick replay of the entire story of Lot and his family as well as Sodom and Gomorrah. He said it was not generally known that gonorrhea got its name from Gomorrah, and mentioned once again exhibits in carnival sideshows.

Mary scarcely heard Murray's voice any longer. She had reached the point that Liz had talked about in her letter, the "ping," the moment at which the brain snaps into the locked position. She could excuse or explain anything that Murray did or said, because she understood. She knew why he preached as he did and believed that he was sincere. Every night she went to the crowded tent and sat as in a trance, near the back, joining in the mass adulation. She rose when the others rose and sang the hymns, her mouth moving mechanically. She listened, unhearing, to the Scripture. She went forward and knelt at Murray's marvelous feet when he asked for believers to come forward as witnesses to the undecided, waiting for the magic moment when he would get to her, put his hand on her head, and say, "God bless you, Mary."

Then she would close her eyes and smell his cologne and taste the saliva from his lips and feel the hardness of his groin pressing into her dress, and she would be transported by memories, both real and imagined. No longer did she trust herself to think or judge or reason. She had lived by herself far too long, waited for Murray forever. Already she had requested Monday off work, and Pastor Gordon had agreed without comment, his face grave.

On Sunday morning, at the Faith Holiness Church, Milt Jennings sat down in the pew beside Mary. He came defiantly, as though daring anyone to stop him. He held the hymn book for her when they sang and, when they were leaving the church afterwards, firmly took her elbow and guided her out, shaking the pastor's hand himself but ignoring Murray's altogether. He hustled Mary on down the steps and out to the street.

"What on earth . . . ?" she demanded.

"Mary," he said, "it's time somebody talked sense to you. You're making a spectacle of yourself, and there's not a person in Marbury who doesn't know how you feel about Brother Dawes."

"That's a spectacle?"

"You're acting like a school girl. You've only known the man a week or so, yet the way you look at him during the revival meetings—it's completely shameless—the way he holds onto your hand, right there in front of everybody. It's shocking, a mature woman like you."

"Absolutely," Mary agreed. "I'm not even responsible for myself any longer."

"Mary! Good grief! You don't know what you're saying."

"Yes, I do. And I know how ridiculous it sounds."

"He's leaving next week. What are you going to do then?"

"I don't know. . . ."

She stopped talking as some parishioners approached, said good morning, and moved on.

Milt looked at her in exasperation.

"It's Jake. You haven't been yourself since the day that boy arrived."

"Don't blame anything on Jake, Milt," Mary snapped suddenly. "What I do is my own decision. And whatever I decide has nothing to do with you and me at all."

"You may feel differently about things when Murray's gone," said Milt.

"Never." She turned and walked away.

Verna and Sam were going out to dinner together after church ("like a second honeymoon," Verna told Mary) and brought Grandpa Myles to Mary's for the afternoon. Jake got out a Parcheesi game and tried to teach his grandfather to play. Grandpa Myles could roll the dice but could not seem to add the numbers. Jake did it for him.

"Four, Gramps! Move it four!" he would say, but it became too much for the old man, who seemed confused and then a little upset. So Jake began playing for both of them, cheering when Grandpa Myles' pieces got close to home, and the old man leaned back and watched Jake with delight, chortling at his enthusiasm. When Jake told him that he had won, Grandpa laughed and slapped one hand down on the table, saying, "By gun dingo."

Brick came over at three with his guitar, and the boys decided to teach Grandpa to play a song.

"Now all you have to do," Brick said, setting the guitar across the old man's lap, "is rub your thumb across the strings right here—no, here, by the hole."

With effort and more adjusting of the instrument, Grandpa Myles was able to do it, and soon had a monotonous strum going. Jake sang, "Blowin' in the Wind," awkwardly slowing down or speeding up depending on the steadiness of his grandfather's rhythm.

The old man was obviously delighted. He stared in wonder at Jake kneeling there on the rug, singing, and was almost overcome with emotion at being able to be a part of the music.

Mary watched from the kitchen doorway, touched. "Oh, Jake, he loves you so," she said. "You boys really have a way with Grandpa."

"If we ever move away from here," Jake responded, "I want to take Gramps with us."

"Hey, man, you're not moving, are you?" Brick asked.

Jake glanced at Mary. "Oh, I don't think so. We just talk about it once in a while, is all."

For a long time that evening, before leaving for the last revival service, Mary stood brushing her hair, staring in the mirror as though she were looking at a stranger. She seemed to have lost touch with who she was. Or had she really found herself? How could she tell? If she were really in love with Murray, and he was the man for her, why did she feel so hesitant? Why wasn't she overwhelmed with joy?

Because there are too many unresolved problems, she told herself as they got in the car. *Jake, Dad, myself, even. . . .*

Jake was silent, too, as they drove toward the tent, and Mary knew what he was thinking. *Oh God,* she breathed in panic, *what should I do? Please give me a sign. If Murray is the right man for me, if this is why you've sent him to Marbury, show me somehow. Anything! Let a dove descend with a twig in its beak or the sky suddenly light up or. . . .*

A huge glob of bird droppings splattered on the windshield. Mary frowned and looked away.

FOURTEEN

It was Verna's fervent hope that Bill would appear at the tent on the last night of revival and have a magnificent conversion, like Saul on the road to Damascus. She had not seen him all day and was afraid he might be off drinking somewhere, only to come back and disrupt the final service.

Actually, Mary thought, as she entered the tent with Jake, a tremendous uproar by Bill could only help. The revival had been so successful and the tent so full that people were ready for anything—*expected* something, almost, as a grand finale.

"He say the same thing every night?" Jake asked as they sat down, waving to Sam and Verna a few rows ahead of them.

"Not really. He uses the same theme, but each sermon is a variation of it."

"What's the theme?"

"Sin. Sodom and Gomorrah—sin in Marbury."

"Wow." Jake remained deadpan. "Old Sin City itself! Where the heck does he find any sin around here, I'd like to know."

"You'd be surprised."

Mary was somewhat uneasy about Jake's reaction to a diatribe against Ned and his ilk. But this time Murray scarcely mentioned the carnival at all. Perhaps it was out of deference to Jake, knowing he would be there. Or perhaps Murray had heard the rumors about the number of church members who had been seen at the sideshow tents, and felt it best not to mention them again. Whatever, Murray had changed tactics, and chose only those hymns which were lively and spirited.

"Page two hundred twenty-four, friends," he said, standing up in his snow white suit and holding the hymn book aloft. His warm smile traveled about the tent from face to face 'There's Not a Friend Like the Lowly Jesus.' I want to hear it for all our brothers and sisters in Pisgah and Welcome and Chapel Point and Dentsville—let's sing it for the whole of Charles County, folks, let's let them hear it all the way to Washington, D.C. and let the world know that Marbury, Maryland, is rocking for the Lord."

His baritone voice sang out vibrant and full, and the people present, those in seats and those standing, sang out lustily, smiling back at Murray and at each other:

> *There's not a friend like the lowly Jesus,*
> *No not one! No not one!*
> *None else could heal all our soul's diseases,*
> *No, not one! No not one!*

" 'When the Roll is Called Up Yonder,' " Murray announced next. "Page five hundred. I'll be there, friends, will you? Men sing the first verse, women the second, and we'll all join together on the third verse because we all want to be together on that final day when the roll is called up yonder. Wives and husbands want to be together, mothers and children want to be together, we don't want anybody to be left behind. Page five hundred, men first."

"Weird," muttered Jake.

When the hymn was finally over, Jake was the first one seated again, and Mary could tell by the way he was swinging his feet that he was bored already. She glanced at him and he stopped. Then he amused himself by using one foot to pile sawdust on top of the other. She let him be.

The offering was taken, and Pastor Gordon led his flock in a long prayer, ending with an invitation to those who were not members of the Faith Holiness Church to introduce themselves to him after the service. Bernice Gordon stood up next and made a little speech about the church school program and the wonderful activities they had on Sunday mornings for young people. Jake put one hand over his mouth and silently pretended to vomit. This time Mary nudged him sharply.

Then Murray, in his white suit, loomed large and dominating behind the lectern. He said he wanted to talk to them about guarantees. He said that everyone present had a good chance of getting home that night safely, of waking up to a new day the next morning. But there were no guarantees. The only guarantee any of us had, he said, was that if we gave our souls to Jesus Christ, we would live with him forever in Heaven.

The problem, Murray went on, was that none of us knew just when he would die. Too many people put off that personal talk with their savior until too late. The only sensible way to live was to be ready for whatever might happen.

Then he recounted God's plan to destroy Sodom and Gomorrah, and how Abraham said to the Lord,

"Will you destroy the righteous with the wicked? If there are at least fifty righteous people in Sodom, won't you save it for their sakes?"

Murray, looking like God himself, cast his eyes slowly over the crowd of listeners, "And the Lord said, 'If I find fifty righteous people, I will save Sodom.' But Abraham was worried about his nephew Lot, and he said, 'What about forty-five? If you find forty-five who are righteous, will you destroy it?' And God reconsidered and said if he found forty-five who were righteous, he would save it. But still Abraham was worried, and he bargained further, first for forty, then thirty, then twenty, and finally ten. But the Lord could not find even ten righteous people in Sodom, and so, along with Gomorrah, the city was destroyed and only Lot and his daughters were saved."

Murray leaned heavily on the lectern and his face was sad and serious. "My friends, if the Lord God Almighty should look down on Marbury, Maryland, or the whole of Charles County, how many righteous would he find here? If God should destroy the county tomorrow, how many of you would be ready to meet your maker? Some of you, I know, are ready now. But for others, this may be the last chance to make your peace with God."

Murray stood up straighter. "I want you to meet somebody right now who has just made a decision for Christ. I want you to see with your own eyes a man who, even if he was struck by a car when he left this tent, would be on his way to glory. My friends, this is a man who has lived a life of wanton depravity, a man who has abused his body by lust and his soul with blasphemies and curses against the holy spirit—a man now so completely changed that should he depart from this world this very moment, the gates of heaven would swing wide to let him in. . . ."

He turned and extended his hand to someone who had been sitting in the first row, half-hidden by Bernice Gordon. Verna leaned forward, one hand to her throat. But it was not Bill. A small, wiry-looking man with a bony face and wavy hair bounded up onto the platform beside Murray.

"Curly!" Jake gasped, staring.

Mary turned. "You know him?" she whispered.

"He works at the carnival! He's the guy who takes care of the ponies. Jesus! He seemed all right yesterday!"

Curly faced the audience and for a moment his mind appeared to go blank. He was a head shorter than Murray and seemed dwarfed by the lectern. Finally, however, he straightened his tie, swallowed, licked his dry lips, and then, in a high rapid voice, said that he had known so many women he couldn't count them, had drunk so much booze that his liver was shot, had stolen soft drinks from grocery stores and broken open a Coke machine. He had slept with other men's wives, had robbed a dry cleaning store, had driven a stolen car, and had had carnal knowledge of a thirteen-year-old girl.

The audience gasped, shaking their heads.

Curly looked over at Murray as to whether or not he should continue, got a fatherly nod, and went on: he had burglarized a house, vandalized a school, taken a CB radio from a pickup truck, and had once been drunk an entire week, only to wake up in jail and find himself booked on statutory rape. Until yesterday, he said, he had nothing to look forward to but tending the ponies in a traveling carnival. But then Murray Dawes found him and talked to him and asked him to turn his whole sordid life over to Jesus Christ, and now he stood here for all the world to see, a new man, convinced that his sins had been washed whiter than snow.

"Praise Jesus!" said Verna loudly.

"Thank you, Lord."

"Jesus, Jesus. . . ."

The murmurs traveled around the tent.

Jake sat transfixed, his eyes on Curly. "He looks just like he did yesterday except for the tie," he whispered.

When Curly had finished his short talk, he sat down again by Bernice Gordon who hugged him, and Murray stood up.

He told the crowd that revivals need money to keep going. He said that the Faith Holiness Church, sponsors of this revival, needed extra money to survive. He said that they all knew that far more money was going to the carnival down the road than was being contributed here, and it was a shame that sideshows could keep going when church revivals could scarcely make ends meet.

"Folks," Murray said. "I know you don't have much money, and I know that some of you gave all you could tonight—gave till it hurt. I know you don't have it, but if you did have an extra hundred dollars to spare, how many of you would give it to the Lord?"

Almost every hand went up except Jake's.

"I knew you people in Marbury had hearts of

gold, even if there isn't any in your pockets," Murray went on. "Well, I want to tell you something, I've been praying for you folks, and I've had a vision. Yes, a vision. I've had a vision that you marvelous people are going to get something extra. Maybe it will be two dollars on your birthday. Maybe it will be an insurance refund or a raise in salary. I don't know just when it will come and I don't know how much it will be, but the Good Lord is sending it. It's on its way. And all I want you to do, my friends, when it comes, is to give half of it to the Lord. I know you said you'd give a hundred dollars if you had it, but the Lord knows that Charles County isn't Manhattan, and He's willing to take just half. That's all. Give half to the Lord, just to show your appreciation, and keep half for yourselves. If it's two dollars, keep one and give the other to the Lord. If it's fifty dollars, keep twenty-five and give the Lord twenty-five."

Murray handed a box of envelopes to Bernice Gordon and asked her to pass them out. Mary had spent the previous Friday stamping addresses on them: half of the envelopes were addressed to Pastor Gordon at the church, half to Murray Dawes at a post office box in Missouri.

"Thank you, Sister Gordon," Murray said. "There you are, brothers and sisters, there's your 'Thank you, God' envelope. All you do is put in half your blessing and send it along for God's work. It doesn't matter whose name is on the envelope—whether it goes to me or to Pastor Gordon, we'll see that it sanctifies His name forever, praise Jesus."

"Praise Jesus," said Verna, leading the pack.

The organist had been playing, "Softly and Tenderly Jesus is Calling," on the portable organ, and as the music rose in volume, the tent grew quieter.

"Friends," said Murray, "this is the last night of our great revival. This is the last chance for many of you folks. I want to ask all of you here who haven't yet made that decision for the Lord to come down here now to the altar."

The Solomon Singers stood up and began humming along with the music, finally adding the words:

> Come home, come ho-o-ome.
> Ye who are weary come ho-o-ome,
> Earnestly, tenderly, Jesus is calling,
> Calling, O Sinner, come home!

"I invite you now, brothers and sisters, young people, anybody out there who hasn't made that decision yet, to come right down here to the front. We don't care who you are. We don't know your sins, and you don't have to tell us. This is just between you and Jesus. All you have to do, my friends, is come. . . ."

Slowly, one by one, then in two's and three's, people began to stand up and come forward, down to where Murray Dawes stood with his hands outstretched, his eyes tightly closed, head tilted back, face toward heaven. . . . They came weeping, dabbing at their eyes, and hands reached out to help them along, to pat them, to offer encouragement and comfort.

Pastor Gordon began mingling with the kneelers up by the platform, whispering to them, touching their heads, kneeling down and praying beside them one by one while the music went on. But Murray himself started down the center aisle.

"I know there are still some of you out here who don't have the courage," he said. "I know that some of you are ready, but you just can't make yourselves get up in front of all these good people and go down to meet your Jesus. So I'm going to make it easy for you, friends. I'm going to come down the rows, one by one. If you're saved already, God bless you. But if you need Jesus—and we all need Jesus, friends—you just raise your hand a little bit, and I'm going to kneel right down beside you. I'll be right there with you, brothers and sisters, right down there in your row, no one else will hear, and we'll go together, friends—you and I will go to Jesus together and tell him you're ready. You don't have to do it alone."

Slowly, row by row, he came, leaning over, talking, patting some on the head, bending down and whispering to others. Sometimes he encountered a raised hand and knelt down, squeezed between the two rows, and prayed softly, earnestly. Some, seeing him coming, decided it would be better to join the crowd at the platform and hastily got up and went forward. All the while the Solomon Singers sang on:

> *Why should we tarry when Jesus is pleading.*
> *Pleading for you and for me?*
> *Why should we linger and heed not his mercies,*
> *Mercies for you and for me?*

As Murray reached the row where Mary was sitting, she could feel Jake fidget beside her.

"You going to raise your hand?" he whispered to her.

She shook her head.

Jake pressed himself against the back of his chair as Murray approached, and suddenly the big man was standing right in front of him, bending over Mary, one large hand over hers, and then he was turning to Jake.

"Bug off," muttered Jake through clenched teeth. Murray moved on.

The moon was almost full and the air warm when they headed home later. There was perfect stillness in the car for the first few blocks. Finally Mary broke it.

"That was totally unnecessary," she said. "All you had to do was shake his hand or something. He wasn't going to embarrass you. He wouldn't have made a scene."

"How was *I* supposed to know?" Jake said. "I've never been to a revival before. I see some big guy in a white suit coming at me and I get nervous, okay?"

She didn't answer.

"I still can't understand about Curly," Jake went on, talking almost to himself. "I went to the back of the tent afterwards to talk to him but he was gone." He waited. Still Mary did not respond. "Maybe it was like Murray said," Jake chuckled. "Maybe the gates of heaven opened wide and swallowed Curly right up. Maybe he was hit by a truck or something. One minute he was there and the next he wasn't."

He got no reply for his effort, however, so he gave up trying. When they reached the house, each went to his own room and closed the door.

Breakfast that morning was polite but reserved. Neither Mary nor Jake seemed in the mood for controversy, and so they talked about only those things they could agree upon—the toast and the orange juice and the fact that it looked as though it would be a beautiful day.

Mary tried to sound casual as she put the dishes in the sink. "Since Murray's leaving tomorrow, I'm taking the day off. It's possible I'll be home quite late, and I'd feel better if you could arrange to spend the night at Brick's."

She could feel his eyes riveted on her from behind. For a long time he didn't answer. Then, barely opening his lips, he said, "I'll ask."

She scrubbed quickly at cups and saucers that needed no scrubbing. "I just don't like you coming home to an empty house at that hour of the night."

"I'll be working till midnight anyway," Jake said. "Will you be getting home later than that?"

"It's possible, so please ask Brick if you can stay at his place. Then I won't worry about you."

Jake got up from the table. "You don't have to worry about *me*," he said, and went off down the hall to his room.

She took a long time in dressing. First she bathed, using some bath oil she'd received at Christmas. She chose her underwear carefully, slipped on white sandals over stockingless feet, then stepped into a pale pink dress with pleated tucks over the bosom. It was the most feminine thing she owned, and she wished to be all woman on Murray's last day.

She was waiting for him when he arrived at ten, her hair falling softly down her back. He came up the steps in his white trousers and dark blue shirt, but this time without either coat or tie. He looked at her with warmth and tenderness that Mary had never seen in a man's eyes before. She felt as though they were leaving to be married. Jake sat in a chair across the room, ankles crossed, watching.

Murray came inside to say hello.

"Jake will be staying at a friend's house tonight, Murray, in case we get back late," Mary told him.

"Good idea," Murray smiled at the boy. "It's a beautiful morning, Jake. Can we drop you off anywhere?"

"No. I don't have to be at work till eleven."

"That's right, I forgot. Well, I'll take good care of your aunt." He strode across the room and extended his hand. "It was a pleasure to meet you, Jake. I can certainly understand why Mary's so fond of you."

"Thanks." Jake shook his hand without getting up. He was not smiling.

As she went out to the car, Mary had a sudden impulse to go back and say something else to her nephew, something loving or pleasant. But she was peeved at his sullenness. Wasn't this the kid who had been asking her if she never really cut loose? Why she didn't go out and do something she'd always wanted to do? Okay, she was doing just that. Jake was jealous, that's all. He'd be jealous of any man she ever picked. Well, he'd have to get over it. She did him no favor by coddling him.

Inside the Dodge, Murray leaned over and kissed her lightly on the cheek.

"Can you walk in those shoes?"

"Yes. If they bother me, I'll go barefoot."

"Ah. That's my girl. This is a day for walking and talking, Mary, for getting to know each other."

He put one big arm around her, and she leaned against him. There was a dark half-circle of perspiration under his arm, and Mary felt drawn to it. It was him. She wanted to taste his saliva, feel his sweat. She wanted him to infiltrate her pores so that forever after Murray Dawes would be a part of her.

They headed southeast through Pisgah to Chapel Point. There the old St. Ignatius Church stood on a hilltop overlooking the junction of the Potomac and Port Tobacco Rivers. For a long time they wandered silently hand in hand through the graveyard, stopping now and then to look out over the panoramic view below, closing their eyes to the sun, letting the breeze blow through their hair. It was utterly silent except for the wind in the trees overhead and the occasional buzz of an insect. They turned toward each other finally and embraced, kissing long and tenderly, haltingly, holding back the torrent that was bound to come.

"I want you, Mary," Murray said, simply and directly, pressing her to him.

"Then take me," she whispered, and instantly felt the warmth of her own wetness.

"Not now," he said gently. "We'll wait. . . ."

They walked on, his arm around her, her head on his shoulder. They would play it out to its full intensity. They would talk about it, anticipate it, flirt with it, fantasy it, and finally, when they had found a place, they would make love. It seemed splendid and wonderful and right.

Inside the old Catholic Church, candles burned beneath a statue of the Virgin. At the back of the sanctuary, on the right, stood the confessional. No one was about. It was as though only the dead came to worship.

Mary walked curiously over to the dark booths and opened the door to the priest's cubicle. She half expected to find a monk staring back at her with ossified eyes, but the chair was empty, like Santa's chair in a department store the day after Christmas. A sheet of paper with printed prayers of absolution was tacked on the wall above the small screen through which the priest addressed the penitent. Somehow Mary thought of Jake and what he would say about it all.

"I've always wondered about Catholics and the confession," she told Murray. "I'd love to sit in there, just to see what it's like."

"Go ahead," Murray laughed. "You be the priest and I'll be the penitent."

"Oh, Murray, I couldn't. What if someone walked in?"

"They won't. The monks are all at prayers."

"How do you know?"

"Monks are always at prayers. They're not anything like traveling preachers."

She laughed, and slipped inside the priest's cubicle. Murray went into the adjoining box. She could just make him out through the layered screen and saw him kneel down.

"Father . . . ," he began.

"Mother," Mary corrected.

"Mother Mary Martha," said Murray. "I've come to confess my sins."

"Then speak, child," said Mary, and they both laughed aloud then. But Murray's voice grew serious again.

"I've got this awful craving for you, Mother."

"What is it like? You'll have to describe it."

"I want to lie on you."

Mary's face flushed slightly. Yet it was so easy hearing it here in the darkness. How natural it was to talk to someone you could not see, be close to someone you could not touch. It must be the next best thing to talking to God. . . .

"Is that all?" Mary asked.

"I want to lie on you naked and feel your skin against mine."

"Then I will come out and we'll lie naked," said Mary. "There's no harm in that."

"But I want to do more than that, Mother," said Murray. "I want to touch your holy parts."

"Touching is no sin, my child." She was surprised at her boldness, her spontaneity.

"You don't understand, Mother. I want to penetrate you. . . . I want to bury myself in your secret place. . . ."

Mary felt weak with wanting him, and she leaned back heavily against the wall. It was not play any longer. "Oh, Murray. . . ."

He was opening the door of the priest's cubicle and taking her hand.

"Let's find a place," said Mary.

"No," Murray said again. "We're going to do it right. We'll have lunch first. We've got all day." But his voice was husky. They walked slowly around the church once more, then drove down to Pope's Creek and ate at a crab house overlooking the water.

They could not seem to talk until their bodies were in tune. There was so much to say, Mary thought, and yet none of it could be said, it seemed, until they were lying flesh against flesh on the same pillow. She ached with wanting him. It was as though it were easier for their bodies to be intimate than their minds, as though they could reach a physical rapport more easily than they could resolve the unspoken disparities in their lives.

She did not know afterwards what exactly she had eaten. She could not seem to remember if she had eaten at all. She remembered looking at a menu with cranberry juice stains on one corner, watching a sailboat out on the river, and seeing some birds fight over a biscuit on the wharf. And then Murray was paying the cashier and they were in the car again, and Murray was looking at her intently and saying, "We're going to find a place now, Mary."

Like the Biblical Joseph looking for an inn for his wife, they could wait no longer. It was time for her to be delivered—a deliverance from convention, from chastity, from piety—from the joylessness of being good. The old restrictions seemed evil somehow; the old rules had warped her, and now she would be cleansed and healed and made whole at last.

There was a motel set back off the road south of Faulkner on 30.

"Are there likely to be any members of Faith Holiness down here?" Murray asked her.

"No. The Baptist church is big on revivals. These people would go to theirs rather than come up to Marbury. We're probably safe."

"We'll take a chance." Murray went in and was back a few minutes later with the key. They drove to the second door on the right.

There were no clothes to hang in the closet, no suitcase to unpack, no toiletries to set on the sink in the bathroom. Murray drew the drapes and they stood there in the half light of early afternoon facing each other.

Then she felt his strong hands on her back, and the hardness of his penis pressing through her dress. His lips were firmly over her own, and her body seemed to leap out to meet him, begging to be taken. Tenderly he unbuttoned her dress until it was loose and hung only on her bare arms. He backed away from her to let it fall, and the dress dropped at her feet.

Slowly, soberly, Murray undressed her all the way, his face solemn yet tense. It was a religious celebration, Mary thought—a special, sacred, ritual in which no more than two, these two—could participate. He took off her brassiere and gently kissed each breast in turn. She felt her nipples stand out at the touch of his lips, straining to meet his mouth, and little bumps stood up around the areola, shivering under Murray's touch.

She had never thought of herself as beautiful, but she felt beautiful here. She had no apprehension as she stepped out of her panties. She was not self-conscious about the mole on her knee or her thighs that were a trifle fleshy. She was imperfect, standing there in her white sandals, but woman still.

"Lie down," Murray whispered. She obeyed, stepping out of her shoes, and lay on her back with her legs slightly apart. He watched her as he took off his shirt, now moving more quickly. He wore no undershirt, but stood bare-chested in his white trousers. Soon those, too, and his shorts, lay in a heap on the floor.

For a man of Murray's size, she had expected a monstrous phallus. But the penis was thick and short and stuck out at a perfect right angle to his body. She could, she mused, hang her dress on it.

"You're smiling," he said, as he lay beside her.

She touched him lovingly. "I'm thinking that I could hang my dress on this."

He laughed. "I want to lie on you, Mother Mary

Martha," he whispered breathlessly at her ear, and she felt his hardness digging against one thigh.

"Is that all?" Mary whispered back, her eyes closing.

"I want to lie on you naked and feel your skin against mine," he said, rolling on top of her, and his penis found the space between her legs.

"What else?" asked Mary.

And then he was in her, she was a virgin no longer, and it was irrelevant whether or not she had been one all along.

"I want to bury myself in you," said Murray, speaking in quick, hesitant phrases, his breath coming faster and faster against the side of her neck. "I want to find all . . . your . . . secret . . . places. . . ."

Mary felt her knees lift and her legs part, and then his body thrust forward. His hands were under the arch of her back, and the two of them rocked sideways, this way and that, as a trickle of sweat dropped off the side of his face and onto Mary's cheek.

"Oh, Mary, my Mary," he said, and they rolled over on their sides, locked together, and lay still.

Their heartbeats gradually slowed, but still they clung to each other. One of Murray's big hands moved up and caressed Mary's ear.

"I couldn't wait, Mary. I'll do better next time."

Was there something better? Mary wondered. Was there anything more beautiful than lying here locked in the embrace of Murray Dawes, the man beneath the white suit? Was there anything more wonderful than having such a man go into a frenzy over her body, feeling his muscles tighten and his buttocks harden until his whole being, it seemed, went into spasm—all because of her, because of her secret places?

"Murray," she breathed, moving her lips up to his, "I've wanted you for so long—I've wanted you all my life and didn't know it."

"You knew it," Murray told her. "I just wasn't here. It took this long to get us together."

For several minutes they lay together without talking. And yet Mary knew that it had to come.

"I don't want you to leave tomorrow," she said finally. "I don't want you ever to go."

Murray rolled over on his back and lay with one hand under his head, the other on Mary's thigh, stroking her skin. "I know."

"I almost wish . . . that this was my fertile period . . . and that you'd left me with a baby. . . ."

He glanced at her quickly.

"It's not," she said, "and I'm not that foolish, but . . . it's strange. I've let you touch me—love me—and I hardly even know you, Murray. Yet I trust you."

He smiled and patted her leg. "I could have a wife back in Missouri," he said.

"And seven kids. . . ."

"I could have a mistress in every town I'd ever held a revival. . . ."

"Or you could run off with all the money and leave Ralph a worthless check for his half. . . ." There. That took care of all the reservations Liz had voiced about him.

"Right. I could be or do all these things, and Mary Martha would go on trusting. . . ." He turned and pulled her to him again. Now his penis was soft and sticky, and it nestled against her groin like a small mouse seeking protection. "I've had women before, Mary—not many, but some—but I've never known any like you. I love you, Mary. I really believe I love you."

"Oh, Murray."

That solved everything, didn't it? Mary thought as he kissed her. If there was love, wouldn't it find a way? If they were destined for each other, couldn't they compromise somehow?

But still Murray seemed troubled. "I've got commitments, Mary. I've got a schedule of revivals right through November. Would you really want to come with me? Every few weeks a new place? You'd get tired of it very soon—and of me in the bargain."

She was realistic enough to know that a life of motel rooms would not suit her. "Not of you, Murray. Not ever."

"But of motels, you would. I've seen some places you wouldn't believe. . . ." He propped himself up on his pillow and looked around. They both surveyed the room for the first time and found it far shabbier than it had appeared from the outside—linoleum floor, frayed chair, one scratched-up dresser with the bathroom beyond.

"This is luxury compared to some of the places I've stayed," said Murray. "I've been in motels, Mary, where you could hear every groan of the mattress, every squeak of the springs from the bed on the other side of the wall." He laughed with the memory. "I've gone into bathrooms, where, when the folks on the other side turned on their water, mine stopped coming. I've been in rooms where the place looked as clean as a grandmother's kitchen, and as soon as the lights went out, the roaches started crawling. Oh, Mary, I wouldn't ask you to live a life like that for me. . . ."

"It wouldn't have to be all the time, would it?" Mary asked. "Couldn't you travel a few months of the year and stay home the rest of the time?"

He took a deep breath and lay still. "I tried staying home once, working in one place. But after two months, looking at those same walls, meeting the same people, I was restless to go again, Mary. It's in my blood. If I was home, I'd be wanting to go. But on the road, I'd be thinking of you. There's no satisfying me. I'm not a good man for marrying. I'm just not. . . ."

"Have you ever been married, Murray?'

"Yes. It was a teenage marriage—a girl I'd known since I was seventeen. We married a couple years later, and it only lasted six months. I thought she was the one girl in the world for me, but I couldn't stand those four walls. No children. Thank Jesus for that."

Again they lay quietly. It was possible to make the sacrifice, Mary was thinking, but it was not possible to make yourself love it. She had expected this response. Still, there ought to be a way to work it out.

"Would you get tired of me if I traveled with you?" she asked.

"I can't imagine it, Mary. To come back to my room and find you there—it would seem like God's blessing going along with me. I'd preach better, I'd feel better—it would change my life, I know. But think of all you'd be giving up."

"Jake," said Mary.

"Yes, Jake. And more."

"I couldn't ask him to travel, Murray. A young boy has to have roots—friends—some kind of stability. He'd have to go to school. He has no one else to take him except Verna, and he'd never stay with her. I promised he could count on me. . . ."

"I know that, Mary, and love you for it. You don't have to explain or apologize."

"Oh, Murray, I want you, too," Mary said, and there were tears in her eyes. She pressed up against him and felt the stirrings of his penis once more. A trace of anger toward Jake flashed through her briefly. It wasn't fair! Relatives had ruled her life already for too long. . . .

"Mary, you don't know me yet. You think you do, but. . . ." Murray sighed, lying quietly for a while, stroking her hair. "It's an ego trip, you know. I come into a small town in my white suit like the Savior himelf, Jesus help mé. People look at me and they think I'm going to solve everything—build up church attendance, increase membership, cement their marriages, bring back their runaway children. I'm going to stop them from gambling and drinking and sleeping around, and they really think I can do it. But most of it doesn't stick, you know. I do what I can, but it amounts to very little. A month after I'm gone—the next week, even—things are back to the way they were before. I'm no miracle man, Mary. They want to see me that way, though, and I let them, that's all. Churches want revivals so I give them all I've got. But when the white suit comes off, and the shirt's hung up, and I step out of dirty underwear and crawl in bed in a cheap motel, I know who I am. I don't fool myself. I'm the kid with the cleft lip who couldn't wait till he was old enough to grow a mustache and hide the scar. I'm still the boy who was left in a strange Indiana town and told to sell a dozen cans of shoe polish, or my Dad wouldn't pick me up at three. I'm the kid who was out selling once and a woman wouldn't let him use her toilet, so he did it in his pants. Now, by God, I come into town in a snow-white suit without a spot on the trousers anywhere. And I don't go around knocking on doors—the people come to me. I'm not selling shoe polish, I'm selling salvation. I'm not shining up their feet, Mary, I'm glorifying their souls, and I don't come back again and ring the doorbell twice. I come through a town once and, by God, when I'm through, they know that Murray Dawes was there."

He stopped talking suddenly and grew very quiet. Then, "Listen to me, Mary. I'm still the little boy. I'm not what I seem to be at all. You'd find out more and more about me until I'd shrunk pretty small in your eyes. I'm not the big man in the white suit all the time. I'm skin and stains and snot and semen and. . . ."

"Oh, Murray, Murray. . . ." She pressed herself against him as his hand caressed her back, her buttocks, her thighs—slowly working up her flank to the edge of her breast. She loved him, she knew—loved him even more for his confession. It made him so human, so real, that it did not seem at all impossible that he was here now with her or that he loved her. She let herself be carried away, almost to the point of sleep, with his hypnotic touch.

"Thy two breasts are like two young roes that are twins, which feed among the lilies," Murray whispered. "Until the day break, and the shadows flee away, I will get me to the mountain of myrrh, and to the hill of frankincense. Thou art all fair, my love; there is no spot in thee."

Those words . . . when had she heard them last? How remarkable that mere syllables could arouse her so!

"Those were always my favorite verses, Warren," she murmured.

Instantly her eyes opened and her heart pounded with the realization of what she had said. Had he noticed? Had he heard? How could she have let a memory follow her here, undress her, and slip into the bed beside her?

She felt her throat constricting, her face growing hot. Would she ever be whole until she confessed, and if not to Murray, then who?

She realized that she was crying. Murray felt the hot tears on his arm and turned over.

"Mary?" he said, tilting her face up toward him.

She closed her eyes, but the tears gushed out under the lashes. He caressed her gently.

"Was he somebody special, Mary?" he asked softly.

"Oh, God, Murray!" she wept, and hid her face against him. "He was my brother."

His hand paused only a moment on her shoulder and then began stroking her again.

"Jake's father?"

"Y . . . yes."

"Tell me about him." His voice soothed like salve on an open wound.

Her breath came jerkily. She felt as though she were twelve again, confessing her very soul to one of those summer evangelists in a white suit, their thighs touching there at the altar, while one of his big hands rested on her shoulder. . . .

"He used to read me verses from the book of Solomon," she began. "I never said anything . . . just listened. But he enjoyed watching me as he read, and I . . . I enjoyed his eyes on me. Afterwards I would think about it . . . about him."

She could not see Murray's face above her on the pillow, and this made it easier.

"We always felt the same way about things—about Marbury, and Verna, and Mother, and the church. We both wanted out, Murray. I'm not the saint I appear to be. But Warren never did anything to me. It was all fantasy. There was more sexuality in his eyes and in his walk than in all the boys I ever dated. When I was alone . . . in bed . . . you know . . . it was always Warren who came to mind, never the others. I knew it was sinful, but the sin only made it better. . . ."

Murray chuckled and Mary felt her body relax.

"Then one night," she continued, "he was discovered in a neighbor's barn having intercourse with a local girl. He had to stand up before the congregation in a special service of penitence, and—toward the end—he suddenly bolted out the door. A minute or two later, I ran after him. . . ."

Murray rolled over and rested his head in his hand so that he could watch her, intent on her story.

"I didn't see where he went, but somehow I felt that he wouldn't go home—that he would go back to that barn. The girl was gone—had been sent away—but I felt he would go there anyway, just to defy them." Mary too, turned over, facing Murray. "I went, Murray, ready to do anything for him. I wanted to share his humiliation, comfort him . . . but he wasn't there. I took off all my clothes and waited, but he didn't come. And so . . . there in the dark . . . I . . . danced . . . like a wicked, Satanic thing. I did all the things I could think of that were awful and lewd—all for Warren's sake. And when I got home later, I discovered he had gone. While I had been dancing, he had packed and left for California without even saying goodbye. . . ."

"And all these years," said Murray, "you've kept it secret in your heart. All these years you've been dutiful and godly and virtuous and quiet, knowing what was inside you. . . ."

"Yes, that was it. All these years, Murray, I never told anyone. . . ."

He turned her over on her back. She lay still, looking at him as he sat up and ran one hand over her stomach, her ribs, her breasts. In the half-light of the motel room she could see his penis standing up again, stiff and glistening wet on the end.

He leaned over and kissed her, his tongue searching out her mouth, forcing itself through her lips and exploring her teeth. His hand roamed over her legs, her belly, until the fingers had penetrated her secret place once more to find her wet and willing. Slowly, very slowly, he began to caress her there rhythmically, kissing her all the while, stopping the kiss occasionally to lay his cheek against hers, but still the fingers continued their steady movements, the pace quickening, and then his lips were on hers once more.

Mary felt as though her eyes were rolling back in their sockets. She sensed a familiar swelling and an urgency that she knew from her own bed, her own touch. Her mouth opened and she felt her legs stiffen, her back arch, her pelvis thrust forward to meet Murray's fingers, and then he was on her like a rider springing on his mount. His penis took over the rhythm of his hand, and he thrust himself deep, watching her face.

"Murray! Oh, Murray!" Her mouth contorted with pleasure as she tilted her head backwards, the muscles of her neck stretching, stretching, as though the orgasm were in her throat. And then her face fell to one side and she lay there limp, happy.

Still Murray towered over her. He pressed her to the bed again, his body tense and strong, hands coming up under her shoulders, fingers holding her fast.

"All these years," he said, "you've been waiting to be set free. . . ."

". . . Waiting for you, Murray," she breathed.

"Don't close your eyes, Mary. Look at me." He moved her body with his own, his pelvis rising and falling—a huge falcon soaring and dipping over her, in her, a bird of prey, a bird of peace. . . .

"Who am I, Mary?"

"Murray . . . Murray Dawes. . . ."

"Where am I, Mary?"

"In me, in me." Her heart was beginning to pound again, and again her neck stiffened, as though someone had grabbed her hair and was pulling her head back.

On and on he went, his energy limitless, his back tense, his groin twisting, turning and pressing, the muscles on his arms bulging as he supported his weight. Suddenly Mary felt a new rush of warmth, and again the heady dizziness of pleasure. And then Murray was exploding inside her with such frenzy that they rolled together to one edge of the bed, hung for a moment over the side, and then settled back on the sheets wet and spent, obliterating the past.

"Murray," she murmured. "Murray, my darling, my

love. . . ." And as their bodies relaxed, she felt cleansed and pure and born again—washed white as snow in Murray's love. Her obsession was no more. She closed her eyes and saw only Murray. She felt only his touch and thought only of him. With his body he had chased the incubus from her soul.

"Come with me," Murray whispered. "Come with me for just a few weeks to see what works out." Then he reached down and put one finger over her lips. "No, think about it first, Mary. Don't answer now. You might say yes, and it wouldn't be fair."

FIFTEEN

She remembered thinking before she fell asleep, that perhaps their problems would solve themselves—that traveling about with Murray while Jake was away at the ocean would help her decide. Murray was already asleep, one hairy leg thrown over her body, his arm under her breasts. Every so often he twitched. Mary smiled and stroked his arm, and then she too drifted off.

She remembered turning over an hour or so later. She remembered Murray getting up once to urinate, then coming back and caressing her again. She remembered snuggling against him and thinking perhaps they would make love still a third time, but then Murray's slow, deliberate breathing told her that love would have to wait. When she woke at last, rested, she judged by the shadows on the wall and the lights which had come on outside that it was almost seven o'clock. They had slept and loved away most of the afternoon and the dinner hour as well. She laughingly rubbed one bare foot up the calf of Murray's leg. He grunted with pleasure, fondled her breasts, and sighed contentedly.

A plane went by overhead, a truck barreled down 301, a dog somewhere barked furiously for a moment or two and then stopped. Other occupants of the motel were pulling in, pulling out, and there was a party or something going on a few doors away. These were all sounds of the here and now, but Mary pretended they weren't there.

"We ought to go out for something to eat," Murray said at last.

"I'm a mess."

"We'll shower together, go get dinner, and come back. Or I could go alone and pick something up. We could eat it in bed."

Mary rolled over and embraced him. "I'm not hungry."

"I am. I'm always hungry. Hungry for you."

"You've had me twice."

"Just got started."

"You'll have a stroke."

"Not if I get some food in me."

Mary had never bathed with a man before. She had never actually thought about it. In all her years of growing up, a bathroom was a private place where people went one at a time—to brush their teeth, even. You knocked, and then you waited. You cleaned the tub of pubic hair when you were through, opened the window to freshen the room, kept to your own towel and wash cloth, and wrapped all personal discards in toilet paper before putting them in the wastebasket. No one was to know anything at all about the inner workings of your body. You left a bathroom as a Boy Scout leaves a forest, with little evidence at all that human life had been there.

The experience of standing in the shower stall with Murray, their bodies pressed against each other as water cascaded over their shoulders and backs, was so new, so wonderful to Mary that she laughed aloud, her voice childishly high. She knelt before him, blinking through the water that pelted her eyelids, as she gently washed his penis, holding it lovingly in her hands. She spread her fingers through the hair on his belly, and the short thick penis began to rise and point toward her again, like the needle of a compass. She kissed it and then laughed. Murray laughed with her.

"He's got to learn to wait," Murray said. "I know my limits—he doesn't."

He lathered her breasts slowly, then her thighs and the cleft of her buttocks. She leaned against the tiled wall, her eyes closed, and shivered as she felt the swelling once more of her own vulva, drenched on the outside by the water from the shower and on the inside by her own slippery wetness.

They dressed slowly, leisurely, helping each other button and fasten. There was considerable noise now from the nearby room, and they heard the motel manager yelling for the ruckus to stop.

"Maybe we should go somewhere else after dinner," Murray said, "some place that's quiet."

"But you've already paid, Murray. At least they don't know us here. The next place might be worse." She was wrapping her long wet hair in a towel, turban-fashion. "How's this? It'll take hours to dry. I don't know what else to do with it."

He laughed. "Then you will come with me and sit in the car. I'll go in a restaurant as a Moor from the East, asking nourishment for my bride who speaks Turkish only and hides her hair from the eyes of other men. . . ."

Mary laughed delightedly. "Are you always this way, Murray?"

"No. Sometimes I'm depressive and boring and dull and, like Lazareth, my breath is foul and my body stinketh. But you bring out the good in me, Mary. I wonder how much I could change if you came with me. . . ."

As Mary put on her sandals, she noticed the flash of a blue light on the bedroom walls. "What is it?" she asked, when Murray looked through the drapes.

"Squad car. I think the manager's called the police about that party."

"Should we wait a few minutes?"

"No. Take advantage of the distraction. That's the first rule of thieves, spies, and pickpockets."

Laughing softly, the huge turban-like towel tilting precariously on Mary's head, they stepped outside. Murray discovered he didn't have the room key and went back in to find it.

There was a small crowd on the sidewalk two doors down, illuminated by the light of the squad car.

"I don't care whether you paid or not; get the hell out of here," the manager was yelling. He stood with his back to Mary, hands on his hips, looking inside an open door. "Drunken louts! Wrecking up the place. Go on. Get out."

There were sounds of cursing and scuffling inside, and then two officers emerged with a young man between them. A girl, looking confused and blank, followed after them, half dressed.

The young man wrenched one arm free, turned his body sideways, and in that brief instant his eyes, half-glazed, fell on Mary. It was Bill.

She froze, as in a dream, rooted to the sidewalk, her feet paralyzed, unable to move.

"Je-*sus!*" said Bill, coming to a dead stop. "Jesus fuckin' Christ, if it ain't my Aunt Mary, with a cast on her head!"

One of the policemen looked over at her. The other officer held open the door of the squad car.

Mary turned away quickly, eyes down, and attempted to get back in the room, but collided with Murray who had already stepped out and locked the door.

"Hey, Char-*lene!* Bill said over his shoulder to the intoxicated girl behind him. "You know who's been screwin' in this place? My aunt! Auntie Mary Martha!"

Murray put his arm around Mary and walked her quickly in the other direction toward the Dodge.

"Jesus! I never would have guessed!" Bill's voice came rolling after them. "She's been fuckin' that preacher in the white suit." He was shouting it now, and the crowd was peering after them through the darkness. "He must be some lay, Aunt Mary! Blew the top off her head, that's what! Wheeeee! Atta girl, Mary! Go to it! Ya-hooooo!"

Mary fell into the car, Murray beside her, and he backed it out of the space and onto the highway. A block down the road, he pulled over on the shoulder and turned off the engine. Mary was crying.

"Oh, my God," she kept saying. "Oh, my God."

"They won't pay attention to him, Mary," Murray soothed. "He was so drunk he could hardly stand up."

She shook her head violently. The towel fell off and she held it listlessly in her lap. Then she covered her face with her hands. "I recognized one of the policemen—a friend of Milt's. He knows me—

knows all of us. It'll be all over Marbury by nine to-morrow morning."

Murray held her close. "Mary, Mary . . . I wish you'd come with me. Get out of this place. I can't leave you behind with all this. . . ."

"It would be worse if I went away. Then they'd all say my sins had driven me out. And my father . . . oh, God, to lose two of us. . . . But you, Murray! What they'll say about you! And they admired you so!" She continued to weep.

He did not answer, just held her as though to protect her. But Mary knew that even his strong arms could not keep out the gossip.

"Mary, they don't even know me," he said. "Not really. But they know you, and they love you. I think I should take you home. That's probably the best thing. If anyone else sees us together this evening, it will only confirm it. When you get home, call someone and talk for a while. It will establish the fact that you were there. Then perhaps Bill's story won't have much effect."

"I guess so. I guess I should go home. People will start calling just to see. . . ."

He reached into his pocket and wrote something on a card. "Listen, darling, this is my next address. Write to me and tell me whether or not you'll come. You could wait a week, then come. Ignore the gossip—everything they say about you—go about your business as usual, and then come to me and we'll make up for this evening. I promise you that."

Mary tucked the card in her purse. For several miles they drove without speaking. One of Murray's big hands rested on Mary's there on the seat between them, squeezing it and caressing her fingers. Mary felt as though his strength were flowing into her.

"I'll survive, Murray," she said at last. "Please don't worry about me. I would do it all again. . . ."

"Would you, Mary?"

"Yes. Especially today."

He pulled her over to him, and she curled up on the seat and put her head against him like a small child. He drove slowly beneath the early evening sky, stroking her hair, caressing her arm, and a sadness filled her, almost choking her.

She could tell by the turns in the road and the clumps of trees passing by the windows when they were approaching her home. The car slowed and stopped.

"I won't come in," Murray said. "I don't want to make it harder for you than it is. I'm sorry the day ended like this, Mary."

"I'm glad we had what time we did. I don't regret a minute of it."

They sat looking straight ahead, their hands locked tightly together there on the front seat. Mary felt her eyes filling with tears, and when the tears rolled down her face, she let them come. Murray reached over and wiped them away. Then he pulled her quickly to him and kissed her tenderly, then passionately, then tenderly once more. And then he backed away and let her go.

She held onto his fingers for one final moment, then turned and ran up the walk to the porch. She leaned against the door frame while his car drove away, the tears running down her face again. He was gone, and finally even the sound of the motor had faded away to nothing.

"Aunt Mary?"

Turning around, she saw someone jump down

from the maple tree in the front yard, and a moment later Jake came slowly up the steps.

She was both surprised and angered at finding him there. He was, and he wasn't, the reason she had not just driven off into the sunset with Murray Dawes. But Jake showed no eagerness to battle with her. He stood on a lower step, his face drawn, saying nothing.

"I thought you were going to stay overnight with Brick," she said, her nose clogged and her eyes swollen.

"I didn't feel so good. I came home about two. Ned said I could have the rest of the day off."

She avoided looking at him as she fumbled with the key. "What's the matter? Stomach?"

He shrugged. "I guess so. Just didn't feel so good."

She opened the door and turned on a lamp. "Then why didn't you come inside and lie down?"

"I wanted to wait for you."

She felt exasperated with him. She didn't want him there—didn't want to talk with him. This was a time for being alone with her own feelings.

"Well, why couldn't you wait for me in the house, for heaven's sake? If you're sick, you ought to be in bed! How long have you been sitting up in that tree?"

At first he didn't answer. He stood with his back to her. "Since six. . . ."

Mary glanced at the clock on the mantel. "You've been in that tree for two and a half hours?" She stared at him, but got only his back in response.

There was something, however, about the slump of his shoulders and the sound of his voice that told her this wasn't just Jake being perverse or peevish or jealous or ornery—this was something else.

She sat down on the arm of the chair and her voice grew softer. "Why were you waiting for me, Jake?"

He didn't answer. A slight movement of his neck and jaw told her that he was crying and didn't want her to know, so she gave him time to recover. He gulped loudly.

"I told you I'd be home late," she continued gently. "As it happens, I decided to come home early. But if I hadn't, you would have been in that tree one heck of a long time."

When he finally answered, his voice was so soft she could hardly hear it. "I wanted to be sure you came back."

And suddenly Mary remembered another time that Jake had waited for someone—when a nine-year-old boy had sat on the steps outside a strange apartment because he'd forgotten his lunch money, waiting for his mother to come out.

"Of course I'd come back, Jake! You're here! How on earth could I ever go off and leave you?" It seemed hypocritical, but it made her feel better to say the words aloud.

He still stood with his back to her and swiftly wiped his eyes with one hand. "You looked like you'd been crying," he said.

"I was. It was sad seeing Murray go."

He turned around. "He's not coming back?"

"No."

He studied her carefully. "Aren't you ever going to see him again?"

"I was thinking about spending a few weeks with him while you're at the ocean with Brick."

Jake's face seemed to blanch again. The gaunt look returned to his eyes.

She started to tell him that she wasn't his mother, that he could count on her, that she wouldn't be leaving him forever. But at that moment there was the sound of a car in the driveway and a door opening. Jake went over to the window to look out. "I'll bet he *is* coming back." he said.

Mary hurried to the door. Two figures were making their way up the sidewalk. Verna and her father. Her heart sank heavily, and the beat seemed dull, deadened. She opened the screen. Had they heard already? Was this the first contingent?

They had not heard.

"Mary, Dad has to go to the bathroom. We were visiting Louella Kramer, and no sooner had we started home than he's got to go. Why he doesn't tell me these things before we leave, I don't know."

"Come on in, Dad," Mary said.

"Hi, Gramps," said Jake, smiling wanly.

Hearing Jake's voice, the old man turned and grinned broadly. His voice shook and he slowly held out one hand. "Chollie ing boy see you."

Jake took his grandfather's arm and helped him down the hallway.

"What did you do to your hair?" Verna asked, looking at Mary curiously.

"Washed it. I'll set it later."

"Well, that's a strange way to do it. Now you'll have to wet it all over again." Verna slumped heavily down in the chair by the door, hunched over, arms crossed on her knees.

"Sam's gone back to the farm, Mary," she said, and

there was no expression in her voice one way or the other. "It didn't work out."

Mary looked at her. "Already? He'd only been home one day."

"One day and two nights," Verna corrected. "It was the nights. I just wasn't meant to love a man, that's all. I just can't do it. I'm too old for pretending."

It was as though, now that Murray was gone, Mary was inheriting the problems he was supposed to have solved. Everyone needed comfort, everyone needed reassurance, everyone needed to know that somebody cared. Mary the earth mother. Maybe that was her destiny.

"I'm sorry, Verna," she said. There was absolutely nothing else to say. She had no advice, no suggestions, no cures. It was happening just as Murray had said it would. A week or so after the revival was over, everything would be just as it was before. It was all an illusion.

Another car came to a stop outside. There was the quick slam of a door and deliberate footsteps coming up the walk.

Milt Jennings walked in. He did not even knock, but stepped inside unannounced and stared grimly at Mary, his face strangely contorted. Verna turned around and looked at him, her mouth open.

"You slut," said Milt, and spit out the words as though they were poison.

Verna wheeled around completely, her face aghast.

Grandpa and Jake were coming back down the hall from the bathroom, and Mary hoped that Milt would have the good sense to turn on his heels, now that the venom was out, and not upset her father. But Milt had no such scruples.

Verna looked from Milt to Mary. "What is wrong with you, Milt?"

"It's a personal matter," Mary said hastily.

Milt sneered. "It's hardly personal, Mary, when it's spreading all over town. If you want to live that kind of life, you shouldn't live in Marbury."

Grandpa Myles saw Milt standing by the door and stopped, looking at him hard.

Milt turned to Verna. "Do you know what your sister was doing this evening?"

"Milt, for heaven's sake!" cried Mary.

"How should I know what she was doing?" Verna said. "I've been over at Louella's."

"Fornicating. Fornicating with Brother Murray Dawes."

Verna turned slowly and looked at Mary, her face blank.

"Milt," said Mary coldly. "If you don't mind. . . ."

"Jake and your father should know exactly what sort of woman you are," Milt exploded, and now his whole face seemed purple. His eyes were mere dots of rage, the lids looked puffy. He looked sick, as though he had some awful disease.

"Who told you that?" Verna demanded, disbelieving.

"A man who was there—Jim Stewart. He was called to a motel on 301 because your son was wrecking up the place, and they saw Mary and Murray Dawes coming out of one of the rooms together."

"I don't *believe* it!" said Verna. "She's been home

washing her hair. Look at her!" She turned to Mary again. "What's this all about?"

Mary looked straight at Milt as she answered. "Milt has just told you," she said. "He has a marvelous knack for details. He is positively fascinated with other people's lives."

This admission came unexpectedly, and Milt looked quickly about the room for support.

"Mary, you mean to stand there and tell me that all this is true?" Verna questioned.

"Yes, I mean to stand here and say that it was Murray's last day in Marbury, and our final chance to be together."

"It runs in the family," Milt crowed in triumph, "and a good thing someone found out, too! First Warren, then Bill, and now Mary. . . ."

"Y . . . You! You!" A cry came from Grandpa Myles, and he took several halting steps toward Milt and stopped. His voice shook and the fury on his face matched Milt's. "You . . . you . . . neng . . . you neng nang in barn . . . you spy neng Warren . . . you told ch . . . cholliebody . . . it was you!" He turned desperately to Mary, frantic to communicate the message.

And then it came to her, and Mary understood. All these years her father had kept the knowledge from her, knowing she might marry Milt, not wanting to upset her life. But now he could hold it back no longer. She turned slowly back to Milt.

"So it was you," she said, "*you* who sat in the deacon's barn that night, all those years ago, waiting to see who had been making love on Saturday nights."

"Chollie!" cried Grandpa Myles, hitting one fist

against his thigh, delighted that he had made himself understood.

Milt's breath came in short, shallow pants and his jaw flinched. He did not answer.

"So it was you," Mary said again, nodding. "I always wondered who it was who sat so still in the barn that night, waiting, watching. . . . I always wondered what that person thought, seeing the sights and hearing the noises of two people making love. I always wondered what kind of charge he got out of seeing others do what he had only fantasied in secret. And what did you do after you had gone to the deacon and told him it was Warren? What did you do after you got back to the safety of your own sanitized bed? Were you good to yourself that night, Milt?"

"Mary! For God's sake, there's a child present," he snarled.

"There's no child present, Milt. Not after what he has been through and seen and heard."

"You whore!" Milt said.

Jake charged. Like a small hornet, he attacked the surprised Milt with his fists, drumming on the pudgy man's chest, eyes closed in blinded fury.

"Wait a minute, Jake," Mary said, pulling him away, "there's something else. Something more that Milt should know." She stood with her arm around Jake, whose shoulders heaved up and down with exertion, little gasps of rage coming from his throat. Milt's eyes traveled warily from one to the other.

"You missed the best scene of all in that barn, did you know that? The night of the penitential service, when Warren rushed out, and I followed. . . . Do you know what happened then?"

"Good heavens, Mary!" Verna said. "Not that!"

"No. Not that. Only in fantasy. I went to that barn

to comfort my brother, sure he was there, but he wasn't. So I danced, Milt. I danced as I'd never danced before. I took off my clothes. Milt—all of them—and Satan himself never saw such a dance. Oh, you should have been there—hiding back in the hay, keeping your little notes. Think what all you'd have to tell. . . ."

"Mary, God help us," said Verna, her hands over her eyes.

Milt continued to stare at Mary, watching for some sign of humiliation, of embarrassment, but there was none.

"You can go now Milt," she said. "You've such a delicious story to tell. Where will you start first? Louella Kramer's, perhaps? Or the Gordons? Mr. Buddinger is right across the street. Why not start with him? Think of all the ground you've got to cover—the post office, the diner, the barbershop—oh, you're going to have such a marvelous time!"

Milt swung around, flushing, and burst out the screen, slamming it hard behind him.

"Chollie bo!" Grandpa Myles cried victoriously. "Milt no neng good. Knew . . . I knew . . . no nung good . . . for . . . good!"

Mary could feel her pulse pounding in her temples. One down. She expected to clash with Verna next, but when she turned, Verna sat where she was, hands limply in her lap. Mary sank down on the edge of the chair.

"Your turn, Verna," she said warily. "Jake? Anybody?"

Verna shook her head. "I've nothing to say, Mary. Should I wish the way I've lived my life on you? And Murray. . . . Well, one never knows." She got up. "Dad's pretty excited. He's had a long evening and ought to be in bed." She took her father's arm and walked toward the door. "You know what's going to come of this, don't you? You know what will happen when Pastor Gordon and the board of trustees hear the story?"

"Yes. . . ."

"Are you prepared to go through with it?"

"No, Verna. I won't."

"They'll throw you out, Mary! You'll lose your job!"

"I know."

Mary followed her sister and father out onto the dark porch, watched them drive away, and sat down in the swing. Jake seemed to crumple on the top step and leaned against the post. In the light from the living room, his eyes looked sad and old, and Mary wanted to cry out that a fourteen-year-old's eyes ought not to look that way, but she waited for him to speak first, to let him say what was in his heart without any prompting.

"That's why you came home, then," he said finally, softly.

"Yes, that's why I came home. We knew the gossip would be all over Marbury, and it would be better if I came back here."

"I thought it was because . . . because you found out. . . ."

"Found out what?"

"About Murray. . . ."

The boldness, the bravado she had felt earlier

evaporated suddenly. It was as though someone had placed a catheter in her soul and all hope and joy were draining away. Mary wondered if she had enough strength to open her mouth, to breathe, even.

"What about Murray, Jake?" Was that her voice— that awful hollow sound?

Even in the half-light from the door she could see tears spring up in the boy's eyes. He pressed his lips together, as though pressing would hold back the words. He looked like a disturbed child in a TV documentary.

"Jake!" she said, alarmed for him and all he had been through. "You can tell me what it is. I won't be angry with you. I can take it." *Lies. All lies.* "What about Murray? Tell me."

His jaw hunk slack and he stared down at his hands. "C . . . Curly told me this morning," he said finally.

"The man who testified at the revival? He came back?" A strange flicker of doubt crossed her mind, as though she were sitting in the shadow of some awful thing she already knew, but preferred not to face.

"No. I found out where he was staying. I went to see him. I wanted to know about last night."

Mary waited. "He *wasn't* saved, after all. Is that it?"

Jake nodded. Still he did not look up.

Again the fear raced through her. "What else did he tell you?"

"How Murray travels around with the carnival. They g . . . go to the same towns, only they never arrive or leave together, so people won't get suspicious. The more Murray preaches against the carnival, the more popular it gets. And when the carnival's over, Ned gives Murray a percentage."

Mary sat with her lips open, her body cold. "Jake, this *can't* be true! It's malicious gossip! I just can't believe it!"

"It's true. Wherever they go, Curly comes to revival on the last night and testifies. He says he's been saved fifteen times in the last year."

Mary stood up and started for the door, shaking her head. "That *can't* be! Murray even gave me his next address."

"Aunt Mary, you've got to believe it. He goes wherever Ned goes. The carnival goes to West Virginia the week after next—to Elkins. . . ."

Like a mechanical woman, she opened the screen, went inside and reached in her purse. Slowly she came back out on the porch, holding the little card. Her eyes did not seem to focus. She found she was holding the card sideways and turned it around. *General Delivery, Elkins, West Virginia*, it read. *I'll love you always, Murray.*

She collapsed in one corner of the swing, her lips trembling. "Oh my God, oh my God," she said.

Murray must have known that Curly might tell Jake. Why had he used Curly's testimonial in this particular town, taking that risk? Did he know that by the time the secret was out, he'd be gone, and he didn't care? Or had he wanted her to know, realizing that things would never be right between them until she knew, and either rejected or forgave him. Yet, if he had wanted forgiveness, he could have told her that afternoon—he could have confessed to her, as she had confessed to him. The only possible answer was that he did not think he could change—not even with her love.

It was as though the room had disappeared, taking its light forever. The future was closing in on her like four walls, squeezing the breath from her lungs. She would go on being Mary Martha Myles of Marbury, Maryland, forever and ever. She had been born in Charles County thirty-four years ago, and she had just this moment died, but it would be years yet before they buried her.

Meanwhile, she would have to go through this charade of living. She would spend her days mimeographing in the church office and her nights dreaming of a single afternoon in a cheap motel. Now that she knew about Murray, was there any point in defending him, or herself? She would stand up before the whole congregation of the Faith Holiness Church, just as Warren did before her, and publicly acknowledge her sin. They would forgive her, and her job would be secure. Liz would come back from Bucharest, marry Greg, and have children, while Mary's own vagina would shrivel and grow dry with no one to penetrate it. As the years passed, people would nod to her and smile and go on squeezing her arm at weddings, and every so often someone would whisper to another, "There goes Mary Martha. They say that once, some time in her thirties. . . ."

Suddenly Jake sprang up from the steps and flung himself beside her on the swing, his arms around her neck, his face against her cheek.

"I didn't want to have to t . . . tell you," he wept. "I was hoping he'd tell you himself. . . ."

"It's all right, honey," she said, crying too. "Perhaps he did tell me in his own way, and I just didn't understand. It's all right."

Skin against skin. . . . Mary felt the warmth of Jake's breath on her neck as she gently caressed his hair, holding him tightly.

The pale pink dress that she had so carefully put on that morning was rumpled, the white sandals lay in a heap by her feet. Her faith and hope and love now lay with this young half-man in her lap—Warren's flesh, the love-child born of an unconsummated wish.

"Are you still going to go to him?" Jake asked, clutching her shoulder.

"I don't think I can—not now."

"He loves you."

"Perhaps. Maybe he'll write . . . I just don't know."

She felt his tense body slump, and his head sank down on her breasts. She remembered the feel of Murray against her body, and a swift electric charge raced through her, making her ache with desolation.

Jake reached up and kissed her on the neck.

"Let's move away from here, Aunt Mary! Let's you and me and Grandpa go off in the woods and live by ourselves."

Gently she stroked his arm. "No one can live all to themselves, Jake."

"I don't ever want to go to that church again," he said determinedly. "I don't ever want to go to a revival. I don't think I believe in their God, Aunt Mary. I *know* I don't."

The courage she had thought was gone was stirring again. She could feel it. Jake, the wonder boy, had called it back. Perhaps it wasn't too late.

"Maybe I don't either, Jake. Maybe we've been mistaken all along. Somewhere there's a God who's loving—a God who understands that people can be confused and uncertain and still be good. We just haven't found him yet, that's all."

"I'm not going to the ocean with Brick, either. I'm going to stay home and be with you. I'm going to take care of you and love you, and you won't even care that Murray's gone away. I promise!"

He was offering her his soul, his very life, something neither Warren nor Murray had ever done. She held it, she knew, in the palm of her hand.

How easy it would be! By a few choice words here and there over the years, a few gestures, a sigh, a look, she could capture this man-child with guilt and make him hers. She could take this fledgling boy, still so unsure of his coming manhood, and set his feet in a circle around herself. She could answer his own yearning for love and security with an attachment so deep that he would want no other, and they would weave a web around them so strong that it would be more and more difficult to break with each passing year. He was like a branch from a green willow tree—she could bend him into any shape she desired.

But all these months he in turn had nourished her, and now that strength surged through her cells as a life-sustaining force. She took him by the arms and held him out away from her, looking at his narrow elfin face, so earnest in its love.

"We both look like we have one heck of a cold," she said, and handed him her tissue. "Of course you're going to the ocean with Brick. He's expecting you, and I know two girls who would be very disappointed if you weren't there. I don't know what I'll do while you're gone. Perhaps I'll do some looking around."

"For what?"

"A place of our own, maybe. I don't mean just a house, I mean a whole new community. How would you like to live in Virginia?"

He studied her carefully before answering. "How far's that?"

"Not so far we couldn't get back to see Brick and Grandpa pretty often. An hour's drive, maybe. I was thinking of Fairfax. I think I could get a job in a clinic there. Dr. Dobbs would recommend me."

"We'd still have a house and a yard and everything?"

"We'd choose it together."

"What about Murray?"

"It's too early to tell, Jake. I'll wait to see if he writes me. But somehow . . . I don't think that he will." A wave of sadness washed over her.

Jake hugged her again. "I don't care if we move," he said, and then, echoing her own words: "I'm strong. I can take it."

"I know you are. We're both tough, you know it? If we weren't, we sure wouldn't have made it this far, would we?"

Jake leaned back in the swing and pushed against the floor with his feet, a slow steady rhythm. Thigh against thigh. . . . But it induced in her no tingle, no longing for Warren—the man was dead.

"I was . . . afraid . . . that you were going to come back and pack a suitcase while I was at work . . . and go off with Murray," Jake said finally. "That's why I came home."

"Ah! And so you sat in the tree waiting."

He smiled a little at his foolishness.

"But I did come home, didn't I? And I didn't even know then what I know now." They sat together, pushing their feet, keeping the rhythm of the swing steady.

"Do you still love him?" Jake asked.

"Yes. I love him for what I thought he was—for what I wanted him to be. He was wonderful to me—for me. How could I not love him?" She paused and then asked the question that was struggling to get out. "Did you find out anything else about him, Jake? Did Curly say that . . . that Murray had other women when he traveled?'

Jake shook his head. "I did ask him that, but Curly said no. He said Murray never fell for a woman like this before, and they were all afraid he might settle down here. Of course, Curly's only been with the carnival a couple years. . . ."

"So we don't really know for sure then, do we, and I can believe whatever I like. I'd like to believe that Murray loved me."

"You know he did, Aunt Mary. Everyone knew it. Everyone could tell. . . ."

Jake sat leaning against her for another minute or two and then, as though waking from a dream, got up somewhat self-consciously, stumbling awkwardly over her sandals.

"Oops! Careful there," Mary said, steadying him.

"I'm tired," Jake said. "Guess I'll go to bed."

She nodded. But still he stood, reluctant to leave.

"Aunt Mary, I don't think we ought to have any secrets between us, do you?"

"I'm not sure, Jake. I don't think I ought to know all your private thoughts. . . ."

"Yeah, well, there's something else you should know, though. Not about Murray . . . about me. . . ."

He took a big breath, held it, and then let it go.

"When the lawyer called and said that Dad had told me I should come and live with you. . . ."

"Yes, I remember. . . ."

"Well, he didn't. Dad never said that at all. I just made it up. It's . . . still legal, isn't it? They wouldn't take me away or anything?"

All myths were self-destructing this night; all fantasies, all daydreams, all delusions. . . . No, Warren had not thought of her all these years. He had not told her goodbye when he left Marbury because, though he liked her, she hadn't meant that much. And he did not, as a final gesture of love, send her his only begotten son; Jake himself had made it up. But did it matter anymore, now that Murray had loved her—now that the big man in the white suit, however faulty, had replaced forever the lover who could never be? No. It mattered not at all.

Mary shook her head. "Jake, nobody will every try to take you away. I wouldn't let them. You're safe with me for as long as you want to stay."

He smiled with relief and yawned, simultaneously—emotionally exhausted. "I was afraid Verna might get her hands on me."

Mary laughed. "No chance. But why did you choose me over her? You hardly knew either of us."

"Well . . . when you both came out to visit us once, Aunt Verna kept grabbing me—squeezing the breath out of me. You just sat on the sofa and waited till I came to you."

He opened the screen, yawned again—an enormous yawn—and said good-night, then padded on down the hall to his room. She heard the thud of his closet door, the squeak of his bed springs.

So he had liked her all these years because she hadn't grabbed him, hadn't squeezed him, hadn't

tried to make him hers. She would remember that
when it came time to let him go. If she did nothing
else in her life, she would send this boy out strong
and confident, and perhaps, unlike Warren, he would
come back now and then.

Mary closed her eyes, but there were no tears. She
opened them again, surprised. She had expected that
once Jake had gone inside, the floodgates of her soul
would open. Instead, she felt as though she were on
the edge of a discovery—a new and possibly wonderful
thing. She was being born again, and again, and
again, but she didn't know where the feeling was
coming from.

And then she realized that the death of Warren
had set her free—not the death of his body, but the
death of his power. He had teased her, shocked her,
sat beside her and tantalized her, but it was not her
he had ravished in the barn, and her dance that night
had never made it so. It was not she with whom Jake
had been conceived, and having the boy here would
never make him hers. She did not belong to her
brother any more, and never had. Murray, in a single
afternoon, had broken the attachment forever, eased
the parasitic grip on her soul, and washed away the
lingering fantasies in the fluid of his body. She had
been loved and penetrated by a new man, and when
she closed her eyes now in the darkness of the porch,
in the shadow of the maple, or later in her room, it
would no longer be a young man of long ago whose
image seduced and caressed, but Murray.

How long, then, would she go on thinking of Murray, wanting him, reliving that afternoon together? She did not know. Perhaps, some day, Murray would decide his life was too empty without her and come back. Maybe he would confess and give up all deceits. She doubted it, but then, anything was possible. If he did not, perhaps another man would take his place. But con-man or miracle maker, Murray had worked a small spell upon her for which she would always be grateful.

He had been mistaken. Not everything would go back to the way it was before. The big man in the white suit had come into Marbury and gone again, but she herself had changed, and Murray had helped bring it about. Only moments before she had felt desolate, and yet there was excitement surfacing already.

She, Mary Martha Myles, had actually stood there on the rug in her own living room and admitted not only fornication, but an incestuous fantasy as well—a fantasy she had kept secret so long that it had held her prisoner here in Marbury. She had not even told it to Dr. Dobbs, who would have understood it, or to Liz, who would have laughed at it. She had boldly, enthusiastically, spilled it out to Verna and Milt, loving it, reveling in it, and no lightning bolt had struck her, no blob of bird shit, even. And once it had been told, it loosened its grip upon her soul. She laughed aloud with the discovery.

"Dear Liz," she would write that night, "I dreamed I was dancing without my Maidenform bra . . . except that it really happened once, and I've just told Milt and Verna, and they're still in shock. I am thinking of selling this house, leaving the church and resigning my job—having spent the afternoon in orgiastic ecstasy with a gentle con-man. How's Bucharest?"

She felt as if she were molting, shedding her old tight, scaly skin and crawling out pink and new, sensitive to a million stimuli she had never experienced before.

They would go on exploring, she and Jake—a new place, new home, new school, new job—and perhaps, in their travels, separate or together, they would discover that their souls belonged neither in Marbury nor the beach house in Malibu, but somewhere, of their own choosing, in between.

ONE WOMAN AND ONE MAN...
AND A LOVE SO RELENTLESS THAT
IT CHANGED THEIR LIVES FOREVER...

THE Bleeding Heart

by MARILYN FRENCH

Marilyn French is a writer of exceptional talent. In her international bestseller, THE WOMEN'S ROOM, she gave
millions of women a true portrayal of their lives. Now, in THE
BLEEDING HEART, she has written a love story both
moving and powerful – a classic of modern fiction that marks a
milestone in our understanding of human relationships.

'A monumental achievement by any standard' *Cosmopolitan*

'Brilliantly constructed...not so much a novel as an act of communication: it deals in home truths rather than literary truths...
I am Marilyn French's fervent admirer' *Fay Weldon, Punch*

GENERAL FICTION   0 7221 0568 1   £1.75

And, look out for Marilyn French's
THE WOMEN'S ROOM
also available in Sphere Books

by Ellen Roddick

Nina is the thirty-nine-year-old wife of a successful lawyer and
the mother of their beautiful, bright children. And she's happy
with life and her teaching job – until the arrival of Mort Hinks,
headmaster at the school where she teaches. As Nina faces her
growing attraction to Mort – and her consequent estrangement
from husband and home – she experiences the perils and joys of
a secret relationship that divides her loyalties between lover and
loved ones. But, unbeknown to Nina and Mort, their mutual
partners have also embarked on a voyage of passion, as secret as
their own, which could offer the ultimate solution – or disaster
– for them all.

'Delightful ... an honest and touching story'
PUBLISHERS WEEKLY

ROMANCE   0 7221 7431 4   £1.25

STEPPING

NANCY THAYER

Stepping isn't easy. It means making friends with two blue-eyed, angel-faced enemies – your husband's children from a former marriage. And taking the steps that bring you close to what you want – home, husband, children, career, friends . . . **everything.**

For Zelda, loving, irresistible, a woman firmly grounded in the eighties, the journey requires a special kind of courage to face the pain and exhilaration of relationships bound by ties that are both more and less than blood.

STEPPING is a powerful and compulsively readable story which explodes the myths of stepmotherhood and crystallises the experiences of the modern woman in today's world.

'It's hard to do **Stepping** *justice, hard to define why it's so good; apart from being funny and sad and often actually painful and completely compulsive, it has that quality peculiar to American books of making the texture and substance of daily life absolutely vivid and interesting. It's just brilliantly written, that's all.' COSMOPOLITAN*

GENERAL FICTION   0 7221 8419 0   £1.25

BY MEREDITH RICH

TYGER HAYES IS ON HER WAY TO THE TOP!

In the glossy world of high fashion, perfume is big business.
Each year conglomerates spend millions in the eternal search
for the sweet scent of success . . . the ultimate fragrance.

Then a multi-national decided to go one better. And hired
a stunning jet-set beauty to create a scent that would capture
the imagination of the dazzling élite. Heading a team picked
from the cream of the world's leading designers and
perfumers, Tyger Hayes was determined to make 'Jazz' the
most irresistible and exclusive aroma ever launched.
An ambition equalled only by a burning desire that drove her
from lover to lover until she found one man who would fulfil
her impossible dream and share her need for love.

BARE ESSENCE – the sensational story of a woman
determined to fight her way to the top of the fabulous world
of high-fashion fragrance. A world of sensual sophistication,
make-or-break intrigue, and ultra-chic luxury . . .

GENERAL FICTION   0 7221 7333 4   £1.35

Special Effects

BY HARRIET FRANK

Ever had the feeling that just about everything is collapsing around you? Well that's the starting-point for Harriet Frank's remarkable new novel *Special Effects*, the story of a very special lady. Her name is Emma, and things – and come to that, people! – have a habit of collapsing around her. But Emma's speciality is survival, and this story of how she faces up to everything that life can throw at her – with the help of her own specially effective blend of panache and earthy common sense – makes riveting and thoroughly entertaining reading. If you enjoy the very best of contemporary women's fiction, you'll be knocked out by Harriet Frank's *Special Effects*, it's the kind of novel that will leave no reader unaffected.

GENERAL FICTION   0 7221 3652 8   £1.25

and don't miss
SINGLE
also by Harriet Frank in Sphere Books

Sometimes you have to
lose everything before
you can begin...

TO LOVE AGAIN

— the latest captivating romance from

Danielle Steel

Isabella and Amadeo. The toast of international society and
the undisputed leaders of Rome couture. Together they ruled
the House of San Gregorio, a monument to Isabella's fabulous
design and stunning beauty, to Amadeo's unerring flair and
golden Florentine elegance. And beyond their enchanted
world of splendour shone their boundless, undying love for
one another.

Then suddenly their dream was shattered, Amadeo was gone
— forever. And Isabella fled Rome for a new life of bitter
struggles and haunting memories. With her proud courage
and all her zest for living, could she ever say goodbye to the
past and dare . . .
TO LOVE AGAIN

CONTEMPORARY ROMANCE   0 7221 8107 8   £1.25

And if you love **To Love Again**, you'll be captivated by
Danielle Steel's six other bestselling romance novels:

A SELECTION OF BESTSELLERS FROM SPHERE

FICTION

TUNNEL WAR	Joe Poyer	£1.50	☐
FAMINE	Graham Masterton	£1.75	☐
THE NIGHT BOAT	Robert R. McCammon	£1.25	☐
THE BLEEDING HEART	Marilyn French	£1.75	☐
INNOCENT BLOOD	P. D. James	£1.50	☐

FILM AND TV TIE-INS

THE PROMISE	Danielle Steel	£1.25	☐
SOMEWHERE IN TIME	Richard Matheson	£1.25	☐

NON-FICTION

WILL	G. Gordon Liddy	£1.75	☐
THIS HOUSE IS HAUNTED	Guy Lyon Playfair	£1.50	☐
MY LIFE AND GAME	Bjorn Borg	£1.25	☐
WAR IN 2080	David Langford	£1.50	☐
A MATTER OF LIFE	R. Edwards & P. Steptoe	£1.50	☐

All Sphere books are available at your local bookshop or newsagent, or can be ordered direct from the publisher. Just tick the titles you want and fill in the form below.

Name _____

Address _____

_____

Write to Sphere Books, Cash Sales Department, P.O. Box 11, Falmouth, Cornwall TR10 9EN

Please enclose a cheque or postal order to the value of the cover price plus:

UK: 40p for the first book, 18p for the second book and 13p for each additional book ordered to a maximum charge of £1.49.

OVERSEAS: 60p for the first book plus 18p per copy for each additional book.

BFPO & EIRE: 40p for the first book, 18p for the second book plus 13p per copy for the next 7 books, thereafter 7p per book.

Sphere Books reserve the right to show new retail prices on covers which may differ from those previously advertised in the text or elsewhere, and to increase postal rates in accordance with the PO.